The Best
AMERICAN
SHORT
STORIES
1991

GUEST EDITORS OF
The Best American Short Stories

1978 Ted Solotaroff
1979 Joyce Carol Oates
1980 Stanley Elkin
1981 Hortense Calisher
1982 John Gardner
1983 Anne Tyler
1984 John Updike
1985 Gail Godwin
1986 Raymond Carver
1987 Ann Beattie
1988 Mark Helprin
1989 Margaret Atwood
1990 Richard Ford
1991 Alice Adams

The Best AMERICAN SHORT STORIES 1991

Selected from
U.S. and Canadian Magazines
by ALICE ADAMS
with KATRINA KENISON

With an Introduction by Alice Adams

HOUGHTON MIFFLIN COMPANY
BOSTON •

ISSN 0067-6233
ISBN 0-395-54410-6
ISBN 0-395-54409-2 (PBK.)

Printed in the United States of America

AGM 10 9 8 7 6 5 4 3

Contents

Foreword

WHAT IS THE SECRET of a good short story?

When I took on the job of series editor of *The Best American Short Stories,* I expected that a year of reading would result in some answers to that age-old question. Now, nearly two thousand stories later, I am beginning to suspect that it is the question itself that will keep me reading through the years ahead, for each good story offers a unique answer, not a formula that can be handily lifted and applied to some other piece of fiction. A good story has a way of announcing itself, rendering irrelevant any preconceived maxims or standards of excellence. When you're done reading, you don't have to ask yourself whether it worked or not.

However, the very process of reading and winnowing that narrowed 2000 stories to 120, and then 120 to the 20 that Alice Adams selected for this volume, gives rise to the temptation to generalize. What are writers writing about? Where are the good stories coming from? What are the trends? I'm happy to report that I had only to identify a trend tentatively for it to vanish into thin air. The more I read, the more variety I encountered, in voice, theme, and setting. One cannot read this collection without a deepening respect for the sheer range of human experience.

And yet, these stories do have something in common. All of them give voice to our universal quest for connection. If there is one sweeping statement that can legitimately be made about these twenty stories, it is this: each is about a struggle to connect. There is a Vietnamese woman, happily transplanted to America yet fervently awaiting the arrival of her grandfather, the only person still alive who knew her as a child; an aging film actress whose self-esteem has ebbed so low that she can no longer reach out to anyone who might genuinely care for her; a widow who knows that her own time on earth is short but who nevertheless treats even her most casual acquaintances with unfailing respect; an amateur fighter who suspects that his relationship with his merciless trainer may be the closest he will ever come to love. "Only connect!" wrote E. M. Forster — and most of us spend our lives endeavoring to do just that. This volume features stories of connections lost and found, avoided and embraced, mourned and celebrated.

Alice Adams reveals in her introduction that reading a good story often provokes her to go and write one of her own. Perhaps we should all give thanks, then, for the inspiration writers draw from each other — one good story begets another. Surely this is a testament to the power of fiction to call forth our own creative impulses. For most of us, I suspect, this inspiration takes another form. In the afterglow of a good short story, consciousness is heightened — we see more clearly, gain fresh perspective, seek to live more thoughtfully and independently. A few years ago, there was concern in certain quarters that the proliferation of writing schools and workshops would result in homogenized fiction, technically proficient but lacking in passion and originality. The stories of 1990 offer compelling evidence that our best fiction writers are in no danger. Here are writers who know what they need to say, who are willing to risk all in the telling, and who suffer no crises of influence. Their stories will kindle your imagination. In the Contributors' Notes, the authors offer us a welcome glimpse into the creative process, as they describe the genesis of the stories collected here.

With this volume, I become the fourth series editor of *The Best American Short Stories,* following in the footsteps of three dedicated readers and friends of the short story: Edward O'Brien, who launched the series in 1915 and presided over it until 1941; Martha Foley, who, when she died in 1977, at the age of eighty, was at work on what would have been her thirty-seventh volume; and Shannon Ravenel, who, over the past thirteen years, has helped the series achieve the prominence it enjoys today. Since 1978, a different writer or critic has served each year as guest editor of the anthology, thereby ensuring its continued diversity. The variety of viewpoints has enlivened the series and resulted in volumes that reflect the passions and predilections of some of the finest writers at work today.

The stories chosen for this year's anthology were originally published in magazines issued between January 1990 and January 1991. The qualifications for selection are: (1) original publication in nationally distributed American or Canadian periodicals; (2) publication in English by writers who are American or Canadian, or who have made the United States or Canada their home; and (3) publication as short stories (novel excerpts are not knowingly considered). A list of the magazines consulted for this volume appears at the back of the book. Publications that want to make sure that their contributors will be considered each year should include the series editor on their subscription list (Katrina Kenison, *The Best American Short Stories,* Houghton Mifflin Company, 2 Park Street, Boston, MA 02108).

K.K.

Introduction

I AM DEEPLY enamored of short stories. The form delights me. Both reading and writing short stories have for many years given me much pleasure. And so I came to the task of reading a great many stories for this collection with an agreeable sense of anticipation. I looked forward to the sheer joy that a good story, a good read, brings — and also, since this work would involve some critical evaluation in making selections, I hoped that my critical standards would become more clearly formulated in the process.

In the first expectation I have to say that I was somewhat disappointed. I had imagined very difficult choices. I saw myself choosing twenty excellent stories from hundreds of good ones, imagined the ambivalence, the painful indecision. As things turned out, though, the choices were not all that difficult; the excellent stories made their presence felt very strongly, on first reading. (I should say too that the pleasure I derived from that reading, in many cases the discovery of a new voice, was all that I could have hoped for.)

But there should have been more first-rate stories from which to choose. What has happened to the wonderful renaissance of the short story that we have heard so much about for the past few years?

I would not pretend to know why, as it seems to me, fewer really good stories are being written now than, say, ten or fifteen years ago, but as I looked over the list of magazines from which I made my selection, I felt that at least one clue was offered. Six stories are from *The New Yorker*, one of the most visible and highest-paying magazines on the market (and one that continues to treat writers with great respect); the remaining fourteen are from quarterlies — some distinguished, some relatively unknown, most with a small circulation, and all, to my knowledge, very low- or nonpaying.

Where are the stories from the women's magazines, many of which were publishing good short fiction as recently as ten years ago? It is my impression that these magazines, though they continue from time to time to declare great interest in serious fiction, are publishing much less of it (if any), and that their editorial policies, always condescending toward their readership, have gotten considerably worse. They have always wanted stories, and especially the endings of stories, to be spelled out, explained, as though the women who read these magazines are wholly uneducated and/or mildly retarded, incapable of appreciating a subtle or, God help us, an ambiguous ending. My own most recent encounter with one of these magazines was so appalling — I was pelted with questions like "Why are they drinking Perrier?" and "Why does he kiss her just now?" — that I had to withdraw the story. For me this whole bout was extremely annoying, time- and energy-consuming; it surely would have been far worse for a younger, less experienced writer, say a young woman with a couple of part-time jobs and/or baby sitters to arrange for and pay. For such writers it must indeed be discouraging simply to send out stories, knowing how extremely poor their chances are. In a way I do not wonder that fewer and fewer good writers seem to be writing short stories.

There is, of course, a more or less alternate group of magazines, the male slicks. They pay extremely well, and occasionally, still, one of them will publish a good story. But as with the women's magazines, this apparently happens less and less frequently.

The sheer economics of short story writing, then, might to some degree explain why many writers decide not to take it up. I find it sad to recall that in the distant forties, writing short stories was a plausible full-time trade and, for many of us who started out then, an extremely attractive one. In those days there was not only *The New Yorker* but a whole array of high-exposure, high-paying magazines, as well as an enormous number of smaller, prestigious "little" magazines and reviews. How one laments their demise!

I am not saying that short stories are written primarily (or even secondarily) to earn money for their writers; still, it seems in some sense deeply wrong for someone who has taken several months to write a good story to be compensated with a hundred dollars or less, or with no dollars and a subscription to a magazine.

One encouraging sign is that book publishers are becoming more generous about bringing out volumes of stories by relatively unknown writers. Until fairly recently, writers had to bribe their publishers with promises of novels to come in order to have such a book published. It is possible that publishers have become aware of excellent writers of short stories who simply do not write novels, do not wish to and never will. Raymond Carver, of course, comes first to mind; it seems vastly to his credit that he chose to spend his energies and intelligence in trying to perfect his skill in the form he loved. And it worked — his excellent stories got better and better and better. In any case, it is good to see so many volumes of stories, and extremely interesting to note that in many cases, despite the excellence of the work, it has never been published before, in any magazine or review.

Book reviewers, I have sometimes felt, do not like collections of short stories. For one thing, you have to read them all; you cannot just skim for plot and tone and then turn in your review. Also, a good collection, even by a single writer, is apt to contain considerable variety; you can't just read one or two stories and come to strong conclusions as to theme, intention, use of energy, whatever. Although heaven knows this has been attempted. My favorite personal instance is that of a reviewer who insisted that in a collection of my stories *all* the heroines left their husbands/ lovers for frivolous reasons. There was one story, however, that he liked in spite of himself, whose heroine he described as a widow; the only problem was that I had described her as having been somewhat cruelly and very intentionally dumped by her husband.

Wallace Stegner says in the introduction to the recently published edition of his collected stories that short stories are a young writer's form, "made for discoveries and nuances and epiphanies and superbly adapted for trial synthesis." I am not at all sure what this means, but it strikes me generally as a highly personal view, and one with which I cannot agree. My own experience aside (I *know* that I am writing better stories now than I did at thirty), much short story literature disproves his point. Perhaps the greatest living practitioner of the form, V. S. Pritchett, is over ninety, and many people writing good short stories now are at least over fifty — John Updike, Joyce Carol Oates, Millicent Dillon (I hope I am not off about anyone's age). And as for the brilliant young — say, Lorrie Moore, or Rick Bass — it seems most likely that they, like Pritchett, will simply get better and better.

Which brings us to my second aim from all this reading: more clarity about what that elusive marvel the good short story actually is. Anne Lamott, a remarkable young novelist who, alas, does not write short stories, shares my enthusiasm for the stories of Alice Munro, and she thus describes her pleasure in a Munro story: "It's like a perfect meal at Chez Panisse, exotic and delicate and imaginative, really beautiful, and afterwards you're perfectly satisfied and happy and comforted. Not stuffed and never bored." I quite agree, although I am not at all sure that this standard can be applied to all good stories — in fact, I know that it cannot. Mary Gordon's "Separation," for example, leaves one almost gasping with pain at the same time that one admires its devastating skill and the pure compassion that informs its creation.

One obviously important factor (true in any fiction, novels as well as stories) is that of sheer interest, or narrative curiosity; one wants to find out what happens. In this volume, I think, this is most clearly true in the stories by Millicent Dillon and Leonard Michaels — very different stories in terms of style and governing sensibility, but both fairly long narratives that one reads with extreme curiosity. Whatever will happen to that young woman who has chosen such an aberrant milieu? one wonders, reading Ms. Dillon's "Oil and Water." And in Leonard Michaels's ornate, exotic, and baroquely structured "Viva la Tropicana," one reads quite feverishly about the extraordinary events surrounding a most curious inheritance.

"It's simply a question of what grabs you" I have heard as an explanation of taste in short stories, a remark that is usually accompanied by its corollary (which we all know too), "and of course in a short story that has to happen right away." I suppose that this is true, for who could not go on with a story that begins "My mother had me sort the eyes. Blue in the biggest box, green in the middle, brown in the smallest box" — the opening lines of Elizabeth Graver's "The Body Shop"? But then, all the stories in this collection have wonderful opening lines. How about "In the middle of the eulogy at my mother's boring and heartbreaking funeral, I started to think about calling off the wedding," from "Love Is Not a Pie," by Amy Bloom? Or "So often, at weddings, one kisses and hugs the bride and groom and then stands there dumbstruck, grinning with dread," from "Dog Stories," by Francine Prose? And no, I do not have a special fondness for stories having to do with weddings.

I do have an important private criterion, though, which is a very particular sort of excitement, familiar (I have been aware of this for over forty years) but hard to describe, that comes with certain stories. What I can most accurately say is that on reading these stories, I am seized with a desire to write a story of my own. The story that I long to write is not necessarily in any sense "like" or even influenced by the story that set off its impulse. Often, for example, I have felt this urgency on reading stories by Joyce Carol Oates; I have come away from reading one of them highly excited, inspired, and have written, though slowly, one of my own, a story that no one would ever suspect of having been inspired by Ms. Oates. Further back, in the forties, which is when I first began to read stories, I was excited in just that way by the work of Elizabeth Bowen, Katherine Anne Porter, Scott Fitzgerald, Mark Schorer — to name a few of the marvelous writers publishing then.

But obviously this is not a reliable criterion for selecting stories. I might (I hope I would) recognize an excellent story about the recent Gulf war; however, I don't think I would have to such a story the sort of response that triggers new work in myself. And so we are left with our private criteria, what grabs us — our individual and sometimes collectively inexplicable reasons for enthusiasm for certain stories.

I would like, though, to thank all the writers of the stories collected here for the pleasure I have taken in their work, and in many cases for the inspiration. And I want to thank, too, Katrina Kenison, who did the preliminary reading for this enterprise, which is to say that she read several thousand stories, probably, while I only dealt with the couple of hundred that she culled from the rest.

ALICE ADAMS

The Best
AMERICAN
SHORT
STORIES
1991

RICK BASS

The Legend of Pig-Eye

FROM THE PARIS REVIEW

WE USED TO GO to bars, the really seedy ones, to find our fights.
It excited Don. He loved going into the dark old dives, ducking
under the doorway and following me in, me with my robe on, my
boxing gloves tied around my neck, and all the workers inside
the bar turning on their stools, turning as if someday someone
special might be coming through, someone who could even help
them out, perhaps — but Don and I were not there to help them
out.

Don had always trained his fighters this way, all of them: in
bars, with poor lighting and a hostile, hometown crowd. We would
get in his old red truck on Friday afternoons — Don, his wife Betty,
and Jason, their fourteen-year-old son, and my two hounds,
Homer and Ann — and we'd take out driving, heading for either
the coast — Biloxi, Ocean Springs, Pascagoula — or sometimes
up into the woods, to the Wagon Wheel bar in Utica, or, if it had
been a long enough time, long enough for them to have forgotten the speed of the punches and the force and snap of them,
we'd go into Jackson, to the rotting, sawdust-floor bars like the
Body Shop or the Tall Low Man. That was where the most money
could be made, and it was sometimes where the best fighters could
be found, but not always.

Jason would wait out in the truck with the dogs. Sometimes
Betty would stay out there with him, with the windows rolled down,
so that they could tell how the fight was going; but other times
she would come in with Don and me, because that was what would
get the bets up, a woman who had come in with a man and who
was not drinking, who was only there for the fight.

We'd make anywhere from five hundred to a thousand dollars per fight, from our bets.

"Anybody, any size, any age, man or woman," Don would say, standing behind the bar with his notepad, taking bets, though I never fought a woman. The people in the bar would pick their best fighter, and they'd watch Betty, and watch Don, or they'd watch their fighter — but they didn't ever watch me the way they should have if they were going to bet on it; and I would look around, I would wish there was better lighting, and then I'd take my robe off, I'd have my gold trunks on underneath, and sometimes a few of them, drunk or sober, would begin to realize that they had done the wrong thing. But by that time things were in motion, the bets had already been made, and there was nothing to do but play it out.

Don had said that when I won a hundred bar fights, I could go to New York. He knew a man up there, a promoter to whom he sometimes sent his better fighters after training them, and that was what I had to do to get up there: win a hundred fights.

Don was forty-four — Betty, thirty-eight — and Don only trained one fighter at a time. Don hadn't boxed in almost twenty years. Betty had made him promise, swear on all sorts of things, to stop, when they got married. Don had been very good, but he had started seeing double after one fight, a fight he'd won but had been knocked down in three times, and he still saw double, twenty years later, when he got tired.

Whenever we talked about the fights, after they were over, it was always *us, we, ours.* My parents thought fighting was the worst thing a person could do, and so I liked the way Don always said "we": it was like I wasn't misbehaving all by myself, like it was someone else's wrongdoing, too. Don knew that. We'd come back out to the truck after a fight, carrying the money in a cigar box. A light mist might be falling, in the summer, and Don would be holding my robe over Betty's head to keep her dry, and we'd be hurrying to get out of the rain, but also to get away from the bar.

"How'd it go?" Jason would ask.

"We smoked 'em," Don would say. "We had a straight counterpuncher, a good man, but we kept our gloves up, worked on his body, and then got him with an overhand right. He didn't know what hit him. When he came to, he wanted to check our gloves, to see if we had put *lead* in them."

Jason would squeal, then smack his forehead, wishing that he'd been able to see it, wishing that he'd been old enough to go into the bar.

We'd put the dogs, black-and-tan pups, in the back of the truck. The faithful Homer-dog would be frantic at having been separated from me and would scramble around in the back, howling, pawing and leaping; but fat Ann would curl up on a burlap sack and fall quickly asleep — and we'd go out for pizza, then, or to a drive-through hamburger place, and we'd talk about the fight, as we waited for our order, and we'd count the money to make sure it was all there, though if it wasn't, we sure weren't going back after it. We used the old rattle-truck so that when the drunks, angry that their fighter had lost, came out into the parking lot, throwing bottles and rocks at us as we drove a way, it would not matter too much if they hit the truck.

Usually we could tell just from looking at the outside what a place was going to be like, if it was the kind of place where we would have to leave Betty in the truck with Jason — sometimes with the engine running — and where we did not know for sure if we would win or lose.

We looked for the backwoods nightspots, more gathering-place than bar, and with huge, angry men — men who either worked hard for a living and hated their jobs or who did not work and hated that, too, or who hated everything, usually beginning with some small incident a long time ago — these were the kinds of men and places we wanted to find, because they were as much of a challenge as any pro fighter would be.

Some nights we would not find the right kind of bar, the one we were looking for, until almost midnight, and Betty would be asleep with her head in Don's lap, and Jason would be driving so I could rest, and the dogs would be asleep on the floorboard. Then, finally, there would be the glow of lights in the fog, the crunch of a crushed-shell parking lot beneath our tires, and a cinder-block tavern, sometimes near the Alabama state line and set back in the woods, with loud music coming through the doors, seeping through the roof and into the night, and the clack of pool balls between songs, It was an angry, caged sound, and we'd feel a little fear in our hearts, it would be just perfect.

"We'll be out in a while," Don would tell Jason. "Pistol's in the glove box. Leave the engine running. Watch after your mother."

The noise would rush out at us like wild dog when we opened the door, and the smell of beer, the smell of anger, the hostile, attacking eyes turning on us when we were swallowed up inside. . . .

We kept a tag hanging on the rearview mirror that told us how many fights in a row we had won, what the magic number was, and after each fight, it was Jason's job to take down the old tag and put the new one up.

Eighty-six. Eighty-seven. Eighty-eight.

Driving home, back to Don's little farm in the woods: Jason with the radio on, steering the truck with just one hand and with the other arm thrown up over the seat next to him like a little man, already like a farmer driving the truck to market on a Saturday. He was a good driver.

We kept rocking chairs in the back of the truck, for the long drives, and sometimes after a fight Don and I would sit in the back like that, with our backs to the cab, and we'd lean back, looking up at the night, and watch the stars and the tops of the big trees that formed tunnels over the lonely back roads. We'd whistle down the road as Jason bombed along, driving hard, with the windows down and his mother asleep in the front. The dogs would be asleep at my feet.

When we drove through the creek bottoms the fog would rise all around us, so we could barely see, and Jason would slow down slightly, and the air would be warm and damp, and the stars would be gone, but when we'd be going fast again, getting back up into the hills, and the air would be clean and cool, we'd see stars once more, and we'd be driving sixty, seventy miles an hour.

We'd lean back and talk about fighting. I was twenty, but I wanted to be fourteen again. I wanted to be like Jason, and I wondered what it would have been like to drive my father and mother around like that, to be able to do something for them, something right. Jason was already like a little man. My parents lived in Chickasay, Oklahoma, and raised cattle, and owned a store.

I thought it would be nice if I could win the one hundred fights and go to New York and turn pro and send my parents money. Don got to keep all of the bar fight money, and he was going to get to keep a quarter of the New York money, if there ever was any. I wanted to buy my parents a new house or some more cattle

or something, the way I read other athletes did, once they made
it big. My childhood had been wonderful, and already I was beginning to miss it, and I wanted to give them something.

When I took the robe off and moved in on the bar-fighter, there
was Don and Betty and Jason to think of, too. They were just
making expenses, barely — nothing more. I could not bear to
think of letting them down. I did not know what my parents
wanted for sure but I did know what Don and Jason and Betty
wanted, so that made it easier, and after a while it became easier
to pretend that it was all the same, that everyone wanted the same
thing, and all I had to do was go out there and fight.

Don had been a chemist once for the coroner's lab in Jackson.
He knew about chemicals, drugs. He knew how to dope my blood,
days before a fight, so that I would feel clean and strong, new
blood, a new man. He knew how to give me smelling salts, sniffs
of ammonia vials broken under my nose when I was fighting
sloppily, sniffs that made my eyes water and my nose and lungs
burn but that focused me, made me remember what everyone
wanted. And even in training, Don would sometimes feint, sparring without gloves, and would catch me off-guard, going one
way when I should have been going the other, and then he would
slip in and clasp a chloroform handkerchief over my face; I'd see
a mixed field of black, and of sparkling, night-rushing stars, and
then I'd be down, collapsed in the pine needles down by the lake
where we did our sparring, and I'd feel the sun on my shoulders,
the sun on my back, feel a delicious sense of rest, lying there, and
I'd want to stay down forever, but I'd hear Don shouting, counting, ". . . Three! FOUR! FIVE!" and I'd have to roll over, get my
knees beneath me, and rise, stagger-kneed, and the lake a hard
glimmer of heat all around me, and Don would be moving in on
me, dancing around me like a demon, moving in and slapping
me with that tremendous reach of his and then dancing back,
and I had to get my gloves up and stay up, had to follow the blur
of him, with that backdrop of deep woods and lake, with everything looking new and different suddenly, making no sense, and
that, Don said, was what it was like to get knocked out, and he
wanted me to practice it occasionally so that I would know what
to do when it finally happened: in New York, or Philadelphia, or
even in a bar.

We shaved my body hair before each fight, me sitting in a chair down by the lake in my shorts, while the three of them, with razors and buckets of soapy water, shaved my legs, my back, my chest, arms, everything, so that the blows would slide away from me rather than cutting, and so that I would move faster, or at least *feel* faster — that new feeling, the feeling of being someone else, newer, younger, and with a fresher start.

After they had me all shaved, I would walk out on the pier and dive into the lake, plunging deep, ripping the water with my new slipperiness, and I would swim a few easy strokes, swimming out into the middle, where I would tread water, feeling how unbelievably slippery I was, how free and unattached, and then I would swim back in, and some days, walking with Don and Betty and Jason back up to the house, my hair slicked back and dripping, clean and shaven, with the woods smelling good in the summer and the pine needles dry and warm beneath my bare feet — some days, then, with the lake behind me, and feeling changed, I could almost tell what it was that everyone wanted, which was nothing, and I was very happy.

After our bar fights, we'd get back home around two or three in the morning; I'd nap on the way, though, in the rocker in the back of the truck, rocking slightly, pleasantly, whenever we hit a bump in the road. Sometimes I would dream, completely relaxed, with my robe wrapped around me and the wind whipping my hair; but whenever I woke up and looked at Don, he would be awake.

He would be watching the stars still, or looking back, watching the darkness and trees slide in across the road behind our taillights, filling in behind us as the road thinned and then disappeared, with Jason driving like a bat out of hell, driving with the windows down so that coffee cups and bits of hay and gum wrappers swirled around inside the cab.

Sometimes Don would have turned his chair around, so that he was looking into the cab, looking in over Jason's shoulder watching him drive, watching his wife sleep. Don had been a good boxer but the headaches and double vision had just gotten too bad. I wondered what it would take for me to stop. I could not imagine anything would. It was the only thing I could do well.

On the long narrow gravel road leading into Don's farm, with

the smell of night honeysuckle and the calls of chuck-will's-wid-
ows, Jason would slow the truck down and drive carefully, respecting the value of home, and the near-sacredness of the place.
. . . Trees formed a tunnel over the gravel lane here, too, and it
was dark and cool.

At the crest of the hill he would turn the engine and lights off,
up above the lake, and coast the rest of the way, pumping the
squeaky brakes, turning the radio off, and in silence we'd glide
down the hill. The dogs would smell the lake and scramble to
their feet and leap over the sides of the truck and race down to
the lake to inspect it, to hunt for frogs.

The porch light would be on, and I had never lost a fight. There
was no feeling like it in the world. Part of me wanted to win the
one hundred fights and go to New York and see how far I could
go, and part of me did not.

I slept in a little bunkhouse, a guest cottage they had built for
their boxers down by the lake. Don's and Betty's and Jason's home
was up on the hill, a larger home, with a picnic table out front,
and a garage — it was a regular-looking house, a cabin. But I liked
my cottage. I didn't even have a phone. I had stopped telling my
parents about the fights. There was not much else to tell them
about, other than the fights, but I tried to think of other things
that might interest them. Sometimes I would write them about
the lake. Nights, after Don and Betty and Jason had gone to bed,
I would go out into the water by myself, and would swim out into
the middle, and with the moon burning bright above me, almost
like a sun, I'd float on my back, and fill my lungs with air, and I'd
just float there, sometimes for thirty minutes or an hour.

The dogs would be swimming in circles around me, loyal and
panting, dog-paddling in frantic but determined circles, sneez-
ing water at times, and I could feel the currents passing beneath
me as they paddled. They would stay out there with me for however long I was out there. I admired them for staying out there
like that, not knowing how to float, always paddling, but staying
out there. I felt like I was their father. I felt like an old man, but
with my young man's health.

I'd float like that until I felt ready again, until I felt as if I'd
never won a fight in my life, and as if it was all new, and I was just
starting over, as if I had everything to prove, and had never done

anything; that was the way I liked to feel, and I would float there until I was reassured that that was how it really was.

I was free, then, and I would break for shore, then swimming again in long slow strokes, and I'd get out and walk through the trees over to my cottage, with the dogs following, shaking water from their coats and rattling their collars, and I know the air felt as cool on them as it did on me. We couldn't see the stars, down in the trees like that. It felt very safe, very cool, even though the night was hot.

I'd walk through the woods like that, with my own blood in me, but also another man's, another woman's, too, and another boy's; and I'd snap on my yellow porch light as I went into the cottage, so that it would attract moths, and I'd go into my back room and lie down on the mattress, damp, with all the windows and doors open and the breezes passing over me, cooling me, burying me, with sleep coming like a certain kind of safety.

The porch light pulled in every moth in the county. Homer and Ann would stand on their hind feet and dance, snapping for hours, leaping up at the moths into the smallest hours, teeth clicking, snapping, jumping. There were frogs down on the lake, drumming all night, and crickets and katydids; the noise was like that at a baseball game on a hot day, always some insistent noises above others, rising and falling. I could hear the dogs crunching June bugs as they caught them.

Right before daylight Betty would ring a bell to wake me for breakfast. Don and I ate at the picnic table, a light breakfast, because we were about to run — me on foot, and Don on horseback.

Don was a genius trainer.

"You will miss me when you get up to New York," he said. "They'll lock you in a gym and work on your *technique,*" he said. "You'll never see the light of day. But you'll have to do it."

I did not want to leave Betty and Jason, did not even want to leave Don, despite the training sessions. It would be fun to fight in a real ring, with paying spectators, a canvas mat, a referee, and ropes, safety ropes to hold you in — I would not mind leaving the bar fights behind at all — but I could not tell Don about my fears. I was half horrified that a hundred wins in Mississippi would

mean nothing, and that I would be unable to win even one fight
in New York.

Don said I was "a fighter, not a boxer."

He had had other fighters who had gone on to New York and
who had done well, who had won many fights; one of them, his
best before me, Pig-Eye Reeves, had been ranked as high as fifth
as a W.B.A. heavyweight. Pig-Eye was a legend, and in Mississippi there were stories and tales about him almost everywhere.
Don knew all of them.

Pig-Eye had swum in the lake I swam in; Pig-Eye ate at the very
same picnic table. Pig-Eye had lived in my cottage, Pig-Eye had
run the trails I ran, daily, the ones Don chased me down, riding
his big black stallion, Killer, and cracking his bullwhip, trying to
run me down.

That was how we trained: after breakfast, Don would head for
the barn, to saddle Killer, and I'd whistle the dogs up and start
down toward the lake. The sun would be coming up on the other
side of the woods, burning steam and mist off of the lake, and
things would be getting clearer, the individual shapes of trees
through the mist on the far side, and I'd be walking, feeling for
once, or at least briefly, good and healthy, as if I would never let
anyone down, and then I would hear the horse running down
the hill through the trees, coming after me, snorting, and I'd hear
his hooves, the saddle creaking, with Don riding silently, posting,
and then when he spotted me, he'd crack the whip once, that short
mean "pop!" and I would have to run.

Don made me wear leg weights and wrist weights. The dogs,
running beside me, sometimes ahead of me, thought it was a game.
It was not. Sometimes for punishment, when I didn't run fast
enough and Don and Killer got too close to me, Don would catch
my shoulder with the tip of the whip, would cut a small stripe
into my sweaty back, which I could feel in the form of heat, but
which I knew meant nothing, because he was only doing it to
protect me, to make me run faster, to keep me from being trampled by the horse.

Don wore spurs, big Mexican rowels he'd bought in an antique
store, and he rode Killer hard, and I ran hard, not wanting to let
Don down, not wanting to be trampled — and I'd leave the trail
sometimes, leaping over logs and dodging around trees and re-

versing my direction, but still Killer stayed with me, leaping the
same logs, galloping through the same brush, though I was better at turning corners and could stay slightly ahead of him that
way, whenever it got too close.

This would go on for an hour or so, until the sun was up over
the trees, and the sky bright and warm, and then, too, when Don
figured the horse was getting too tired, too bloody from the spurs,
he would shout "Swim!" and that meant that it was over, that I
could go into the lake.

"The Lake of Peace!" Don would roar, snapping the whip and
spurring Killer, and the dogs and I would splash out into the reeds,
gasping, scattering frogs and red-winged blackbirds in all directions, the mud warm around my ankles, and then we'd be out
into the shallows, me running awkwardly, high-stepping the way
you do going into the waves at the beach, and then the dogs were
floating, swimming, and it was waist-deep on me, I was leaning
forward too, into the warm water, and would feel the weeds
brushing my knees, and would hear Killer right behind us, still
coming: but we would be swimming hard, swimming for our
lives — the dogs would be whining and rolling their eyes back
like Chinese dragons, paddling furiously, trying to see behind
them. Killer would be swimming too by then, blowing hard
through his nostrils and grunting, much too close to us, trying to
swim right over the top of us, but the dogs stayed with me, as if
they thought they could protect me, and with the leg weights trying
to weigh me down and pull me under, I'd near the middle of the
lake, the deepest part, where the water turned cold.

I'd swim across that dark cold center, and that was where the
horse, frightened, slowed down, sometimes panicking at the
water's coldness and swimming in circles rather than pushing on.
The chase was forgotten then, by the time I made it out to the
center, and the dogs and I would keep swimming, with the other
side of the lake drawing closer finally, and Jason and Betty standing on the shore jumping and cheering, waving pennants. The
water would begin to get shallow again, we'd feel land beneath
our feet, good clean gravel on that side of the lake, and wet and
heavy, we'd come crawling out of the lake, and Betty would hand
me a towel, Jason would dry off the dogs, and then we'd walk up
the hill toward the cabin for lunch, which would already be pre-

pared, spread out on a checkered tablecloth and waiting for me as if there had never been any doubt that I would make it.

Don would still be laboring, in the lake, shouting and cursing the horse now, trying to rein Killer out of the angry, confused circles he was still swimming, cracking the whip and giving him muted, underwater jabs of the spurs, until finally, with his last breath, Killer would recognize that the far shore was as good as the near one, that in fact the far shore had somehow *become* the near one, and they'd make it in finally, struggling, twenty or thirty minutes behind the dogs and me.

Killer would lie on his side, gasping, coughing up seaweed, ribs rising and falling, and Don would come up the hill to join us for lunch: fried chicken, cream gravy, hot biscuits with honey, string beans from the garden, great wet red quarter-sections of water-melons, and long cool slices of cantaloupe, and a pitcher of iced tea for each of us . . . we ate shirtless, barefooted, and threw the rinds to the dogs, who wrestled and fought over them like wolves.

It would be straight-up noon. The sun would press down through the trees, reflecting off of the cabin, off of the table-cloth, off of the ground itself, the pine needles; and out through the trees, down the hill and in the opening in the woods, it would glint off of the Lake of Peace.

We'd change into our bathing suits, all of us, and inflate our air mattresses and carry them down to the lake, and we'd wade out into the lake's warm water, and with suntan oil on our backs and our legs, our cheeks and foreheads, and chests, we'd float directly beneath the sun, wearing sunglasses, our arms trailing loosely in the water, and we'd nap as if stunned after the heavy meal, while the dogs whined and paced the shore, afraid we might not come back.

Killer, still lying on the shore, would stare glassy-eyed at noth-ing, ribs still rising and falling in the sun. He would stay like that until midafternoon, when he would finally roll over and get to his feet, and then he would trot up the hill as if nothing had hap-pened.

We drifted all over the lake, in our half-stupor, our sated, sum-mer-day sleep. My parents wanted me to come home and take over the hardware store. But there was nothing in the world that could make me stop fighting. I wished that there was, because I liked the hardware store, but that was simply how it was. I felt that if I could not fight, I might stop breathing, or I might go down: I imagined that it was like drowning; like floating in the lake, and then exhaling all my air, and sinking, and never being heard from again.

I could not see myself ever giving up fighting, and I wondered how Don had done it.

We floated and lazed, dreaming, each of us spinning out across the lake in different directions whenever a small breeze would blow, eventually drifting farther and farther apart, but on the shore, the dogs followed only me, tracking me around the lake, following, staying with me, whining for me to come back in to the shore.

Some afternoons, after an especially good run and an exhausting swim, I would be unable to even lift my arms. I would just float and perspire, greasy in the sun, with minnows nibbling at my toes, the tips of my fingers, and nothing mattered, I would never move again, and I would sometimes think the blasphemy that this is how I can give up, this is how I can never fight again. I can drop out, raise a family, and float on the lake in the bright sun all day, the Lake of Peace. This is maybe how I can do it, I'd think. Perhaps my son could be a boxer.

Fights number eighty-nine, ninety, ninety-one; I tore a guy's jaw off in the Body Shop. I felt it give way and then detach, heard the ripping sound that sounded as if it came from somewhere else, and it was sickening — we left without any of the betting money, gave it all to his family for the hospital bill, but it certainly did not stop me from fighting, or even from hitting hard. I was very angry about something, but did not know what. I'd sit in the back of the truck with Don on the ride home, the dogs' heads in my lap, the wind ruffling their fur, and I'd know that I wanted something, but did not know what. I assumed it was boxing. Boxing helped.

Sometimes Don would have to lean forward and massage his temples, his head hurt so badly. He ate handfuls of aspirin, ate them like M&M's, chewing them, so bad was the pain, and he chased them down with beer, with two beers, with three or four. I would panic when he did that and think that he was dying, and

I wondered if that was where my anger came from, if I fought so wildly and viciously in an attempt, somehow and with no logic, to keep things from changing.

On the evenings that we did not have a fight, we would spar a little, in the barn. Killer watching us wild-eyed from his paddock, waiting to get to me. Don made me throw a bucket of lake water on him each time I went into the barn to make sure that his hate for me did not wane. Killer would scream whenever I did this and Jason would howl and blow on the noisemaker and bang two metal garbage can lids together, a deafening sound inside the barn, while Killer, dripping from the bucket of water, would scream and rear up on his hind legs and try to break free, but the stables were built strongly, solidly, and he couldn't get out — and then, after sparring (Jason with a stopwatch, sitting in the corner, banging the garbage can lids together whenever a round was over), we would go back up to the house, and Betty would fix us supper.

We grilled corn from Betty's garden and a huge porterhouse steak from cattle Don had slaughtered himself, and lima beans and Irish potatoes, also from the garden. It felt like I was family. We ate at the picnic table as bats skimmed and dove, climbed and twisted over the lake, which would be disappearing as the evening fog moved in from out of the woods. When the lake steamed like that, it was as if everyone could see what I was thinking: my thoughts bare and exposed, out in the middle like that, but it didn't matter, because Don and Betty and Jason cared for me, and also because I was not going to fail.

Owls would be calling, back in the woods. We could hear Killer in the stables, chewing his oats noisily, still angry. The dogs would be lying under the picnic table, eyes closed, breathing heavily, sometimes twitching, chasing rabbits. Someday I wanted a family like Don's.

After dinner we would watch old fight films. We used a sheet strung between two pine trees for the screen. We set the projector up on the picnic table and Don used a crooked branch for a pointer. Some of the films were of past champions, but some were old movies of Don fighting. We could make the film go in slow motion to show the combinations that led to knockdowns, and Betty would always have to get up and leave whenever we watched one of the old splintery films of Don's fights. It just wasn't any fun for her, even though she knew he was going to win, or was going to get back up again after going down — and she couldn't ever seem to acknowledge the fact that it wasn't really happening, that it was twenty years old, and that the blows from the past had long ago stopped hurting anyone.

I had seen all of Don's fights a hundred times, and had watched all the films of the greatest fighters thousands of times, and I would get bored. Fighting is not films. It's experience, repetition. I knew what to do, when to do it. I'd look out past the bedsheet, and past the flickering washes of light — Jason and Don would be leaning forward, breathless, watching Don stalk his victim, everything silent except for the clicking of the projector and the crickets and the frogs and sometimes the owls — and I'd wonder what New York was going to be like, if it was going to be anything like this.

Some nights, after the movies had ended, we would talk about Pig-Eye Reeves. Don's best fighter before me. It had only been a few years ago, so Jason even remembered him, though not as clearly as Don did. We were so familiar with the stories that it seemed to all of us, even to me, who had never met him, that we remembered it clearly; both Jason and I knew almost all of the Pig-Eye stories by heart.

Pig-Eye had knocked out one of Don's trained fighters in a bar up in the Delta one night, the Green Frog. That was how Don had found him, he had beaten Don's challenger, had just stepped up out of the crowd. Don's fighter, whose name Don always pretended he could not remember, threw the first punch, a wicked, winging right, not even bothering to set up with a jab — Don says he covered his face with his hands and groaned, knowing what was going to happen — and Pig-Eye, full of beer, was still able to duck it, evidently, because Don heard nothing but the rip of air, and then, a little delayed, the sound of another glove hitting a nose, a grunt, and the sound of a body falling in the sawdust.

Don and Jason and Betty left the fighter there in the Green Frog, semiconscious, with blood all over his chest and trunks and a broken nose. They drove home with no money and Pig-Eye.

They flipped the numbers on the truck mirror, from wherever they had been before — forty-five or fifty — back to one. Pig-Eye had won one fight.

He rode in the back with Don, the way I do now, and they looked at the stars. Betty drove. Jason says he can remember it, but he would have only been about six, and he probably was asleep.

"You just left your other fighter sitting there?" I asked the first time I heard the story, though I know better than to ask now.

Don had seemed confused by the question. "He wasn't my fighter anymore," he said finally.

Sometimes Jason would ask the question for me, so I didn't have to, and so I could pretend it didn't matter, as if I wasn't even thinking about it.

"Is Mack a better fighter than Pig-Eye?" he'd ask after watching the movies, whenever we got to talking about Pig-Eye.

Don would answer like a coach, every time. He was wonderful; he was the best.

"Mack is better than Pig-Eye ever dreamed of being," he'd say, clapping a big hand on my shoulder and neck and giving me the Vulcan death squeeze, his hand the size of a license plate. Jason would grin. Jason would never have to fight for his father's love, or have to prove his own.

"Tell him about the balloon," Jason would cry, almost every night, when he had reached a fever pitch for Pig-Eye stories. There were many stories, but the balloon was perhaps the best.

Don would lean back against a tree and smile at his son. He would rub his temples slightly, and I'd wonder if he was seeing double, as if he had two sons, twins, waiting to hear his story. The old projector would be cooling down, making ticking sounds in the summer night, and the lights would be off in the house. Betty would have gone to bed. Moths around the porch light, fluttering and falling, and down below us, in the darkness, the Lake of Peace, with bullfrogs drumming, and no other sound.

"Pig-Eye won his last five fights down here with one hand tied behind his back," Don said, closing his eyes and remembering, smiling, and I'd wonder if I could do that, wondered if in fact I'd *have* to do that, to ride down the legend of Pig-Eye, and pass over it.

"We sent him up to New York, to a promoter I knew" — he looked over at me, quickly, it seemed, and I realized for the first time that the summer was almost over, and I would be going even farther away from my home, farther than I had ever been, and I was not sure I wanted to leave, not for any reason — "the same one we'll be sending Mack to, if he wins the rest of his fights" — Jason squirmed with pleasure, thinking, I suppose, of the excitement of it — "and this promoter, Big Al Wilson, set him up in a penthouse in Manhattan, brought all his meals to him. He had masseuses, masseurs, everything. He was the *champ*," Don said. "Everyone was excited about him."

"Tell him about the scars," Jason said, leaning forward, then moving in and leaning against his dad, moving so that his back was right against the same tree, and it was as if they were both telling me the story now, though I knew it too, we all knew it.

It was late, and there was no moon, a field of stars above us, like far-off cities, cities seen down in a valley at night from a long way off, from up in the mountains, and Jason would be yawning, and I would be too.

"Pig-Eye had all these scars from his bar fights, and from his jobs," Don said. "He'd been in Vietnam, too, and had gotten a lot of scars there; and he flew those crazy hot air balloons for a hobby once he started winning some fights and making some money, and he was always having rough landings, always crashing the balloons and getting cut up that way."

"The big balloons," Jason said. "Eighty feet tall."

"It was a very disturbing thing to Pig-Eye's opponents, whenever he first stepped in the ring against them. They'd all heard about him, but he really had to be seen to be believed."

"Like a zipper," Jason would say, sleepily, but delighted. "He looked like a zipper. I remember."

"Pig-Eye won fourteen fights in New York. He was ranked fifth, and was fighting well. I went to a few of his fights, but then he changed."

"He got different," Jason cautioned.

"He stopped calling, stopped writing, and he started getting a little fat, a little slow. No one else could tell it, but I could."

"He needed Dad for a trainer," said Jason. Killer nickered in his stall, kicked the paddock once.

"He lost," Don said, shaking his head. "He was fighting a nobody fighter, some kid from Japan, and he just didn't have it, one night. He got knocked down four times, until finally he just couldn't get back up. I saw tapes of it later, and he was sitting up, like one of those bears in a zoo, still trying to get up for a fifth time, but he just couldn't do it — it was like he didn't know where his legs were, didn't know what his feet were for, couldn't remember how to do it."

I thought about the ammonia, the chloroform handkerchiefs Don would sometimes place over my face when we were sparring; I wondered if he had gotten that idea after watching Pig-Eye, his best, part of himself, forget how to stand up. I thought that I surely knew how Pig-Eye had felt.

"The balloon," said Jason. There was as wind in the trees, many nights, and it made me feel young and old at the same time: younger than Pig-Eye but older than Jason, and with no turning back, not ever. "The balloon," Jason would say again, punching his father on the shoulder. "This is the best part."

"Pig-Eye was crushed," Don said, sleepy, detached, as if it was no longer Pig-Eye he was talking about, no longer one of his fighters, and I thought again of how they had walked off and left the other fighter, the nameless one, up in the Delta that night, sitting in the sawdust holding his broken nose in the Green Frog Café. "It was the only time Pig-Eye had ever been knocked out, the only time he'd ever lost, and it devastated him," said Don.

"One hundred and fourteen and one," said Jason. "A hundred and fifteen fights, and he'd only lost one."

"But it was my fault," said Don. "It was how I trained him, it was wrong."

"The balloon," said Jason.

"He rented one," Don said, looking up at the stars, speaking to the night. "He went out over the countryside the next day, his face all bandaged up, with a bottle of wine and his girlfriends, and he took it up as high as it could go, and then he cut the strings to the gondola."

"He was good," Jason said solemnly.

"He was too good," said Don.

All that summer, I trained hard for New York. I knew that I would win my hundred fights. I knew that I could win them with one arm tied behind my back, either arm, if Don and Jason wanted it. I was not worried about winning my one hundred bar fights. I was worried about going up to New York, to a strange place, someplace different. Sometimes I did not want to fight anymore, but I never let anyone see that.

Jason was getting older, filling out, that summer, and sometimes Don let Jason ride Killer. We'd all have breakfast, as usual — a small glass of orange juice, half a cantaloupe, two eggs, a strip of bacon, and some toast. Then Jason would saddle Killer, and I'd wake the dogs, and we'd start down toward the lake, moving lazily through the trees toward the water but knowing that in a minute or two we were going to be running.

Don would sit in a chair down by the lake to watch us with his binoculars. He had a whistle he'd blow, to warn me when I was about to be trampled.

The dogs and I would hear the horse, the hard fast hooves coming straight down the hill, and without looking back, we'd start to run.

It would be almost six o'clock then. The sun would just be coming up, and we'd see things as we raced through the woods: turkeys taking dust baths in the center of the trail, and deer slipping back into the woods, and cottontails diving into the brush. The dogs would break off and chase all of these things, briefly, and sometimes they'd rejoin me later on the other side of the lake, with a rabbit hanging from their jaws, and they'd be fighting over it, really wrestling and growling — Ann usually the one who'd caught it, but Homer sometimes taking it away from her.

All of this would be going past at what seemed like ninety miles an hour: trees, vines, logs; greens, browns, blacks, and blue — flashes of the lake, flashes of the sky, flashes of logs on the trail. I knew the course well, knew when to jump, when to dodge. It's said that a healthy man can outrun a horse, over enough distance, but that first mile was the hardest, all that dodging.

Jason shouting, imitating his father, and cracking the whip. The sun up, orange over the tops of the trees, the start of another day of perfection. And then the cry, "The Lake of Peace!" and it would be over, either the horse would be tiring or Jason would be, and I'd rush out into the shallows, a dog on either side of me, tripping and falling, the lake at my ankles, at my knees, coming up around my waist then, and we'd be swimming, with Killer plunging in after us, and Jason still cracking the whip.

Actually there were two stories about Pig-Eye Reeves. I was the only person Don told about the second one. I did not know which one was true. Don said it was possible that the balloon story was not the true one.

If it was, Pig-Eye recovered, survived — and, still distraught over losing, came south, tried to come home, back to Don, to start all over again. But Don already had another fighter, he said, and would not train Pig-Eye anymore.

Don rubs his temples when he tells me this. He is not sure if this is how it went or not.

So Pig-Eye despaired even more, and began drinking bottles of wine, sitting out on the dock and drinking them down the way a thirsty man might drink water; he drank far into the night, singing at the top of his lungs, and Don and Betty had to put pillows over their heads to get to sleep, after first locking the doors.

I think this is how it went.

Then Don woke up around midnight — he never could sleep through the night — and he heard splashing.

He went outside and saw that Pig-Eye had on his wrist and ankle weights, and was swimming, out toward the middle of the lake.

Don said he could see Pig-Eye's wake, could see Pig-Eye at the end of it, stretching it out, splitting the lake in two — and then he disappeared. He'd just gone down and hadn't come up. The lake became smooth again.

Don said that he — Don — sleepwalked sometimes, and thought perhaps that was what it was, but he wasn't sure. They'd had the sheriff's department come out and drag the lake, but never found the body. It was possible that he was still down there, and would be, forever.

Sometimes, as Jason and the horse chased me across the lake, I would think about a game I used to play as a child, in the small town in Oklahoma where I grew up.

When I was in the municipal swimming pool, I would hold my breath, pinch my nose, and duck under the water and shove off from the pool wall's pale blue side, like a frog, breast-stroking, eyes wide and bulging in the reddening chlorine, and I would try to make it all the way to the other side without having to come up for air.

That was the trick, to get all the way to the other side. As the water deepened, there'd be a drumming in the back of my head, and the sinister whine of my ears, pressure, and too, the heart and throat clawing tightly, about halfway across.

I thought about that game, as I swam with Jason and Killer close behind me, I seemed to remember my dogs being with me then, swimming in front of me, as if trying to show me the way, half pulling me across. I know it was not that way at all, because this was many years before their time, and I knew nothing about dogs, or boxing, or living, or trying to hold onto a thing you loved, and letting go of other things to do it.

I only understood what it was like to swim through deeper and deeper water, trying as hard as I could to keep from losing my breath, sucking in water, forever, and trying, still, to make it to the deep end.

CHARLES BAXTER

The Disappeared

FROM THE MICHIGAN QUARTERLY REVIEW

WHAT HE FIRST NOTICED about Detroit and therefore America was the smell. Almost as soon as he walked off the plane, he caught it: an acrid odor of wood ash. The smell seemed to go through his nostrils and take up residence in his head. In Sweden, his own country, he associated this smell with autumn, and the first family fires of winter, the smoke chuffing out of chimneys and settling familiarly over the neighborhood. But here it was midsummer, and he couldn't see anything burning.

On the way in from the airport, with the windows of the cab open and hot stony summer air blowing over his face, he asked the driver about it.

"You're smelling Detroit," the driver said.

Anders, who spoke very precise school English, thought that perhaps he hadn't made himself understood. "No," he said. "I am sorry, I mean the burning smell. What is it?"

The cab driver glanced in the rearview mirror. He was wearing a knitted beret, and his dreadlocks flapped in the breeze. "Where you from?"

"Sweden."

The driver nodded to himself. "Explains why," he said. The cab took a sharp right turn on the freeway and entered the Detroit city limits. The driver gestured with his left hand toward an electronic signboard, a small windowless factory at its base, and a clustered group of cramped clapboard houses nearby. When he gestured, the cab wobbled on the freeway. "Fire's here most all the time," he said. "Day in and day out. You get so you don't notice. Or maybe you get so you do notice and you like it."

"I don't see any fires," Anders said.

"That's right."

Feeling that he was missing the point somehow, Anders decided to change the subject. "I see a saxophone and a baseball bat next to you," he said, in his best English. "Do you like to play baseball?"

"Not in this cab, I don't," the driver said quietly. "It's no game then, you understand?"

The young man sat back, feeling that he had been defeated by the American idiom in his first native encounter with it. An engineer, he was in Detroit to discuss his work in metal alloys that resist oxidation. The company that had invited him had suggested that he might agree to become a consultant on an exclusive contract, for what seemed to him an enormous, American-sized fee. But the money meant little to him. It was America he was curious about, attracted by, especially its colorful disorderliness.

Disorder, of which there was very little in Sweden, seemed sexy to him: the disorder of a disheveled woman who has rushed down two flights of stairs to offer a last long kiss. Anders was single, and before he left the country he hoped to sleep with an American woman in an American bed. It was his ambition. He wondered if the experience would have any distinction. He had an idea that he might be able to go home and tell one or two friends about it.

At the hotel, he was met by a representative of the automobile company, a gray-haired man with thick glasses who, to Anders' surprise, spoke rather good Swedish. Later that afternoon, and for the next two days, he was taken down silent carpeted hallways and shown into plush windowless rooms with recessed lighting. He showed them his slides and metal samples, cited chemical formulas, and made cost projections; he looked at the faces looking back at him. They were interested, friendly, but oddly blank, like faces he had seen in the military. He saw corridor after corridor. The building seemed more expressive than the people in it. The lighting was both bright and diffuse, and a low-frequency hum of power and secrecy seemed to flow out from the ventilators. Everyone complimented him on his English. A tall woman in a tailored suit, flashing him a secretive smile, asked him if he intended to stay in this country for long. Anders smiled, said that his plans on that particular point were open, and managed to work the name of his hotel into his conversation.

At the end of the third day, the division head once again shook Anders' hand in the foyer of the hotel lobby and said they'd be getting in touch with him very soon. Finally free, Anders stepped outside the hotel and sniffed the air. All the rooms he had been in since he had arrived had had no windows, or windows so blocked by drapes or blinds that he couldn't see out.

He felt restless and excited, with three days free for sightseeing in a wide-open American city, not quite in the wild West but close enough to it to suit him. He returned to his room and changed into a pair of jeans, a light cotton shirt, and a pair of running shoes. In the mirror, he thought he looked relaxed and handsome. His vanity amused him, but he felt lucky to look the way he did. Back out on the sidewalk, he asked the doorman which direction he would recommend for a walk.

The doorman, who had curly gray hair and sagging pouches under his eyes, removed his cap and rubbed his forehead. He did not look back at Anders. "You want my recommendation? Don't walk anywhere. I would not recommend a walk. Sit in the bar and watch the soaps." The doorman stared at a fire hydrant as he spoke.

"What about running?"

The doorman suddenly glanced at Anders, sizing him up. "It's a chance. You might be okay. But to be safe, stay inside. There's movies on the cable, you want them."

"Is there a park here?"

"Sure, there's parks. There's always parks. There's Belle Isle. You could go there. People do. I don't recommend it. Still and all, you might enjoy it if you run fast enough. What're you planning to do?"

Anders shrugged. "Relax. See your city."

"You're seeing it," the doorman said. "Ain't nobody relaxed, seeing this place. Buy some postcards, you want sights. This place ain't built for tourists and amateurs."

Anders thought that perhaps he had misunderstood again and took a cab out to Belle Isle; as soon as he had entered the park, he saw a large municipal fountain and asked the cabbie to drop

him off in front of it. On its rim, children were shouting and
dangling their legs in the water. The ornamentation of the stone
lions was both solemn and whimsical and reminded him of the
forced humor of Danish public sculpture. Behind the fountain
he saw families grouped in evening picnics on the grass, and many
citizens, of various apparent ethnic types, running, bicycling, and
walking. Anders liked the way Americans walked, a sort of busy-
ness in their step, as if, having no particular goal, they still had
an unconscious urgency to get somewhere, to seem purposeful.

He began to jog, and found himself passing a yacht club of
some sort, and then a small zoo, and more landscaped areas where
solitaries and couples sat on the grass listening to the evening
baseball game on their radios. Other couples were stretched out
by themselves, self-absorbed. The light had a bluish-gold quality.
It looked like almost any city park to him, placid and decorative,
a bit hushed.

He found his way to an old building with a concession stand
inside. After admiring the building's fake Corinthian architecture, he bought a hot dog and a cola. Thinking himself disguised
as a native — America was full of foreigners anyway — he walked
to the west windows of the dining area to check on the unattached women. He wanted to praise, to an American, this evening, and this park.

There were several couples on this side of the room, and what
seemed to be several unattached men and women standing near
the open window and listening to their various earphones. One
of these women, with her hair partially pinned up, was sipping a
lemonade. She had just the right faraway look. Anders thought
he recognized this look. It meant that she was in a kind of sus-
pension, between engagements.

He put himself in her line of sight and said, in his heaviest accent, "A nice evening!"

"What?" She removed the earphones and looked at him. "What
did you say?"

"I said the evening was beautiful." He tried to sound as foreign
as he could, the way Germans in Sweden did. "I am a visitor here,"
he added quickly, "and not familiar with any of this." He motioned his arm to indicate the park.

"Not familiar?" she asked. "Not familiar with what?"

"Well, with this park. With the sky here. The people."

"Parks are the same everywhere," the woman said, leaning her hip against the wall. She looked at him with a vague interest. "The sky is the same. Only the people are different."

"Yes? How?"

"Where are you from?"

He explained, and she looked out the window toward the Canadian side of the Detroit River, at the city of Windsor. "That's Canada, you know," she said, pointing a finger at the river. "They make Canadian whiskey right over there." She pointed at some high buildings and what seemed to be a grain elevator. "I've never drunk the whiskey. They say it tastes of acid rain. I've never been to Canada. I mean, I've seen it, but I've never been there. If I can see it from here, why should I go there?"

"To be in Canada," Anders suggested. "Another country."

"But I'm *here*," she said suddenly, turning to him and looking at him directly. Her eyes were so dark they were almost colorless. "Why should I be anywhere else? Why are *you* here?"

"I came to Detroit for business," he said. "Now I'm sightseeing."

"Sightseeing?" She laughed out loud, and Anders saw her arch her back. Her breasts seemed to flare in front of him. Her body had distinct athletic lines. "No one sightsees here. Didn't anyone tell you?"

"Yes. The doorman at the hotel. He told me not to come."

"But you did. How did you get here?"

"I came by taxi."

"You're joking," she said. Then she reached out and put her hand momentarily on his shoulder. "You took a taxi to this park? How do you expect to get back to your hotel?"

"I suppose," he shrugged, "I will get another taxi."

"Oh no you won't," she said, and Anders felt himself pleased that things were working out so well. He noticed again her pinned-up hair and its intense black. Her skin was deeply tanned or naturally dark, and he thought that she herself might be black, or Hispanic, he didn't know which, being unpracticed in making such distinctions. Outside he saw fireflies. No one had ever mentioned fireflies in Detroit. Night was coming on. He gazed up at the sky. Same stars, same moon.

"You're here *alone*?" she asked. "In America? And in this city?"

"Yes," he said. "Why not?"

"People shouldn't be left alone in this country," she said, leaning toward him with a kind of vehemence. "They shouldn't have left you here. It can get kind of weird, what happens to people. Didn't they tell you?"

He smiled and said that they hadn't told him anything to that effect.

"Well, they should have." She dropped her cup into a trash can, and he thought he saw the beginning of a scar, a white line, traveling up the underside of her arm toward her shoulder.

"Who do you mean?" he asked. "You said 'they.' Who is 'they'?"

"Any they at all," she said. "Your guardians." She sighed. "All right. Come on. Follow me." She went outside and broke into a run. For a moment he thought that she was running away from him, then realized that he was expected to run with her; it was what people did now, instead of holding hands, to get acquainted. He sprinted up next to her, and as she ran, she asked him, "Who are you?"

Being careful not to tire — she wouldn't like it if his endurance was poor — he told her his name, his professional interests, and he patched together a narrative about his mother, father, two sisters, and his Aunt Ingrid. Running past a slower couple, he told her that his aunt was eccentric and broke china by throwing it on the floor on Fridays, which she called "the devil's day."

"Years ago, they would have branded her a witch," Anders said. "But she isn't a witch. She's just moody."

He watched her reactions and noticed that she didn't seem at all interested in his family, or any sort of background. "Do you run a lot?" she asked. "You look as if you're in pretty good shape."

He admitted that, yes, he ran, but that people in Sweden didn't do this as much as they did in America.

"You look a little like that tennis star, that Swede," she said. "By the way, I'm Lauren." Still running, she held out her hand, and, still running, he shook it. "Which god do you believe in?"

"Excuse me?"

"Which god?" she asked. "Which god do you think is in control?"

"I had not thought about it."

"You'd better," she said. "Because one of them is." She stopped suddenly and put her hands on her hips and walked in a small circle. She put her hand to her neck and took her pulse, timing it on her wristwatch. Then she placed her fingers on Anders' neck and took his pulse. "One hundred fourteen," she said. "Pretty good." Again she walked away from him and again he found himself following her. In the growing darkness he noticed other men, standing in the parking lot, watching her, this American with pinned-up hair, dressed in a running outfit. He thought she was pretty, but maybe Americans had other standards so that here, in fact, she wasn't pretty, and it was some kind of optical illusion.

When he caught up with her, she was unlocking the door of a blue Chevrolet rusting near the hubcaps. He gazed down at the rust with professional interest — it had the characteristic blister pattern of rust caused by salt. She slipped inside the car and reached across to unlock the passenger side, and when he got in — he hadn't been invited to get in, but he thought it was all right — he sat down on several small plastic tape cassette cases. He picked them out from underneath him and tried to read their labels. She was taking off her shoes. Debussy, Bach, 10,000 Maniacs, Screamin' Jay Hawkins.

"Where are we going?" he asked. He glanced down at her bare foot on the accelerator. She put the car into reverse. "Wait a minute," he said. "Stop this car." She put on the brake and turned off the ignition. "I just want to look at you," he said.

"Okay, look." She turned on the interior light and kept her face turned so that he was looking at her in profile. Something about her suggested a lovely disorder, a ragged brightness toward the back of her face.

"Are we going to do things?" he asked, touching her on the arm.

"Of course," she said. "Strangers should always do things."

She said that she would drop him off at his hotel, that he must change clothes. This was important. She would then pick him up. On the way over, he saw almost no one downtown. For some reason, it was quite empty of shoppers, strollers, or pedestrians of any kind. "I'm going to tell you some things you should know," she said. He settled back. He was used to this kind of talk on dates:

everyone, everywhere, liked to reveal intimate details about themselves. It was an international convention.

They were slowing for a red light. "God is love," she said, downshifting, her bare left foot on the clutch. "At least I think so. It's my hope. In the world we have left, only love matters. Do you understand? I'm one of the Last Ones. Maybe you've heard of us."

"No, I have not. What do you do?"

"We do what everyone else does. We work and we go home and have dinner and go to bed. There is only one thing we do that is special."

"What is that?" he asked.

"We don't make plans," she said. "No big plans at all."

"That is not so unusual," he said, trying to normalize what she was saying. "Many people don't like to make —"

"It's not liking," she said. "It doesn't have anything to do with liking or not liking. It's a faith. Look at those buildings." She pointed toward several abandoned multistoried buildings with broken or vacant windows. "What face is moving behind all that? Something is. I live and work here. I'm not blind. *Anyone* can see what's taking place here. You're not blind either. Our church is over on the east side, off Van Dyke Avenue. It's not a good part of town but we want to be near where the face is doing its work."

"Your church?"

"The Church of the Millennium," she said. "Where they preach the Gospel of Last Things." They were now on the freeway, heading up toward the General Motors Building and his hotel. "Do you understand me?"

"Of course," he said. He had heard of American cult religions but thought they were all in California. He didn't mind her talk of religion. It was like talk of the sunset or childhood; it kept things going. "Of course I have been listening."

"Because I won't sleep with you unless you listen to me," she said. "It's the one thing I care about, that people listen. It's so damn rare, listening I mean, that you might as well care about it. I don't sleep with strangers too often. Almost never." She turned to look at him. "Anders," she said, "what do you pray to?"

He laughed. "I don't."

"Okay, then, what do you plan for?"

"A few things," he said.

"Like what?"

"My dinner every night. My job. My friends."

"You don't let accidents happen? You should. Things reveal themselves in accidents."

"Are there many people like you?" he asked.

"What do you think?" He looked again at her face, taken over by the darkness in the car but dimly lit by the dashboard lights and the oncoming flare of traffic. "Do you think there are many people like me?"

"Not very many," he said. "But maybe more than there used to be."

"Any of us in Sweden?"

"I don't think so. It's not a religion over there. People don't . . . They didn't tell us in Sweden about American girls who listen to Debussy and 10,000 Maniacs in their automobiles and who believe in gods and accidents."

"They don't say 'girls' here," she told him. "They say 'women.' "

She dropped him off at the hotel and said that she would pick him up in forty-five minutes. In his room, as he chose a clean shirt and a sport coat and a pair of trousers, he found himself laughing happily. He felt giddy. It was all happening so fast; he could hardly believe his luck. I am a very lucky man, he thought.

He looked out his hotel window at the streetlights. They had an amber glow, the color of gemstones. This city, this American city, was unlike any he had ever seen. A downtown area emptied of people; a river with huge ships going by silently; a park with girls who believe in the millennium. No, not girls: women. He had learned his lesson.

He wanted to open the hotel window to smell the air, but the casement frames were welded shut.

After walking down the stairs to the lobby, he stood out in front of the hotel doorway. He felt a warm breeze against his face. He told the doorman, Luis, that he had met a woman on Belle Isle who was going to pick him up in a few minutes. She was going to take him dancing. The doorman nodded, rubbing his chin with his hand. Anders said that she was friendly and wanted to show him, a foreigner, things. The doorman shook his head. "Yes, I agree," Luis said. "Dancing. Make sure that this is what you do."

"What?"

"Dancing," Luis said, "yes. Go dancing. You know this woman?"

"I just met her."

"Ah," Luis said, and stepped back to observe Anders, as if to remember his face. "Dangerous fun." When her car appeared in front of the hotel, she was wearing a light summer dress, and when she smiled, she looked like a melancholy baby he had heard about in an American song. As they pulled away from the hotel, he looked back at Luis, who was watching them closely, and then Anders realized that Luis was reading the numbers on Lauren's license plate. To break the mood, he leaned over to kiss her on the cheek. She smelled of cigarettes and something else — soap or cut flowers.

She took him uptown to a club where a trio played soft rock and some jazz. Some of this music was slow enough to dance to, in the slow way he wanted to dance. Her hand in his felt bony and muscular; physically, she was direct and immediate. He wondered, now, looking at her face, whether she might be an American Indian, and again he was frustrated because he couldn't tell one race in this country from another. He knew it was improper to ask. When he sat at the table, holding hands with her and sipping from his drink, he began to feel as if he had known her for a long time and was related to her in some obscure way.

Suddenly he asked her, "Why are you so interested in me?"

"Interested?" She laughed, and her long black hair, no longer pinned up, shook in quick thick waves. "Well, all right. I have an interest. I like it that you're so foreign that you take cabs to the park. I like the way you look. You're kind of cute. And the other thing is, your soul is so raw and new, Anders, it's like an oyster."

"What?" He looked at her near him at the table. Their drinks were half finished. "My soul?"

"Yeah, your soul. I can almost see it."

"Where is it?"

She leaned forward, friendly and sexual and now slightly elegant. "You want me to show you?"

"Yes," Anders said. "Sure."

"It's in two places," she said. "One part is up here." She released his hand and put her thumb on his forehead. "And the other part is down here." She touched him in the middle of his stomach. "Right there. And they're connected."

"What are they like?" he asked, playing along.

"Yours? Raw and shiny, just like I said."

"And what about your soul?" he asked.

She looked at him. "My soul is radioactive," she said. "It's like plutonium. Don't say you weren't warned."

He thought that this was another American idiom he hadn't heard before, and he decided not to spoil things by asking her about it. In Sweden, people didn't talk much about the soul, at least not in conjunction with oysters or plutonium.

In the dark he couldn't make out much about her building, except that it was several floors high and at least fifty years old. Her living room window looked out distantly at the river — once upstairs, he could see the lights of another passing freighter — and through the left side of the window he could see an electrical billboard. The name of the product was made out of hundreds of small incandescent bulbs, which went on and off from left to right. One of the letters was missing.

It's today's CHEVR LET!

All around her living room walls were brightly framed watercolors, almost celebratory and Matisse-like, but in vague shapes. She went down the hallway, tapped on one of the doors, and said, "I'm home." Then she returned to the living room and kicked off her shoes. "My grandmother," she said. "She has her own room."

"Are these your pictures?" he asked. "Did you draw them?"

"Yes."

"I can't tell what they are. What are they?"

"They're abstract. You use wet paper to get that effect. They're abstract because God has gotten abstract. God used to have a form but now He's dissolving into pure light. That's what you see in those pictures. They're pictures of the trails that God leaves behind."

"Like the vapor trails," he smiled, "behind jets."

"Yes," she said. "Like that."

He went over to her in the dark and drew her to him and kissed her. Her breath was layered with smoke, apparently from cigarettes. Immediately he felt an unusual physical sensation inside his skin, like something heating up on a fry pan.

She drew back. He heard another siren go by on the street outside. He wondered whether they should talk some more in the living room — share a few more verbal intimacies — to be really civilized about this and decided, no, it was not necessary, not when strangers make love, as they do, sometimes, in strange cities, away from home. They went into her bedroom and undressed each other. Her body, by the light of a dim bedside lamp, was as beautiful and as exotic as he hoped it would be, darker than his own skin in the dark room, native somehow to this continent. She had the flared shoulders and hips of a dancer. She bent down and snapped off the bedside light, and as he approached her, she was lit from behind by the billboard. Her skin felt vaguely electrical to him.

They stood in the middle of her bedroom, arms around each other, swaying, and he knew, in his arousal, that something odd was about to occur: he had no words for it either in his own language or in English.

They moved over and under each other, changing positions to stay in the breeze created by the window fan. They were both lively and attentive, and at first he thought it would be just the usual fun, this time with an almost anonymous American woman. He looked at her in the bed and saw her dark leg alongside his own, and he saw that same scar line running up her arm to her shoulder, where it disappeared.

"Where did you get that?" he asked.

"That?" She looked at it. "That was an accident that was done to me."

Half an hour later, resting with her, his hands on her back, he felt a wave of happiness; he felt it as a wave of color traveling through his body, surging from his forehead down to his stomach. It took him over again, and then a third time, with such force that he almost sat up.

"What is it?" she asked.

"I don't know. It is like . . . I felt a color moving through my body."

"Oh, that?" She smiled at him in the dark. "It's your soul, Anders. That's all. That's all it is. Never felt it before, huh?"

"I must be very drunk," he said.

She put her hand up into his hair. "Call it anything you want to. Didn't you feel it before? Our souls were curled together."

"You're crazy," he said. "You are a crazy woman."

"Oh yeah?" she whispered. "Is that what you think? Watch. Watch what happens now. You think this is all physical. Guess what. You're the crazy one. Watch. Watch."

She went to work on him, and at first it was pleasurable, but as she moved over him it became a succession of waves that had specific colorations, even when he turned her and thought he was taking charge. Soon he felt some substance, some glossy blue possession entangled in the air above him.

"I bet you're going to say that you're imagining all this," she said, her hand skidding across him.

"Who are you?" he said. "Who in the world are you?"

"I warned you," she whispered, her mouth directly over his ear. "I warned you. You people with your things, your rusty things, you suffer so bad when you come into where *we* live. Did they tell you we were all soulless here? Did they say that?"

He put his hands on her. "This is not love, but it —"

"Of course not," she said. "It's something else. Do you know the word? Do you know the word for something that opens your soul at once? Like that?" She snapped her fingers on the pillow. Her tongue was touching his ear. "Do you?" The words were almost inaudible.

"No."

"Addiction." She waited. "Do you understand?"

"Yes."

In the middle of the night he rose up and went to the window. He felt like a stump, amputated from the physical body of the woman. At the window he looked down, to the right of the billboard, and saw another apartment building with heavy decorations with human forms near the roof's edge, and on the third floor he saw a man at the window, as naked as he himself was but almost completely in shadow, gazing out at the street. They were so far away from each other that being unclothed didn't matter. It was vague and small and impersonal.

"Do you always stand at the window without clothes on?" she asked, from the bed.

"Not in Sweden," he said. He turned around. "This is odd," he said. "At night no one walks out on the streets. But there, over on that block, there's a man like me, at the window, and he is looking out, too. Do people stand everywhere at the windows here?"

"Come to bed."

"When I was in the army, the Swedish army," he said, still looking out, "they taught us to think that we could *decide* to do anything. They talked about the will. Your word 'willpower.' All Sweden believes this — choice, will, willpower. Maybe not so much now. I wonder if they talk about it here."

"You're funny," she said. She lay in bed and watched until he returned to her.

In the morning he watched her as she dressed. His eyes hurt from sleeplessness. "I have to go," she said. "I'm already late." She was putting on a light blue skirt. As she did, she smiled. "You're a lovely lover," she said. "I like your body very much."

"What are we going to do?" he asked.

"We? There is no 'we,' Anders. There's you and then there's me. We're not a couple. I'm going to work. You're going back to your country soon. What are you planning to do?"

"May I stay here?"

"For an hour," she said, "and then you should go back to your hotel. I don't think you should stay. You don't live here."

"May I take you to dinner tonight?" he asked, trying not to watch her as he watched her. "What can we do tonight?"

"There's that 'we' again. Well, maybe. You can teach me a few words of Swedish. Why don't you hang around at your hotel and maybe I'll come by around six and get you, but don't call me if I don't come by, because if I don't, I don't."

"I can't call you," he said. "I don't know your last name."

"Oh, that's right," she said. "Well, listen. I'll probably come at six." She looked at him lying in the bed. "I don't believe this," she said.

"What?"

"You think you're in love, don't you?"

"No," he said. "Not exactly." He waited. "Oh, I don't know."

"I get the point," she said. "Well, you better get used to it. Welcome to our town. We're not always good at love but we are good at that." She bent to kiss him and then was gone. Happiness and agony simultaneously reached down and pressed against his chest. They, too, were like colors, but when you mixed the two together, you got something greenish-pink, excruciating.

He stood up, put on his trousers, and began looking into her dresser drawers. He expected to find trinkets and whatnot, but all she had were folded clothes, and, in the corner of the top drawer, a small turquoise heart for a charm bracelet. He put it into his pocket.

In the bathroom, he examined the labels on her medicines and facial creams before washing his face. He wanted evidence but didn't know for what. He looked, to himself, like a slightly different version of what he had once been. In the mirror his face had a puffy look and a passive expression, as if he had been assaulted during the night.

After he had dressed and entered the living room, he saw Lauren's grandmother sitting at a small dining room table. She was eating a piece of toast and looking out of the window toward the river. The apartment, in daylight, had an aggressively scrubbed and mopped look, quite obviously an apartment where only women lived. On the kitchen counter a small black-and-white television was blaring, but the old woman wasn't watching it. Her black hair was streaked with gray, and she wore a ragged pink bathrobe decorated with pictures of orchids. She was very frail. Her skin was as dark as her granddaughter's. Looking at her, Anders was once again unable to guess what race she was. She might be Arabic, or a Native American, or Hispanic, or black. Because he couldn't tell, he didn't care.

Without even looking at him, she motioned at him to sit down.

"Want anything?" she asked. She had a high, distant voice, as if it had come into the room over wires. "There are bananas over there." She made no gesture. "And grapefruit, I think, in the refrigerator."

"That's all right." He sat down on the other side of the table and folded his hands together, studying his fingers. The sound of traffic came up from the street outside.

"You're from somewhere," she said. "Scandinavia?"

"Yes," he said. "How can you tell?" Talking had become a terrible effort.

"Vowels," she said. "You sound like one of those Finns up north of here. When will you go back? To your country?"

"I don't know," he said. "Perhaps a few days. Perhaps not. My name is Anders." He held out his hand.

"Nice to meet you." She touched but did not shake his hand. "Why don't you know when you're going back?" She turned to look at him at last. It was a face on which curiosity still registered. She observed him as if he were an example of a certain kind of human being in which she still had an interest.

"I don't know . . . I am not sure. Last night, I . . ."

"You don't finish your sentences," the old woman said.

"I am trying to. I don't want to leave your granddaughter," he said. "She is" — he tried to think of the right adjective — "amazing to me."

"Yes, she is." The old woman peered at him. "You don't think you're in love, do you?"

"I don't know."

"Well, don't be. She won't ever be married, so there's no point in being in love with her. There's no point in being married *here*. I see them, you know."

"Who?"

"All the young men. Well, there aren't many. A few. Every so often. They come and sleep here with her and then in the morning they come out for breakfast with me and then they go away. We sit and talk. They're usually very pleasant. Men are, in the morning. They should be. She's a beautiful girl."

"Yes, she is."

"But there's no future in her, you know," the old woman said. "Sure you don't want a grapefruit? You should eat something."

"No, thank you. What do you mean, 'no future'?"

"Well, the young men usually understand that." The old woman looked at the television set, scowled, and shifted her gaze to the window. She rubbed her hands together. "You can't invest in her. You can't do that at all. She won't let you. I know. I know how she thinks."

"We have women like that in my country," Anders said. "They are —"

"Oh no you don't," the old woman said. "Sooner or later they want to get married, don't they?"

"I suppose most of them."

She glanced out the window toward the Detroit River and the city of Windsor on the opposite shore. Just when he thought that she had forgotten all about him, he felt her hand, dry as a winter leaf, taking hold of his own. Another siren went by outside. He felt a weight descending in his stomach. The touch of the old woman's hand made him feel worse than before, and he stood up quickly, looking around the room as if there were some object nearby he had to pick up and take away immediately. Her hand dropped away from his.

"No plans," she said. "Didn't she tell you?" the old woman asked. "It's what she believes." She shrugged. "It makes her happy."

"I am not sure I understand."

The old woman lifted her right hand and made a dismissive wave in his direction. She pursed her mouth; he knew she had stopped speaking to him. He called a cab, and in half an hour he was back in his hotel room. In the shower he realized that he had forgotten to write down her address or phone number.

He felt itchy: he went out running, returned to his room, and took another shower. He did thirty pushups and jogged in place. He groaned and shouted, knowing that no one would hear. How would he explain this to anyone? He was feeling passionate puzzlement. He went down to the hotel's dining room for lunch and ordered Dover sole and white wine but found himself unable to eat much of anything. He stared at his plate and at the other men and women consuming their meals calmly, and he was suddenly filled with wonder at ordinary life.

He couldn't stand to be by himself, and after lunch he had the doorman hail a cab. He gave the cab driver a fifty and asked him to drive him around the city until all the money was used up.

"You want to see the nice parts?" the cabbie asked.

"No."

"What is it you want to see then?"

"The city."

"You tryin' to score, man? That it?"

Anders didn't know what he meant. He was certain that no sport was intended. He decided to play it safe. "No," he said.

The cab driver shook his head and whistled. They drove east

and then south; Anders watched the water-ball compass stuck to the front window. Along Jefferson Avenue they went past the shells of apartment buildings, and then, heading north, they passed block after block of vacated or boarded-up properties. One old building with Doric columns was draped with a banner.

PROGRESS! THE OLD MUST MAKE WAY FOR THE NEW
Acme Wrecking Company

The banner was worn and tattered. Anders noticed broken beer bottles, sharp brown glass, on sidewalks and vacant lots, and the glass, in the sun, seemed perversely beautiful. Men were sleeping on sidewalks and in front stairwells; one man, wearing a hat, urinated against the corner of a burned-out building. He saw other men — there were very few women out here in the light of day — in groups gazing at him with cold slow deadly expressions. In his state of mind, he understood it all; he identified with it. All of it, the ruins and the remnants, made perfect sense.

At six o'clock she picked him up and took him to a Greek restaurant. All the way over, he watched her. He examined her with the puzzled curiosity of someone who wants to know how another person who looks rather attractive but also rather ordinary could have such power. Her physical features didn't explain anything.

"Did you miss me today?" she asked, half jokingly.

"Yes," he said. He started to say more but didn't know how to begin. "It was hard to breathe," he said at last.

"I know," she said. "It's the air."

"No, it isn't. Not the air."

"Well, what then?"

He looked at her.

"Oh, come on, Anders. We're just two blind people who staggered into each other and we're about to stagger off in different directions. That's all."

Sentences struggled in his mind, then vanished before he could say them. He watched the pavement pass underneath the car.

In the restaurant, a crowded and lively place smelling of beer and roasted meat and cigars, they sat in a booth and ordered an antipasto plate. He leaned over and took her hands. "Tell me, please, who and what you are."

She seemed surprised that he had asked. "I've explained," she said. She waited, then started up again. "When I was younger I had an idea that I wanted to be a dancer. I had to give that up. My timing was off." She smiled. "Onstage, I looked like a memory of what had already happened. The other girls would do something and then I'd do it. I come in late on a lot of things. That's good for me. I've told you where I work. I live with my grandmother. I go with her into the parks in the fall and we watch for birds. And you know what else I believe." He gazed at the gold hoops of her earrings. "What else do you want to know?"

"I feel happy and terrible," he said. "Is it you? Did you do this?"

"I guess I did," she said, smiling faintly. "Tell me some words in Swedish."

"Which ones?"

"House."

"Hus."

"Pain."

"Smärta."

She leaned back. "Face."

"Ansikte."

"Light."

"Ljus."

"Never."

"Aldrig."

"I don't like it," she said. "I don't like the sound of those words at all. They're too cold. They're cold-weather words."

"Cold? Try another one."

"Soul."

"Själ."

"No, I don't like it." She raised her hand to the top of his head, grabbed a bit of his hair, and laughed. "Too bad."

"Do you do this to everyone?" he asked. "I feel such confusion."

He saw her stiffen. "You want to know too much. You're too messed up. Too messed up with plans. You and your rust. All that isn't important. Not here. We don't do all that explaining. I've told you *everything* about me. We're just supposed to be enjoying ourselves. Nobody has to explain. That's freedom, Anders. Never telling why." She leaned over toward him so that her

shoulders touched his, and with a sense of shock and desperation, he felt himself becoming aroused. She kissed him, and her
lips tasted slightly of garlic. "Just say hi to the New World," she
said.

"You feel like a drug to me," he said. "You feel experimental."

"We don't use that word that way," she said. Then she said,
"Oh," as if she had understood something, or remembered another engagement. "Okay. I'll explain all this in a minute. Excuse
me." She rose and disappeared behind a corner of the restaurant, and Anders looked out the window at a Catholic church the
color of sandstone, on whose front steps a group of boys sat, eating popsicles. One of the boys got up and began to ask passers-
by for money; this went on until a policeman came and sent the
boys away. Anders looked at his watch. Ten minutes had gone by
since she had left. He looked up. He knew without thinking about
it that she wasn't coming back.

He put a ten-dollar bill on the table and left the restaurant,
jogging into the parking structure where she had left the car. Although he wasn't particularly surprised to see that it wasn't there,
he sat down on the concrete and felt the floor of the structure
shaking. He ran his hands through his hair, where she had grabbed
at it. He waited as long as he could stand to do so, then returned
to the hotel.

Luis was back on duty. Anders told him what had happened.

"Ah," Luis said. "She is disappeared."

"Yes. Do you think I should call the police?"

"No," Luis said. "I do not think so. They have too many disappeared already."

"Too many disappeared?"

"Yes. All over this city. Many many disappeared. For how many
times do you take this lady out?"

"Once. No, twice."

"And this time is the time she leave you?"

Anders nodded.

"I have done that," Luis said. "When I get sick of a woman, I
too have disappeared. Maybe," he said suddenly, "she will re-
appear. Sometimes they do."

"I don't think she will." He sat down on the sidewalk in front
of the hotel and cupped his chin in his hands.

"No no," Luis said. "You cannot do that in front of the hotel. This looks very bad. Please stand up." He felt Luis reaching around his shoulders and pulling him to his feet. "What you are acting is impossible after one night," Luis said. "Be like everyone else. Have another night." He took off his doorman's cap and combed his hair with precision. "Many men and women also disappear from each other. It is one thing to do. You had a good time?"

Anders nodded.

"Have another good time," Luis suggested, "with someone else. Beer, pizza, go to bed. Women who have not disappeared will talk to you, I am sure."

"I think I'll call the police," Anders said.

"Myself, no, I would not do that."

He dialed a number he found in the telephone book for a local precinct station. As soon as the station officer understood what Anders was saying to him, he became angry, said it wasn't a police matter, and hung up on him. Anders sat for a moment in the phone booth, then looked up the Church of the Millennium in the directory. He wrote down its address. Someone there would know about her, and explain.

The cab let him out in front. It was like no other church he had ever seen. Even the smallest places of worship in his own country had vaulted roofs, steeples, and stained glass. This building seemed to be someone's remodeled house. On either side of it, two lots down, were two skeletal homes, one of which had been burned and which now stood with charcoal windows and a charcoal portal where the front door had once been. The other house was boarded up; in the evening wind, sheets of newspaper were stuck to its south wall. Across the street was an almost deserted playground. The saddles had been removed from the swing set, and the chains hung down from the upper bar and moved slightly in the wind. Four men stood together under a basketball hoop, talking together. One of the men bounced a basketball occasionally.

A signboard had been planted into the ground in front of the church, but so many letters had been removed from it that Anders couldn't make out what it was supposed to say.

Ch rch of   e Mill   ni m
Rev. H rold T. oodst th, Pas or

Everyo e   elco e!
"Love on   other, lest ye f ll to d t le for r le m!"

On the steps leading up to the front door, he turned around and saw, to the south, the lights of the office buildings of downtown Detroit suspended in the darkness. After hearing what he thought was some sound in the bushes, he opened the front door of the church and went inside.

Over a bare wood floor, folding chairs were lined up in five straight rows, facing toward a front chest intended as an altar, and everywhere there was a smell of incense, of ashy pine. Above the chest, and nailed to the far wall where a crucifix might be located in a Protestant church, was a polished brass circle with a nimbus of rays projecting out from its top. The rays were extended along the wall for a distance of four feet. One spotlight from a corner behind him lit up the brass circle, which in the gloom looked either like a deity-sun or some kind of explosion. The bare walls had been painted with flames: buildings of the city, some he had already seen, painted in flames, the earth in flames. There was an open Bible on the chest, and in one of the folding chairs a deck of playing cards. Otherwise, the room was completely empty. Gazing at a side door, he decided that he had never seen a church so small, or one that filled him with a greater sense of desolation. Behind him, near the door, was a bench. He had the feeling that the bench was filled with the disappeared. He sat down on it, and as he looked at the folding chairs it occurred to him that the disappeared were in fact here now, in front of him, sitting or standing or kneeling.

He composed himself and went back out onto the street, thinking that perhaps a cab would go by, but he saw neither cabs nor cars, not even pedestrians. After deciding that he had better begin walking toward the downtown area, he made his way down two blocks, past a boarded-up grocery store and a vacated apartment building, when he heard what he thought was the sound of footsteps behind him.

He felt the blow at the back of his head; it came to him not as a sensation of pain but as an instant crashing explosion of light in his brain, a bursting circle with a shooting aura irradiating from it. As he turned to fall, he felt hands touching his chest and his trousers; they moved with speed and almost with tenderness, until they found what they were looking for and took it away from him.

He lay on the sidewalk in a state somewhere between consciousness and unconsciousness, hearing the wind through the trees overhead and feeling some blood trickling out of the back of his scalp, until he felt the hands again, perhaps the same hands, lifting him up, putting him into something, taking him somewhere. Inside the darkness he now inhabited, he found that at some level he could still think: *Someone hit me and I've been robbed.* At another, later, point, he understood that he could open his eyes; he had that kind of permission. He was sitting in a wheelchair in what was clearly a hospital emergency room. It felt as though someone were pushing him toward a planetary corridor. They asked him questions, which he answered in Swedish. "Det gör ont," he said, puzzled that they didn't understand him. "Var är jag?" he asked. They didn't know. English was what they wanted. He tried to give them some.

They x-rayed him and examined his cut; he would need four stitches, they said. He found that he could walk. They told him he was lucky, that he had not been badly hurt. A doctor, and then a nurse, and then another nurse, told him that he might have been killed — shot or knifed — and that victims of this type, strangers who wandered into the wrong parts of the city, were not unknown. He mentioned the disappeared. They were polite, but said that there was no such phrase in English. When he mentioned the name of his hotel, they said, once again, that he was lucky: it was only a few blocks away, walking distance. They smiled. You're a lucky man, they said, grinning oddly. They knew something but weren't saying it.

As the smaller debris of consciousness returned to him, he found himself sitting in a brightly lit room, like a waiting room, near the entryway for emergency medicine. From where he sat, he could see, through his fluent tidal headache, the patients arriving, directed to the Triage Desk, where their condition was judged.

They brought in a man on a gurney, who was hoarsely shouting. They rushed him through. He was bleeding, and they were holding him down as his feet kicked sideways.

They brought in someone else, a girl, who was stumbling, held up on both sides by friends. Anders heard something that sounded like Odie. Who was Odie? Her boyfriend? Odie, she screamed. Get me Odie.

Anders stood up, unable to watch any more. He shuffled through two doorways and found himself standing near an elevator. From a side window, he saw light from the sun rising. He hadn't realized that it was day. The sun made the inside of his head shriek. To escape the light, he stepped on the elevator and pressed the button for the fifth floor.

As the elevator rose, he felt his knees weakening. In order to clear his head, he began to count the other people on the elevator: seven. They seemed normal to him. The signs of this were coats and ties on the men, white frocks and a stethoscope on one of the women, and blouses and jeans on the other women. None of them looked like her. From now on, none of them ever would.

He felt that he must get home to Sweden quickly, before he became a very different person, unrecognizable even to himself.

At the fifth floor the doors opened and he stepped out. Close to the elevators was a nurses' station, and beyond it a long hallway leading to an alcove. He walked down this hallway, turned the corner, and heard small squalling sounds ahead. At the same time, he saw the windows in the hallway and understood that he had wandered onto the maternity floor. He made his way to the viewer's window and looked inside. He counted twenty-five newborns, each one in its own clear plastic crib. He stared down at the babies, hearing, through the glass, the cries of those who were awake.

He was about to turn around and go back to his hotel when one of the nurses saw him. She raised her eyebrows quizzically and spread her hands over the children. He shook his head to indicate no. Still she persisted. She pointed to a baby with white skin and a head of already-blond hair. He shook his head no once again. He would need to get back to the hotel, call his bank in Sweden, get money for the return trip. He touched his pants pocket and found that the wallet was still there. What had they taken? The nurse, smiling, nodded as if she understood, and motioned toward the newborns with darker skin, the Hispanics and light-skinned blacks and all the others, babies of a kind he never saw in Sweden.

Well, he thought, why not? Now that they had done this to him.

He felt himself nodding. Sure. That American word. His right arm rose. He pointed at a baby whose skin was the color of clay, Lauren's skin, the color of polished bronze, or flames. Now the nurse was wheeling the baby he had pointed to closer to the window. When it was directly in front of him, she left it there, returning to the back of the nursery. Standing on the other side of the glass, staring down at the sleeping infant, he tapped on the panel twice and waved, as he thought fathers should. The baby did not awaken. Anders put his hand in his pocket and touched the little turquoise heart, then pressed his forehead against the glass of the window and recovered himself. He stood for what seemed to him a long time, before taking the elevator down to the ground floor and stepping out onto the front sidewalk, and to the air, which smelled as it always had, of powerful combustible materials and their traces, fire and ash.

AMY BLOOM

Love Is Not a Pie

FROM ROOM OF ONE'S OWN

IN THE MIDDLE of the eulogy at my mother's boring and heart-breaking funeral, I started to think about calling off the wedding. August 21 did not seem like a good date, John Wescott did not seem like a good person to marry and I couldn't see myself in the long white silk gown Mrs. Wescott had offered me. We had gotten engaged at Christmas, while my mother was starting to die. She died in May, earlier than we had expected. When the minister said, "She was a rare spirit, full of the kind of bravery and joy that inspires others . . . ," I stared at the pale blue ceiling and thought, "My mother would not have wanted me to spend my life with this man." He had asked me if I wanted him to come from Boston to the funeral, and I said no. So he didn't, respecting my autonomy and so forth. I think he should have known that I was just being considerate.

After the funeral, we took the little box of ashes back to the house and entertained everybody who came by to pay their respects. Lots of my father's colleagues, other law professors, a few of his former students, my Uncle Steve and his new wife, my cousins (whom my sister and I always referred to as Thing One and Thing Two), friends from the old neighborhood, before my mother's sculpture started selling, my mother's art world friends, her sisters, some of my friends from high school, some people I used to baby-sit for, my best friend from college, some friends of my sister's, a lot of people I didn't recognize. I've been living away from home for a long time, first at college, now at law school.

My sister, my father and I worked the room. And everyone
that came in, my father embraced. It didn't matter whether they
started to pat him on the back or shake his hand, he pulled them
to him and hugged them so hard, I saw some people's feet lift
right off the floor. My sister and I took the more passive route,
letting people do whatever they wanted to us — patting, stroking, embracing, cupping our faces in their hands.

My father was in the middle of squeezing Mrs. Ellis, our cleaning lady, when he saw Mr. DeCuervo come in, still carrying his
suitcase. He about dropped Mrs. Ellis and went charging over to
Mr. DeCuervo, wrapped his arms around him, and the two of
them moaned and rocked together, in a passionate, musicless waltz.
My sister and I sat down on the couch, our arms pressed against
each other, watching our father cry all over his friend, our mother's lover.

When I was eleven and my sister was eight, her last naked summer, Mr. DeCuervo and his daughter, Gisela, who was just about
to turn eight, spent part of the summer with us at the cabin in
Maine. The cabin was from the Spencer side, my father's side of
the family, and he and my Uncle Steve were co-owners. We went
there every July (colder water, better weather) and they came in
August. My father felt about his brother the way we felt about
our cousins, so we would only overlap for lunch on the last day
of our stay.

That July, the DeCuervos came, but without Mrs. DeCuervo,
who had to go visit a sick someone in Argentina, where they were
from. That was okay with us; Mrs. DeCuervo was a professional
mother, a type that made my sister and me very uncomfortable.
She told us to wash the berries before we ate them, to rest after
lunch, to put on more suntan lotion, to make our beds. She was
a nice lady; she was just always in our way. My mother had a few
very basic summer rules: don't eat food with mold or insects on
it; don't swim alone; don't even think about waking your mother
before 8 A.M., unless you are fatally injured or ill. That was about
it and Mrs. DeCuervo was always amending and adding to the
list, one apologetic eye on my mother. Our mother, as usual, was
pleasant and friendly and did things the way she always did. She
made it pretty clear that if we were cowed by the likes of Mrs.

DeCuervo, we were on our own. They got divorced when Gisela was a sophomore at Mount Holyoke.

We liked pretty, docile Gisela, and bullied her a little bit, and liked her even more because she didn't squeal on us, on me in particular. We liked her father, too. We saw the two of them, sometimes the three of them, at occasional picnics and lesser holidays. He always complimented us, never made stupid jokes at our expense and brought us unusual, perfect little presents. Silver barrettes for me, the summer I was letting my hair grow out from my pixie cut; a leather bookmark for Lizzie, who learned to read when she was three. My mother would stand behind us as we unwrapped the gifts, smiling and shaking her head at his extravagance.

When they drove up, we were all sitting on the porch; Mr. DeCuervo got out first, his curly brown hair making him look like a giant dandelion, with his yellow T-shirt and brown jeans. Gisela looked just like him, her long, curly brown hair caught up in a bun, wisps flying around her tanned little face. As they walked toward us, she took his hand and I felt a rush of warmth toward her, for showing how much she loved her daddy, like I loved mine, and for showing that she was a little afraid of us, of me, probably. People weren't often frightened of Lizzie, she never left her books long enough to bother anyone.

My parents got down from the porch, my big father in his faded blue trunks, drooping below his belly, his freckled back pink and moist in the sun, as it was every summer. The sun caught the red hair on his head and shoulders and chest and he shone. The Spencers were half Viking, he said. My mother was wearing her summer outfit, a black two-piece bathing suit. I don't remember her ever wearing a different suit. At night, she'd add one of my father's shirts and wrap it around her like a kimono. Some years, she looked great in her suit, waist nipped in, skin smooth and tan; other years, her skin looked burnt and crumpled and the suit was too big in some places and too small in others. Those years, she smoked too much and went out on the porch to cough. But that summer, the suit fit beautifully, and when she jumped off the porch into my father's arms, he whirled her around and let her black hair whip his face, while he smiled and smiled.

They both hugged Mr. DeCuervo and Gisela; my mother took

her little flowered suitcase and my father took his duffel bag and
they led them into the cabin.

The cabin was our palace; Lizzie and I would say, very grandly,
"We're going to the cabin for the summer, come visit us there, if
it's okay with your parents." And we loved it and loved to act as
though it was nothing special, when we knew, really, that it was
magnificent. The pines and birches came right down to the lake,
with just a thin lacing of mossy rocks before you got to the smooth,
cold water, and little gray fish swam around the splintery dock
and through our legs, or out of reach of our oars when we took
out the old blue rowboat.

The cabin itself was three bedrooms and a little kitchen and a
living room that took up half the house. The two small bedrooms
had big beds with pastel chenille spreads; yellow with red roses
in my parents' room, white with blue pansies in the other. The
kids' room was much bigger, like a dormitory, with three sets of
bunk beds, each with its own mismatched sheets and pillowcases.
The pillows were always a little damp and smelled like salt and
pine and mine smelled of Ma Griffe perfume as well, because I
used to sleep with my mother's scarf tucked under my pillow.
The shower was outside, with a thin green plastic curtain around
it, but there was a regular bathroom inside, next to my parents'
room.

Mr. DeCuervo and Gisela fit into our routine as though they'd
been coming to the cabin for years, instead of just last summer.
We had the kind of summer cabin routine that stays with you
forever as a model of leisure, of life being enjoyed. We'd get up
early, listening to the birds screaming and trilling, and make ourselves some breakfast: cold cereal or toast if the parents were up,
cake or cold spaghetti or marshmallows, if they were still asleep.
Then the parents would get up, my mother first, usually. She'd
make a cup of coffee and brush and braid our hair and set us
loose. If we were going exploring, she'd put three sandwiches
and three pieces of fruit in a bag, with an army blanket. Otherwise, she'd just wave to us as we headed down to the lake.

We'd come back at lunchtime and eat whatever was around and
then go out to the lake, or the forest, or down the road to see if
the townie kids were around and in a mood to play with us. I
don't know what the grown-ups did all day; sometimes they'd come

out to swim for a while, and sometimes we'd find my mother in the shed she used for a studio. But when we came back at around five or six, they all seemed happy and relaxed, drinking gin-and-tonics on the porch, watching us run toward the house. It was the most beautiful time.

At night, after dinner, the fathers would wash up and my mother would sit on the porch, smoking a cigarette, listening to Aretha Franklin or Billie Holiday or Sam Cooke, and after a little while, she'd stub out her cigarette and the four of us would dance. We'd twist and lindy and jitterbug and stomp, all of us copying my mother. And pretty soon, the daddies would drift in, with their dishtowels and their beers, and they'd lean in the doorway and watch. My mother would turn first to my father, always to him, first.

"What about it, Danny? Care to dance?" And she'd put her hand on his shoulder and he'd smile, tossing his dishtowel to Mr. DeCuervo, resting his beer on the floor. And my father would lumber along, gamely, shuffling his feet and smiling. Sometimes, he'd wave his arms around and pretend to be a fish or a bear, while my mother swung her body, easily and dreamily, sliding through the music. They'd always lindy together, to Fats Domino. That was my father's favorite and then he'd sit down, puffing a little.

My mother would stand there, snapping her fingers, shifting back and forth.

"Gaucho, you dance with her, before I have a coronary," said my father.

Mr. DeCuervo's real name was Bolivar, which I didn't know until Lizzie told me after the funeral. We always called him Mr. DeCuervo because we felt embarrassed to call him by a nickname.

So, Mr. DeCuervo would shrug gracefully, and toss the two dishtowels back to my father. And then he'd bop toward my mother, his face still turned toward my father.

"We'll go running tomorrow, Dan, get you back into shape, so you can dance all night."

"What do you mean, 'back'? I've been exactly this same svelte shape for twenty years. Why fix it if it ain't broke?"

And they all laughed and Mr. DeCuervo and my mother rolled

their eyes at each other and my mother walked over and kissed my father, where the sweat was beading up at his temples. Then she took Mr. DeCuervo's hand and they walked to the center of the living room.

When she and my father danced, my sister and I giggled and interfered and treated it like a family badminton game in which they were the core players but we were welcome participants. When she danced with Mr. DeCuervo, we'd sit on the porch swing or lean on the windowsill and watch, not even looking at each other.

They only danced the fast dances, and they danced as though they'd been waiting all their lives for each song. My mother's movements got deeper and smoother and Mr. DeCuervo suddenly came alive, as though a spotlight had hit him. My father danced the way he was — warm, noisy, teasing, a little overpowering; but Mr. DeCuervo, who was usually quiet and thoughtful and serious, became a different man when he danced with my mother. His dancing was light and happy and soulful, edging up on my mother, turning her, matching her every step. They would smile at all of us, in turn, and then face each other, too transported to smile.

"Dance with Daddy some more," my sister said, speaking for all three of us. They had left us too far behind.

My mother blew Lizzie a kiss. "Okay, sweetheart."

She turned to both men, smiling, and said, "That message was certainly loud and clear. Let's take a little break, Gauch', and get these monkeys to bed. It's getting late, girls."

And the three of them shepherded the three of us through the bedtime rituals, moving us in and out of the kitchen for water, the bathroom for teeth, potty and calamine lotion, and finally to our big bedroom. We slept in our underwear and T-shirts, which impressed Gisela.

"No pajamas?" she had said, the first night.

"Not necessary," I said smugly.

We would lie there after they kissed us, listening to our parents talk and crack peanuts and snap cards; they played gin and poker while they listened to Dinah Washington and Odetta.

One night, I woke up at around midnight and crossed the living room to get some water in the kitchen and see if there was

any strawberry shortcake left. I saw my mother and Mr. De-
Cuervo hugging, and I remember being surprised, and puzzled,
too. I had seen movies; if you hugged someone like you'd never
let them go, surely you were supposed to be kissing, too. It wasn't
a Mommy-Daddy hug, partly because their hugs were defined by
the fact that my father was eight inches taller and a hundred
pounds heavier than my mother. These two looked all wrong to
me; embraces were a big pink-and-orange man enveloping a
smaller, leaner black-and-white woman who looked up at him.
My mother and Mr. DeCuervo looked like sister and brother,
standing cheek-to-cheek, with their broad shoulders and long,
tanned, bare legs. My mother's hands were under Mr. De-
Cuervo's white T-shirt. She must have felt my eyes on her because she opened hers slowly.

"Oh, honey, you startled us. Mr. DeCuervo and I were just saying goodnight. Do you want me to tuck you in after you go potty?"
Not quite a bribe, certainly a reminder that I was more important
to her than he was. They had moved apart so quickly and smoothly
I couldn't even remember how they had looked together. I nodded to my mother; what I had seen was already being transformed into a standard goodnight embrace, the kind my mother
gave to all of her close friends.

When I came back from the bathroom, Mr. DeCuervo had disappeared and my mother was waiting, looking out at the moon.
She walked me to the bedroom and kissed me, first on my forehead, then on my lips.

"Sleep well, pumpkin pie. See you in the morning."

"Will you make blueberry pancakes tomorrow?" It seemed like
a good time to ask.

"We'll see. Go to sleep."

"Please, Mommy."

"Okay, we'll have a blueberry morning. Go to sleep, now.
Goodnight, nurse." And she watched me for a moment, from the
doorway, and then she was gone.

My father got up at five to go fishing with some men at the
other side of the lake. Every Saturday in July, he'd go off, with a
big red bandanna tied over his bald spot, his Mets T-shirt, and
his tackle box, and he'd fish until around three. Mr. DeCuervo
said that he'd clean them, cook them and eat them, but he wouldn't

spend a day with a bunch of guys in baseball caps and white socks to catch them.

I woke up smelling coffee and butter. Gisela and Liz were already out of bed and I was aggrieved; I was the one who had asked for the pancakes and they were probably all eaten by now.

Mr. DeCuervo and Liz were sitting at the table, finishing their pancakes. My mother and Gisela were sitting on the blue couch in the living room, while my mother brushed Gisela's hair. She was brushing it more gently than she brushed mine, not slapping her on the shoulder to make her sit still. Gisela didn't wiggle and she didn't scream when my mother hit a knot.

I was getting ready to be mad when my mother winked at me over Gisela's head and said, "There's a plate of pancakes for you on top of the stove, bunny. Gauch', would you please lift them for Ellen? The plate's probably hot."

Mr. DeCuervo handed me my pancakes, which were huge brown wheels studded with smashed, purply berries; he put my fork and knife on top of a folded paper towel and patted my cheek. His hand smelled like coffee and cinnamon. He knew what I liked and pushed the butter and the honey and the syrup toward me.

"Juice?" he said.

I nodded, trying to watch him when he wasn't looking; he didn't look like the man I thought I saw in the moonlight, giving my mother a funny hug.

"Great pancakes, Lila," he said.

"Great, Mom." I didn't want to be outclassed by the De-Cuervos' habitual good manners. Even Gisela remembered her please and thank you for every little thing.

My mother smiled and put the barrettes in Gisela's hair. It was starting to get warm, so I swallowed my pancakes and kicked Liz to get her attention.

"Let's go," I said.

"Wash your face, then go," my mother said.

I stuck my face under the kitchen tap and my mother and Mr. DeCuervo laughed. Triumphantly, I led the two little girls out of the house, snatching our towels off the line as we ran down to the water, suddenly filled with longing for the lake.

"Last one in the water's a fart," I screamed, cannonballing off the end of the dock. I hit the cold blue water, shattering its sur-

face. Liz and Gisela jumped in beside me and we played water
games until my father drove up in the pickup with a bucket of
fish. He waved to us and told us we'd be eating fish for the next
two days, and we groaned and held our noses as he went into the
cabin, laughing.

There was a string of sunny days like that one: swimming, fishing with Daddy off the dock, eating peanut-butter-and-jelly
sandwiches in the rowboat, drinking Orange Crush on the porch
swing.

And then it rained for a week. We woke up the first rainy
morning, listening to it tap and dance on the roof. My mother
stuck her head into our bedroom.

"It's monsoon weather, honeys. How about cocoa and cinnamon toast?"

We pulled on our overalls and sweaters and went into the
kitchen, where my mother had already laid out our mugs and
plates. She was engaged in her rainy-day ritual: making sangria.
First she poured the orange juice out of the big white plastic pitcher
into three empty peanut-butter jars, then she started chopping
up all the oranges, lemons and limes we had in the house. She let
me pour the brandy over the fruit, Gisela threw in the sugar and
Lizzie came up for air long enough to pour the big bottle of red
wine over everything. I cannot imagine drinking anything else
on rainy days.

That day, my mother went out onto the porch for her morning
cigarette and when my father came down, he joined her on the
porch, while we played Go Fish; I could see them snuggling on
the wicker settee. After a while, Mr. DeCuervo came down, looked
out on the porch and picked up an old magazine and started
reading.

We decided to play Monopoly in our room, since the grown-
ups didn't want to entertain us. After two hours, in which I rotted in jail and Lizzie forgot to charge rent, little Gisela beat us
and the three of us went back to the kitchen for snacks. Rainy
days were basically a series of snacks, more and less elaborate,
punctuated by board games, card games and whining. We drank
soda and juice all day, ate cheese, bananas, cookies, bologna, gra-
ham crackers, Jiffy popcorn, hard-boiled eggs. The grown-ups
ate cheese and crackers and drank sangria.

The daddies were reading in the two big armchairs; my mother had gone off to her room to sketch. We were getting bored, so I started writing my name in the honey that had spilled on the kitchen table, while Gisela and Liz pulled the stuffing out of the hole in the bottom of the blue couch.

My mother came downstairs for a cigarette and started swearing. "Jesus Christ, Ellen, get your hands out of the goddamned honey. Liz, Gisela, that's absolutely unacceptable, you know that. Leave the poor couch alone. If you're so damned stir-crazy, go outside and dance in the rain."

The two men looked up, slowing focusing, from a great distance.

"Lila, really," said my father.

"Lila, it's pouring. We'll keep an eye on them, now," said Mr. DeCuervo.

"Right. Like you were." My mother was grinning.

"Can we, Mommy, can we go in the rain? Can we take off our clothes and go in the rain?"

"Sure, go naked, there's no point in getting your clothes wet and no point in suits. There's not likely to be a big crowd in the yard."

We ran to the porch and, before my mother could get rational, stripped and ran whooping into the rain, leaping off the porch onto the muddy lawn, screaming and feeling superior to every child in Maine who had to stay indoors.

We played goddesses-in-the-rain, which consisted of caressing our bodies and screaming the names of everyone we knew, and we played ring-around-the-rosie and tag and red light, green light and catch, all of which were deliciously slippery and surreal in the sheets of gray rain. Our parents watched us from the porch.

When we finally came in, thrilled with ourselves and the extent to which we were completely, profoundly wet, in every pore, they bundled us up and told us to dry our hair and get ready for dinner.

My mother brushed our hair and then she made sauce for spaghetti, while my father made a salad and Mr. DeCuervo made a strawberry tart, piling the berries into a huge, red, shiny pyramid in the center of the pastry. We were in heaven. The grown-ups were laughing a lot, sipping their rosy drinks, tossing the vegetables back and forth.

After dinner, my mother took us into the living room to dance and then the power went off.

"Shit," said my father in the kitchen.

"Double shit," said Mr. DeCuervo, and we heard them stumbling around in the dark, laughing and cursing until they came in with two flashlights.

"The cavalry is here, ladies," said Daddy, bowing to us all and twirling his flashlight.

"American and Argentinian divisions, senora y senoritas." I had never heard Mr. DeCuervo speak Spanish before, not even that little bit.

"Well, then, I know I'm safe — from the bad guys, anyway. On the other hand . . ." My mother laughed, and the daddies put their arms around each other, and they laughed, too.

"On the other hand, what? What, Mommy?" I tugged at her the way I did when I was afraid of losing her in a big department store.

"Nothing, honey. Mommy was just being silly. Let's get ready for bed, munchkins. Then you all can whisper in bed for a while. We're shut down for the night, I'm sure."

The daddies accompanied us to the bathroom and whispered that we could skip everything except peeing, since there was no electricity. The two of them kissed us goodnight, my father's moustache tickling, Mr. DeCuervo's sliding over my cheek. My mother came into the room a moment later, and her face was as smooth and warm as a velvet cushion. We didn't whisper for long; the rain dance and the eating and the storm had worn us out.

It was still dark when I woke up, but the rain had stopped and the power had returned, so that there was a light burning in our hallway. It made me feel very grown-up and responsible, getting out of bed and going around the house turning out the lights that no one else knew were on; I was conserving electricity.

I went into the bathroom and was squeezed by stomach cramps, probably from all the burnt popcorn kernels I had eaten. I sat on the toilet for a long time, watching a brown spider crawl along the wall; I'd knock him down and then watch him climb back up again toward the towels. My cramps were better, but not gone, so

I decided to wake my mother. My father would have been more sympathetic, but he was the heavier sleeper, and by the time he understood what I was telling him my mother would have her bathrobe on and be massaging my stomach, kindly, but without the excited concern that I felt was my due as a victim of illness.

I walked down to my parents' room, turning the hall light back on. I pushed open the creaky door and saw my mother spooned up against my father's back, as she always was, and Mr. De-Cuervo spooned up against her, his arm over the covers, his other hand resting on the top of her head.

I stood up and looked and then backed out of the bedroom. They hadn't moved, the three of them breathing deeply, in unison. What was that, I thought, what did I see? I wanted to go back and take another look, to see it again, to make it disappear, to watch them carefully, until I understood.

My cramps were gone. I went back to my own bed, staring at Liz and Gisela, who looked, in their sleep, like little girl versions of the two men I had just seen. Just sleeping, I thought, the grown-ups were just sleeping. Maybe Mr. DeCuervo's bed collapsed, like ours did two summers ago, or maybe it got wet in the storm. I thought I would never be able to fall asleep, but the next thing I remember is waking up to more rain and the sounds of Liz and Gisela begging my mother to take us to the movies in town. We went to see *The Sound of Music*, which had been playing at the Bijou for about ten years.

I don't remember much else about the summer; all of the images run together. We went on swimming and fishing and taking the rowboat out for little adventures, and when the DeCuervos left, I hugged Gisela, but wasn't going to hug him, until he whispered in my ear, "Next year, we'll bring up a motorboat and I'll teach you to water-ski," and then I hugged him very hard and my mother put her hand on my head, lightly, giving benediction.

The next summer, I went off to camp in July and wasn't there when the DeCuervos came. Lizzie said they had a good time without me. Then they couldn't come for a couple of summers in a row, and by the time they came again, Gisela and Lizzie were at camp with me in New Hampshire; the four grown-ups spent about a week together, but then I heard my father say that another vacation with Elvira DeCuervo would kill him or he'd kill her. My mother said she wasn't so bad.

We saw them a little less after that. They came, Gisela and Mr. DeCuervo, to my high school graduation, to my mother's opening in Boston, to my father's fiftieth birthday party and then to Lizzie's graduation. When my mother went down to New York, she'd have dinner with the three of them, she said, but sometimes her plans would change and they'd have to substitute lunch for dinner.

Gisela couldn't come to the funeral; she was in Argentina for the year, working with the architectural firm that Mr. DeCuervo's father had started.

After all the mourners left, Mr. DeCuervo gave us a sympathy note from Gisela, with a beautiful pen-and-ink of our mother inside it. The two men went into the living room and took out a bottle of Scotch and two glasses. It was like we weren't there; they put on Billie Holiday singing "Embraceable You," and they got down to serious drinking and grieving. Lizzie and I went into the kitchen and decided to eat everything sweet that people had brought over: brownies, strudel, pfeffernuss, sweet potato pie, Mrs. Ellis' chocolate cake, with chocolate mousse in the middle. We laid out two plates and two mugs of milk and got to it.

Lizzie said, "You know, when I was home in April, he called every day." She jerked her head toward the living room.

I couldn't tell if she approved or disapproved, and I didn't know what I thought about it either.

"She called him 'Bolivar.' "

"What? She always called him 'Gaucho' and so we didn't call him anything."

"I know, but she called him 'Bolivar.' I heard her talk to him every fucking day, El; she called him 'Bolivar.' " Tears were running down Lizzie's face, and I wished my mother was there to pat her soft, fuzzy hair and keep her from choking on her tears. I held her hand across the table. I was still holding my fork in my other hand and I could feel my mother looking at me, smiling and narrowing her eyes a little, the way she did when I was balking. I dropped the fork onto my plate and went over and hugged Lizzie, who leaned into me as though her spine had collapsed.

"I asked her, after the third call, about his calling," she said, into my shoulder.

"What'd she say?" I straightened Lizzie up, so I could hear what she was saying.

"She said, 'Of course, he calls at noon, he knows that's when I'm feeling strongest.' And I told her that's not what I meant, that I hadn't known they were so close."

"You said that?"

"Yeah. And she said, 'Honey, nobody loves me more than Bolivar.' And I didn't know what to say, so I just sat there feeling like 'Do I really want to hear this?' and then she fell asleep."

"So what do you think?"

"I don't know. I was getting ready to ask her again . . ."

"You're amazing, Lizzie," I interrupted. She really is, she's so quiet but she goes out and has conversations that I can't even imagine having.

"But I didn't have to ask because she brought it up herself, the next day after he called. She got off the phone, looking just so exhausted, she was sweating, but she was smiling. She was looking out at the crabapple trees in the yard, and she said, 'There were apples trees in bloom when I met Bolivar, and the trees were right where the sculpture needed to be in the courtyard, so he offered to get rid of the trees, and I said that seemed arrogant, and he said that they'd replant them. So I said okay and he said, 'What's so bad about arrogance?' And the first time he and Daddy met, the two of them drank Scotch and watched soccer while I made dinner. And then they washed up, just like at the cabin. And when the two of them are in the room together and you two girls are with us, I know that I am living in a state of grace.' "

"She said that? She said 'in a state of grace'? Mommy said that?"

"Yes, Ellen. Christ, what do you think, I'm making up interesting deathbed statements?" Liz hated to be interrupted, especially by me.

"Sorry. Go on."

"Anyway, we were talking and I sort of asked what were we actually talking about. I mean, close friends or very close friends, and she just laughed. You know how she'd look at us like she knew exactly where we were going when we said we were going to a friend's house for the afternoon but we were really going to drink Boone's Farm and skinny-dip at the quarry? Well, she looked just like that and she took my hand. Her hand was so light, El. And she said that the three of them loved each other, each differently, and that they were both amazing men, each special, each deserving love and appreciation. She said that she thought Daddy was the most wonderful husband a woman could have and that she was very glad that we had him as a father. And I asked her how she could do it, love them both, and how they could stand it. And she said, 'Love is not a pie, honey. I love you and Ellen differently, because you are different people, wonderful people, but not at all the same. And so who I am with each of you is different, unique to us. I don't choose between you. And it's the same way with Daddy and Bolivar. People think that it can't be that way, but it can. You just have to find the right people.' And then she shut her eyes for the afternoon. Your eyes are bugging out, El."

"Well, Jesus, I guess so. I mean, I knew . . ."

"You knew and you didn't tell me?"

"You were eight or something, Lizzie, what was I supposed to say? I didn't even know what I knew then."

"So what did you know?" Lizzie was very serious. It was a real breach of our rules not to share inside dirt about our parents, especially our mother; we were always trying to figure her out.

I didn't know how to tell her about the three of them; that was even less normal than her having an affair with Mr. DeCuervo with Daddy's permission. I couldn't even think of the words to describe what I had seen, so I just said, "I saw Mommy and Mr. DeCuervo kissing one night after we were in bed."

"Really? Where was Daddy?"

"I don't know. But wherever he was, obviously he knew what was going on. I mean, that's what Mommy was telling you, right? That Daddy knew and that it was okay with him."

"Yeah. Jesus."

I went back and sat down and we were halfway through the strudel when the two men came in. They were drunk, but not incoherent. They just weren't their normal selves, but I guess we weren't either, with our eyes puffy and red and all this destroyed food around us.

"Beautiful girls," Mr. DeCuervo said to my father. They were hanging in the doorway, one on each side.

"They are, they really are. And smart, couldn't find smarter girls." My father was going on and on about how smart we were. Lizzie and I just looked at each other, embarrassed but not displeased.

"Ellen has Lila's mouth," Mr. DeCuervo said. "You have your mother's mouth, with the right side going up a little more than the left. Exquisite."

My father's nodding his head, like this is the greatest truth ever told. And Daddy turns to Liz and says, "And you have your mother's eyes. Since the day you were born and I looked right into them, I thought, 'My God, she's got Lila's eyes, but blue, not green.'"

And Mr. DeCuervo is nodding away, of course. I wondered if they were going to do a complete autopsy, but they stopped.

My father came over to us at the table and put one hand on each of us. "You girls made your mother incredibly happy. There was nothing she ever created that gave her more pride and joy than you two. And she thought that you were both so special . . ." He started crying and Mr. DeCuervo put an arm around his waist and picked up for him.

"She did, she had two pictures of you in her studio, nothing else. And you know, she expected us all to grieve, but you know how much she wanted you to enjoy, too. To enjoy everything, every meal, every drink, every sunrise, every kiss . . ." He started crying too.

"We're gonna lie down for a while, girls. Maybe later we'll have dinner or something." My father kissed us both, wet and rough, and the two of them went down the hall.

Lizzie and I just looked at each other.

"Wanna get drunk?" I said.

"No, I don't think so. I guess I'll go lie down for a while unless you want my company." She looked like she was about to sleep standing up, so I shook my head. I was planning on calling John anyway.

Lizzie came over and hugged me, hard, and I hugged her back and brushed the chocolate crumbs out of her hair.

Sitting alone in the kitchen, I thought about John, about telling him about my mother and her affair and how the two men were sacked out in my parents' bed, probably snoring. And I could hear John's silence and I knew that he would think my father must not have really loved my mother, if he'd let her go with another man; or that my mother must have been a real bitch, forcing my father to tolerate an affair "right in his own home," John would think, maybe even say. I thought I ought to call him, before I got myself completely enraged over a phone call that hadn't taken place. Lizzie would say I was projecting anyway.

I called John and he was very sweet, asking how I was feeling, how the memorial service had gone, how my father was. And I told him all that and then I knew I couldn't tell him the rest and that I couldn't marry a man I couldn't tell this story to.

"I'm so sorry, Ellen," he said. "You must be very upset. What a difficult day for you."

I realize that that was a perfectly normal response; it just was all wrong for me. I didn't come from a normal family, I wasn't ready to get normal.

I felt terrible, hurting John, but I couldn't marry him just because I didn't want to hurt him, so I said, "And that's not the worst of it, John. I can't marry you, I really can't. I know this is pretty hard to listen to, over the phone . . ." I couldn't think of what else to say.

"Ellen, let's talk about this when you get back to Boston. I know what kind of a strain you must be under. I had the feeling that you were unhappy about some of Mother's ideas. We can work something out when you get back."

"I know that you think this is because of my mother's death and it is, but not the way you think, John, I just can't marry you. I'm not going to wear your mother's dress and I'm not going to marry you and I'm very sorry." He was quiet for a long time and then he said, "I don't understand, Ellen. We've already ordered the invitations." And I knew that I was right. If he had said, "Fuck this, I'm coming to see you tonight," or even "I don't know what you're talking about, but I want to marry you anyway," I would have probably changed my mind before I got off the phone. But as it was I said goodbye sort of quietly and hung up.

It was like two funerals in one day. I sat at the table, poking the cake into little shapes and then knocking them over. My mother would have sent me out for a walk. I started to clear the stuff away when my father and Mr. DeCuervo appeared, looking more together.

"How about some gin, El?" my father said.

"If you're up for it," said Mr. DeCuervo.

"Okay," I said. "I just broke up with John Wescott."

"Oh?" I couldn't tell which one spoke.

"I told him that I didn't think we'd make each other happy."
Which was what I had meant to say.

My father hugged me and said, "I'm sorry if it's hard for you."
Then he turned to Mr. DeCuervo and said, "Did she know how
to call them or what? Your mother knew you weren't going to
marry that guy."

"She was almost always right, Dan."

"Almost always, not quite," said my father, and the two of them
laughed at some private joke and shook hands like a pair of old
boxers.

"So it's your deal," my father said, leaning back in his chair.

"Penny a point," said Mr. DeCuervo.

KATE BRAVERMAN

Tall Tales from the Mekong Delta

FROM STORY

IT WAS IN THE FIFTH MONTH of her sobriety. It was after the
hospital. It was after her divorce. It was autumn. She had even
stopped smoking. She was wearing pink aerobic pants, a pink T-
shirt with KAUAI written in lilac across the chest, and tennis shoes.
She had just come from the gym. She was walking across a parking lot bordering a city park in West Hollywood. She was carrying cookies for the AA meeting. She was in charge of bringing
the food for the meeting. He fell into step with her. He was short,
fat, pale. He had bad teeth. His hair was dirty. Later, she would
freeze this frame in her mind and study it. She would say he
seemed frightened and defeated and trapped, "cagey" was the
word she used to describe his eyes, how he measured and evalu-
ated something in the air between them. The way he squinted
through hazel eyes, it had nothing to do with the sunlight.

"I'm Lenny," he said, extending his hand. "What's your name?"

She told him. She was holding a bag with packages of cookies
in it. After the meeting, she had an appointment with her psychiatrist, then a manicure. She kept walking.

"You a teacher? You look like a teacher," he said.

"I'm a writer," she told him. "I teach creative writing."

"You look like a teacher," Lenny said.

"I'm not just a teacher," she told him. She was annoyed.

"Okay. You're a writer. And you're bad. You're one of those
bad girls from Beverly Hills. I've had my eye on you," Lenny said.

She didn't say anything. He was wearing blue jeans, a black
leather jacket zipped to his throat, a long red wool scarf around

his neck, and a Dodgers baseball cap. It was too hot a day for the
leather jacket and scarf. She didn't find that detail significant. It
caught her attention, she touched it briefly and then let it go. She
looked but did not see. They were standing on a curb. The meeting was in a community room across the boulevard. She wasn't
afraid yet.

"You do drugs? What do you do? Drink too much?" he asked.

"I'm a cocaine addict," she told him.

"Me too. Let's see your tracks. Show me your tracks." Lenny
reached out for her arm.

"I don't have any now." She glanced at her arm. She extended
her arm into the yellow air between them. The air was already
becoming charged and disturbed. "They're gone."

"I see them," Lenny told her, inspecting her arm, turning it
over, holding it in the sunlight. He touched the part of her arm
behind her elbow where the vein rose. "They're beautiful."

"But there's nothing there," she said.

"Yeah, there is. There always is if you know how to look," Lenny
told her. "How many people by the door? How many steps?"

He was talking about the door across the boulevard. His back
was turned. She didn't know.

"Four steps," Lenny said. "Nine people. Four women. One old
man. I look. I see."

She was counting the people on the steps in front of the meeting. She didn't say anything.

"Let's get a coffee later. That's what you do, right? You can't
get a drink? You go out for coffee?" Lenny was studying her face.

"I don't think so," she said.

"You don't think so? Come on. I'll buy you coffee. You can
explain AA to me. You like that Italian shit? That French shit?
The little cups?" Lenny was staring at her.

"No, thank you. I'm sorry," she said. He was short and fat and
sweating. He looked like he was laughing at her with his eyes.

"You're sorry. I'll show you sorry. Listen. I know what you want.
You're one of those smart-ass teachers from Beverly Hills," Lenny
said.

"Right," she said. She didn't know why she bothered talking to
him.

"You want to get in over your head. You want to see what's on the other side. I'll show you. I'll take you there. It'll be the ride of your life," Lenny said.

"Goodbye," she answered.

Lenny was at her noon meeting the next day. She saw him immediately as she walked through the door. She wondered how he knew that she would be there. As she approached her usual chair, she saw a bouquet of long-stemmed pink roses.

"You look beautiful," Lenny said. "You knew I'd be here. That's why you put that crap on your face. You didn't have that paint on yesterday. Don't do that. You don't need that. Those whores from Beverly Hills need it. Not you. You're a teacher. I like that. Sit down." He picked the roses up. "Sit next to me. You glad to see me?"

"I don't think so." She sat down. Lenny handed to roses to her. She put them on the floor.

"Yeah. You're glad to see me. You were hoping I'd be here. And here I am. You want me to chase you? I'll chase you. Then I'll catch you. Then I'll show you what being in over your head means." Lenny was smiling.

She turned away. When the meeting was over, she stood up quickly and began moving, even before the prayer was finished. "I have to go," she said, softly, over her shoulder. She felt she had to apologize. She felt she had to be careful.

"You don't have to go," Lenny said. He caught up with her on the steps. "Yeah. Don't look surprised. Lenny's fast, real fast. And you're lying. Don't ever lie to me. You think I'm stupid? Yeah, you think Lenny's stupid. You think you can get away from me? You can't get away. You got an hour. You don't pick that kid up for the dance school until four. Come on. I'll buy you coffee."

"What are you talking about?" She stopped. Her breath felt sharp and fierce. It was a warm November. The air felt like glass.

"I know all about you. I know your routine. I been watching you for two weeks. Ever since I got to town. I saw you my first day. You think I'd ask you out on a date and not know your routine?" Lenny stared at her.

She felt her eyes widen. She started to say something but she changed her mind.

"You live at the top of the hill, off of Doheny. You pick up that kid, what's her name, Annie something? You pick her up and take her to dance school. You get coffee next door. Table by the window. You read the paper. Then you go home. Just the two of you. And that Mex cleaning lady. Maria. That her name? Maria? They're all called Maria. And the gardener Friday afternoons. That's it." Lenny lit a cigarette.

"You've been following me?" She was stunned. Her mouth opened.

"Recon," Lenny said.

"I beg you pardon?"

"In Nam. We called it recon. Fly over, get a lay of the land. Or stand behind some trees. Count the personnel. People look but they don't see. I'll tell you about it. Get coffee. You got an hour. Want to hear about Vietnam? I got stories. Choppers? I like choppers. You can take your time, aim. You can hit anything, even dogs. Some days we'd go out just aiming at dogs. Or the black market? Want to hear about that? Profiteering in smack? You're a writer, right? You like stories. I got some tall tales from the Mekong Delta for you, sweetheart. Knock your socks off. Come on." He reached out and touched her arm. "Later you can have your own war stories. I can be one of your tall tales. I can be the tallest."

The sun was strong. The world was washed with white. The day seemed somehow clarified. He was wearing a leather jacket and shaking. It occurred to her that he was sick.

"Excuse me. I must go," she said. "If you follow me, I shall have someone call the police."

"Okay. Okay. Calm down," Lenny was saying behind her. I'll save you a seat tomorrow, okay?"

She didn't reply. She sat in her car. It was strange how blue the sky seemed, etched with the blue of radium or narcotics. Or China blue, perhaps. Was that a color? The blue of the China Sea? The blue of Vietnam. When he talked about Asia, she could imagine that blue, luminescent with ancient fever, with promises and bridges broken, with the harvest lost in blue flame. Always there were barbarians, shooting the children and dogs.

She locked her car and began driving. It occurred to her, suddenly, that the Chinese took poets as concubines. Their poets slept with warlords. They wrote with gold ink. They ate orchids and

smoked opium. They were consecrated by nuance, by birds and
silk and the ritual birthdays of gods and nothing changed for a
thousand years. And afternoon was absinthe yellow and almond,
burnt orange and chrysanthemum. And in the abstract sky, a lit-
any of kites.

She felt herself look for him as she walked into the meeting the
next day at noon. The meeting was in the basement of a church.
Lenny was standing near the coffeepot with his back to the wall.
He was holding two cups of coffee as if he was expecting her. He
handed one to her.

"I got seats," he said. He motioned for her to follow. She followed. He pointed to a chair. She sat in it. An older woman was
standing at the podium, telling the story of her life. Lenny was
wearing a white warm-up suit with a green neon stripe down the
sides of the pants and the arms of the jacket. He was wearing a
baseball cap. His face seemed younger and tanner than she had
remembered.

"Like how I look? I look like a lawyer on his way to tennis, right?
I even got a tan. Fit right in. Chameleon Lenny. The best, too."
He lit a cigarette. He held the pack out to her.

She shook her head, no. She was staring at the cigarette in his
mouth, in his fingers. She could lean her head closer, part her
lips, take just one puff.

"I got something to show you," Lenny said.

The meeting was over. They were walking up the stairs from
the basement of the church. The sun was strong. She blinked in
the light. It was the yellow of a hot autumn, a yellow that seemed
amplified and redeemed. She glanced at her watch.

"Don't do that," Lenny said. He was touching the small of her
back with his hand. He was helping her walk.

"What?"

"Looking at that fucking watch all the time. Take it off," Lenny
said.

"My watch?" She was looking at her wrist as if she had never
seen it before.

"Give it here, come on." Lenny put his hand out. He motioned
with his fingers. She placed her watch in the palm of his hand.

"That's a good girl," Lenny was saying. "You don't need it. You don't have to know what time it is. You're with me. Don't you get it? You're hungry, I feed you. You're tired, I find a hotel. You're in a structured environment now. You're protected. I protect you. It doesn't matter what time it is." He put her watch in his pocket. "Forget it. I'll buy you a new one. A better one. That was junk. I was embarrassed for you to wear junk like that. Want a Rolex?"

"You can't afford a Rolex," she said. She felt intelligent. She looked into his face.

"I got a drawerful," Lenny told her. "I got all the colors. Red. Black. Gold."

"Where?" She studied his face. They were walking on a side street in Hollywood. The air was a pale blue, bleeding into the horizon, taking the sky.

"In the bank," Lenny said. "In the safety deposit with everything else. All the cash that isn't buried." Lenny smiled.

"What else?" She put her hands on her hips.

"Let's go for a ride," Lenny said.

They were standing at the curb. They were two blocks from the church. A motorcycle was parked there. Lenny took out a key.

"Get on," he said.

"I don't want to get on a motorcycle." She was afraid.

"Yes, you do," Lenny told her. "Sit down on it. Wrap your arms around me. Just lean into me. Nothing else. You'll like it. You'll be surprised. It's a beautiful day. It looks like Hong Kong today. Want to go to the beach? Want lunch? I know a place in Malibu. You like seafood? Crab? Scampi? Watch the waves?" Lenny was doing something to the motorcycle. He looked at her face.

"No," she said.

"How about Italian? I got a place near the Marina. Owner owes for ten kilos. We'll get a good table. You like linguini?" Lenny sat down on the motorcycle.

She shook her head, no.

"Okay. You're not hungry. You're skinny. You should eat. Come on. We'll go around the block. Get on. Once around the block and I'll bring you back to the church." Lenny reached out his hand through the warm white air.

She looked at his hand and how the air seemed blue near his fingers. It's simply a blue glaze, she was thinking. In Malibu, in

Hilo, in the China Sea, forms of blue, confusion and remorse, a
dancing dress, a daughter with a mouth precisely your own and
it's done, all of it.

Somewhere it was carnival night in the blue wash of a village
on the China Sea. On the river, boats passed with low-slung antique masts sliding silently to the blue of the ocean, to the inverted delta where the horizon concluded itself in a rapture of
orchid and pewter. That's what she was thinking when she took
his hand.

She did not see him for a week. She changed her meeting sched-
ule. She went to women's meetings in the Pacific Palisades and
the Valley. She went to meetings she had never been to before.
She trembled when she thought about him.

She stopped her car at a red light. It occurred to her that it was
an early afternoon in autumn in her thirty-eighth year. Then she
found herself driving to the community center. The meeting was
over. There was no one left on the street. Just one man, sitting
alone on the front steps, smoking. Lenny looked up at her and
smiled.

"I was expecting you," Lenny said. "I told you. You can't get
away from me."

She could feel his eyes on her face, the way when she lived with
a painter, she had learned to feel lamplight on her skin. When
she had learned to perceive light as an entity. She began to cry.

"Don't cry," Lenny said, his voice soft. "I can't stand you crying.
Let's make up. I'll buy you dinner."

"I can't." She didn't look at him.

"Yeah. You can. I'll take you someplace good. Spago? You like
those little pizzas with the duck and shit? Lobster? You want the
Palm? The Rangoon Racket Club? Yeah. Don't look surprised. I
know the places. I made deals in all those places. What did you
think?" He was lighting a cigarette and she could feel his eyes on
her skin.

She didn't say anything. They were walking across a parking
lot. The autumn made everything ache. Later, it would be worse.
At dusk, with the subtle irritation of lamps.

"Yeah. I know what you think. You think Lenny looks like he
just crawled out from a rock. This is a disguise. Blue jeans, sneak-

ers. I fit right in. I got a gang of angry Colombians on my ass.
Forget it." Lenny stared at her. "You got a boyfriend?"

"What's it to you?"

"What's it to me? That's sharp. I want to date you. I probably
want to marry you. You got a boyfriend, I got to hurt him." Lenny
smiled.

"I can't believe you said that." She put her hands on her hips.

"You got a boyfriend? I'm going to cut off his arm and beat
him with it. Here. Look at this." He was bending over and removing something from his sock. He held it in the palm of his
hand.

"Know what this is?" Lenny asked.

She shook her head, no.

"It's a knife, sweetheart," Lenny said.

She could see that now, even before he opened it. A push-but-
ton knife. Lenny was reaching behind to his back. He was pulling
out something from behind his belt, under his shirt. It was another knife.

"Want to see the guns?"

She felt dizzy. They were standing near her car. It was early in
December. The Santa Anas had been blowing. She felt that it had
been exceptionally warm for months.

"Don't get in the car," Lenny said. "I can't take it when you
leave. Stay near me. Just let me breathe the same air as you. I love
you."

"You don't even know me," she said.

"But you know me. You been dreaming me. I'm your ticket to
the other side, remember?" Lenny had put his knives away. "Want
to hear some more Nam stories? How we ran smack into Honolulu? You'll like this. You like the dope stories. You want to get
loaded?"

She shook her head, no.

"You kidding me? You don't want to get high?" Lenny smiled.

"I like being sober," she said.

"Sure," Lenny said. "Let me know when that changes. One
phone call. I got the best dope in the world."

They were standing in front of her car. The street beyond the
parking lot seemed estranged, the air was tarnished. She hadn't
thought about drugs in months. Lenny was handing her some-

thing, thin circles of metal. She looked down at her hand. Two dimes seemed to glare in her palm.

"For when you change your mind," Lenny said. He was still smiling.

They were sitting on the grass of a public park after a meeting. Lenny was wearing Bermuda shorts and a green T-shirt that said CANCÚN. They were sitting in a corner of the park with a stucco wall behind them.

"It's our anniversary," Lenny told her. "We been in love four weeks."

"I've lost track of time," she said. She didn't have a watch anymore. The air felt humid, green, stalled. It was December in West Hollywood. She was thinking that the palms were livid with green death. They could be the palms of Vietnam.

"I want to fuck you," Lenny said. "Let's go to your house."

She shook her head, no. She turned away from him. She began to stand up.

"Okay. Okay. You got the kid. I understand that. Let's go to a hotel. You want the Beverly Wilshire? I can't go to the Beverly Hills Hotel. I got a problem there. What about the Four Seasons? You want to fuck in the Four Seasons?"

"You need to get an AIDS test," she said.

"Why?" Lenny looked amused.

"Because you're a heroin addict. Because you've been in jail," she began.

"Who told you that?" Lenny sat up.

"You told me," she said. "Terminal Island. Chino. Folsom? Is it true?

"Uh-huh," Lenny said. He lit a cigarette. "Five years in Folsom. Consecutive. Sixty months. I topped out."

She stared at him. She thought how easy it would be, to reach and take a cigarette. Just one, once.

"Means I finished my whole sentence. No time off for good behavior. Lenny did the whole sixty." He smiled. "I don't need an AIDS test."

"You're a heroin addict. You shoot cocaine. You're crazy. Who knows what you do or who you do it with?" She was beginning to be afraid.

"You think I'd give you a disease?" Lenny looked hurt.

Silence. She was looking at Lenny's legs, how white the exposed skin was. She was thinking that he brought his sick body to her, that he was bloated enormous with pathology and bad history, with jails and demented resentments.

"Listen. You got nothing to worry about. I don't need a fucking AIDS test. Listen to me. Are you hearing me? You get that disease, I take care of you. I take you to Bangkok. I keep a place there, on the river. Best smack in the world. Fifty cents. I keep you loaded. You'll never suffer. You start hurting, I'll take you out. I'll kill you myself. With my own hands. I promise," Lenny said.

Silence. She was thinking that he must be drawn to her vast emptiness, could he sense that she was aching and hot and always listening? There is always a garish carnival across the boulevard. We are born, we eat and sleep, conspire and mourn, a birth, a betrayal, an excursion to the harbor, and it's done. All of it, done.

"Come here." Lenny extended his arm. "Come here. You're like a child. Don't be afraid. I want to give you something."

She moved her body closer to his. There are blue enormities, she was thinking, horizons and boulevards. Somewhere, there are blue rocks and they burn.

"Close your eyes," Lenny said. "Open your mouth."

She closed her eyes. She opened her mouth. There was something pressing against her lip. Perhaps it was a flower.

"Close your mouth and breathe," Lenny said.

It was a cigarette. She felt the smoke in her lungs. It had been six months since she smoked. Her hand began to tremble.

"There," Lenny was saying. "You need to smoke. I can tell. It's okay. You can't give up everything at once. Here. Share it. Give me a hit."

They smoked quietly. They passed the cigarette back and forth. She was thinking that she was like a sacked capital. Nothing worked in her plazas. The palm trees were on fire. The air was smoky and blue. No one seemed to notice.

"Sit on my lap. Come on. Sit down. Closer. On my lap," Lenny was saying. "Good. Yeah. Good. I'm not going to bite you. I love you. Want to get married? Want to have a baby? Closer. Let me kiss you. You don't do anything. Let me do it. Now your arms.

Yeah. Around my neck. Tighter. Tighter. You worried? You got
nothing to worry about. You get sick, I keep you whacked on
smack. Then I kill you. So what are you worried? Closer. Yeah.
Want to hear about R and R in Bangkok? Want to hear about
what you get for a hundred bucks on the river? You'll like this.
Lean right up against me. Yeah. Close your eyes."

"Look. It's hot. You want to swim. You like that? Swimming? You
know how to swim?" Lenny looked at her. "Yeah? Let's go. I got
a place in Bel Air."

"You have a place in Bel Air?" she asked. It was after the meeting. It was the week before Christmas. It was early afternoon.

"Guy I used to know. I did a little work for him. I introduced
him to his wife. He owes me some money. He gave me the keys."
Lenny reached in his pocket. He was wearing a white-and-yellow
warm-up suit. He produced a key ring. It hung in the hot air
between them. "It's got everything there. Food. Booze. Dope. Pool.
Tennis court. Computer games. You like that? Pac Man?"

She didn't say anything. She felt she couldn't move. She lit a
cigarette. She was buying two packages at a time again. She would
be buying cartons soon.

"Look. We'll go for a drive. I'll tell you some more war stories.
Come on. I got a nice car today. I got a brand-new red Ferrari.
Want to see it? Just take a look. One look. It's at the curb. Give
me your hand." Lenny reached out for her hand.

She could remember being a child. It was a child's game in a
child's afternoon, before time or distance were factors. When you
were told you couldn't move or couldn't see. And for those moments you are paralyzed or blind. You freeze in place. You don't
move. You feel that you have been there for years. It does not
occur to you that you can move. It does not occur to you that you
can break the rules. The world is a collection of absolutes and
spells. You know words have a power. You are entranced. The
world is a soft blue.

"There. See. I'm not crazy. A red Ferrari. A hundred forty
grand. Get in. We'll go around the block. Sit down. Nice interior,
huh? Nice stereo. But I got no fucking tapes. Go to the record
store with me? You pick out the tapes, okay? Then we'll go to Bel
Air. Swim a little. Watch the sunset. Listen to some music. Want

to dance? I love to dance. You can't get a disease doing that, right?" Lenny was holding the car door open for her.

She sat down. The ground seemed enormous. It seemed to leap up at her face.

"Yeah. I'm a good driver. Lean back. Relax. I used to drive for a living," Lenny told her.

"What did you drive? A bus?" She smiled.

"A bus? That's sharp. You're sharp. You're one of those sharp little Jewish girls from Beverly Hills with a cocaine problem. Yeah. I know what you're about. All of you. I drove some cars on a few jobs. Couple of jewelry stores, a few banks. Now I fly," Lenny said.

Lenny turned the car onto Sunset Boulevard. In the gardens of the houses behind the gates, everything was in bloom. Patches of color slid past so fast she thought they might be hallucinations. Azaleas and camellias and hibiscus. The green seemed sullen and half asleep. Or perhaps it was opiated, dazed, exhausted from pleasure.

"You fly?" she repeated.

"Planes. You like planes? I'll take you up. I got a plane. Company plane," Lenny told her. "It's in Arizona."

"You're a pilot?" She put out her cigarette and immediately lit another.

"I fly planes for money. Want to fly? I'm going next week. Every second Tuesday. Want to come?" Lenny looked at her.

"Maybe," she said. They had turned on a street north of Sunset. They were winding up a hill. The street was narrow. The bougainvillea was a kind of net near her face. The air smelled of petals and heat.

"Yeah. You'll come with me. I'll show you what I do. I fly over a stretch of desert looks like the moon. There's a small manufacturing business down there. Camouflaged. You'd never see it. I drop some boxes off. I pick some boxes up. Three hours' work. Fifteen grand," Lenny said. "Know what I'm talking about?"

"No."

"Yeah. You don't want to know anything about this. Distribution," Lenny said. "That's federal."

"You do that twice a month?" she asked. They were above Sunset Boulevard. The bougainvillea was a magenta web. There were sounds of birds and insects. They were winding through pine trees. "That's thirty thousand dollars a month."

"That's nothing. The real money's the Bogotá run," Lenny said. "Mountains leap up out of the ground, out of nowhere. The Bogotá run drove me crazy. Took me a month to come down. Then the Colombians got mad. You know what I'm talking about?"

"No."

"That's good. You don't want to know anything about the Colombians," Lenny said again.

She was thinking about the Colombians and Bogotá and the town where Lenny said he had a house, Medellín. She was thinking they would have called her *gitana,* with her long black hair and bare feet. She could have fanned herself with handfuls of hundred-dollar bills like a green river. She could have borne sons for men crossing borders, searching for the definitive run, the one you don't return from. She would dance in bars in the permanently hot nights. They would say she was intoxicated with grief and dead husbands. Sadness made her dance. When she thought about this, she laughed.

The driveway seemed sudden and steep. They were approaching a walled villa. Lenny pushed numbers on a console. The gate opened.

He parked the red Ferrari. He opened the car door for her. She followed him up a flight of stone steps. The house looked like a Spanish fortress.

A large Christmas wreath with pine cones and a red ribbon hung on the door. The door was unlocked. The floor was tile. They were walking on an Oriental silk carpet, past a piano, a fireplace, a bar. There were ceiling-high glass cabinets in which Chinese artifacts were displayed, vases and bowls and carvings. They were walking through a library, then a room with a huge television, stereo equipment, a pool table. She followed him out a side door.

The pool was built on the edge of the hill. The city below seemed like a sketch for a village, something not quite formed beneath the greenery. Pink and yellow roses had been planted around two sides of the pool. There were beds of azaleas with ferns between them and red camellias, yellow lilies, white daisies, and birds-of-paradise.

"Time to swim," Lenny said.

She was standing near the pool, motionless. "We don't have suits," she said.

"Don't tell nobody, okay?" Lenny was pulling his shirt over his head. He stared at her, a cigarette in his mouth. "It's private. It's walled. Just a cliff out here. And Bernie and Phyllis aren't coming back. Come on. Take off your clothes. What are you? Scared? You're like a child. Come here. I'll help you. Daddy'll help you. Just stand near me. Here. See? Over your head. Over baby's head. Did that hurt? What's that? One of those goddamn French jobs with the hooks in front? You do it. What are you looking at? I put on a few pounds. Okay? I'm a little out of shape. I need some weights. I got to buy some weights. What are you? Skinny? You're so skinny. You one of those vomiters? I'm not going to bite. Come here. Reach down. Take off my necklace. Unlock the chain. Yeah. Good. Now we swim."

The water felt strange and icy. It was nothing like she expected. There were shadows on the far side of the pool. The shadows were hideous. There was nothing ambiguous about them. The water beneath the shadows looked remote and troubled and green. It looked contaminated. The more she swam, the more the infected blue particles clustered on her skin. There would be no way to remove them.

"I have to leave," she said.

The sun was going down. It was an unusual sunset for Los Angeles, red and protracted. Clouds formed islands in the red sky. The sprinklers came on. The air smelled damp and green like a forest. There were pine trees beyond the rose garden. She thought of the smell of camp at nightfall, when she was a child.

"What are you? Crazy? You kidding me? I want to take you out," Lenny said. He got out of the pool. He wrapped a towel around his waist. Then he wrapped a towel around her shoulders. "Don't just stand there. Dry off. Come on. You'll get sick. Dry yourself."

He lit a cigarette for her. "You want to get dressed up, right? I know you skinny broads from Beverly Hills. You want to get dressed up. Look. Let me show you something. You'll like it. I know. Come on." He put out his hand for her. She took it.

They were walking up a marble stairway to the bedroom. The bedroom windows opened onto a tile balcony. There were sunken tubs in the bathroom. Everything was black marble. The faucets were gold. There were gold chandeliers hanging above them. Every wall had mirrors bordered by bulbs and gold. Lenny was standing in front of a closet.

"Pick something out. Go on. Walk in. Pink. You like pink? No. You like it darker. Yeah. Keep walking. Closet big as a tennis court. They got no taste, right? Looks like Vegas, right? You like red? No. Black. That's you. Here. Black silk." Lenny came out of the closet. He was holding an evening gown. "This your size? All you skinny broads wear the same size."

Lenny handed the dress to her. He stretched out on the bed. "Yeah. Let go of the towel. That's right. Only slower."

He was watching her. He lit a cigarette. His towel had come apart. He was holding something near his lap. It was a jewelry box.

"After you put that crap on your face, the paint, the lipstick, we'll pick out a little something nice for you. Phyllis won't need it. She's not coming back. Yeah." Lenny laughed. "Bernie and Phyllis are entertaining the Colombians by now. Give those boys from the jungle something to chew on. Don't look like that. You like diamonds? I know you like diamonds."

Lenny was stretched out on the bed. The bed belonged to Bernie and Phyllis but they weren't coming back. Lenny was holding a diamond necklace out to her. She wanted it more than she could remember wanting anything.

"I'll put it on you. Come here. Sit down. I won't touch you. Not unless you ask me. I can see you're all dressed up. Just sit near me. I'll do the clasp for you," Lenny offered.

She sat down. She could feel the stones around her throat, cool, individual, like the essence of something that lives in the night. Or something more ancient, part of the fabric of the night itself.

"Now you kiss me. Come on. You want to. I can tell. Kiss me. Know what this costs?" Lenny touched the necklace at her throat with his fingertips. He studied the stones. He left his fingers on her throat. "Sixty, seventy grand maybe. You can kiss me now."

She turned her face toward him. She opened her lips. Outside, the Santa Ana winds were startling, howling as if from a mouth. The air smelled of scorched lemons and oranges, of something delirious and intoxicated. When she closed her eyes, everything was blue.

She didn't see him at her noon meeting the next day or the day after. She thought, Well, that's it. She wasn't sorry. She got a manicure. She went to her psychiatrist. She began taking a steam bath after her aerobics class at the gym. She went Christmas shopping. She bought her daughter a white rabbit coat trimmed with blue fox. She was spending too much money. She didn't care.

It was Christmas Eve when the doorbell rang. There were carols on the radio. She was wearing a silk robe and smoking. She told Maria that she would answer the door.

"You promised never to come here." She was angry. "You promised to respect my life. To recognize my discrete borders."

"Discrete borders?" Lenny repeated. "I'm in serious trouble. Look at me. Can't you see there's something wrong? You look but you don't see."

There was nothing unusual about him. He was wearing blue jeans and a black leather jacket. He was carrying an overnight bag. She could see the motorcycle near the curb. Maybe the Colombians had the red Ferrari. Maybe they were chewing on that now. She didn't ask him in.

"This is it," Lenny was saying. He brushed past her and walked into the living room. He was talking quickly. He was telling her what had happened in the desert, what the Colombians had done. She felt like she was being electrocuted, that her hair was standing on end. It occurred to her that it was a sensation so singular that she might come to enjoy it. There were small blue wounded sounds in the room now. She wondered if they were coming from her.

"I disappear in about five minutes." Lenny looked at her. "You coming?"

She thought about it. "I can't come, no," she said finally. "I have a child."

"We take her," Lenny offered.

She shook her head, no. The room was going dark at the edges, she noticed. Like a field of blue asters, perhaps. Or ice when the sun strikes it. And how curious the blue becomes when clouds cross the sun, when the blue becomes broken, tawdry.

"I had plans for you. I was going to introduce you to some people. I should of met you fifteen years ago. I could have retired. Get me some ice," Lenny said. "Let's have a drink."

"We're in AA. Are you crazy?" She was annoyed.

"I need a drink. I need a fix. I need an automatic weapon. I need a plane," he said. He looked past her to the den. Maria was watching television and wrapping Christmas presents.

"You need a drink, too," Lenny said. "Don't even think about it. The phone. You're an accessory after the fact. You can go to jail. What about your kid then?"

They were standing in her living room. There was a noble pine tree near the fireplace. There were wrapped boxes beneath the branches. Maria asked in Spanish if she needed anything. She said not at the moment. Two glasses with ice, that was all.

"Have a drink," Lenny said. "You can always go back to the meetings. They take you back. They don't mind. I do it all the time. All over the world. I been doing it for ten years."

"I didn't know that," she said. It was almost impossible to talk. It occurred to her that her sanity was becoming intermittent, like a sudden stretch of intact road in an abandoned region. Or radio music, blatant after months of static.

"Give me the bottle. I'll pour you one. Don't look like that. You look like you're going down for the count. Here." Lenny handed the glass to her. She could smell the vodka. "Open your mouth, goddamn it."

She opened her mouth. She took a sip. Then she lit a cigarette.

"Wash the glass when I leave," Lenny said. "They can't prove shit. You don't know me. You were never anywhere. Nothing happened. You listening? You don't look like you're listening. You look like you're on tilt. Come on, baby. Listen to Daddy. That's good. Take another sip."

She took another sip. Lenny was standing near the door. "You're getting off easy, you know that? I ran out of time. I had plans for you," he was saying.

He was opening the door. "Some ride, huh? Did Daddy do like he said? Get you to the other side? You catch a glimpse? See what's there? I think you're starting to see. Can't say Lenny lied to you, right?"

She took another sip. "Right," she agreed. When this glass was finished she would pour another. When the bottle was empty, she would buy another.

Lenny closed the door. The night stayed outside. She was surprised. She opened her mouth but no sound came out. Instead, blue things flew in, pieces of glass or tin, or necklaces of blue diamonds, perhaps. The air was the blue of a pool when there are shadows, when clouds cross the turquoise surface, when you suspect something contagious is leaking, something camouflaged and disrupted. There is only this infected blue enormity elongating defiantly. The blue that knows you and where you live and it's never going to forget.

ROBERT OLEN BUTLER

The Trip Back

FROM THE SOUTHERN REVIEW

I AM JUST a businessman, not a poet. It is the poet who is supposed to see things so clearly and to remember. Perhaps it is only
the poets who can die well. Not the rest of us. I drove from my
home in Lake Charles, Louisiana, to the airport in Houston, Texas,
to pick up my wife's grandfather. And what is it that I experienced on that trip? What is it that struck me as I got off the inter-
state highway in Beaumont, knowing the quick route to the airport as I do? I was driving through real towns in Texas. One was
named China, another Nome. One was Liberty. If I were a man
who believed in symbols and omens, I would have smiled at this.
I was passing through Liberty to pick up my wife's grandfather
whose own liberty my wife and I and the man's nephew in San
Francisco had finally won, after many years of trying. He was arriving this very day from the West Coat after living thirteen years
under Communist rule in our home country of Vietnam. Perhaps a poet would think of those things — about Liberty, Texas,
and my wife's grandfather — and write a memorable poem.
Though maybe not. I am ignorant of these matters. Maybe it is
only the bird taking flight or the frog jumping into the pond that
the poet is interested in.

All I know is that for me I drove the two-lane highway across
Texas and I just noticed the businesses — the little ones that
seemed so Vietnamese to me in the way the people always looked
for some new angle, some empty corner in the marketplace. I
noticed the signs for stumpgrinding and for house leveling and
for mud pumping, the different stands along the way — fire-

works, fruit and vegetables, hubcaps, and antiques. The Paradise
Club had a miniskirt contest, the Bait Barn had a nightcrawler
special, and Texas Winners had a baseball trophy sale. There was
a Donut Delight and a Future Star Twirling Academy and a hand-
painted sign on a post saying that the finest porch swings were a
mile down this dusty road. The Mattress Man said on his sign,
right underneath his business name, "Jesus Is Lord."

I am a Catholic and I must say that this made me smile. The
Lord of the Universe, the Man of Sorrows, turned into the Lord
of the Mattress, the Mattress Man. But even so, I understood what
this owner was trying to do, appealing specially to those of his
own kind. This is good business practice, when you know your
sales area. I have done very well for myself in Lake Charles in the
laundry and dry cleaning business. It is very simple. People sweat
a lot in the climate of southern Louisiana, and there was a place
for a very good laundry and dry cleaner. I have two locations in
Lake Charles, and I will soon open one in Sulphur. So it was this
that interested me as I drove through Texas, as it always does. I
am a businessman. It is my way.

And if I were a man who believed in symbols and omens, I
would have been very interested toward the end of my journey
when I came to a low highway bridge that took me across the
wide converging of two rivers, for as I entered the bridge, the
sign said, "Lost and Old Rivers." These two rivers were full of
little islands and submerged trees, and it was hard to see how the
two ran together, for they looked more like one sprawling thing,
like perhaps a large lake, something that was bound in and not
moving, not flowing. Lost and old.

I had not given much serious thought to Mr. Chinh, my wife's
grandfather. I knew this: my wife loved him very much. We are
all like that in Vietnam. We honor our families. My four children
honor me very much, and I honor them. My wife is devoted to
me, and I am devoted to her. I love her. We were very lucky in
that our parents allowed us to marry for love. That is to say, my
mother and father and my wife's mother allowed it. Her father
was dead. We still have a little shrine in our house and pray for
him, which is the way of all Vietnamese, even if they are Catholic.
As Catholics we understand this as the communion of saints. But
my wife has no clear memory of her father. He died when she

was very young. He drowned swimming in the South China Sea. And after that, Mr. Chinh became like a father for my wife.

She wept the night before my trip to the airport. She was very happy to have her grandfather again and very sorry that she missed all those years with him. I heard her muffling the sound of her crying in the pillow, and I touched her on the shoulder and felt her shaking, and then I switched on the light by the bed. She turned her face sharply away from me, as if I would reproach her for her tears, as if there was some shame in it. I said to her, "Mai, it is all right. I understand your feeling."

"I know," she said, but she did not turn back to me. So I switched the light off once more, and in the dark she came to me and I held her.

You must wait to understand why it is important, but at this point I must confess one thing. My wife came to me in the dark and I held her, and her crying slowed and stopped, and of course I was happy for that. I was happy to hold my wife in the dark in this moment of strong feeling for her and to be of help, but as I lay there, my mind could not focus on this woman that I love. My mind understood that she was feeling these things for a man of her own blood who had been very important to her and who then disappeared from her life for more than a decade and now was coming back into it. But these are merely bloodless words, things of the mind. And that was all they were to me even lying there in the dark. I made those words run in my head, but what was preoccupying me at that moment was an itching on my heel that I could not scratch and the prices of two different types of paint for the outer shop of the new dry cleaning store. My wife was a certain pressure, a warmth against me, but there was also a buzz in the electric alarm clock that I was just as conscious of.

Do not misjudge me. I am not a cold man. I drew my wife closer as she grew quieter, but it was a conscious decision, and even saying that, I have to work hard to remember the moment, and the memory that I have is more like a thought than a memory of my senses. And it's not as if the itching on my heel, the buzz of the clock, are any more vivid. I have to work extremely hard to reconstruct this very recent night so that I can even tell you with assurance that there was a clock in the room or that there was a foot at the end of my leg.

But you will see that it is Mr. Chinh who has put me in this present state of agitation. After a time, as I held her in the bed, my wife said, "My tears are mostly happy. Don't worry for me, Khanh. I only wish I was small enough and his back was strong enough that I could ride upon it again."

At the airport gate I looked at the people filing through the door from the jetway. The faces were all white or Spanish, and they filed briskly through the door and rushed away, and then there were a long few moments when no one appeared. I began to think that Mr. Chinh had missed the plane. I thought of the meal that my wife was preparing at home. She and my children and our best friends in Lake Charles had been working since dawn on the house and on the food for this wonderful reuniting, and when the door to the jetway gaped there with no one coming through, that is the only thought I had, that the food would be ruined. I did not worry about Mr. Chinh or wonder what the matter could really be.

I looked over to the airline agents working behind their computers, checking in the passengers for the next flight. I was ready to seek their help when I glanced back to the door and there was Mr. Chinh. He was dressed in a red-and-black plaid sport shirt and chino pants, and he was hunched a little bit over a cane, but what surprised me was that he was not alone. A Vietnamese man about my age was holding him up on the side without the cane and bending close and talking into his ear. Then the younger man looked up and saw me, and I recognized a cousin of my wife, the son of Mr. Chinh's nephew. He smiled at me and nodded a hello, and he jiggled the old man into looking at me as well. Mr. Chinh raised his head, and an overhead light flashed in his glasses, making his eyes disappear. He too smiled, so I felt that it was all right.

They approached me, and I shook Mr. Chinh's hand first. "I am so happy you have come to visit us," I said.

I would have said more — I had a little speech in my head about my wife's love for him, and how she is so sorry she is not at the airport, and how much his great-grandchildren want to see him. But my wife's cousin cut in before I had a chance. "This is Mr. Khanh," he said to the old man. "The one I told you about who would meet you."

Mr. Chinh nodded and looked at me and repeated my name. He spoke no more, and I looked to the cousin, who said, "I'm Huong," and he bowed to me very formally.

"I remember you," I said, and I offered my hand. He took it readily, but I knew from his formality that there could be things I did not know about Mr. Chinh. It is the custom of Vietnamese, especially of the old school of manners, not to tell you things that are unpleasant to hear. The world need not be made worse than it is by embracing the difficult things. It is assumed that you wish to hear that all is well, and many people will tell you this no matter what the situation really is. Huong struck me as being of this tradition — as surely his father must, too, for this is how an otherwise practical people learns an attitude such as this.

But I am a blunt man. Business has made me that way, particularly business in America. So I said to Mr. Huong, "Is there something wrong with Mr. Chinh?"

He smiled at me as if I were a child asking about the thunder. "I came with our dear uncle to make sure he traveled safely. He is very old."

I suddenly felt a little uncomfortable talking about the man as if he wasn't there, so I looked at him. He was leaning contentedly on his cane, gazing around the circle of gates. I bent nearer to him and said, "Mr. Chinh, do you like the airport?"

He turned to me at once and said, "This is a fine airport. The best I have seen."

The man's voice was strong, and this reassured me. I liked his appreciation of the airport, which I too admired, so I said to Mr. Huong, "Is he a little frail, physically?"

"Yes," said Mr. Huong, happy, I suppose, to have words put in his mouth sufficient to answer my blunt question. I did not like this cousin Huong.

But I was compelled to ask, "Will you be coming to Lake Charles to join us?"

"No. I must decline your gracious invitation. I return by a flight later this day."

I was blunt again. "You came all this way never to leave the airport? Just to return at once?"

Mr. Huong shrugged. "It is my pleasure to make sure our beloved uncle arrives safely. My father said that if you should wish to discuss Uncle Chinh's permanent home after perhaps a week or so, he will await your call."

I didn't know the details of all that, except that I was prepared for my wife's sake and the sake of our country's family tradition to make him part of our household. So I just nodded and took Mr. Chinh by the arm and said a brief goodbye to Mr. Huong, and the old man and I started off for the baggage check.

Mr. Chinh was enchanted with the airport, gawking about as we moved, and his interest was so intense and his pleasure so evident from the little clucks and nods he made that I did not try to speak with him. Twice he asked me a question, once about where they would take the luggage, answered by our arrival at the carousel, which caused him to laugh loudly when the bell rang and the silver metal track began to run. Mr. Chinh stood at the opening, and he watched each bag emerging through the plastic flaps as closely as a customs inspector. The second question was if I had a car. And when I said yes, he seemed very pleased, lifting his cane before him and tapping it down hard. "Good," he said. "Don't tell me what kind. I will see for myself."

But in the parking garage, he was baffled. He circled the car and touched it gently with the rubber tip of his cane, touched it several places, on a taillight, a hubcap, the front bumper, the name on the grille. "I don't know this car," he said. "I don't know it at all."

"It's an Acura," I said.

He shook the name off as if a mosquito had just buzzed his ear. "I thought you would own a French car. A Citröen, I had predicted. A 15CV sedan."

"No, Mr. Chinh. It's an Acura. It's a very good car," and I stopped myself from telling him it was from Japan.

Mr. Chinh lifted his shoulders and let them drop heavily, like he was greatly disappointed and perhaps even a little scornful. I put his bags in the trunk and opened the door for him, and we made it out of the airport and back onto the two-lane highway before any more words were spoken. I was holding my eyes on the road, trying to think of small talk, something I'm not very good at, when Mr. Chinh finally said, "The inside is very nice."

I didn't understand. I glanced over to him, and he was running his hand along the dashboard, and I realized that he'd been thinking about the car all this time. "Good, " I said. "I'm glad you like it."

"Not as nice as many others," he said. "But nice."

There's no car interior short of a Rolls that is nicer than my Acura, but I nodded at the old man, and I told myself that there was no need to debate with him or entertain him but just to be cordial to him. Let him carry the conversation, if he wished one. But the trip looked very long ahead of me. We hadn't even gotten out into the country of stump grinders and fruit stands. It was still franchised fast food and clusters of gas stations and mini-malls and car dealerships. There were many miles to go.

Then up ahead I saw the work of a clever man, a car dealer who had dangled a big luxury car from the top of what looked like at least a seventy-foot crane. I said to Mr. Chinh, "There's something the Citröens don't do," and I motioned the man's attention to the car in the sky. He bent down and angled his head up to look, and his mouth gaped open. He said nothing but quickly shifted to the side window as we passed the car dealership, and then he turned around to watch out the back window until the car on the crane was out of sight.

I expected Mr. Chinh to remark on this. Perhaps a word on how no one would ever do such a thing to a French car. There would be no need. Something like that. But he said nothing, and after a time, I decided to appreciate the silence. I just concentrated on covering these miles before the old man would be reunited with the granddaughter he loved. I found that I myself was no longer comfortable with the old ways. Like the extended family. Like other things, too. The Vietnamese indirectness, for instance. The superstition. I was a good American now, and though I wished I could do more for this old man next to me, at least for my wife's sake, it was not an unpleasant thought that I had finally left Vietnam behind.

And I'd left behind more than the customs. I don't suppose that struck me as I was driving home from the airport. But it is clear to me now. I grew up, as did my wife, in Vung Tau. Both our families were pretty well off and we lived year-round in this seaside resort on the South China Sea. The French had called it Cap St. Jacques. The sand was white and the sea was the color of jade. But I say these things not from any vivid recollection, but from a thought in my head, as real only as lines from a travel brochure. I'd left behind me the city on the coast and the sea as well.

But you must understand that ultimately this doesn't have anything to do with being a refugee in the United States. When I got to the two rivers again, Old and Lost, I could recognize the look of them, like a lake, but it was only my mind working.

Perhaps that is a bad example. What are those two rivers to me? I mention them now only to delay speaking of the rest of my ride with Mr. Chinh. When we crossed the rivers, I suppose I was reminded of him somehow. Probably because of the earlier thoughts of the rivers as an omen. But now I tried once more to think of small talk. I saw a large curl of rubber on the shoulder of the road and then another a little later on, and I said to Mr. Chinh, "Those are retreads from trucks. In Vietnam some enterprising man would have already collected those to make some use of them. Here no one cares."

The old man did not speak, but after a few moments I sensed something beside me, and I glanced and found him staring at me. "Do we have far to go?" he asked.

"Perhaps an hour and a half," I said.

"May I roll down the window?"

"Of course," I said. I turned off the air conditioning, and as he made faint grabbing motions at the door, I pressed the power button and lowered his window. Mr. Chinh turned his face to me with eyes slightly widened in what looked to me like alarm. "They're power windows," I said. "No handle."

His face did not change. I thought to explain further, but before I could, he turned to the window and leaned slightly forward so that the wind rushed into his face, and his hair — still more black than gray — rose and danced, and he was just a little bit scary to me for some reason. So I concentrated again on the road, and I was happy to let him stay silent, watching the Texas highway, and this was a terrible mistake.

If I'd forced him into conversation earlier, I would've had more time to prepare for our arrival in Lake Charles. Not that I could have done much, though. As it was, we were only fifteen minutes or so from home. We'd already crossed the Sabine River into Louisiana and I'd pointed it out to Mr. Chinh, the first words spoken in the car for an hour. Even that didn't start the conversation. Some time later the wandering of his own mind finally made him speak. He said, "The air feels good here. It's good when you can feel it on your face as you drive."

I naturally thought he was talking to me, but when I said, "Yes, that's right," he snapped his head around as if he'd forgotten that I was there.

What could I have said to such a reaction? I should have spoken of it to him right away. But I treated it as I would treat Mai waking from a dream and not knowing where she is. I said, "We're less than twenty miles from Lake Charles, Mr. Chinh."

He did not reply, but his face softened, as if he were awake now.

I said, "Mai can't wait to see you. And our children are very excited."

He did not acknowledge this, which I thought was rude for the grandfather who was becoming the elder of our household. Instead, he looked out the window again, and he said, "My favorite car of all was a Hotchkiss. I had a 1934 Hotchkiss. An AM80 tourer. It was a wonderful car. I would drive it from Saigon to Hanoi. A fine car. Just like the car that won the Monte Carlo rally in 1932. I drove many cars to Hanoi over the years. Citröen, Peugeot, Ford, DeSoto, Simca. But the Hotchkiss was the best. I would drive to Hanoi at the end of the year and spend ten days and return. It was eighteen hundred kilometers. I drove it in two days. I'd drive in the day, and my driver would drive at night. At night it was very nice. We had the top down, and the moon was shining, and we drove along the beach. Then we'd stop and turn the lights on, and rabbits would come out, and we'd catch them. Very simple. I can see their eyes shining in the lights. They we'd make a fire on the beach. The sparks would fly up, and we'd sit and eat and listen to the sea. It was very nice, driving. Very nice."

Mr. Chinh stopped speaking. He kept his face to the wind, and I was conscious of the hum of my Acura's engine, and I felt very strange. This man beside me was rushing along the South China Sea. Right now. He had felt something so strong that he could summon it up and place himself within it, and the moment would not fade, the eyes of the rabbits still shone, and the sparks still climbed into the sky, and he was a happy man.

Then we were passing the oil refineries west of the lake, and we rose on the I-10 bridge, and Lake Charles was before us, and I said to Mr. Chinh, "We are almost home now."

And the old man turned to me and said, "Where is it that we are going?"

"Where?"

"You're the friend of my nephew?"

"I'm the husband of Mai, your granddaughter," I said, and I tried to tell myself he was still caught on some beach on the way to Hanoi.

"Granddaughter?" he said.

"Mai. The daughter of your daughter Diem." I was trying to hold off the feeling in my chest that moved like the old man's hair was moving in the wind.

Mr. Chinh slowly cocked his head, and he narrowed his eyes, and he thought for a long moment and said, "Diem lost her husband in the sea."

"Yes," I said, and I drew a breath in relief.

But then the old man said, "She had no daughter."

"What do you mean? Of course she had a daughter."

"I think she was childless."

"She had a daughter and a son." I found that I was shouting. Perhaps I should have pulled off to the side of the road at that moment. I should have pulled off and tried to get through to Mr. Chinh. But it would have been futile, and then I would still have been forced to take him to my wife. I couldn't very well just walk him into the lake and drive away. As it was, I had five more minutes as I drove to our house, and I spent every second trying carefully to explain who Mai was. But Mr. Chinh could not remember. Worse than that. He was certain I was wrong.

I stopped at the final stop sign before our house, and I tried once more. "Mai is the daughter of Nho and Diem. Nho died in the sea, just as you said. Then you were like a father to Mai. . . . You carried her on your back."

"My daughter Diem had no children. She lived in Nha Trang."

"Not in Nha Trang. She never lived in Nha Trang."

Mr. Chinh shook his head no, refuting me with the gentleness of absolute conviction. "She lived on the beach of Nha Trang, a very beautiful beach. And she had no children. She was just a little girl herself. How could she have children?"

I felt weak now. I could barely speak the words, but I said, "She had a daughter. My wife. You love her."

The old man finally just turned his face away from me. He sat with his head in the window as if he were patiently waiting for the wind to start up again.

I felt very bad for my wife. But it wasn't that simple. I've become a blunt man. Not like a Vietnamese at all. It's the way I do business. So I will say this bluntly. I felt bad for Mai, but I was even more concerned for myself. The old man frightened me. And it wasn't in the way you might think, with my saying to myself, Oh that could be me over there sitting with my head out the window and forgetting who my closest relatives are. It was different from that, I knew.

I drove the last two blocks to our house on the corner. The long house with the steep roof and the massively gnarled live oak in the front yard. My family heard my car as I turned onto the side street and then into our driveway. They came to the side door and poured out, and I got out of the car quickly, intercepting the children. I told my oldest son to take the others into the house and wait, to give their mother some time alone with her grandfather whom she hadn't seen in so many years. I have good children, obedient children, and they disappeared again even as I heard my wife opening the car door for Mr. Chinh.

I turned and looked, and the old man was standing beside the car. My wife embraced him, and his head was perched on her shoulder, and there was nothing on his face at all, no feeling except perhaps the faintest wrinkling of puzzlement. Perhaps I should have stayed at my wife's side as the old man went on to explain to her that she didn't exist. But I could not. I wished to walk briskly away, far from this house, far from the old man and his granddaughter. I wished to walk as fast as I could, to run. But at least I fought that desire. I simply turned away and moved off, along the side of the house to the front yard.

I stopped near the live oak and looked about, trying to see things. Trying to see this tree, for instance. This tree as black as a charcoal cricket and with great lower limbs, as massive themselves as the main trunks of most other trees, shooting straight out and then sagging and rooting again in the ground. A monstrous tree. I leaned against it, and as I looked away, the tree faded within me. It was gone, and I envied the old man, I knew. I envied him driving his Hotchkiss along the beach half a century ago. Envied him his sparks flying into the air. But my very envy frightened me. Look at the man, I thought. He remembered his car, but he can't remember his granddaughter.

And I demanded of myself: Could I? Even as I stood there? Could I remember this woman whom I loved? I'd seen her just moments ago. I'd lived with her for more than twenty years. And certainly if she was standing there beside me, if she spoke, she would have been intensely familiar. But separated from her, I could not picture her clearly. I could construct her face accurately in my mind. But the image did not burn there, did not rush upon me and fill me up with the feelings that I genuinely held for her. I could not put my face into the wind and see her eyes as clearly as Mr. Chinh saw the eyes of the rabbits in his headlights.

Not the eyes of my wife and not my country either. I'd lost a whole country, and I didn't give it a thought. Vung Tau was a beautiful city, and if I put my face into the wind I could see nothing of it clearly, not its shaded streets or its white sand beaches, not the South China Sea lying there beside it. I can speak these words, and perhaps you can see these things clearly because you are using your imagination. But I cannot imagine these things because I lived them, and to remember them with the vividness I know they should have is impossible. They are lost to me.

Until perhaps when I am as old as Mr. Chinh. Perhaps he, too, moved through his life as distracted as me. Perhaps only after he forgot his granddaughter did he remember his Hotchkiss. And perhaps that was necessary. Perhaps he had to forget the one to remember the other. Not that I think he'd made that conscious choice. Something deep inside him was sorting out his life as it was about to end. And that is what frightens me the most. I am afraid that deep down I am built on a much smaller scale than the surface of my mind aspires to. When something finally comes back to me with real force, perhaps it will be a luxury car hanging on a crane or the freshly painted wall of a new dry cleaning store or the faint buzz of the alarm clock beside my bed. Deep down, secretly, I may be prepared to betray all that I think I love the most.

This is what brought me to the slump of grief against the live oak in my front yard. I leaned there, and the time passed, and then my wife crept up beside me. I turned to her, and she was crying quietly, her head bowed and her hand covering her eyes.

"I'm sorry," I said.

"I put him in the guest room," she said. "He thanked me as he would an innkeeper." She sobbed faintly, and I wanted to touch her, but my arm was very heavy, as if I was standing at the bottom of the sea. It rose only a few inches from my side. Then she said, "I thought he might remember after he slept."

I could neither reassure her with a lie nor make her face the truth. But I had to do something. I had thought too much about this already. A good businessman knows when to stop thinking and to act instead. I drew close to my wife, but only briefly did my arm rise and hold her. That was the same as all the other forgotten gestures of my life. Suddenly I surprised myself and my wife, too. I stepped in front of her and crouched down, and before either of us could think to feel foolish, I had taken Mai onto my back and straightened up, and I began to move about the yard, walking at first, down the long drooping lower branch of the oak tree and then faster along the sidewalk and then up the other side of the house, and I was going faster, and she only protested for a moment before she was laughing and holding on tighter, clinging with her legs about my waist and her arms around my neck, and I ran with her, ran as fast as I could so that she laughed harder, and I felt her clinging against me, pressing against me, and I felt her breath on the side of my face as warm and moist as a breeze off the South China Sea.

CHARLES D'AMBROSIO, JR.

The Point

FROM THE NEW YORKER

I HAD BEEN lying awake after my nightmare, a nightmare in which
Father and I bought helium balloons at a circus. I tied mine around
my finger and Father tied his around a stringbean and lost it.
After that, I lay in the dark, tossing and turning, sleepless from
all the sand in my sheets and all the uproar out in the living room.
Then the door opened, and for a moment the blade of bright
light blinded me. The party was still going full blast, and now
with the door ajar and my eyes adjusting I glimpsed the silver
smoke swirling in the light and all the people suspended in it,
hovering around as if they were angels in heaven — some kind
of heaven where the host serves highballs and the men smoke
cigars and the women all smell like rotting fruit. Everything was
hysterical out there — the men laughing, the ice clinking, the
women shrieking. A woman crossed over and sat on the edge of
my bed, bending over me. It was Mother. She was backlit, a vague,
looming silhouette, but I could smell lily of the valley and something else — lemon rind from the bitter twist she always chewed
when she reached the watery bottom of her vodka-and-tonic.
When Father was alive, she rarely drank, but after he shot himself you could say she really let herself go.

"Dearest?" she said.

"Hi, Mom," I said.

"Your old mother's bombed, dearest — flat-out bombed."

"That's O.K.," I said. She liked to confess these things to me,
although it was always obvious how tanked she was, and I never
cared. I considered myself a pro at this business. "It's a party,'" I
said, casually. "Live it up."

"Oh, God," she laughed. "I don't know how I got this way."

"What do you want, Mom?"

"Yes, dear," she said. "There was something I wanted."

She looked out the window — at the sail-white moon beyond the black branches of the apple tree — and then she looked into my eyes. "What was it I wanted?" Her eyes were moist, and mapped with red veins. "I came here for a reason," she said, "but I've forgotten it now."

"Maybe if you go back you'll remember," I suggested.

Just then, Mrs. Gurney leaned through the doorway. "Well?" she said, slumping down on the floor. Mrs. Gurney had bright-silver hair and a dark tan — the sort of tan that women around here get when their marriages start busting up. I could see the gaudy gold chains looped around Mrs. Gurney's dark-brown neck winking in the half-light before they plunged from sight into the darker gulf between her breasts.

"That's it," Mother said. "Mrs. Gurney. She's worse off than me. She's really blitzo. Blotto? Blitzed?"

"Hand me my jams," I said.

I slipped my swim trunks on underneath the covers.

For years I'd been escorting these old inebriates over the sandy playfield and along the winding boardwalks and up the salt-whit-ened steps of their homes, brewing coffee, fixing a little toast or heating leftovers, searching the medicine cabinets for aspirin and Vitamin B, setting a glass of water on the nightstand, or the cof-fee table if they'd collapsed on the couch — and even, once, tucking some old fart snugly into bed between purple silk sheets. I'd guide these drunks home and hear stories about the alma ma-ter, Theta Xi, Boeing stock splits, Cadillacs, divorce, Nembutal, infidelity, and often the people I helped home gave me three or four bucks for listening to all their sad business. I suppose it was better than a paper route. Father, who'd been a medic in Viet-nam, made it my job when I was ten, and at thirteen I considered myself a hard-core veteran, treating every trip like a mission.

"O.K., Mrs. Gurney," I said. "Upsy-daisy."

She held her hand out, and I grabbed it, leaned back, and hoisted her to her feet. She stood there a minute, listing this way, that way, like a sailor who hadn't been to port in a while.

Mother kissed her wetly on the lips and then said to me, "Hurry home."

"I'm toasted," Mrs. Gurney explained. "Just toasted."

"Let's go out the back way," I said. It would only take longer if we had to navigate our way through the party, offering excuses and making those ridiculous promises adults always make to one another when the party's over. "Hey, we'll do it again," they assure each other, as if that needed to be said. And I'd noticed how, with the summer ending and Labor Day approaching, all the adults would acquire a sort of desperate, clinging manner, as if this were all going to end forever, and the good times would never be seen again. Of course I now realize that the end was just an excuse to party like maniacs. The softball tournament, the salmon derby, the cocktails, the clambakes, the barbecues, would all happen again. They always had and they always would.

Anyway, out the back door and down the steps.

Once I'd made a big mistake with a retired account executive, a friend of Father's. Fred was already falling-down drunk, so it didn't help at all that he had two more drinks on the way out the door, apologizing for his condition, which no one noticed, and boisterously offering bad stock tips. I finally got Fred going and dragged him partway home in a wagon, dumping his fat ass in front of his house — close enough, I figured — wedged in against some driftwood so the tide wouldn't wash him out to sea. He didn't get taken out to sea, but the sea did come to him, as the tide rose, and when he woke he was lassoed in green kelp. Fortunately, he'd forgotten the whole thing — how he'd got where he was, where he'd been before that — but it scared me that a more or less right-hearted attempt on my part might end in such an ugly mess.

By now, though, I'd worked this job so long I knew all the tricks.

The moon was full and immaculately white in a blue-black sky. The wind funneled down Saratoga Passage, blowing hard, blowing south, and Mrs. Gurney and I were struggling against it, tacking back and forth across the playfield. Mrs. Gurney strangled her arm around my neck and we wobbled along. Bits of sand shot in our eyes and blinded us.

"Keep your head down, Mrs. Gurney! I'll guide you!"

She plopped herself down in the sand, nesting there as if she were going to lay an egg. She unbuckled her sandals and tossed them behind her. I ran back and fetched them from the sand. Her skirt fluttered in the wind and flew up in her face. Her silver

hair, which was usually shellacked with spray and coiffed to re-
semble a crash helmet, cracked and blew apart, splintering like a
clutch of straw.

"Why'd I drink so damned much?" she screamed. "I'm
toasted — really, Kurt, I'm totally toasted. I shouldn't have drunk
so damned much."

"Well, you did, Mrs. Gurney," I said, bending toward her.
"That's not the problem now. The problem now is how to get you
home."

"Why, God damn it!"

"Trust me, Mrs. Gurney. Home is where you want to be."

One tip about these drunks: My opinion is that it pays in the
long run to stick as close as possible to the task at hand. We're
just going home, you assure them, and tomorrow it will all be
different. I've found if you stray too far from the simple goal of
getting home and going to sleep, you let yourself in for a lot of
unnecessary hell. You start hearing about their whole miserable
existence, and suddenly it's the most important thing in the world
to fix it all up, right then. Certain things in life can't be repaired,
as in Father's situation, and that's always sad, but I believe there's
nothing in life that can be remedied under the influence of half
a dozen planter's punches.

Now, not everyone on the Point was a crazed rumhound, but
the ones that weren't, the people who accurately assessed their
capacities and balanced their intake accordingly, the people who
never got lost, who never passed out in flower beds or, adrift in
the maze of narrow boardwalks, gave up the search for home
altogether and walked into any old house that was nearby — they,
the people who never did these things and knew what they were
about, never needed my help. They also weren't too friendly with
my mother and didn't participate in her weekly bashes. The Point
was kind of divided that way — between the upright, seaworthy
residents and the easily overturned friends of my mother's.

Mrs. Gurney lived about a half-mile up the beach in a bunga-
low with a lot of Gothic additions. The scuttlebutt on Mrs. Gurney was that while she wasn't divorced, her husband didn't love
her. This kind of knowledge was part of my job, something I didn't
relish but accepted as an occupational hazard. I knew all the gossip, the rumors, the rising and falling fortunes of my mother's

friends. After a summer, I'd have the dirt on everyone, whether I wanted it or not. But I had developed a priestly sense of my position, and whatever anyone told me in a plastered, blathering confessional fit was as safe and privileged as if it had been spoken in a private audience with the Pope. Still, I hoped Mrs. Gurney would stick to the immediate goal and not start talking about how sad and lonely she was, or how cruel her husband was, or what was going to become of us all, etc.

The wind rattled the swings back and forth, chains creaking, and whipped the ragged flag, which flew at half-mast. Earlier that summer, Mr. Crutchfield, the insurance lawyer, had fallen overboard and drowned while hauling in his crab trap. He always smeared his bait box with Mentholatum, which is illegal, and the crabs went crazy for it, and I imagined that in his greed, catching over the limit, he couldn't haul the trap up but wouldn't let go, either, and the weight pulled him into the sea, and he had a heart attack and drowned. The current floated him all the way to Everett before he was found, white and bloated as soggy bread.

Mrs. Gurney was squatting on the ground, lifting fistfuls of sand and letting them course through her fingers, the grains falling away as through an hourglass.

"Mrs. Gurney? We're not making much progress."

She rose to her feet, gripping my pant leg, my shirt, my sleeve, then my neck. We started walking again. The sand was deep and loose, and with every step we sank down through the soft layers until a solid purchase was gained in the hard-packed sand below, and we could push off in baby steps. The night was sharp, and alive with shadows — everything, even the tiny tufted weeds that sprouted through the sand, had a shadow — and this deepened the world, made it seem thicker, with layers, and more layers, and then a darkness into which I couldn't see.

"You know," Mrs. Gurney said, "the thing about these parties is, the thing about drinking is — you know, getting so damnably blasted is . . ." She stopped, and tried to mash her wild hair back down into place, and, no longer holding on to anything other than her head, fell back on her ass into the sand.

I waited for her to finish her sentence, then gave up, knowing it was gone forever. Her lipstick, I noticed, was smeared clownishly around her mouth, fixing her lips into a frown, or maybe a smirk. She smelled different from my mother — like pepper, I thought, and bananas. She was taller than me, and a little plump, with a nose shaped exactly like her head, like a miniature replica of it right in the middle of her face.

We finally got off the playfield and onto the boardwalk that fronted the seawall. A wooden wagon leaned over in the sand. I tipped it upright.

"Here you go, Mrs. Gurney," I said, pointing to the wagon. "Hop aboard."

"I'm O.K.," she protested. "I'm fine. Fine and dandy."

"You're not fine, Mrs. Gurney."

The caretaker built these wagons out of old hatches from P.T. boats. They were heavy, monstrous, and made to last. Once you got them rolling, they cruised.

Mrs. Gurney got in, not without a good deal of operatics, and when I finally got her to shut up and sit down I started pulling. I'd never taken her home before, but on a scale of one to ten, ten being the most obstreperous, I was rating her about a six at this point.

She stretched out like Cleopatra floating down the Nile in her barge. "Stop the world," she sang, "I want to get off."

I vaguely recalled that as a song from my parents' generation. It reminded me of my father, who shot himself in the head one morning — did I already say this? He was sitting in the grass parking lot above the Point. Officially, his death was ruled an accident, a "death by misadventure," and everyone believed that he had in fact been cleaning his gun, but Mother told me otherwise one night. Mother had a batch of lame excuses she tried on me, but it only made me sad to see her groping for an answer and falling way short. I wished she'd come up with something, just for herself. Father used to say that everyone up here was *dinky dow*, which is Vietnamese patois for "crazy." At times, after Father died, I thought Mother was going a little *dinky dow* herself.

I leaned forward, my head bent against the wind. Off to starboard, the sea was black, with a line of moonlit white waves continually crashing on the shore. Far off, I could see the dark headlands of Hat Island, the island itself rising from the water like a breaching whale, and then, beyond, the soft, blue, irresolute lights of Everett, on the distant mainland.

I stopped for a breather, and Mrs. Gurney was gone. She was sitting on the boardwalk, a few houses back.

"Look at all these houses," Mrs. Gurney said, swinging her arms around.

"Let's go, Mrs. Gurney."

"Another fucking great summer at the Point."

The wind seemed to be refreshing Mrs. Gurney, but that was a hard one to call. Often drunks seemed on the verge of sobering up, and then, just as soon as they got themselves nicely balanced, they plunged off the other side, into depression.

"Poor Crutchfield," Mrs. Gurney said. We stood in front of Mr. Crutchfield's house. An upstairs light — in the bedroom, I knew — was on, although the lower stories were dark and empty. "And Lucy — God, such grief. They loved each other, Kurt." Mrs. Gurney frowned. "They loved each other. And now?"

Actually, the Crutchfields hadn't loved each other — information I alone was privy to. Lucy's grief, I was sure, had to do with the fact that her husband died in a state of absolute misery, and now she would never be able to change things. In Lucy's mind, he would be forever screwing around, and she would be forever waiting for him to cut it out and come home. After he died, she spread the myth of their reconciliation, and everyone believed it, but I knew it to be a lie. Mr. Crutchfield's sense of failure over the marriage was enormous. He blamed himself, as perhaps he should have. But I remember, one night earlier in the summer, telling him it was O.K., that if he was unhappy with Lucy, it was fine to fuck around. He said, You think so? I said, Sure, go for it.

Of course, you might ask, what did I know? At thirteen, I'd never even smooched with a girl, but I had nothing to lose by encouraging him. He was drunk, he was miserable, and I had a job, and that job was to get him home and try to prevent him from dwelling too much on himself.

It was that night, the night I took Mr. Crutchfield home, as I walked back to our house, that I developed the theory of the black hole, and it helped me immeasurably in conducting this business of steering drunks around the Point. The idea was this — that at a certain age, a black hole emerged in the middle of your life, and everything got sucked into it, and you knew, forever afterward, that it was there, this dense negative space, and yet you

went on, you struggled, you made your money, you had some
babies, you got wasted, and you pretended it wasn't there and
never looked directly at it, if you could manage the trick. I imagined that this black hole existed somewhere just behind you and
also somewhere just in front of you, so that you were always leaving it behind and entering it at the same time. I hadn't worked
out the spatial thing too carefully, but that's what I imagined.
Sometimes the hole was only a pinprick in the mind, often it was
vast, frequently it fluctuated, beating like a heart, but it was always there, and when you got drunk, thinking to escape, you only
noticed it more. Anyway, when I discovered this, much like an
astronomer gazing out at the universe, I thought I had the key —
and it became a policy with me never to let one of my drunks
think too much and fall backward or forward into the black hole.
We're going home, I would say to them — we're just going home.

I wondered how old Mrs. Gurney was, and guessed thirty-seven.
I imagined her black hole was about the size of a sewer cap.

Mrs. Gurney sat down on the hull of an overturned life raft. She
reached up under her skirt and pulled her nylons off, rolling them
down her legs, tossing the little black doughnuts into the wind. I
fetched them, too, and stuffed them into the straps of her sandals.

"Much better," she said.

"We're not far now, Mrs. Gurney. We'll have you home in no
time."

She managed to stand up on her own. She floated past me,
heading toward the sea. A tangle of ghostly gray driftwood —
old tree stumps, logs loosed from booms, planks — barred the
way, being too treacherous for her to climb in such a drunken
state, I thought, but Mrs. Gurney just kept going, her hair exploding in the wind, her skirt billowing like a sail, her arms wavering like a trapeze artist's high up on the wire.

"Mrs. Gurney?" I called.

"I want —" she started, but the wind tore her words away. Then
she sat down on a log, and when I got there, she was holding her
head in her hands and vomiting between her legs. Vomit, and
the spectacle of adults vomiting, was one of the unpleasant aspects of this job. I hated to see these people in such an abject

position. Still, after three years, I knew in which closets the mops and sponges and cleansers were kept in quite a few houses on the Point.

I patted Mrs. Gurney's shoulder and said, "That's O.K., that's O.K., just go right ahead. You'll feel much better when it's all out."

She choked and spat, and a trail of silver hung from her lip down to the sand. "Oh, damn it all, Kurt. Just damn it all to hell." She raised her head. "Look at me, just look at me, will you?"

She looked a little wretched, but all right. I'd seen worse.

"Have a cigarette, Mrs. Gurney," I said. "Calm down."

I didn't smoke, myself — thinking it was a disgusting habit — but I'd observed from past experience that a cigarette must taste good to a person who has just thrown up. A cigarette or two seemed to calm people right down, giving them something simple to concentrate on.

Mrs. Gurney handed me her cigarettes. I shook one from the pack and stuck it in my mouth. I struck half a dozen matches before I got one going, cupping the flame against the wind in the style of old war movies. I puffed the smoke. I passed Mrs. Gurney the cigarette, and she dragged on it, abstracted, gazing off. I waited, and let her smoke in peace.

"I feel god-awful," Mrs. Gurney groaned.

"It'll go away, Mrs. Gurney. You're drunk. We just have to get you home."

"Look at my skirt," she said.

True, she'd messed it up a little, barfing on herself, but it was nothing a little soap and water couldn't fix. I told her that.

"How old am I, Kurt?" she retorted.

I pretended to think it over, then aimed low.

"Twenty-nine? Good God!" Mrs. Gurney stared out across the water, at the deep, black shadow of Hat Island, and I looked, too, and it was remarkable, the way that darkness carved itself out of the darkness all around. But I could marvel over this when I was off duty.

"I'm thirty-eight, Kurt," she screamed. "Thirty-eight, thirty-eight, thirty-eight!"

I was losing her. She was heading for ten on a scale of ten.

"On a dark night, bumping around," she said, "you can't tell the difference between thirty-eight and forty. Fifty! Sixty!" She pitched her cigarette in a high, looping arc that exploded against a log in a spray of gold sparks. "Where am I going, God damn it?"

"You're going home, Mrs. Gurney. Hang tough."

"I want to die."

A few boats rocked in the wind, and a seal moaned out on the diving raft, the cries carrying away from us, south, downwind. A red warning beacon flashed out on the sandbar. Mrs. Gurney clambered over the driftwood and weaved across the wet sand toward the sea. She stood by the shoreline, and for a moment I thought she might hurl herself into the breach, but she didn't. She stood on the shore's edge, the white waves swirling at her feet, and dropped her skirt around her ankles. She was wearing a silky white slip underneath, the sheen like a bike reflector in the moonlight. She waded out into the water and squatted down, scrubbing her skirt. Then she walked out of the water and stretched herself on the sand.

"Mrs. Gurney?"

"I've got the fucking spins."

Her eyes were closed. I suggested that she open them. "It makes a difference," I said. "And sit up, Mrs. Gurney. That makes a difference, too."

"You've had the spins?" Mrs. Gurney asked. "Don't tell me you sneak into your mother's liquor cabinet, Kurt Pittman. Don't tell me that. Please, just please spare me that. Jesus Christ, I couldn't take it. Really, I couldn't take it, Kurt. Just shut the fuck up about that, all right?"

I'd never taken a drink in my life. "I don't drink, Mrs. Gurney."

"I don't drink, Mrs. Gurney," she repeated. "You prig."

I wondered what time it was, and how long we'd been gone.

"Do you know how suddenly life can turn?" Mrs. Gurney asked. "How bad it can get?"

At first I didn't say anything. This kind of conversation didn't lead anywhere. Mrs. Gurney was drunk and belligerent. She was looking for an enemy. "We need to get you home, Mrs. Gurney," I said. "That's my only concern."

"Your only concern," Mrs. Gurney said, imitating me again. "Lucky you."

I stood there, slightly behind Mrs. Gurney. I was getting tired, but sitting down in the sand might indicate to her that where we were was O.K., and it wasn't. We needed to get beyond this stage, this tricky stage of groveling in the sand and feeling depressed, and go to sleep.

"We're not getting anywhere like this," I said.

"I've got cottonmouth," Mrs. Gurney said. She made fish movements with her mouth. She was shivering, too. She clasped her knees and tucked her head between her legs, trying to ball herself up like a potato bug.

"Kurt," Mrs. Gurney said, looking up at me, "do you think I'm beautiful?"

I switched the sandals I was holding to the other hand. First I'll tell you what I said, and then I'll tell you what I was thinking. I said yes, and I said it immediately. And why? Because I sensed that questions that didn't receive an immediate response fell away into silence and were never answered. They got sucked into the black hole. I'd observed this, and I knew the trick was to close the gap in Mrs. Gurney's mind, to bridge that spooky silence between the question and the answer. There she was, drunk, sick, shivering, loveless, sitting in the sand and asking me, a mere boy, if I thought she was beautiful. I said yes, because I knew it wouldn't hurt, or cost me anything but one measly breath, though that wasn't really my answer. The answer was in the immediacy, the swiftness of my response, stripped of all uncertainty and hesitation.

"Yes," I said.

Mrs. Gurney lay down again in the sand. She unbuttoned her blouse and unfastened her brassiere.

I scanned the dark, and fixed my eyes on a tug hauling a barge north through the Passage, up to the San Juans.

Mrs. Gurney sat up. She shrugged out of her blouse and slipped her bra off and threw them into the wind. Again I fetched her things from where they fell, and held the bundle at my side, waiting.

"That's better," Mrs. Gurney said, arching her back and stretching her hands in the air, waggling them as if she were some kind of dignitary in a parade. "The wind blowing, it's like a spirit washing over you."

"We should go, Mrs. Gurney."

"Sit, Kurt, sit," she said, patting the wet sand. The imprint of her hand remained there a few seconds, then flattened and vanished. The tide was coming in fast, and it would be high tonight, with the moon full.

I crouched down, a few feet away.

"So you think I'm beautiful?" Mrs. Gurney said. She stared ahead, not looking at me, letting the words drift in the wind.

"This really isn't a question of beauty or not beauty, Mrs. Gurney."

"No?"

"No," I said. "I know your husband doesn't love you, Mrs. Gurney. That's the problem here."

"Beauty," she sang.

"No. Like they say, beauty is in the eye of the beholder. You don't have a beholder anymore, Mrs. Gurney."

"The moon and the stars," she said, "the wind and the sea."

Wind, sea, stars, moon: we were in uncharted territory, and it was my fault. I'd let us stray from the goal, and now it was nowhere in sight. I had to steer this thing back on course, or we'd end up talking about God.

"Get dressed, Mrs. Gurney; it's cold. This isn't good. We're going home."

She clasped her knees, and rocked back and forth. She moaned, "It's so far."

"It's not far," I said. "We can see it from here."

"Someday I'm leaving all this to you," Mrs. Gurney said, waving her hands around in circles, pointing at just about everything in the world. "When I get it from my husband, after the divorce, I'm leaving it to you. That's a promise, Kurt. I mean that. It'll be in my will. You'll get a call. You'll get a call and you'll know I'm dead. But you'll be happy, you'll be very happy, because all of this will belong to you."

Her house was only a hundred yards away. A wind sock, full of the air that passed through it, whipped back and forth on a tall white pole. Her two kids had been staying in town most of that summer. I wasn't sure if they were up this weekend. She'd left the porch light on for herself.

"You'd like all this, right?" Mrs. Gurney asked.

"Now is not the time to discuss it," I said.

Mrs. Gurney lay back down in the sand. "The stars have tails," she said. "When they spin."

I looked up; they seemed fixed in place to me.

"The first time I fell in love I was fourteen. I fell in love when I was fifteen, I fell in love when I was sixteen, seventeen, eighteen. I just kept falling, over and over," Mrs. Gurney said. "This eventually led to marriage." She packed a lump of wet sand on her chest. "It's so stupid — you know where I met him?"

I assumed she was referring to Jack, to Mr. Gurney. "No," I said.

"On a golf course, can you believe it?"

"Do you golf, Mrs. Gurney?"

"No! Hell no."

"Does Jack?"

"No."

I couldn't help her — it's the stories that don't make sense that drunks like to repeat. From some people, I'd been hearing the same stories every summer for the last three years — the kind everyone thinks is special, never realizing how everyone tells pretty much the same one, never realizing how all those stories blend, one to the next, and bleed into each other.

"I'm thirsty," Mrs. Gurney said. "I'm so homesick."

"We're close now," I said.

"That's not what I mean," she said. "You don't know what I mean."

"Maybe not," I said. "Please put your shirt on, Mrs. Gurney."

"I'll kill myself," Mrs. Gurney said. "I'll go home and I'll kill myself."

"That won't get you anywhere."

"It'll show them."

"You'd just be dead, Mrs. Gurney. Then you'd be forgotten."

"Crutchfield isn't forgotten. Poor Crutchfield. The flag's at half-mast."

"This year," I said. "Next year it'll be back where it always is."

"My boys wouldn't forget."

That was certainly true, I thought, but I didn't want to get into it.

Mrs. Gurney sat up. She shook her head back and forth, wildly, and sand flew from it. Then she stood, wobbling. I held the shirt out to her, looking down. She wiggled her toes, burrowing them into the sand.

"Look at me," Mrs. Gurney said.

"I'd rather not, Mrs. Gurney," I said. "Tomorrow you'll be glad I didn't."

For a moment we didn't speak, and into that empty space rushed the wind, the waves, the moaning seal out on the diving raft. I looked up, into Mrs. Gurney's eyes, which were dark green and floating in tears. She stared back, but kind of vaguely, and I wondered what she saw.

I had the feeling that the first to flinch would lose.

She took the shirt from my hand.

I looked.

In this I had no experience, but I knew what I saw was not young flesh. Her breasts sagged away like sacks of wet sand, slumping off to either side. They were quite enormous, I thought, although I had nothing to compare them with. There were long whitish scars on them, as if a wild man or a bear had clawed her. The nipples were purple in the moonlight, and they puckered in the cold wind. The gold, squiggling loops of chain shone against the dark of her neck, and the V of her tan line made everything else seem astonishingly white. The tan skin of her chest looked like parchment, like the yellowed, crinkled page of some ancient text, maybe the Bible, or the Constitution, the original copy, or even the rough draft.

Mrs. Gurney slipped the shirt over her shoulders and let it flap there in the wind. It blew off and tumbled down the beach. She sighed. Then she stepped closer and leaned toward me. I could smell her — the pepper, the bananas.

"Mrs. Gurney," I said, "let's go home now." The tide was high enough for us to feel the first foamy white reaches of the waves wash around our feet. The receding waves dragged her shirt into the sea, and then the incoming waves flung it back. It hung there in the margin, agitated. We were looking into each other's eyes. Up so close, there was nothing familiar in hers; they were just glassy and dark and expressionless.

It was then, I was sure, that her hand brushed the front of my trunks. I don't remember too much of what I was thinking, if I was, and this, this not thinking too clearly, might have been my downfall. What is it out there that indicates the right way? I might have gone down all the way. I might have sunk right there. I knew all the words for it, and they were all short and brutal. Fuck, poke, screw. A voice told me I could get away with it. Who will know the difference, the voice asked. It said, Go for it. And I knew the voice, knew it was the same voice that told Mr. Crutchfield to go ahead, fuck around. We were alone — nothing out there but the moon and the sea. I looked at Mrs. Gurney, looked into her eyes, and saw two black lines pouring out of them and running in crazy patterns down her cheeks.

I felt I should be gallant, or tender, and kiss Mrs. Gurney. I felt I should say something, then I felt I should be quiet. It seemed as if the moment were poised, as if everything were fragile, and held together with silence.

We moved up the beach, away from the shore and the incoming tide, and the sand beneath the surface still held some of the day's warmth.

I took off my T-shirt. "Put this on," I said.

She tugged it on, inside out, and I gathered up her sandals and stockings and her bra. We kept silent. We worked our way over the sand, over the tangle of driftwood, the wind heaving at us from the north.

We crossed the boardwalk, and I held Mrs. Gurney's elbow as we went up the steps of her house. Inside, I found the aspirin and poured a glass of apple cider, and brought these to her in bed, where she'd already curled up beneath a heavy Mexican blanket. She looked like she was sleeping underneath a rug. "I'm thirsty," she said, and drank down the aspirin with the juice. A lamp was on. Mrs. Gurney's silver hair splayed out against the pillow, poking like bike spokes, every which way. I knelt beside the bed, and she touched my hand and parted her lips to speak, but I squeezed her hand and her eyes closed. Soon she was asleep.

As I was going downstairs, her two boys, Mark and Timmy, came out of their bedroom and stared at me from the landing.

"Mommy home?" asked Timmy, who was three.

"Yeah," I said. "She's in bed, she's sleeping."

They stood there on the lighted landing, blinking and rubbing knuckles in their eyes, and I stood below them on the steps in the dark.

"Where's the sitter?" I asked.

"She fell asleep," Timmy said.

"You guys should be asleep, too."

"I can't sleep," Timmy said. "Tell a bedtime story."

"I don't know any bedtime stories," I said.

Back home, inside our house, the bright light and smoke stung my eyes. The living room was crowded, but I knew everybody — the Potters, the Shanks, the Capstands, etc. It was noisy and shrill, and someone had cranked up the Victrola, and one of my grandfather's old records was sending a sea of hissing static through the room. I could see on the mantel, through the curling smoke, the shrine Mother had made for Father: his Silver Star and Purple Heart, which he got in Lao Bao, up near Khe Sanh, near the DMZ when he was a medic. His diploma from medical school angled cockeyed off a cut nail. A foul ball he'd caught at a baseball game, his reading glasses, a pocketknife, a stethoscope, a framed Hippocratic oath with snakes wreathed around what looked like a barber pole. I saw Mother flit through the kitchen with a silver cocktail shaker, jerking it like a percussion instrument. She just kept pacing like a caged animal, rattling cracked ice in the shaker. I couldn't hear any distinct voices above the party noise. I stood there awhile. No one seemed to notice me until Fred, three sheets to the wind, as they say, hoisted his empty glass in the air and said, "Hey, Captain!"

I went into the kitchen. Mother set down the shaker and looked at me. I gave her a hug. "I'm back," I said.

Then I crossed into my room and stripped the sheets from my bed. I hung them out the window and shook the sand away. I tossed the sheets back on the bed and stretched out, but I couldn't get to sleep. I got up and pulled one of Father's old letters out from under my mattress. I went out the back door. It was one of those nights on the Point when the blowing wind, the waves breaking in crushed white lines against the shore, the grinding sand, the moon-washed silhouettes of the huddled houses, the slapping of buoys offshore — when all of this seems to have been going on for a long, long time, and you feel eternity looking down on you. I sat on the swing. The letter was torn at the creases, and

I opened it carefully, tilting it into the moonlight. It was dated 1966, and written to Mother. The print was smudged and hard to see.

First, the old news: thank you for the necktie. I'm not sure when I'll get a chance to wear it, but thanks. Now for my news. I've been wounded, but don't worry. I'm O.K.

For several days a company had been deployed on the perimeter of this village — the rumor was that somehow the fields had been planted with VC mines. The men work with tanks — picture tanks moving back and forth over a field like huge lawnmowers. They clear the way by exploding the mines. Generally VC mines are antipersonnel, and the idea is that the tanks are supposed to set off the mines and absorb the explosions. Tanks can easily sustain the blows, and the men inside are safe. A textbook operation. Simple. Yesterday they set off twelve mines. Who knows how they got there?

Clearing the perimeter took several days. Last night they thought they were done. But as the men were jumping off the tanks, one of them landed right on a mine. I was the first medic to reach him. His feet and legs were blown off, blown away up to his groin. I've never seen anything so terrible, but here's what I remember most clearly: a piece of shrapnel had penetrated his can of shaving cream, and it was shooting a stream of white foam about five feet in the air. Blood spilling everywhere, and then this fountain of white arcing out of his back. The pressure inside the can kept hissing. The kid was maybe nineteen. "Doc, I'm a mess," he said. I called in a medevac. I started packing dressings, then saw his eyes lock up, and tried to revive him with heart massage. The kid died before the shaving cream was done spraying.

Everything became weirdly quiet, considering the havoc, and then suddenly the LZ got hot and we took fire — fifteen minutes of artillery and incoming mortar fire, then quiet again. Nothing, absolutely nothing. I took a piece of shrapnel in my back, but don't worry. I'm all right, though I won't have occasion to wear that tie soon. I didn't even know I was wounded until I felt the blood, and even then I thought it was someone else's.

Strange, during that fifteen minutes of action I felt no fear. But there's usually not much contact with the enemy. Often you don't see a single VC the whole time. Days pass without any contact. They're out there, you know, yet you never see them. Just mines, booby traps. I'm only a medic, and my contact with the enemy is rarely direct — what I see are the wounded men and the dead, the bodies. I see the destruction, and I have begun to both fear and hate the Vietnamese — even here in South Vietnam, I can't tell whose side they're on.

Every day I visit a nearby village and help a local doctor vaccinate children. The morning after the attack I felt the people in the village were laughing at me because they knew an American had died. Yesterday I returned to the same village. Everything quiet, business as usual, but I stood there, surrounded by hooches, thinking of that dead kid, and for a moment I felt the urge to even the score somehow.

What am I saying, sweetie? I'm a medic, trained to save lives. Every day I'm closer to death than most people ever get, except in their final second on earth. It's a world of hurt — that's the phrase we use — and things happen over here, things you just can't keep to yourself. I've seen what happens to men who try. They're consumed by what they've seen and done, they grow obsessive, and slowly they lose sight of the job they're supposed to be doing. I have no hard proof of this, but I think in this condition men open themselves up to attack. You've got to talk things out, get everything very clear in your mind. Lucky for me I've got a buddy over here who's been under fire too, and can understand what I'm feeling. That helps.

I'm sorry to write like this, but in your letter you said you wanted to know everything. It's not in my power to say what this war means to you or anyone back home, but I can describe what happens, and if you want, I'll continue doing that. For me, at least, it's a comfort to know someone's out there, far away, who can't really understand, and I hope is never able to. I'll write again soon.

All love,
Henry

I'd snagged this letter from a box Mother kept in her room, under the bed. There were other kinds of letters in the box, letters about love and family and work, but I didn't think Mother would miss this one, which was just about war. Father never talked much about his tours in Vietnam, but he would if I asked. Out of respect, I learned not to ask too much, but I knew about Zippo raids, trip flares, bouncing bettys, hand frags, satchel charges, and such, and when he was angry, or sad, Father often peppered his speech with slang he'd picked up, like *titi*, which means "little," and *didi mow*, which means "go quickly," and *xin loi*, meaning "sorry about that."

I tucked the letter away. I got the swing going real good, and I rose up, then fell, rose and fell, seeing, then not seeing. When the swing was going high enough I let go and sailed through the open air, landing in an explosion of soft sand. I wiped the grains out of my eyes. My eyes watered, and everything was unclear. Things toppled and blew in the wind. A striped beach umbrella rolled across the playfield, twirling like a pinwheel. A sheet from someone's clothesline flapped loose and sailed away. I thought of my nightmare, of Father's balloon tied to a stringbean. I looked up at the sky, and it was black, with some light. There were stars, millions of them like tiny holes in something, and the moon, like a bigger hole in the same thing. White holes. I thought of Mrs. Gurney and her blank eyes and the black pouring out of them. Was it the wind, a sudden gust kicking up and brushing my trunks? It happened so quickly. Had she tried to touch me? Had she? I stretched out in the sand. The wind gave me goose bumps. Shivering, I listened. From inside the house, I heard the men laughing, the ice clinking, the women shrieking. Everything in there was still hysterical. I'd never get to sleep. I decided to stay awake. They would all be going home, but until then I'd wait outside.

I lay there, very quietly. I brushed some sand off me. I waited.

It was me who found Father, that morning. I'd gone up to get some creosote out of the trunk of his car. It was a cold, gray, misty morning, the usual kind we have, and in the grass field above the parking lot there was a family of deer, chewing away, looking around, all innocent. And there he was, sitting in the car. I opened the passenger door. At first my eyes kind of separated from my brain, and I saw everything real slow, like you might see a movie, or something far away that wasn't happening to you. Some of his face was gone. One of his eyes was staring out. He was still breathing, but his lungs worked like he'd swallowed a yard of chunk gravel or sand. He was twitching. I touched his hand and the fingers curled around mine, gripping, but it was just nerves, an old reaction or something, because he was brain-dead already. My imagination jumped right out of its box when he grabbed me. I knew right away I was being grabbed by a dead man. I got away. I ran away. In our house I tried to speak, but there were no words. I started pounding the walls and kicking over the furniture and breaking stuff. I couldn't see, I heard falling. I ran around the house holding and ripping at my head. Eventually Mother caught me. I just pointed up to the car. You understand, I miss Father, miss having him around to tell me what's right and what's wrong, or to talk about *boom-boom*, which is sex, or just to go salmon fishing out by Hat Island and not worry about things, either way, but I also have to say, never again do I want to see anything like what I saw that morning. I never, as long as I live, want to find another dead person. He wasn't even a person then, just a blown-up thing, just crushed-up garbage. Part of his head was blasted away, and there was blood and hair and bone splattered on the windshield. It looked like he'd just driven the car through something awful, like he needed to use the windshield wipers, needed to switch the blades on high and clear the way, except that the wipers wouldn't do him any good, because the mess was all on the inside.

MILLICENT DILLON

Oil and Water

FROM SOUTHWEST REVIEW

IT WAS January something, 1946, and I was in the bus station, waiting to go to the oil field. Though it was five months since the end of the war, there were still a number of servicemen about, some standing, some milling, some on benches, asleep and awake.

When my bus was called, only a few passengers boarded. I went to the back seat and stretched out full length. I had been up too late the night before and I needed sleep badly. I fell asleep and woke up and fell asleep again, the bus making its droning sound, putting me to sleep in the way I don't like to sleep. You try to come out of it, but you can't, you're in and out of the noise, you're in and out of the sleep.

I don't know how long I was lying there, my purse near my head, when suddenly I felt a thing on my leg and I was awake. I saw a guy in a dark jacket beside me on the seat. "Take your goddam hand off of me," I yelled, though he had already taken it off. One passenger turned around, then another, but he had put himself into the corner and was pretending to be asleep. I was so mad at the nerve of this guy putting his hand on me I wasn't able to sleep anymore. Shaking, I sat upright. A whole journey like that, no leaning, no nodding, looking in front of me. The creep in the corner must have got off at some stop in the valley, though I never noticed. By then it was dark and the bus had filled up.

It was almost eleven at night when we got into Avenal, the valley town west of the oil field. At the bus stop, a parking lot beside a diner, a station wagon was waiting, marked with the company name and logo, a series of jagged peaks in a circle on a dusty green ground. The driver, a lean man wearing a greasy cap, threw my suitcase into the front seat and motioned to me to get in back. He remained silent as we drove out of town, along a straight unlit road. After about twenty minutes we began to climb into the hills. He took the curves very fast in the darkness. I felt myself growing carsick. I tried to stop the nausea by fixing firmly on something outside. I saw lights gleaming on the tops of high still derricks. Around them and beneath them rows of squat metal beams moved in shadow through semicircular arcs, looking like a herd of blind horses rocking in the night.

I don't know what I would have done, where I would have thrown up, I was beginning to feel desperate, but finally we came to a stop. Before us a group of one-story buildings were huddled together in the dark.

"Women's bunkhouse," the driver announced loudly, as if he were addressing a carload of people. He jumped out and took my bag out of the front and set it on the railed porch. Then he got back in the car.

"Which is my room?" I whispered to him, worried that I might wake somebody up, since there wasn't a single other sound I could hear.

"Fourth door to the left. Bathroom's at the end. And the cookhouse is over there." He pointed vaguely left. "Whistle blows at six."

I dragged my suitcase into number four and turned on the overhead light. A single bed with a white chenille cover, an unpainted wooden table with a metal lamp, a bare floor, a bureau, a small closet curtained off from the rest of the room by material marked with those jagged peaks.

It was the idea of the desert that had appealed to me when I had heard about the job. Just the words, "the desert" and "an oil field," had sounded like adventure. And then, too, I had figured I could save some money if I could just make myself stay a little while. I thought of that road winding down to the valley, then straight as a shot back to where I had just come from and then further back. Who needed that? I was finished with that. I fell back on the bed without taking my clothes off. I wasn't even sleepy. My stomach was gurgling, empty, I hadn't brought any food with me. I hadn't thought things out well, but then I hadn't known what to expect. At least I was here. I'd gotten on the bus, I'd gotten off the bus. There was a beginning, a middle, and an end — that's what I liked about journeys.

At the middle, or close to the beginning, was that creep who put his hand on my leg. What did he think when I yelled? He had jumped away, backed away. He cowered in that corner, pretending that he'd been sleeping all along. Did he even know why he did what he did? He saw a leg lying there. Was it my fault that I had good legs? It was there, to be touched. Is that what he thought? It had nothing to do with thinking, probably. He saw it, his hand moved to it, it went, it was going, it was touching, he thought, he did not think. That this person, myself, was asleep, did that excite him? What was he on his way to? What had he been? He was no soldier. He looked too young, didn't look as though he could have been a soldier . . .

It was still dark when the cookhouse whistle blew and woke me up. At first I didn't know where I was. Then I remembered. I lay for a few minutes listening to the sounds around me, someone going past the window, the footsteps heavy on the wooden porch, a door slamming, a radio on, loud. New sounds, new day, come on get up, for some reason I was filled with hope as I almost always was in the morning. People are getting up, a whistle has blown, in a way it's a little like the army, I told myself.

I dressed and went outside. The building next door with all the lights had to be the cookhouse. I crossed the path and entered a large room with many rows of long tables and straight chairs, a steam table along one wall and behind it the kitchen, partially enclosed. There were only a few men sitting at the tables. As I walked over to the serving line, several of the men turned and looked at me. They didn't smile, they only stared, then turned back again and said something in low voices to each other.

The food at the steam table was overwhelming: great huge slabs of ham covered with a dark thick raisin sauce, mounds of bacon, more mounds of scrambled eggs, boxes of cereal, loaves and loaves of white bread, containers full of milk, coffee, more milk, enough for a regiment. Next to me in line was a small neat woman with a braid wrapped around her head. She was wearing a sensible dress and sensible shoes. She had on her tray a bowl of cereal and milk, a glass of orange juice, and coffee. I took the same.

After I got out of the serving line, I looked around. I didn't feel like just going over to the men's table and barging in. I had the feeling those men wouldn't like it. Instead I went over to where the sensible woman was sitting by herself. I introduced myself, I said I was new here, I said, "They certainly give you a lot of food."

"They sure do. Too much. Maybe if you're a roughneck, but for someone working in the office, it's ridiculous. So just don't eat it." She held out her hand. "My name is Udell Banks Henry. It was plain Udell Banks until last year when I married Frank Henry. I always call myself Udell Banks Henry. Do you think that's peculiar?" she asked belligerently.

"Not at all," I said. "I think it's admirable."

Mollified, she went on. "Frank Henry lives in Fresno, where he works in a clothing store. I go there every weekend. I don't much care for all the driving but I'd be nuts to give up my job here as a bookkeeper. I save a lot and there's no rent and no expenses for food. I figure a couple more years of this and I'll have a real nest egg socked away. Frank Henry agrees with me. A good thing too, because if he didn't it wouldn't matter. I am very independent in my thinking." She finished off her glass of juice. "So you're new here. How do you like it? Did you meet anybody yet?"

"The driver. He picked me up at the bus station last night. He wasn't very — talkative," I added.

"Talkative? Are you kidding? They're all sphinxes. None of them talk."

She turned around and looked around the room. All the men were gone now. "Those men. What a weird bunch they are. They stay on in this godforsaken place that's already beginning to run out of oil, when they could be making three times as much doing the same thing in Saudi Arabia. I think they're afraid, that's what I think."

She circled her coffee cup with both palms. "I'll tell you one thing, they are definitely afraid of women. Oh sure, they'll get drunk and go to a whore for a quickie, but a real woman? a long-term woman? They want nothing to do with her. I went out a couple of times with some of them before I met Frank Henry. What a drag. You ask them how they feel about something, anything, and they say, 'What do you want to know for?' I mean, you're not asking them for their most intimate private business. I'd ask them, 'Do you have a brother?' or 'What is your hobby?' You know what this one guy said to me? He said, 'I don't ask you anything about yourself. You don't need to ask me anything.' What have they got to hide? But who cares? I quit asking. I mean, who needs it? Who needs them? Anonymous jerks. My advice to you is to do like I do. Keep to yourself, keep your nose to the grindstone, when you're grinding, that is. I do my real living in Fresno. If you want to go there any weekend, just let me know, I'll give you a ride."

"Thanks," I said. "I'll keep that in mind." I only said that out of politeness. I had just arrived. I couldn't even think of leaving yet.

At seven-twenty-five, as I came out of the women's bunkhouse, the sun was already well up. Across the valley to the east, a great dry plain extended as far as I could see. In the far distance, I could just make out a range of snow-topped mountains. At the north end of the valley, a body of water glistened in the slanting light. It looked as if it were a square lake. How could a lake be square? In the air was an odd smell, as if something heavy and invisible had oozed in on the night air.

Some men came out of a nearby building in their tan work outfits and got into a company car. They sped off, the dust circling behind them. From another building across the way I heard men's voices calling out to each other. I felt as if I were a fly on a wall, watching, listening, in a space permeated by maleness. Had these men been in the war? I wondered. Maybe that accounted for their silence, for their being what Udell had called "weird."

I found Mr. Redfern, my supervisor, in his office seated behind a long narrow table. On each side of him and opposite him were a number of chairs, all unoccupied. There was something very pale and pinched-looking about Mr. Redfern. (How did he stay so pale in the desert?) He did not ask me to sit down. His first words were not welcoming words. "We didn't expect you so early."

"But I thought we were supposed to start at seven-thirty."

"I mean so early in the week, in the month. We're not ready for you." What does he expect me to do, go back? I wondered.

"Well," he went on with asperity, "I suppose now that you're

here we'll have to find something for you to do. Your predecessor was working on depth pressure readings. I suppose you can
do that."

"Depth pressure?"

"You don't know what depth pressure is?"

"No, but I — I'm eager to learn."

"What is the matter with those people at the central office? Do
they think I'm running a school here? Have you ever been in an
oil field before? Have you?"

"No, but I —"

"I thought not. At least you do know how to measure and plot,
don't you? You do know how to do that?"

"Yes, I think so."

"She thinks so," he said loudly, as if he were addressing an audience seated in the empty chairs. "Either you do or you don't,
there's no halfway about it."

"Yes, I do."

"I hope so."

Grumbling again about the central office, he led me out of his
office into a small cubicle with a desk in it. "Sit there." He went
away and came back with a stack of small pieces of metallic paper, each with a staggered line engraved on it. He placed before
me a wooden holder. The paper was to be slipped into it and
then tightened into position with two small wing nuts. When
everything was firmly in place, I was to measure the deviation of
the jagged line from the center line every quarter of an inch and
then plot the readings on a chart.

"Think exactness," Mr. Redfern said. I watched him go out of
the cubicle, amazed at how even his back looked pinched.

Okay, I instructed myself. No and, if, or but. Start and start
right. I did like exactitude, I liked to see things fit, to see disorder
vanish. I loved to be in the grip of sudden intuition going toward,
reaching, discovery. Many beginnings, how many middles, one
end.

I began. But to my dismay, each time I took a reading and then
went back to check it (for I was thinking "exactness"), I found the
second reading was different from the first. Not by a lot, but
enough to cause anxiety. Something was out of whack. Maybe
the paper was slipping in the holder. I tightened the wing nuts.

Again, each measurement of the distance from the center line from a particular point was slightly different from the previous measurement at that point. I began to despair of exactness as a fundamental principle. I kept tightening and measuring and tightening and measuring till I was in a sweat. I began to fear that the uncertainty principle had taken hold in a big — an impossibly big — way, that by the act of measuring itself I was causing, had caused, a change in the universe.

Stop that, just write down what you get, I told myself, write down all the different answers, then you'll have a set of answers for each point. It's better than nothing. I wondered if Mr. Redfern would buy the idea of multiple answers with its implication that the world was a maze of possibilities. I myself wasn't sure I could buy it. The need for precision, for the precision of singleness, of single (right) answers, had come on me like a fever. I had the feeling that the slightest inaccuracy would count against me, that it would blemish my record irrevocably, even though, especially because, this was my first day on the job.

Mr. Redfern appeared at my elbow. "This is all, this is all you have done? And what are those extra figures you have written down?"

"I'm having a little problem," I said. In my agitation the words tumbled out about the slipping and sliding of the paper.

"Your predecessor never mentioned that problem."

"Maybe it didn't happen before."

"Nothing has changed. It was always very stable before and it should be now." He bent over the holder, tugged lightly on the metallic paper, and it slipped. He tightened the wing nuts and tugged on the paper again. "That's very peculiar. Did you tighten the nuts too tight?"

"No, no, that's the way they were from the beginning. I didn't do anything."

"You're sure?"

"I'm pretty sure."

"They look stripped to me. You know, I didn't need this. I've got enough on my mind without this."

"But what do you want me to do?"

"What do I want you to do? I want you to be careful. As far as these wing nuts are concerned, you'd better draw up some specifications for new wing nuts and take them over to the shop foreman."

"And what should I do about the different measurements?"

"Average them." Mr. Redfern started toward his office, stopped, and returned to my desk. He cleared his throat. "There is something I think it is my responsibility to say to you, since you have never been in an oil field before. There are certain things that, as a young woman, in this unfamiliar setting, you ought to —" He stopped, bit his lips, and started again. "I — my wife and I go to church in Avenal every Sunday morning at eleven. Would you like to accompany us this Sunday?"

"Thank you very much," I blurted out, "but I don't go to church."

"I see," he said. Just that and nothing more. He went into his office and closed the door.

I felt like an idiot, I felt like a gorilla, I felt it was all my fault. Why did I turn him down so quickly without even thinking? It was a kind offer. Wasn't it kind? I could have just said that I was agnostic. Would that have been better? But that wasn't the truth either. I didn't know what I believed except that God was as inscrutable to me as man — or men. But on the other hand I certainly didn't mean any refusal of Mr. Redfern's religion by my not going. Only it had come upon me so quickly. First all that business about being too early and then about not being exact and then his telling me to average — I hated averaging — was this an acceptable way for a supervisor to act or wasn't it? Who was this man? I didn't know a thing about him except that he looked pinched, and what did that mean, after all? Had he been in the war? I looked at the metallic pieces of paper before me with their jagged lines. I began to feel something akin to dread. It was as if my skin had become porous to the uncertainty of the entire universe and that trying to know, like trying to measure, only increased that uncertainty, made the world a pool of uncertainty, and I, an insect suspended through surface tension alone, at any moment might drown.

Looking out the window beside my desk, I saw that the snow-clad peaks across the valley were no longer visible because of a gathering haze. Out there were derricks and pumps and oil in the ground, black oil made by the disintegration of carbon and whatever over the centuries. I had to take a longer view of things. I had to look at the world the way it was. I had to stop making such a fuss about slipping papers and slipping words.

Coming out of the bathroom of the women's bunkhouse was Udell, a towel with the company insignia wrapped around her head.

"Aren't you coming to dinner at the cookhouse?" I asked.

"Nah. I don't have dinner there every night. Lots of times I just have cottage cheese and fruit in the kitchen. Want to join me?"

"I didn't know we had a kitchen."

"It's right through the living room. How could you miss it?"

"I haven't seen the living room yet."

Udell led me around to the other side of the building, opened a door, and there was a living room with five overstuffed green chairs, very large, unoccupied, one standing lamp with a faded shade, and a number of torn issues of the *Saturday Evening Post* on a wooden table in the corner. "They certainly keep it messy," Udell said. I didn't know who she meant by "they."

She led me through the living room out another door to the kitchen, painted the dusty green of the company logo. In the center of the room was a battered wooden table with six chairs. Had a lot more people once been here, or were they expecting a lot more to arrive?

Udell got the cottage cheese and fruit — apples and pears — out of the refrigerator and took two pale green glass plates from the rusty metal cabinet. She heaped the cottage cheese and fruit on the plates.

"Do the other women eat here too?" I asked.

"Don't ask me what they do," Udell said with irritation. She munched on a pear and then put it down. "I'll tell you what the trouble with the women around here is. There are so many men it makes them greedy. I mean, you'd think they'd want to share, but no, the more they have, the more they want. Take Francine, who's the office manager, and Mattie, who's a pumper —"

"What's a pumper?"

"A pumper goes out to the wells and reads the numbers on the pumps. I wouldn't like to have that job, I'll tell you. Going out and checking at night. God knows how many snakes there are just hiding and waiting. Not for me. I'm glad I've got an office job."

"How old is Mattie?"

"Young. My age. But Francine — have you seen her?"

"No, I haven't seen any of the women."

"Francine's forty-five if she's a day but she gets herself all dolled up in frilly dresses meant for kids."

"What did you say Francine does?"

"She's supposed to manage the office. Some manager. She spends most of her time chasing after the younger guys. In fact," and here Udell leaned closer, "I wouldn't be surprised if Francine and Mattie both had a thriving business going on here. All I know is that she'd better not approach me to be part of her business. I'd spit in her eye. My favors are my own favors. They're not for sale to anyone. I care about my reputation. Don't you?"

Was this what Mr. Redfern had had in mind when he asked me to go to church? Was he really only watching out for me? Why didn't he speak more directly? How was I supposed to know what was going on?

"Don't you?" Udell repeated, louder.

"Yes, yes, of course."

"I'm independent-minded, like I told you, but that doesn't mean I don't give a damn about what other people think. That's just plain common," Udell said as she cleared away the food and began washing up. Her way of washing dishes, I noticed, was to use hot water and no soap.

"Will the dishes get clean that way, with just water?"

"If the water's hot enough, they'll get clean."

"But," I said, thinking of germs, and that surely there are germs in the desert like anywhere else, maybe even more, but I didn't say anything about them. Instead I asked her what she usually did in the evening.

"Usually? Usually I go to sleep. I save myself for Fresno. I used to go up to the employees' clubhouse before I was married. They have pool tables and cards there and a soda fountain. Good malts, the best I've ever had. But that's good reason for me to stay away. Frank Henry doesn't like it if I put on weight. Besides, I go up there now and it's just plain boring. The same thing over and over, those guys feeding you a line. The way I look at it, there's

more to life than that. Don't misunderstand me. I like sex. Frank
Henry likes sex too. I don't have any complaints in that department. But after all, let's face it, there are more important things
in life than sex. Just don't ask me what, right this moment."

I went into my room and shut the door and sat on the bed to
read. There wasn't any other place to sit. I thought of going into
the living room, in fact I went into the living room. I even sat in
one of those large chairs. But after a while it depressed me, just
those large empty chairs and me.

I went outside. The night was very dark, there wasn't any moon.
It was eerie, even frightening. But I didn't want to go back to my
room. The depression, if that's what it was, was wearing off, and
had left me anxious to move. I started walking up the road. From
inside the clubhouse I heard men's voices and sharp clicking noises.
I went on, past the men's bunkhouses, past the storage areas, until finally I was at the end of the camp. Peering out, I could not
penetrate the darkness. There were no pumps or derricks visible
from here. It was as if I had come to the edge of the world. I
thought of vast distances, cold, silent, and uninhabited. I thought
of the snow-covered peaks I had seen that morning that had vanished in the later haze. Only that morning? I felt in some way as
if I had always been here, that there was no other place but here.
The world, all there was of it, ended here, and I had better come
to terms with it, take it for what it was, because there was no other,
because one could fall into darkness as if into a chasm, if one
refused it.

I retraced my steps, but instead of passing by the employee
clubhouse I went inside. At one end of the huge room were a
number of men, standing around the pool tables, talking and
playing. The clicking noises I had heard before, I now realized,
were from the pool balls hitting each other as they shot out on
the green surfaces. In front of me was a group of small tables
with men playing cards, slamming them down, gathering them
up, some laughing, some frowning. A rack with magazines lined
another wall, and to my right was the snack bar and some empty
round tables and chairs.

I ordered a chocolate malted at the snack bar and took it to one
of the round tables. The malted was certainly creamy and rich,

just as Udell had said. It was also huge, and I wondered if I'd be able to finish the whole thing. Looking up, I caught several of the men at the card tables looking at me. Again that wary look, again that turning away and saying something to each other. I felt I had invaded a sanctuary.

"Would you like to play a game of pool?" A short stocky man stood in front of me. He had an open honest face and a friendly grin.

"I don't know how to play," I said.

"I can show you."

"That would be very nice indeed." Even as I said the words, they sounded affected to me, but he didn't seem to notice. He led me to an empty pool table and took a cue down from the wall. "This one looks about the right size for you." He stood it on end on the floor next to me. "Yep, it's fine."

He showed me how to grip the cue with the thumb and first finger of my right hand, and how to place my left hand on the table to make a bridge with my fingers. "Don't hold it so tight, it's not a death grip. Not too loose, either. You have to do it just right. Light with you right hand here at the butt end and tighter where the bridge is. Okay, now what you want to do is try to hit the ball with the cue in this small area at the center. You're going to be aiming for that corner pocket."

I did as he said. I hit the ball and it went straight into the pocket. He took out another ball. I aimed and I got it into the corner pocket again. I felt my luck had turned. No — more than that. I felt I had discovered an unknown talent in myself. No — more than that. There was something about the game, the estimation of the impact and then the actuality of the ball's passage through space and into the proper hole, that touched and excited me.

Two other men came over, one heavyset and middle-aged, the other somewhat younger and very thin. "Why don't you teach her about english, Shorty?" said the heavier one.

"Kelly, just leave me do it my way. I don't want her to get completely confused the first time."

"Why don't we play a game? You and her against me and Al."

"All right with you?" Shorty asked.

"As long as nobody minds a beginner."

"It's just a game," said Kelly.

Though it was just a game, they played with great seriousness, taking a long time to estimate, to judge, to aim. As for my own shots, now and then I would hit a good one and they praised me. When I missed completely, Shorty said, "Never mind. What do you expect the first time? You're doing real good."

The air in the clubhouse was warm and comforting and no one said a word to me that was at all out of the way. Udell had been wrong about that, at least. It's not that they weren't treating me as if I were a woman. They were, but somehow they acted as if I'd been admitted to their fraternity. And I was experiencing a reciprocal sense of comradeship with them. It did pass through my mind that I was not attracted to Shorty or Al or Kelly. In its own way, that was a kind of relief. It came to me that there were, after all, different kinds of maleness, or perhaps different feelings that maleness evoked: this friendly maleness, then the maleness of sexuality — that wasn't friendly — and then there was the third kind of maleness, the one that was all mixed up with death. Had these men been in the war? I wondered.

First thing the next morning I began to draw up the specifications for the new wing nuts. I had never drawn a specification before so I had delayed doing it when Mr. Redfern told me to, but today I decided it must not be that difficult. I did a drawing of the old wing nut, then made the winged section larger, then larger again. The important thing, I decided, is to be able to get a good purchase on it, so I can really screw it down tight. I felt as if I were making substantial progress toward accuracy. I even began to look at averaging with less distaste.

As the day went by, I felt myself falling into place, into my own proper niche. Though I had only the haziest idea of what was involved in depth pressure measurements, I was convinced that what needed to be revealed would be revealed in its own good time. Whatever secrecy there was seemed a natural secrecy, appropriate to this time and place, to these circumstances. I was, after all, a student in the school of learning how to wait. I felt I was being released from all those questions that had been nagging at me so persistently in the recent past, about what I must or should find. The sense of desire itself was altering in me. Even as I felt this way, I noted that I was becoming a little weird, nunlike, almost. But at the same time I was convinced that while I was being helped to wait, I was also being helped over some hump of loathsome vulnerability within myself.

Soon I fell into a comforting and comfortable routine, getting up, having breakfast at the cookhouse, working in the morning, having lunch at the cookhouse, working in the afternoon, then dinner at the bunkhouse with Udell and, to cap off the day, playing pool at night. Shorty was teaching me how to sight along the cue, how to gauge the proper angle and english for a carom shot.

After playing, I would sit at one of the small round tables with Shorty and Al and Kelly, listening to them talk about the old days at the camp. All that other history out there — my own family's history, which I'd just as well not think of, why else did I leave home but to get away from it? — and even the history of the war seemed to be giving way to another kind of history that I began to identify as my own.

Once Shorty said something about the field already beginning to play out. Kelly said that the engineers were damn smart, they'd find a way to extract more oil. In some places they were already forcing water at high pressure into the wells to drive up the oil still left in the rock.

"Still," said Shorty, "there's a limit to what you can do. There's only so much oil in the ground."

"So if it plays out here, I'll go somewhere else," said Al.

"If there is somewhere else."

"There's always a somewhere else."

Shorty shrugged. "For you, maybe."

They were silent for a while. Then Al got up to get another beer.

"Al's a driller, one of the best," said Kelly.

"One of the best," said Shorty. "You ought to go see him work someday. It's an art, the way he guides that block, the way he can tell when the drilling mud is just right."

For a moment I felt a spasm of envy. I couldn't say there was any art to what I was doing on the job, but at least, I reassured myself, you're getting accurate readings. The shop had made the wing nuts exactly to my specifications. The flange of each nut was almost two inches in width, and when I tightened them down on the paper, it never slipped.

Now that it was March there were dust storms every afternoon at the camp. The wind blew relentlessly, and the sun, when it shone, was filtered through grit. One night I was awakened by the sound of rain on the metal roof of the bunkhouse. The water thundered so loud I wondered if the roof would hold. Finally, toward morning, without any tapering off, the rain stopped.

Coming out of the cookhouse into the brilliant washed light, I smelled the unfamiliar moisture over and under the smell of oil. I was afflicted with a vague sense of loss, as if a memory — or more accurately, a memory of a memory — were slipping from my grasp. But I haven't lost anything, I assured myself. I saw in the wash behind the camp a roaring stream, but elsewhere there was dryness as before.

In the evening after an early dinner Udell and I went for a walk. "We'd better keep to the road," said Udell as we passed beyond the end of the camp. "This is snake weather."

"Snakes? Poisonous snakes?"

"Nah. I don't think so, but I steer clear of them anyhow. Like I told you, I don't like snakes. Once I saw a cobra in a zoo. It was all wrapped around itself and one end started to move but the other end hadn't gotten the message yet. Weird. In the next cage was this frog or toad, the ugliest thing I have ever seen. It lay there in this tiny cage like a blob — a blob of shit. I'll tell you, God makes plenty of mistakes."

"Well, maybe not mistakes, exactly." Uncertain as I was about the nature of my own beliefs, I did not want to share in the complicity of this judgment.

"Yes, mistakes," Udell went on doggedly. "Plenty of them. What's the matter? You afraid God will punish me for saying he makes mistakes? Mistakes!" she yelled. "You make plenty of mistakes!" She grinned. "You see, He doesn't strike me dead. Frank Henry, he's a Baptist, always trying to get me to go and be dunked into the church. Not me, I say, not me. I had enough of that fire and brimstone when I was a kid. Meekness, kid, does not inherit the earth. What it does do is turn you into a poor fucked-up toad in a cage."

At that moment I heard a terrible sound behind me, as if the earth were rumbling and the air roaring. Can this be punishment? I thought in a panic. I turned around and saw a riderless horse in full gallop coming toward us. I stared in wonder, I couldn't move, I couldn't believe the power of that horse in motion.

Udell yanked my arm and pulled me off the road. The horse went thundering by and disappeared round a bend in the road. "What's the matter with you, standing there like you were paralyzed? Haven't you ever seen a horse before?"

"I have, but not — not one like that."

"I worry about you, kid. Sometimes I think you need a keeper." She shook her head. "Let's go back, I've had enough walking for today."

A pickup truck drove up with Shorty at the wheel. "You see my gray mare?"

"We sure did," Udell said. "What the hell is it doing running loose like that?"

"She got out of the corral when I wasn't looking," Shorty said sheepishly. "She's only feeling her oats."

"Some oats. You better keep that horse corralled or I'll complain to the management. We could have been killed just walking. Mean, stupid beasts," she said as he drove away. "You can't trust them."

That night I had a dream: I was climbing a steep pass at a great height. At a turn in the path I looked up and saw that a man had grabbed the woman next to him and with a violent gesture was flinging her over the edge of the cliff. I watched in terror as the woman plummeted to earth and finally dropped into a small pool of water. After a long wait, the woman surfaced, safe. In the dream I wondered how it was possible for that man to have so accurately directed his throw, for I didn't doubt that he had intended what had happened. There was something admirable as well as frightening about the sureness of his gesture.

The leftover feelings of the dream stayed with me after I woke up, and fastened themselves somehow onto the image of that horse, galloping, galloping. Two feelings, vague and grave, rode in and out of my brain. First, I felt a sense of awe at the horse, at its — her thundering motion, at its mane that in retrospect seemed

to be like flame, at its quivering nostrils. Then there was the sense
of shame at the thought of how I stood so paralyzed until Udell
pulled me out of its path.

As I worked in my cubicle that morning tightening the wing
nuts, I saw that they were like two misshapen beings, animals with
huge shoulders, too big for their small bodies, clutching at the
metallic paper as if it were a matter of life and death. Why had I
come here and why was I staying? I was a coward, staying on here
like a lump, wasting away my youth, losing the main chance,
throwing it away, being bypassed forever. Stop it, I told myself,
but I was saddled with a burden of regret that I could not shake
off.

Looking out the window, I felt that even the landscape was
putting something over on me. There was the square lake, another cause for shame. I'd asked Kelly about the lake one evening. "What?" he'd said to me in surprise. "You've never seen
a square lake before? That's the only kind we have around
here."

"You're kidding," I said, but he insisted so soberly that he was
serious, I was about to believe him. After all, what did I know
about the desert? But finally Shorty had taken pity on me and
said it was manmade, a storage lake for irrigation, and they'd had
a good laugh at me. Good-naturedly, I'd thought at the time. But
now I felt differently. They were in the know in this, their world,
and I wasn't. They had their secrets that weren't secrets to them
but were to me. And they would not be revealed, except piece-
meal and grudgingly, only at that point when they didn't matter
anymore. All the assumptions I had made about camaraderie were
incorrect, I now saw. Oh come on, I said to myself, all this because of a riderless horse?

I made myself go the clubhouse that night, as if habit could
rectify existence. I found Shorty alone playing solitaire. He seemed
distant, unfamiliar. He put the queen of diamonds on the king
of clubs. He didn't say anything about the horse. I felt I ought to
say something.

"How's your horse?"

"Okay."

"You got her back all right?"

"Yeah." He put the jack of clubs on the queen of diamonds.

"What's her name?"

"Tiny."

"Tiny?" I began to laugh hysterically.

"That's her name," he said stubbornly.

"Sorry," I said, trying to control myself. "I hope I didn't hurt your feelings. I mean, she seems like a very nice horse."

He smiled, old, familiar, decent, friendly Shorty. "Would you like to ride her?"

"I'd love to, but I don't know how to ride."

"I'll teach you. We could go out on rides together."

"Both on one horse?"

"No," he laughed. "I've got two horses. Tiny and a gelding named Curly. Would you like to go on a moonlight ride sometime?"

"A moonlight ride?"

"Sure. Riding with the moon shining and the stars out and the sagebrush and the —"

Right then Al and Kelly came in and the usual pool game started, but I had a hard time concentrating. "What's the matter with you tonight?" Kelly asked. He and I were partners. "You're missing everything."

"Nothing's the matter," I said. But I was upset that Shorty had asked me that question. Maybe at first, for an instant, I was pleased — flattered. I had felt that small sly leap, that inner grin at the proof of my power to attract. But almost at once it had been replaced, covered over, by my conviction that now things were going to be muddier.

As I sighted along the cue for the next shot, I was afraid I was going to miss that one too. I felt I'd lost any ability I'd ever had to judge, to estimate, to aim.

"I wondered how long it was going to take before you had to get away," Udell said as we drove into the outskirts of Fresno. "You can only stand it so long and then you have to get out. It happens to everybody."

"It's certainly nice here," I said, admiring the wide streets and the green trees and the neat small houses.

"It is nice, if I say so myself. Clean, they keep it clean. I get so damned tired of all that dust at the camp. It gets in your nose and your eyes and your mouth. I feel like spitting out all the time. Grit," she said with disgust, then added, "We'll go by the house first. Frank Henry will be wondering what happened to me if I'm late. And I don't like him to worry."

She pulled into the driveway of a small white house on a tree-lined street. The front of the house had a picture window looking out onto a green cement front edged by a low wire fence. "Frank Henry covered the front over with cement. He hates mowing lawns. He made the cement green so it would look like lawn. Don't you think that was a cute idea?"

Udell got out of the car, unloaded her things from the back, and went up on the porch. "Frank Henry," she called out, "I'm here. Come and help me."

There was no answer.

"Don't tell me he's not here yet. Damn — after all that rushing —"

I followed her into the living room. I noticed multicolored afghans everywhere, over the back of the couch and on the backs of the big chairs. I noticed the white frilly curtains pulled back from the picture window by an even frillier sash. Udell, who had gone out into the kitchen, came back and said nervously, "Frank Henry didn't even leave me a note. That's not like him. It's after five. It's almost dinnertime. He has a fit if he doesn't have his food right at six. He's like a kid that way." She smiled fondly, then added, "I hope nothing has happened to him. The first thing I always think about is an automobile accident . . ." Her voice tapered off anxiously. "I'll go ahead and start dinner. He'll be here any moment, I'm sure."

"Can I help you?"

"You can keep me company if you want to. I'm just going to make a big pot of spaghetti."

I leaned against the kitchen counter and watched her get out an enormous pot and fill it with water. "How much spaghetti are you going to make?"

"I make up a big pot for the week. That way he doesn't have to cook when I'm gone."

"He must love spaghetti."

"He's not that particular. Frank Henry eats whatever I give him," she said proudly.

When six o'clock came, the spaghetti and the tomato sauce were done but Frank Henry had not yet arrived. "Where the devil is he? He couldn't have stopped off at Charlie's Bar, could he have? Frank Henry doesn't like me to call to see if he's there, but I don't care, I'm going to call anyhow.

"No, he's not there," she said, hanging up the receiver. "Wait till I get hold of him, I'll —"

At that moment the door between the kitchen and the living room swung open and Frank Henry came in. He was small and thin and bald. He was carrying a large paper bag.

"Where have you been, Frank Henry?" Udell asked, her hands on her hips.

"I've been fishing. I took the afternoon off."

"You took the afternoon off and you didn't let me know? We've been waiting around for hours, keeping the dinner warm —"

"You don't have to make a federal case of it." He put the paper bag on the counter. "I brought you some nice fish." He started out the kitchen door.

"I don't want any fish. What am I going to do with fish? I've already made spaghetti," Udell yelled, following him into the living room.

Even with the kitchen door closed, I could hear them yelling. I tried not to listen to what was being said. I looked at the spaghetti. It seemed to be agglutinating before my eyes. I looked at the window over the counter. More frilly curtains.

Udell shoved open the swinging door. She sat at the table and started spooning out spaghetti on my plate. "Can you imagine the nerve? He says it's my fault that I wasn't here earlier. What good would it have done if I'd been here earlier?"

"That's enough, thank you," I said. The mound before me was intimidating.

"Let him starve, what do I care?" Udell said. "Are you coming in to eat, Frank Henry?" she yelled.

There was a muffled "No."

"Goddammit, after I've been to all this trouble." She got up and went into the living room and slammed the door behind her. I heard a thud and then some yelling, a murmur, a yell, another murmur, and then some knocking sounds. I wondered if I should just go ahead and eat, but I wasn't hungry. The smell of the fish was overpowering. Should I put it in the refrigerator? Would it go bad sitting there on the counter? How long does fresh fish stay fresh?

Udell came back into the kitchen, her face red, her lipstick smeared.

"He'll be in in a minute," she said primly.

At the end of the meal, eaten in silence except for Udell inquiring at frequent intervals if everything was okay for Frank Henry, he sat back and yawned. "This girl is a real big city girl," Udell said, as if now were the appointed time for conversation. "She's never even seen a lamb before, can you imagine? She wanted to get out and touch one."

"Did she touch one?"

"No, I didn't have time to stop. But I guess I could have stopped. As it turns out," she added darkly.

"I think I'll lie down," Frank Henry said.

"We'll do the dishes, while you're resting."

"Quietly, I hope," Frank Henry said as he went out.

"Frank Henry is a maniac about peace and quiet. If there's the slightest sound, he can't sleep. And once he's up, he's up for the rest of the night. Me, I could sleep through an earthquake."

"Are there earthquakes around here?"

"Sure, all over the state. But you're not going to start worrying about that now, are you? You're really a worrier, aren't you?"

"Well —"

Udell lapsed into silence as she washed the dishes, without soap. "Don't bother drying, air drying is better. It's cleaner."

"Can we go to the hotel now, to make sure I have a room?"

"Stop worrying, I'll get you there. Let's go wake up Frank Henry from his beauty sleep."

In the living room Udell leaned over Frank Henry, who was lying on the couch, covered with an afghan in orange and purple and green and red. "Time to go out on the town," she sang out cheerily.

He opened one eye. "I don't want to go out. I'm tired."

"Can you beat it?" Udell turned to me. "He's tired. From fishing." She leaned over Frank Henry again. "I didn't come home to sit around while you sleep. What am I supposed to do? Listen to the radio? Saturday night is my night for excitement. I spend all week at the camp, busting my ass while I work on the accounts and —"

"You don't have to stay there."

"I stay there because I choose to stay there and I get away from there when I choose to get away from there and I can get away from here when I choose to get away from here. Come on, Frank Henry," she said coyly. "Everybody needs a change, everybody needs to get out of the old daily routine —"

"I've had enough excitement to last me for a lifetime," said Frank Henry and closed his eye.

"Okay, Mr. Filled-Up-With-Excitement, if that's the way you feel —" She yanked open the front door. "Come on, let's go," she summoned me.

"What about the fish?" I asked.

"Let him take care of the goddam fish," she said and slammed out.

Frank Henry pulled the afghan up over his head. He looked like a camouflaged mound. I was going to say something to him, but then I decided not to.

"What's Frank Henry doing now?" Udell asked as I climbed into the front seat.

"He's got the afghan over his head. Does that mean he's depressed or something?"

"Why should he be depressed? He's doing what he wants to do. And we're going to do what we want to do. Right?"

The Fresno Hotel was six stories high with a blinking electric sign on the roof. A canopy over the entrance repeated the name in movie marquee letters. To the left of the entrance was a door with a sign, COFFEESHOP, and to the right another door with a sign, TAVERN. The desk in the lobby was unattended. Udell banged a little metal bell on the counter. Waiting for someone to come, I read the announcement behind the desk: *The Fresno Hotel is absolutely fireproof. George R. Edwards, owner, and Edwin C. White, owner.* An elderly clerk with a green nightshade appeared and I registered. "You take your things on up," Udell said. "I'll wait here."

Room 604 was a narrow dark room almost completely filled by a single bed and a large dark wardrobe. The window looked out onto a court. In one of the rooms opposite people — mostly men — were moving back and forth in front of the window. I looked up and saw the sign FRESNO HOTEL, blinking on and off, and I pulled the shade down.

When I got back down to the lobby, Udell wasn't anywhere in sight. Maybe, I thought, she went to the bathroom. I waited a while but she still didn't appear. I went into the coffee shop. No Udell. I went into the tavern. There she was sitting at the bar, a drink in front of her, deep in conversation with a man to her right.

"Oh, there you are, kid. What took you so long? Sit right here." She patted the stool to her left. "Would you like to meet a Lion? They're having a convention right at the hotel, and this fellow is one of the chief Lions. What'll you have? Whiskey sour? Bring the young lady a whiskey sour," she said to the barman. "Of course she's over twenty-one, can't you tell? Show him your ID, kid. How's your room?"

"It's okay. A little small. In fact, it's very small. And it's got this enormous wardrobe in it —" I made a sweeping gesture to the left with my hand, and before I could catch it I had knocked over a drink, not my drink, the drink of the person next to me. The liquid spilled onto the bar and began to leak over the edge.

"Sloppy, sloppy," Udell called out.

I vainly tried to wipe up the liquid with a cocktail napkin.

"Here, bring us a rag," Udell said to the bartender.

"Bring me another Scotch," said the man next to me, as the bartender wiped up the spill.

"I'll be glad to pay for it," I said.

"No need."

Embarrassed by my awkwardness — yes, I was getting sloppier all the time, moving without thinking, doing just what my parents always warned me against — I put my purse down and put both hands around my drink. I heard Udell say to the Lion, "Do you have a hobby?"

In the mirror above the bar I saw the man next to me finish his drink and set it down. He was wearing a suit jacket of a shiny blue material and a khaki (army?) shirt. I stole a glance at him from the side. He was wearing khaki (army?) pants. He had brown hair and a rather sharp nose. I felt I ought to say something but I didn't know what to say. I thought of asking him if he had a hobby but he didn't look like a man who had a hobby.

"I'm sorry about the drink," I said.

"No need to be sorry. It happens all the time, in millions of bars, all over the world." He smiled.

Emboldened, I asked, "Are you a Lion?"

"A what?"

"A Lion. They're having a convention here."

"No, I'm not a Lion."

What are you? I wanted to ask. But how can you ask anybody that? Instead I said, "I don't know anything about Lions, do you?"

"Not much."

"Except that they meet."

"You from around here? You live here?" he asked.

"That Lion is a dope," Udell whispered loudly in my ear. "Come on, let's get out of here."

I picked up my purse and got off the stool. I turned back to the man.

"Goodbye. Sorry about your drink. It was very nice talking to you."

"Do you have to go now? We were just getting acquainted."

"Yes. When you gotta go, you gotta go," Udell said grimly.

"I've been thinking about Frank Henry," Udell said as we walked into the lobby. "I've been thinking of him lying there. I feel terrible that I went off and left him."

"Do you want to go home?"

"I don't know what to do. I can't decide. I told him I was going out and I don't like to go back on my word. It's not a good thing if you don't stand up for what you say. Otherwise you end up being a patsy, and one thing I don't want to be is a patsy. Still —" She shrugged. "Still I have such a sweet need of that man. I don't know . . ."

"You could call him."

"That's a good idea. Let's go on up to your room and I'll call him from there, where it's private."

In room 604 Udell sat at the head of the bed and picked up the receiver. Since there wasn't a chair in the room, I sat at the foot of the bed, turned away from her. I tried not to listen.

"I was just thinking, Frank Henry —" Udell said. I tried to concentrate on the outlines of the monstrous wardrobe. It was dark brown, almost black, it looked to be about ten feet tall, looming there. When you looked up at its top, you saw two round humps, decorations with curlicues and spirals. I heard Udell giggle and say, "Of course I do, you know what I mean —"

At that moment there was a knock on the door. Udell motioned to me to answer. "Of course I want to —"

I went to the door and opened it. Standing there was the man half in and half out of uniform. He was carrying a glass.

"How about having a drink with me?" he asked.

I was so taken aback by the sight of him with the glass in his hand (the reminder of my moving without thinking) that I felt my old terrible awkwardness making havoc with my throat and my tongue. Words spilled out. "Well, actually, I was just about to go to bed — I mean I was just about to retire. I mean, I know it's still early, but my friend and I drove down from the desert after working all day and we — I mean, thank you very much but —"

"Just one drink. What's the harm in that? It'll help you to fall asleep. Besides, tomorrow's Sunday, you can sleep late. Come on," he pleaded. "It will only take a few minutes. I just got my discharge and I —"

I felt something jerk on me and pull me back into the room. It was Udell, who in the same motion shut the door in the man's face. "What's the matter with you, girl? You just say no and shut the goddam door. Don't you know how to say no? You didn't ask him up, did you?"

"Of course not. I don't even know how he got my room number."

"He slipped the clerk two bucks, that's how. Boy, you sure are some innocent. Is it safe to leave you alone?" She picked up her purse. "Frank Henry and me had a good talk. He actually asked me to come home, he even said he was missing me. I should have been more understanding. After all, he had enough excitement during the war, no wonder he —"

"Was Frank Henry in the service?"

"Sure, he was. What do you think he was, a draft dodger?"

"Not everybody who wasn't in the service was a draft dodger. There were people in essential positions, essential to the war effort —"

"Yeah, I know. 4-F."

"Not just —"

"Well, kid," Udell said briskly, "I am on my way. You look as if you could use a rest anyhow. Maybe the big city's too much for you." She grinned and went to the door. Her hand on the knob, she turned. "There's something I feel I ought to say to you. I've noticed something about you. You know what you do? You let people ride all over you."

"No I don't."

"Then why didn't you shut the door in that guy's face?"

"It seemed —"

"What?"

"It seemed impolite."

"Impolite?" Udell scoffed. "What was he being, coming up when he wasn't asked, not going away when you said no? That's politeness?"

"That wasn't exactly what I meant."

"It's exactly Number One that you ought to be paying attention to, otherwise guys like that will wipe up the floor with you." She opened the door and looked out. "The creep's gone, thank goodness. You know what the trouble with you is. You're all over the place. One moment you're going this way, the next moment you're going that way, the next thing you can't move at all. You can't make up your mind about anything, that's the trouble. Oh, you've got a good brain, I've no doubt about that. But you don't use it. Now me, I don't have that good a brain — oh no, that's the truth, I don't pretend to be what I'm not — but I make up for it by using what I have. Like the turtle, I get where I'm going, even though I get there slowly. I look at what's ahead of me in the road. I don't waste my energy wondering about the big picture. Let the world take care of itself. You can't do anything about the world anyway. So keep your eye on your goal. It's the same way with men. If it's somebody that I'm not interested in, I don't give them the time of day. But if it's somebody I like — I mean, they couldn't get rid of me if they tried. You've got to decide what you want, kid. That's what life is really about — deciding. There's always somebody doing the choosing. I figure it'd better be me than someone else."

"But —"

But Udell was already out the door.

*

Downstairs, in the tavern, the bar was crowded almost to bursting with Lions. I made my way to a small round table in the corner. Sitting there alone, I thought of the camp. I hadn't really been ready to leave it. Why had I been so stupid, hasty, judging? So Shorty had asked me to go with him on a moonlight ride. Was that so terrible? I could have just said no — or maybe even gone.

"Well. So you're here, after all." It was the man half in and half out of uniform. He raised his glass to me. "Welcome." He pointed to the chair opposite me. "Do you mind?"

"Where's the Dragon Lady?" he asked as he sat down.

"She left. She went home."

"She your sister or something?"

"No. She's a friend. We work in the same place."

"What's that?"

"In the valley. In an oil field."

"Not many women there, I'll bet," he said admiringly.

"A few."

"What do you do there?"

"I measure things . . . and plot them."

"Oh," he said.

A waitress appeared. "Scotch on the rocks," he said. "And you?"

"The same," I said, though I had never liked Scotch before. But I was going to get what I hadn't gotten. I was going to ask what I wanted to, needed to ask. But not yet. I couldn't ask him here. All around us the Lions were laughing and drinking. I was drinking my Scotch. Would I learn to like it?

He was talking about a trip he was planning to take to the mountains. He was going to go fishing and hunting, things I didn't know anything about. In fact, I always hated the thought of killing an animal for no reason. Looking at him intently, I saw that his eyes were blue and that they were delicately fringed with long lashes.

"I don't know your name. What's your name?"

I gave him my name. I thought, what will happen next? Will I ask him up to my room? No, not to that room. We could go out. We could go to his place.

He was looking down at his drink now. He was smiling. When he finished his drink, he said, "Let's go."

When we walked out together, I looked surreptitiously to the side. For some reason I thought, Perhaps he is limping. But he was not limping. We got into his car. It was a Studebaker, an old Studebaker, the upholstery all torn, two side windows covered over with cloth where there was no glass. We drove through the quiet streets, with houses with lights on in them. He too was a silent driver. He pulled me over to him, closer. I felt his knee against my knee. I felt the thickness, the lubricity of desire multiplying.

We came to a dark place where there were no houses. He pulled off onto a side road. He came to a stop in a place that looked like a field. He turned the headlights off. He sat there, not saying anything, not moving, just sitting there, though now his hand was on my knee. Maybe right then I was thinking of that guy on the bus, the one who had touched my leg, without my choosing. Yes, it was all about choosing, as Udell had said.

"Let's just sit here and talk for a minute." I heard the hesitancy in his voice. After all, he was shy. That made me feel surer. I had noticed this often about myself before. If the other person was very sure, I was unsure. But if they were unsure, I somehow grew bolder.

"Where were you in the war?" I asked.

He was silent for a moment. I prepared myself to listen. I thought about what I'd read and what I'd seen in the movies, about men having to walk for days in mud in the jungle, about how they had to keep looking and looking for anything that moved around them or overhead, how they had to throw themselves into ditches to save themselves, how some were caught and some escaped and some were left behind . . .

"I was on Attu — in the Aleutians."

He stopped. "A cold place," I said.

"A very cold place. Twenty, thirty, forty degrees below zero most of the time. In summer it warms up. Then it's almost up to freezing. Some summer." He laughed nervously.

I waited. "But inside it wasn't like that, was it?"

"No. Inside, in the huts, it was warm enough. But there was nothing going on. There was nothing to do. We just waited and waited. It drove me nuts. I applied for a transfer to the infantry. I didn't care, anything to be out of there. But it didn't come and it didn't come and then finally when it did come and I was shipped to Fort Benning, the war was over. I don't usually talk about it," he added.

"But I asked you."

"Yes, you asked."

Yes, I had asked him, but what he had said was not what I had wanted to know. I had wanted to hear about the fighting, about what it meant to risk death and injury, to be on that edge, to believe that at any minute you could die. I had wanted to know what it meant to have to kill someone, to be ordered to kill someone. But he hadn't told me that. He didn't know that.

"All that snow and ice got to me. It got to my eyes, inside my eyes. Everything looked and felt white. It scared me. I thought it was never going to change, that I was always going to be in that white, my whole life. I still think about it sometimes. Then I'm inside that white all over again."

The way he said it, the edge of panic in his voice — it was the kind of talk that makes you wobble, that makes you feel there's nothing firm anywhere, that makes you distrust the one talking, that makes you fearful about your own judgment, that makes you feel you have to say something to save the situation, him, yourself, even if that saying comes out of your own hide, or wherever it's been hidden.

"Once at the camp, the first night I was there . . ." I told him about looking out into the empty dark and thinking of cold, uninhabited places. I told him how then I'd gone in to play pool with the men, and how then everything was okay.

"Where you from?" he asked.

"Philadelphia."

"Born there?"

"Yes."

"Any sisters?"

"One."

"Any brothers?"

"No."

"Do you — do you believe in God?"

"That's a very personal question. It's not the kind of question you can ask someone and expect them to be able to answer just like that."

"Sorry," he mumbled. He took his hand from my knee.

"Where are we?" I asked desperately.

"We're in a field. If it was light you could see that there's a lake in front of us. Not a lake exactly. It used to be a lake when I was a kid, but now it's mostly dried up and it's more like a pond."

There I was, in a ridiculous car with shreds hanging, looking out over a pond that I couldn't even see, with a man half in and half out of uniform. Something fluid began to rise in me. Was it rage? It came up and up, starting down in me where I never even knew down was, forcing out the embedded, driving up the viscous, till I was flung — no — I threw myself down, precisely, into grief.

HARRIET DOERR

Another Short Day in La Luz

FROM THE NEW YORKER

URSULA BOWLES, with more than half the distance to La Luz left
to travel, recognized a quick stab of pain below her diaphragm,
and turned to contemplate the landscape rolling away behind her
on the right. At the same moment Patricio Gómez, her seven-
teen-year-old driver, as if to confirm that a state of peril existed,
said, "There is a deviation ahead."

Ursula turned to see a barrier, lettered DESVIACIÓN, directly
in front of them. A flagman waved them to the right, where a
rough path, barely wide enough to accommodate a farmer's cart,
had been chopped through cactus and nettles. Its dust-filled ruts
curved out of sight.

"How long is this detour?" Ursula asked, and found that it continued as far as the town of El Refugio. The flagman and Patricio, standing at the road's edge for a better view, waved in the
direction of the southern half of Mexico. Now a pickup truck and
the local bus passed them, entered the detour, and disappeared
in two separate hurricanes of dust.

Patricio, understanding her hesitation, which would never have
been his, leaned into the car and said, "Señora, I know a short-
cut."

When another bus passed them, Ursula said, "Yes, let us go
that way." She imagined a smooth country lane, winding beside
meadows and an occasional peach orchard.

They drove diagonally across an uncultivated field, and Patricio remarked, "Besides, we must consider the car." He looked at
Ursula gravely. "A borrowed American Ford station wagon, only
two years old, with its original paint and tires. Damage might have

occurred on the *desviación* from stones like knives and thorns like spikes."

"Perhaps I should not have sold my car," Ursula said, clinging to the door as they descended into an arroyo. "In that case I would not have to borrow. Perhaps I should have driven to Mexico in my own car on some of those roads I used to know." Then, in less time than it took five goats to cross the dirt track in front of her, she installed herself at the wheel of cars in other places. First she drove skillfully around the blind curves and into the gullies of the Mexican mining town where she was born and raised. After that, without a second's pause, she was splitting the flat red earth of a road in New Mexico, speeding down a mile-long, perfectly straight line, with her husband sitting, perfectly, beside her.

Now the last goat crossed, and the widow Bowles was in Mexico again, here by choice in back country on an unmapped road.

"Where are we?" she asked her driver.

"Do not preoccupy yourself, Señora," Patricio said. "I know this region well." He turned to stare at Ursula, and allowed his glance to rest on her profile. So white-haired, so frail, so slow to decide — was it possible she had steered, accelerated, and applied her brakes on the hazardous thoroughfares of Mexico, fording its *barrancas*, toiling up its mountain grades? Patricio asked Ursula the question she had more than once asked him. "Do you have a driver's license?"

She found the card in her purse and held it out to him, and even as he drove he examined her picture, her name, and her age. He nodded. "So you are permitted to drive." In this same tone, he had commented to his sister Altagracia, when woman's suffrage was made law, "So now you can run for governor."

Ursula glanced at the card. "For two more years," she said, and added, "Someday I'll borrow a car and drive up and down the old roads." And she might have remembered a few of them now, but a sign on the outskirts of a cluster of houses distracted her. "La Soledad," she told Patricio, as if he had no eyes. And ten minutes later she announced, "Los Dolores."

They were traveling along two ruts now, with their right wheels higher than their left, and from her vantage point Ursula discovered herself at eye level with cattle and horses, which looked up from cropping weeds to watch her pass. She put on her distance glasses, and made out a church dome and a silo directly ahead and, when they had almost reached the sign, informed Patricio that this was Las Lágrimas. "These names," she said. "All titles of the Virgin, I suppose."

Patricio said nothing. He had never heard of a Virgin of Tears and doubted that there was one. In any case, he saw no point in discussing religion with a woman nobody had ever seen at Mass.

Ursula believed that the three names had appeared in natural sequence, and repeated them to herself. Solitude, sorrow, and tears.

It was in the town of Tears that Patricio turned left at the cobbled plaza and, as if drawn by a magnet, bounced over potholes and gullies until they arrived at El Refugio and the paved road to La Luz.

Patricio looked back. "The *desviación* is well behind us," he said.

Miles and miles, Ursula silently agreed. But she had enjoyed the detour through the fields, had like lowering her window to touch corn silk, to smell turned earth.

Even before the church and radio towers of La Luz came into view, Patricio asked the widow, "What must be done in the city today?"

Ursula found her list. On it were a number of items — telegraph office, oculist, and pharmacy — which she did not mention to Patricio at this time. She merely said, "The bank, the nursery for plants, and, of course, the market. I will have lunch at the *posada*, while you have a free hour." She believed there was no need for detail. Days in La Luz were all alike, passed in the dim interiors of shops and offices or under noon sun on the crowded, broken sidewalks, in heavy air that smelled of food and flowers.

At the bank, Patricio, who was tall and narrow, stood next to Ursula at a counter marked CAMBIOS and waved her check over the heads of people who had already waited in shifting disorder for more than half an hour.

"We should be given numbers and form a line," Ursula said, but Patricio, extending a long arm and hissing, "Psst, psst," at the cashier, was soon able to hand Ursula her pesos out of turn.

"Dispénseme," Ursula said to the pushing crowd, as Patricio knifed his way through. "I am sorry. Thank you."

A number of people turned their heads to stare. She is old, she is confused, they thought. What does she mean? Why be sorry?

*

"I must send a telegram," Ursula told Patricio, as if the idea had just occurred to her, and a moment later he found a place to park near the office, in the shade.

At Telégrafos Nacionales the dispatcher handed Ursula a form. "You are sending an international message," he said, but his client shook her head.

"The Federal District," she said, and produced from her purse a folded sheet of paper covered with her daughter's dark, emotional script. Frances, hoping to insure privacy, had written her message in English. Without looking at the phrases her daughter had chosen to lure her lover to her bed again, Ursula handed this paper across the counter to the operator, who unfolded it and said, "This message will transmit more accurately in Spanish." He pushed the paper, together with a pencil and a yellow form, back to Ursula. She heard Fran's words of a few hours ago. "Please send it as soon as you can. It must be delivered today. He is about to leave Mexico City." Ursula hesitated, looking into the uninterested eyes of the dispatcher. "I would prefer not to read this," she wanted to say. "It is a message I myself would not send." But she knew such an argument would be useless. Why do mothers do these things for their children, especially their grown children, she asked herself, and took up the pencil and started to print.

"Francisco Alvarado Torres," she wrote, putting down Paco's full name, and under that the address of his apartment on the Avenida Victor Hugo in the capital. Even before she reached her daughter's headlong declarations of love and of her willingness to hide and lie indefinitely, Ursula crowded Paco's rooms with various women she imagined. Husky-voiced, wide-mouthed, honey-skinned, they left an echo of perfume in the hall, of a whisper behind bedroom doors. And now in the telegraph office, with a solitary fly circling her head, Ursula placed in Paco's bed her daughter Fran's latest rival — still in her teens no doubt, product of a convent school, long-lashed, innocent, a virgin until last night.

Frances Bowles, according to her mother's reluctant translation, went on to propose a rendezvous. Wherever you like, whenever you say, she begged. "Please," Fran had written, and *"Querido,"* in Spanish, as her mother was writing it now.

Pride has abdicated, Ursula perceived, and this raging passion has spilled over into its place. She stopped writing for a moment to ask herself, How was I with Phil? Immediately, an image of her husband, dead three years, took shape at her side — his profile, complete with broken nose; the top of his head tan where his hair had thinned. She found herself turning to meet his unshakable blue glance, to reach for his quiet hands, to remember their touch.

What would I do to get him back? she silently inquired of the dispatcher, and, as clearly as she could, went on printing her daughter's words in Spanish. "Please," she translated for the second time.

Patricio entered the office from behind her just too late to read the message over her shoulder.

"Now where, Señora?" he said. "I am illegally parked."

"To the oculist," she said.

Outside the doctor's door a moment later, Ursula had further instructions. "While I'm here, please select a bougainvillea at the nursery. For the señora who has lent us the car."

Halfway back to the car, Patricio, without taking time to turn, lifted an arm in acknowledgment.

The doctor's office, which occupied the two front rooms of his house, was cool and high-ceilinged. The waiting room had chairs for twelve patients, but all were empty when Ursula entered. Behind a desk at one side sat an utterly beautiful young woman, wearing thick horn-rimmed glasses on her sculptured nose and great golden loops swinging from her ears. On the floor at her side a boy of three or four, identical in profile and wearing heavy glasses of his own, played with the boxcars of a wooden train. The woman and child looked up as Ursula entered, and examined her with their myopic spice-brown eyes.

"I have an appointment with the doctor," Ursula told the receptionist, whose name, according to a lettered sign on her desk, was Griselda. But before there was time for a response, the telephone rang and a conversation followed.

Griselda looked up. "Forgive me," she said. "Your appointment is canceled. There has been a death in the doctor's family," and at this, as though a floodgate had burst open, the calls began to come incessantly. Occasionally Griselda had time for a few words of explanation. "The doctor's mother," she would say, or "Eighty-six years old," or "After High Mass, the interment. Gallegos Brothers in charge."

Listening to the receptionist, Ursula reminded herself to talk to her daughter again. Though how could Frances have forgotten? On matters such as this, mother and child were in accord. No services or ceremonies — simple cremation, with the small sealed box that resulted carried across the border to the Southwestern hillside where, three years ago, living in New Mexico, she had taken Phil's. Nothing could have seemed more plain and ordinary at the time she had planned it, but today in La Luz, with church bells tolling the hour of one, a priest and four nuns visible through the doctor's window, and Griselda's repeated references to a cortège and the *panteón,* apprehension began to gnaw at Ursula. Would there be obstacles in a Catholic country? I must tell Frances again exactly what I want, she told herself, even if she is frantic about Paco. I must write it down and sign it.

While Griselda gravely informed callers of funeral details, Ursula, followed by the child, left her chair to study a group of framed pictures on the wall opposite the desk. She was surprised to find they were all of the same subject — a happy woman's round, cheerful face. But each portrait in the series of identical poses was flawed. One was entirely obscured by mist, one streaked by random clouds. An opaque black center half filled another. A wide circle of black hid most of the fourth.

"What do these pictures mean?" Ursula asked Griselda, who at last had found a moment to open her appointment book.

"They show how people see who have diseases of the eye," and Griselda went on to name some of them. "Astigmatism, cataracts, detached retina." She seemed to chant. "Glaucoma, macular degeneration."

Ursula stood before the pictures, hypnotized. Silently the child separated the boxcars, one by one, from his train.

At this moment Patricio burst in, leaving the door open to street dust and sunlight. *"Qué tal?"* he said to the bespectacled child, and *"Vámonos"* to Ursula, who, taking an appointment card from Griselda, hurried after him into the midday crowd.

"Are you losing your sight?" Patricio asked as soon as he and his passenger were in the car.

"Oh, I think not," Ursula said, and then, "What is that smell?" Twisting in her seat, she saw that the entire space at the rear of the station wagon was wound about with a tangle of flowers and vines.

"Besides the bougainvillea, there are three honeysuckles," Patricio said, and he, too, looked back. "They are gifts from the proprietor of the nursery, because you and the other North American señoras buy so much from him."

The combined fragrances of the nurseryman's gifts were almost suffocating. Ursula lowered her window. "Where to now?" asked Patricio, and after a small pause she said, "The pharmacy."

Patricio offered his help. "I can make this purchase for you, while you rest in the patio of the hotel." Ursula shook her head. "I prefer to do it myself," she said.

From the driver's seat, Patricio observed the passenger beside him. So rich and old and weak, he remarked to himself, and so obstinate.

Before entering the pharmacy, Ursula handed him a shopping list and a quantity of money. "This should cover everything," she told him. "What you buy at the market, and your own lunch as well." Then, as though noticing his habitual leanness for the first time, she asked where he ate in La Luz.

Patricio said, "At Un Taco Más," though in actuality he intended to take his midday meal at the house of his mother's cousin and save this money for an emergency.

"Let us meet at the *posada* at three," Ursula said, and watched him turn the corner in the flower-scented car.

The Farmacia Buena Salud was situated next to a music store. Even inside the pharmacy, strains of music could sometimes be heard when a patron of one shop and a patron of the other opened the street doors simultaneously.

Ursula, stepping from the shadeless glare of the sidewalk into the shadowed room, thought at first that she was the pharmacy's only customer. Then she saw the proprietor at the far end of the counter, attending to a bent old woman who was wearing two shawls, two skirts, and no shoes. In his hand was a glass of water and a bottle. His ancient client held up a bony forefinger, and the pharmacist shook out a single pill. Ursula watched the old woman extract coins from a knot in her *rebozo,* lay them on the counter, pick up the pill and the glass, and swallow.

The pharmacist, a man with a brooding air of disillusion, now approached Ursula. "Can I help you, Señora?"

In order to conceal the true purpose of her presence here, she began with ordinary purchases. "Adhesive tape," she said. "Hand lotion, a toothbrush."

The pharmacist collected these things and placed them on the counter. "What more?" he said.

Ursula, looking first at a display of cough syrup, then at an apothecary jar filled with a purple liquid, eventually said, "Something for pain."

"Do you have a doctor's prescription?" he asked, and she shook her head.

Through his somber eyes, the pharmacist examined her face. "Where is the pain?"

Ursula waved vaguely at the area between her shoulders and her hips. "What I need is something stronger than aspirin," she said.

The pharmacist allowed his gaze to rest on the apothecary jar. "Consider this, Señora," he said. "I cannot diagnose the cause of pain. I can only sell the medicine to alleviate it."

"That is all I ask of you," she said.

The pharmacist then disappeared into his dispensary, and came back with white capsules.

"No more than two a day," he instructed her. "And here are the cards of some excellent local doctors."

At this mention of local doctors, an image of the recently installed government intern at Amapolas sprang into Ursula's mind. She saw his young face, his troubled eyes. "Señora, are you losing weight?" the intern asked.

At the moment when Ursula pushed open the pharmacy door, two customers entered the music shop. From the sidewalk she heard a mariachi band playing "Ojos Tapatíos." "How I love that song," she said out loud in English, and a passer-by turned to stare.

The Posada del Sol was only five blocks from the pharmacy, and Ursula was halfway there when she noticed a sign on her left. GALLEGOS HERMANOS, FUNERALES," she read in gold-and-black

letters on the glass front door. Seeing this as a lucky encounter,
Ursula crossed the street. She found the three Gallegos brothers
standing together just inside the door.

They bowed, shook her hand, and asked her to come back at
four. "It is past the hour for lunch," they told her, and pointed
to a clock with golden hands and a golden pendulum as witness.

"I have only one simple question," Ursula said, and held up
her right hand as though to detain them. She merely wished to
know if their services included cremation, but the necessary words
were not in her vocabulary, and in the end she simply said "fire"
and "burn" and, a moment later, "ashes."

The Gallegos brothers, black-suited and bald, were shocked into
silence by this stripping away of euphemism. This old woman, so
close to death and to purgatory, the eyes of each said to the eyes
of the others. So willing to disappear into eternity and leave no
trace behind, their eyes agreed.

"You are disturbed, Señora," said one Gallegos.

"Let us talk later," said another.

"Yes, after lunch — at four o'clock," said the third.

They bowed, escorted her to the door, and called out after her,
"Until then."

Seated in the dining room of the *posada* at a small table in the
rear, Ursula reached into her deep straw bag for the pharmacist's pills. This was the time to take one, for she was alone, had
just now suffered sudden pain, and had a glass of water at hand.
But all at once a man was at her side, saying, "Señora, will you
join me?" and here was Enrique Ortiz de León. Ursula, wearing
her reading glasses for the menu, stared up at him half blindly,
then removed them and noticed how handsome the heir to the
hacienda at Amapolas still was. Straight brows, straight nose,
straight neck — he reminded her of something, perhaps an eagle.

If only Frances were attracted to a stable man like this one, she
found herself thinking, and then, imagining the two together,
Have I gone mad?

Three minutes later she was at his table. Don Enrique, without
wasting time, ordered seviche, tortilla soup, and rice with chicken
for them both. "And *vino blanco*," he told Violeta, the new waitress, long and slender as a sugar-cane stalk.

Ursula protested, "Oh, no, I can't eat so much," but Don Enrique, choosing not to hear, merely passed her the hard rolls. *"Salud,"* they said to each other when the wine came, and they touched glasses.

"Have you accomplished all you wished to do in La Luz?" he asked.

Ursula, thinking of the oculist, the pharmacy, and the Gallegos brothers, shook her head. Only the cashing of the check, the purchase of the bougainvillea, and the sending of the telegram were done. As for the three other matters, much remained unresolved.

"The oculist had been called away," she told him.

Immediately Don Enrique, like Patricio, said, "Are you losing your sight?" and again she answered, "Oh, I think not."

"My mother was blind for a year before she died," Don Enrique said. "Her hearing became so acute that she could identify visitors by their footsteps alone, long before they spoke."

The widow knew she would try this. One day, she would close her eyes and, using the correct name, say "Good morning" to her daughter, to Altagracia and Patricio, the priest, the doctor, the mayor.

Don Enrique ate slowly, and slowly drank three glasses of wine. He spoke of the weather and the economy.

A shadow fell across the table, and Ursula, looking up through the window, observed a gathering of clouds. Certain she could eat no more, she laid down her fork. "You have always lived in this town," she said to her companion.

"No, no," he said. "As a child I traveled abroad with my parents."

"Where did you go?" Ursula asked, and at this, to her astonishment, a torrent of recollection poured from Don Enrique.

"To the Eiffel Tower," he said. "The Tower of London, the Alhambra, Napoleon's tomb." Don Enrique went on. "And the restaurants." He named a few, and Ursula began to recognize, in his voice and in his eyes, the banked embers of nostalgia. At the same moment, as though a contagion had spread in the dining room of the Posada del Sol, the widow fell into her own fever of recall.

"Did you ever eat at the Ferme Saint-Jacques, in the south of France?" she asked him, but he shook his head and went on to remember the Leaning Tower and the Roman Forum. With attentive eyes on her host's face, Ursula Bowles withdrew to a hill above the Mediterranean, where she sat at a table with her husband, Philip, at the outer edge of a flagstone court. On one side of them more diners sat at tables; on the other an abrupt slope, terraced with grapevines and olive trees, dropped straight down to the sea.

Half listening to Don Enrique and wearing a fixed smile, Ursula fished the depths of her memory to discover the exact blue of the sea that day, the precise blue of the sky. How was it then, she asked herself. How was that day in France?

Peering through her memory's eye, she believed she saw short-stemmed field flowers crowded into a shallow bowl on the table. She recalled earthenware plates and copper pans. What were the Gallic miracles they ate? What was the ambrosia that they drank? But clearer than the food, clearer than the wine, what Ursula recovered at this instant, four thousand miles from France, was the accurate image of their waiter on that sapphire day at the Ferme Saint-Jacques. So sharp were the outlines of this hallucination that he might as well have stood beside her here, in this other dining room.

The French waiter was wiry, lithe, and fierce. His eyes blazed a passionate black. He wore a pirate's sweeping black mustache. Ursula watched him bound up and down the steps to the kitchen. She thought she remembered the course he brought — the pâté, the soup, the fish, the young lamb, the wines. "All this is from the *ferme*," the waiter told them. "The wine, too." And the young Ursula and the young Philip nodded, trying to believe. Now the sun sank away from its zenith, the day declined, and the Bowleses asked for their bill.

"We can eat no more," they told their waiter.

"There is still dessert," he said, and he sternly recited the choices.

"We cannot. It is impossible. *L'addition, s'il vous plaît.*"

At this, heads of thrifty French at nearby tables turned to stare, for there was a fixed price.

"One moment," the waiter said.

"He has gone for his cutlass," Ursula told Philip.

But he returned quietly with two plates and five platters. *"Les cinq desserts obligatoires,"* he said, and he placed a spoonful of each on the plates.

From a provincial town in Mexico, the widow Bowles, bending

her glance around the curve of the earth and finding the south of France, conjured up the waiter's quick black eyes, his wide smile white with teeth.

Don Enrique interrupted. "You are smiling," he said. "You, too, have traveled to Copenhagen," and she nodded, though it was a city she had never visited.

"We will both have *flan*," Don Enrique told Violeta, who for half an hour had hovered patiently nearby.

The widow rose from her chair. "Oh, not for me," she said. "Thank you. You have been so kind. But I believe Patricio is here," and as if to prove her truthful, her driver entered the hotel at this instant and could be seen standing restless in the lobby.

"You are late, Señora," he said as they walked to the car. "The lettuce and spinach are wilting and the strawberries beginning to rot." He opened the door on the right.

But halfway there Ursula stopped. "I will drive," she said. Patricio handed her the keys.

And so they traveled the road back to Amapolas. As she drove, Ursula was aware of an unexplained delight trembling in her bones. She made no attempt to analyze this sensation, but for an hour or two it turned her young. She sped down the highway to each arroyo and up the grade to the next rise. The tangle of flowering vines, their fragrance subsiding, occupied the rear of the car; three market baskets, heavy with fruit and vegetables, filled the back seat. Looking straight ahead, Patricio sat somberly beside her as she passed trucks and slowed for burros. Ursula understood his mood. For the time being, his only wish was not to be seen as a passenger in a car she was driving.

They left the highway twice, once to buy gas and once for a detour. At the gas station, a boy of six removed his shoes, climbed onto the hood, and polished her windshield with his shirt-sleeve and a wet newspaper. Patricio watched her hand the child coins.

"Señora, you tip too much," he said, and, a few moments later, "Another *desviación*."

The detour they had to take, unlike this morning's, was short. They traveled through its dust for only a few miles. When they were at midpoint, Patricio said, "On the right is my great-uncle's

farm." And he went on to give Ursula further family information. "When my great-uncle knew he had cancer and could not
wait to die of it, he hanged himself in the *bodega*." Patricio pointed
to the storeroom, a square adobe structure behind the longer,
low adobe house. "In there," he said. "By a rope from a rafter.
One of his grandchildren found him. Carlos, seven years old."
Patricio's eyes were on the widow.

She said, "What a terrible thing."

Patricio had more. "Now Carlos has lost his speech." And Ursula said, "Poor child."

"Two weeks have passed since the suicide," Patricio went on,
"and still not a word from Carlos."

But the widow Bowles did not rage against fate, as he had expected. Instead, she accepted this tragedy. She might have been
Mexican herself.

Ursula understood that Patricio was punishing her, and once
back on the paved road, she changed places with him. So she was
not driving when the pain, now grown familiar, struck again. Later
on, she would take the first pill.

By the time they reached the house on the edge of the mesa at
Amapolas, dusk was coming on. Patricio carried in her basket and
one honeysuckle, and drove away to deliver the rest.

But before leaving he commented on the trip. "Another
short day in La Luz," he said. "Only a few hours, and so much
done."

As soon as he left, Ursula went to her terrace to watch the day
end. She saw that a sunset had begun to streak the western sky
with color, and turned to look for its reflection, like an echo, on
the opposite horizon. Only when she moved a chair to face the
eastern hills did she realize how tired she was, and at the same
time how oddly filled with joy.

Today had stopped happening. Already it had consigned its
events to memory. Untouched by the evening chill, she sat outside until dark, wrapped in the mists of her brief, uncertain future and the brilliant patchwork of her never-ending past.

DEBORAH EISENBERG

The Custodian

FROM THE NEW YORKER

FOR YEARS after Isobel left town (was sent from town, to live with an aunt in San Francisco) Lynnie would sometimes see her at a distance, crossing a street or turning a corner. But just as Lynnie started after her Isobel would vanish, having been replaced by a substitute, some long-legged stranger with pale, floaty hair. And while Lynnie might have been just as happy, by and large, not to see Isobel, at those moments she was felled by a terrible sorrow, as though somewhere a messenger searching for her had been waylaid, or was lost.

It was sixteen years after Lynnie had watched Isobel disappearing from view in the back seat of her father's car when Lynnie really did see her again. And then, although Isobel walked right into Lynnie's shop, several long, chaotic moments elapsed before Lynnie understood who Isobel was. "Isobel," she said, and, as the well-dressed customer browsing meditatively among the shelves and cases of expensive food turned to look full at Lynnie, the face that Lynnie had known so well — a girl's face that drew everything toward it and returned nothing — came forward in the woman's.

"Oh," Isobel said. "It's you. But Mother wrote me you were living in Boston. Or did I make that up?"

"You didn't make it up," Lynnie said.

"Well, then," Isobel said, and hesitated. "You're back."

"That about sums it up," Lynnie said. She let her hand bounce lightly against the counter, twice. "I hear you're still in San Francisco," she said, relenting: they were adults now.

"Mmm," Isobel said. "Yes." She frowned.

Lynnie cleared her throat. "And someone told me you have a baby."

"Oh, yes," Isobel said. "Two. And a husband, of course. All that sort of thing." She and Lynnie smiled at one another — an odd, formal equilibrium.

"And you," Isobel said, disengaging. "What are you doing these days?"

"This —" Lynnie gestured. "Of course, I have help now."

"Heavens," Isobel remarked unheatedly.

" 'Heavens,' " Lynnie said. "I know." But either more of a reaction from Isobel or less would have been just as infuriating. "Heavens" or "How nice" was all that anyone had said when Lynnie retreated from Boston and managed, through effort born of near-panic, to open the store. All her life Lynnie had been assumed to be inadequate to any but the simplest endeavor; then, from the moment the store opened, that was something no one remembered. No one but her, Lynnie thought; she remembered it perfectly.

"Isn't it funny?" Isobel was saying. "I drove by yesterday, and I thought, How nice that there's a place like that up here now. I'll have to stop in and get something for Mother, to cheer her up."

"I'm sorry about your father," Lynnie said.

"Yes," Isobel said. "God. I was just at the hospital. They say the operation was successful, but I don't know what that's supposed to mean. It seemed they might mean successful in the sense that he didn't die during it." Her flat green glance found Lynnie, then moved away.

"Hard to think of him . . . in a hospital," Lynnie said. "He always seemed so —" He'd seemed so big.

"Strong," Isobel said. "Yes, he's strong all right. He and I are still on the most horrible terms, if you can believe it. It's simply idiotic. I suppose he has to keep it up to justify himself. All these years! You know, this is the first time I've been back, Lynnie — he came out for my wedding, and Mother's made him come with her twice to see the boys, but I haven't been back once. Not once. And there I was today — obviously I'd decided to get here before he died. But did he say anything — like he was glad I'd come?

Of course not. Lynnie, he's riddled with tumors, he can't weigh more than a hundred pounds, but he behaved as though he were still sitting in that huge chair of his, telling me what I'd done to him."

Lynnie shook her head. How easily Isobel was talking about these things.

"So," Isobel said.

"Well," Lynnie said.

"Yes," Isobel said.

"I'll wrap up some things for your mother if you want," Lynnie said. "I've got a new pâté I think she'll like. And her favorite crackers have come in."

"Lovely," Isobel said. "Thanks." She pushed back a curving lock of hair and scanned the shelves as though waiting for some information to appear on them. "So Mother comes into your store."

"Oh, yes," Lynnie said.

"Funny," Isobel said. Isobel looked like anyone else now, Lynnie understood with a little shock. Very pretty, but like anyone else. Only her hair, with its own marvelous life, was still extraordinary. "How's your mother, by the way?" Isobel said.

"All right," Lynnie said, and glanced at her. "So far."

"That's good," Isobel said opaquely.

"And at least she's not such a terror anymore," Lynnie said. "She's living up north with Frank now."

"Frank . . ." Isobel said.

"Frank," Lynnie said. She reached up to the roll of thick waxed paper and tore a piece off thunderously. "My brother. The little one."

"Oh, yes," Isobel said. "Of course. You know, this feels so peculiar — being here, seeing you. The whole place stopped for me, really, when I went away."

"I'm sure," Lynnie said, flushing. "Well, we still exist. Our lives keep going on. I have the store, and people come into it. Your mother comes in. Cissy Haddad comes in. Ross comes in, Claire comes in. All six of their children come in. . . ."

"*Six* —" Isobel stared at Lynnie; her laugh was just a breath. "Well, I guess that means they stayed together, anyway."

"Mostly," Lynnie said. But Isobel only waited, and looked at her. "There was a while there, a few years ago, when he moved in with an ex-student of his. Claire got in the van with the four youngest — Emily and Bo were already at school — and took off. It didn't last too long, of course, the thing with the girl, and of course Claire came back. After that they sold the stone house. To a broker, I heard."

"Oh," Isobel said. Absently she picked up an apple from a mound on the counter and looked into its glossy surface as though it were a mirror.

"They're renovating a farmhouse now," Lynnie said. "It's much smaller."

"Too bad," Isobel said, putting down the apple.

"Yes."

"Was she pretty?" Isobel asked.

"Who?" Lynnie said. "Ross's girl? Not especially."

"Ah," Isobel said, and Lynnie looked away, ashamed of herself.

Isobel started to speak but didn't. She scanned the shelves again vaguely, then smiled over at Lynnie. "You know what else is funny?" she said. "When I woke up this morning, I looked across the street. And I saw this woman going out the door of your old house, and just for an instant I thought, There's Lynnie. And then I thought, No, it can't be — that person's all grown up."

For a long time after Isobel had left town, Lynnie would do what she could to avoid running into Ross or Claire; and eventually when she saw them it would seem to her not only that her feeling about them had undergone an alteration but that they themselves were different in some way. Over the years it became all too clear that this was true: their shine had been tarnished by a slight fussiness — they had come to seem like people who were anxious about being rained on.

Newcomers might have been astonished to learn that there was a time when people had paused in their dealings with one another to look as Ross walked down the street with Claire or the children. Recent arrivals to the town — additions to the faculty of the college, the businessmen and bankers who were now able to live in country homes and still work in their city offices from computer terminals — what was it they saw when Ross and Claire passed by? Fossil forms, Lynnie thought. Museum reproduc-

tions. It was the Claire and Ross of years ago who were vivid,
living. A residual radiance clung to objects they'd handled and
places where they'd spent time. The current Ross and Claire were
lightless, their own aftermath.

Once in a while, though — it happened sometimes when she
encountered one of them unexpectedly — Lynnie would see them
as they had been. For an instant their sleeping power would flash,
but then their dimmed present selves might greet Lynnie, with
casual and distant politeness, and a breathtaking pain would cau-
terize the exquisitely reworked wound.

It is summer when Lynnie and Isobel first come upon Ross and
Claire. Lynnie and Isobel live across the street from one another,
but Isobel is older and has better things to do with her time than
see Lynnie. And because Lynnie's mother works at the plant for
unpredictable stretches, on unpredictable shifts, Lynnie frequently must look after her younger brothers. Still, when Lynnie
is free, she is often able to persuade Isobel to do something, particularly in the summers, when Isobel is bored brainless.

They take bicycle expeditions then, during those long summers, often along the old highway. The highway is silent, lined
with birchwoods, and has several alluring and mysterious features — among them a dark green wooden restaurant with
screened windows, and a motel, slightly shabby, where there are
always, puzzlingly, several cars parked. Leading from the highway is a wealth of dirt roads, on one of which Lynnie and Isobel
find a wonderful house.

The house is stone, and stands empty on a hill. Clouds float by
it, making great black shadows swing over the sloping meadows
below with their cows and barns and wildflowers. Inside, in the
spreading coolness, the light flows as variously clear and shaded
as water. Trees seem to crowd in the dim recesses. The house is
just there, enclosing part of the world: the huge fireplace could
be the site of gatherings that take place once every hundred, or
once every thousand, years. The girls walk carefully when they
visit, fearful of churning up the delicate maze of silence.

For several summers, the house has been theirs, but one day,
the summer that Lynnie is twelve and Isobel is just turning fourteen, there is a van parked in front. Lynnie and Isobel wheel their
bicycles stealthily into the woods across the road and walk as close

as they dare, crouching down opposite the house, well hidden, to watch.

Three men and a woman carry bundles and cartons into the house. Bundles and cartons and large pieces of furniture sit outside, where two small children tumble around among them, their wisps of voices floating high into the birdcalls and branches above Lynnie and Isobel. The woman is slight, like a child herself, with a shiny braid of black hair down her back, and there is no question about which of the men she, the furniture, and the children belong to.

Lynnie squints, and seems to draw closer, hovering just too far off to see his face. Then, for just a fraction of a second, she penetrates the distance.

The sun moves behind Lynnie and Isobel, and the man to whom everything belongs waves the others inside, hoisting up the smaller child as he follows. Just as Lynnie and Isobel reach cautiously for their bicycles, the man looks out again, shading his eyes. For a moment he stands there peering out toward them from under his hand, and they freeze, before he turns once again to go inside.

Neither Lynnie nor Isobel suggests going on — to town, or to the gorge, or anywhere. They ride back the way they've come and, without discussion, go upstairs to Isobel's room.

Isobel lies down across her flounced bed while Lynnie wanders around absently examining Isobel's things, which she knows so well: Isobel's books, her stuffed animals, her china figurines.

"Do you think we're the first people to see them?" Lynnie says.

"The first people *ever*?" Isobel says, flopping over onto her side.

Lynnie stares out Isobel's window at her own house. She doesn't know what to do when Isobel's in a bad mood. She should just leave, she thinks.

From here, her house looks as though it were about to slide to the ground. A large aluminum canister clings to its side like a devouring space monster. "Do you want to go back out and do something?" she asks.

"What would we do?" Isobel says, into her pillow. "There's nothing to do. There's not one single thing to do here. And now would you mind sitting down, please, Lynnie? Because you happen to be driving me insane."

As she leaves Isobel's, Lynnie pauses before crossing the street to watch her brothers playing in front of the house. They look weak and bony, but the two older boys fight savagely. A plastic gun lies near them on the ground. Frank, as usual, is playing by himself, but he is just as banged up as they are. His skin is patchy and chapped — summer and winter he breathes through his mouth, and even this temperate sun is strong enough to singe the life out of his fine, almost white hair. She looks just like him, Lynnie thinks. Except chunky. "Chunky" is the word people use.

Inside, Lynnie's mother is stationed in front of the TV. At any hour Lynnie's mother might be found staring at the television, and beyond it, through the front window, as though something of importance were due to happen out on the street. The television is almost always on, and when men friends come to visit, Lynnie's mother turns up the volume, so that other noises bleed alarmingly through the insistent rectangle of synthetic sound.

Lynnie brings a paper napkin from the kitchen and inserts it between her mother's glass of beer and the table. "May I inquire . . . ?" her mother says.

"Isobel's mother says you should never leave a glass on the furniture," Lynnie says. "It makes a ring."

Lynnie's mother looks at her, then lifts the glass and crumples the napkin. "Thank you," she says, turning back to her program. "I'll remember that." A thin wave of laughter comes from the TV screen, and little shapes jump and throb there, but Lynnie is thinking about the people from the stone house.

Lynnie's mother can be annoyed when she knows that Lynnie has been playing with Isobel; Isobel's father works for the same company Lynnie's mother works for, but not in the plant. He works in the office, behind a big desk. Whenever Lynnie is downstairs in Isobel's house and Isobel's father walks in, Lynnie scuttles as though she might be trodden underfoot. In fact, Isobel's father hardly notices her; perhaps he doesn't even know from one of her visits to the next that she is the same little girl. But he booms down at Isobel, scrutinizing her from his great height, and sometimes even lifts her way up over his head.

Isobel's mother is tall and smells good and dresses in neat wool. Sometimes when she sees Lynnie hesitating at the foot of the drive she opens the door, with a bright, special smile. "Lynnie, dear," she says, "would you like to come in and see Isobel? Or have a snack?" But sometimes, when Lynnie and Isobel are playing, Isobel's mother calls Isobel away for a whispered conference, from which Isobel returns to say that Lynnie has to go now, for this reason or that.

When Lynnie looks out the window of the room she shares with Frank, she can see Isobel's large, arched window, and if the light is just right she can see Isobel's bed, too, with its white flounces, and a heavenly blue haze into which, at this distance, the flowers of Isobel's wallpaper melt.

One day, doing errands for her mother in town, Lynnie sees the woman from the stone house coming out of the bakery with the children, each of whom carefully holds a large, icing-covered cookie. The woman bends down and picks up one of the children, smiling — unaware, Lynnie observes, that people are noticing her.

Lynnie sees the woman several times, and then one day she sees the man.

She has anticipated his face exactly. But when he smiles at her, the little frown line between his eyes stays. And the marvelousness of this surprise causes a sensation across the entire surface of her skin, like the rippling of leaves that demonstrates a subtle shift of air.

When Lynnie sees Isobel she can't help talking about the people from the stone house. She describes variations in their clothing or demeanor, compiling a detailed body of knowledge while Isobel lies on her bed, her eyes closed. "Should we give them names?" Lynnie says one afternoon.

"No," Isobel says.

But Lynnie can't stop. "Why not?" she says, after a moment.

" 'Why not?' " Isobel says.

"Don't, Isobel," Lynnie pleads.

" 'Don't, Isobel,' " Isobel says, making her hands into a tube to speak through. Her voice is hollow and terrifying.

Lynnie breathes heavily through her mouth. "Why not?" she says.

"Why *not*," Isobel says, sitting up and sighing, "is because they already have names."

"I know," Lynnie says, mystified.

"Their names," Isobel says, "are Ross and Claire."

Lynnie stares at her.

"They had dinner at Cissy Haddad's house one night," Isobel says. "Ross is going to be teaching medieval literature at the college. He's in Cissy's father's department."

" 'Department'?" Lynnie says.

"Yes," Isobel says.

Lynnie frowns. "How do you know?" she asks. How *long* has Isobel known?

Isobel shrugs. "I'm just telling you what Cissy said." She looks at Lynnie. "I think Cissy has a crush on him."

"What else did Cissy say?" Lynnie asks unhappily.

"Nothing," Isobel says. "Oh. Except that he's thirty-five and Claire's only twenty-three. She used to be one of his students."

"One of his students?" Lynnie says.

" 'One of his—' " Isobel begins, and then flops down on the bed again. "Oh, Lynnie."

One day Lynnie sees Cissy Haddad in the drugstore. Lynnie hurries to select the items on her mother's list, then waits until Cissy goes to the counter. "Hi," she says, getting into line behind Cissy. She feels herself turning red.

"Oh, hi, Lynnie," Cissy says, and smiles wonderfully. "Are you having a fun summer?"

"Yes," Lynnie says.

"What're you doing?" Cissy says.

"Just mostly looking after my brothers," Lynnie says. She feels bewildered by Cissy's dazzling smile, her pretty sundress. "And riding around and things with Isobel."

"That's good," Cissy says. And then, instead of saying something useful about Isobel, which might lead to Ross and Claire, she asks, "Are you coming to high school this year? I can't remember."

"No," Lynnie says. "Isobel is."

Cissy peers into Lynnie's basket of embarrassing purchases.

"What are you getting?" she asks.

"Things for my mother," Lynnie says, squirming. "What about you?"

"Oh," Cissy says. "Just lipstick."

*

One fall day when Lynnie gets home from school, her mother summons her over the noise from the TV. "You got a phone call," she says shortly. "The lady wants you to call her back." And Lynnie knows, while her mother is still speaking, whom the call was from.

Lynnie dials, and the soft, dark shadow of Claire's voice answers. She is looking for someone to help with the children on a regular basis, she explains, several afternoons a week. She got Lynnie's name from Tom Haddad's daughter. She knows that Lynnie is very young, but this is nothing difficult — just playing with the children upstairs or outside so that she can have a couple of hours to paint. "I thought I would be able to do so much here," she says, as though Lynnie were an old friend, someone her own age, "but there's never enough time, is there?"

"I'll need you just as much with the boys," Lynnie's mother says later. "And you'd better remember your homework."

"I will," Lynnie says, though actually, beyond a certain point, it scarcely matters; however hard she tries, she lags far behind in school, and her teachers no longer try to stifle their exclamations of impatience. "I'll do my homework." And her mother makes no further objections; Lynnie will be earning money.

Claire leads Lynnie around in the house that used to be Lynnie and Isobel's. Now it is all filled up with the lives of these people.

Everywhere there is a regal disorder of books, and in the biggest room downstairs, with its immense fireplace, there are sofas and, at one end, a vast table. A thicket of canvases and brushes has sprung up in a corner, and Lynnie sees pictures of the table on whose surface objects are tensely balanced, and sketch after sketch of Ross and the children. "What do you think?" Claire says, and it is a moment before Lynnie realizes what Claire is asking her.

"I like them," Lynnie says. But in fact they frighten her — the figures seem caught, flowing in a webby dimness.

In the kitchen huge pots and pans flash, and a great loaf of brown bread lies out on a counter. Claire opens the door to Ross's study; stacks and stacks of paper, more books than Lynnie has ever seen, breed from its light-shot core.

Upstairs, Bo and Emily are engrossed in a sprawling project of blocks. Emily explains the dreamlike construction to Lynnie, gracefully accepting Bo's effortful elaborations, and when Lynnie leaves both children reach up to her with their tanned little arms.

Twice a week Lynnie goes to the stone house. Bo and Emily have big, bright, smooth wooden toys, some of which were made by Ross. Lynnie strokes the toys; she runs her hand over them like a blind person; she runs her hand over the pictures in Bo and Emily's beautiful storybooks. But then Claire counts out Lynnie's money, and Lynnie is to go. And at the first sight of her own house she is slightly sickened, as upon disembarkation — not by the firm ground underfoot but by a ghostly rocking of water.

When Claire finishes painting for the afternoon, she calls Lynnie and Bo and Emily into the kitchen. For a while, although Bo and Emily chatter and nuzzle against her, Claire seems hardly to know where she is. But gradually she returns, and makes for herself and Lynnie a dense, sweet coffee in a little copper pot, which must be brought to the boil three times. They drink it from tiny identical cups, and Lynnie marvels, looking at Claire, that she herself is there.

Some afternoons Ross is around. He announces that he will be in his study, working, but sooner or later he always appears in the kitchen and talks about things he is reading for his book.

"What do you think, Lynnie?" he asks once. He has just proposed an idea for a new chapter in his book, to which Claire's response was merely "Possible."

Lynnie can feel herself blush. "I don't know," she says.

Amusement begins to spread from behind his eyes. "Do you think it's a good idea?" he asks.

"Yes," she says, wary.

"Why?" he says.

"Because you just said it was," Lynnie says, turning a deeper red.

He laughs happily and gives Lynnie a little hug. "You see?" he says to Claire.

When the snow lies in great drifts around the stone house, students begin to come, too, and sit around the kitchen. They drink beer, and the girls exclaim over Bo and Emily while the boys shyly answer Claire's gentle questions and Lynnie holds her coffee cup tightly in misery. Now and again, as he talks to them, Ross touches the students lightly on the wrist or shoulder.

Late one Saturday afternoon, Lynnie is washing dishes in her own house when her mother walks in with several large grocery bags. "I was just in town," she announces unnecessarily, and grins an odd, questioning grin at Lynnie. "Now, who do you think I saw there?"

"I don't know who you saw," Lynnie says, reaching for a dish-cloth.

"The man you work for," her mother says.

"How do you know who he is?" Lynnie says.

"Everybody knows who he is," her mother says. "He was in the stationery store. I just went in to get some tape, but I stuck around to watch. Muriel Furman was waiting on him. She almost went into a trance. That poor thing." Lynnie's mother shakes her head and begins to unload groceries. "Homeliest white woman I ever saw."

"Mother," Lynnie says. She stares unhappily out the little window over the sink.

"I've seen the wife around a few times, too," Lynnie's mother says. "She's a pretty girl, but I wish her luck with him."

Lynnie has not been to Isobel's house once this year. Isobel comes and goes with Cissy Haddad and other high-school friends. From across the street Lynnie can sometimes see their shapes behind the film of Isobel's window. At night, when Isobel's light is on and her window is transparent, Lynnie watches Isobel moving back and forth until the curtain closes.

One afternoon as Lynnie is arriving home, she almost walks into Isobel. "Wake up, Lynnie," Isobel says. And then, "Want to come over?"

"Lynnie, dear," Isobel's mother says as Lynnie and Isobel go upstairs. "How *nice* to see you."

It has been so long since Lynnie has been in Isobel's room that Isobel's things — the flouncy bed and the china figurines and the stuffed animals she used to see so often — have a new, melancholy lustre. "How's high school?" she asks.

"It's hard," Isobel says. "You won't believe it."

But Lynnie will. She does. Almost every day she remembers that that is where she is going next fall — to the immense, tentacled building that looks like a factory. She has reason to suspect that she will be divided from most of her classmates there, and put into the classes for people who won't be going on to college — the stupid people — with all the meanest teachers. No one has threatened her with this, but everybody knows how it works. Everybody knows what goes on in that building.

Lynnie picks up a stuffed turtle and strokes its furry shell.

"How's school?" Isobel asks. "How's old Miss Fisher?"

"She doesn't like me," Lynnie says. "Miss Fish Face."

"Oh, well," Isobel says. "So what? Soon you'll never have to see her again." She looks at Lynnie and smiles. "What else have you been up to?"

Lynnie feels slightly weak because of what she is about to tell Isobel. She has been saving it up, she realizes, a long time. "Well," she says slowly, "I've been baby-sitting for the kids at the stone house."

"Have you?" Isobel says, but as she says it Lynnie understands that Isobel already knew, and although Isobel is waiting, Lynnie cannot speak.

"You know what —" Isobel says after a moment. "Lynnie, what are you doing to that poor turtle? But do you know what Cissy's father said about that man, Ross? Cissy's father said he's an arrogant son of a bitch." She looks at Lynnie, hugging her pillow expectantly. "I heard him."

Lynnie and Claire and three students watch as Ross describes various arguments concerning a matter that has come up in class. The students look at him with hazy, hopeful smiles. But not Lynnie — she is ashamed to have heard what Isobel said to her.

Ross glances down at her unhappy face. "Apparently Lynnie disagrees," he says, stroking a strand of her pale, flossy hair behind her ear. "Apparently Lynnie feels that Heineman fails to account for the Church's influence over the emerging class of tradesmen."

The students laugh, understanding his various points, and Ross smiles at Lynnie. But Lynnie is ashamed again — doubly ashamed — and leans for comfort into the treacherous hand that still strokes her hair.

Lynnie has two Rosses who blend together and diverge unpredictably. Many mornings begin drowsily encircled in the fleecy protection of one, but sometimes, as Lynnie continues to wake, the one is assumed into the other. He strokes Lynnie's hair, inflicting injury and healing it in this one motion, and she opens her eyes to see her own room, and Frank curled up on the other bed, breathing laboriously, susceptible himself to the devious assaults of dreams.

In the fall, Lynnie is put, as she had feared, into the classes for the slowest students. Had anyone entertained hopes for her, this would have been the end of them.

A few of her old schoolmates are confined to her classes, but most have sailed into classes from which they will sail out again into college, then marriage and careers. She sees them only in the halls and the lunchroom and on the athletic fields. Every day they look taller, more powerful, more like strangers.

Most of those in her classes really are strangers. But in some ways they are as familiar as cousins met for the first time. Their clothes, for instance, are not right, and they are the worst students from all the elementary schools in the area. The boys are rough or sly or helpless, or all three, like her brothers, and the girls are ungainly and bland-looking. They stand in clumps in the halls, watching girls like Isobel and Cissy Haddad with a beleaguered envy and trading accounts of the shocking things such girls have been known to do.

Oddly, Isobel is friendlier to Lynnie at school, in full view of everyone, than she is out of school, despite Lynnie's stigma. "Hi, Lynnie," she calls out with a dewy showpiece of a smile, not too different from her mother's.

"Hi," Lynnie answers, facing a squadron of Isobel's friends.

One afternoon as Lynnie approaches her house, a silence reaches for her like a suction. Her brothers are not outside, and the

television is not on. No one is in the kitchen or upstairs. She
sits without moving while the winter sky goes dark. Across the
street Isobel turns on the light in her room and sits down at her
little desk. After a while she leaves, turning off the light, but Lynnie continues to stare at the blank window. By the time Lynnie
hears her mother's car, her arms and legs feel stiff. She waits
for a moment before going downstairs to be told what has happened.

Frank is in the hospital with a ruptured appendix, her mother
says; her face has a terrible jellylike look. If she could see her
own face, Lynnie wonders, would it look like that?

There will be no more going to the stone house; she will be
needed at home, her mother is saying, staring at Lynnie as though
Lynnie were shrinking into a past of no meaning — the way a
dying person might look at an enemy.

The next day, Lynnie seeks out Isobel in the lunchroom. "A
ruptured appendix," Isobel says. "That's really dangerous, you
know."

"My mother says Frank is going to be all right," Lynnie says
doggedly.

"Poor Lynnie," Isobel says. "So what are you going to do if Ross
and Claire hire someone else?"

Lynnie puts her head down on the lunch table and closes her
eyes. The sweet, unpleasant smell of the lunchroom rises up,
and the din of the students, talking and laughing, folds around
her.

"Poor Lynnie," Isobel says again.

Later that week, Lynnie brings Isobel to the stone house. Claire
makes coffee, and when she brings out a third tiny china cup,
Lynnie is unable to hear anything for several seconds.

Ross comes in, whistling, and lets the door slam behind him.
"What's this?" he asks, indicating Isobel. "Invader or captive?"

"Friendly native," Claire says. "Isobel's going to be our new
Lynnie."

"What's the matter with our old Lynnie?" Ross says. He looks
at Isobel for a moment. "Our old Lynnie's fine with me."

"Oh, Ross." Claire sighs. "I told you. Lynnie's brother is sick."

"Hmm," Ross says.

"He's in the hospital, Ross," Claire says.

"Oh, God," Ross says. "Yes, I'm sorry to hear that, Lynnie."

"First day of the new semester," Claire says to Lynnie. "He's always disgusting the first day. How are your new students, my love?"

"Unspeakable," Ross says.

"Truly," Claire says. She smiles at Isobel.

"Worse than ever," Ross says, taking a beer from the refrigerator. "There isn't *one*. Well, one, maybe. A possibility. A real savage, but she has an interesting quality. Potential, at least."

"I used to have potential," Claire says, "but look at me now."

Ross raises his beer to her. "Look at you now," he says.

Ross holds the door as Lynnie and Isobel leave. "I've seen you in town," he says to Isobel. "You're older than I thought."

She glances up at him and then turns back to Claire. "Goodbye," she says. "See you soon."

"See you soon," Claire says, coming to join them at the door. "I do appreciate this. I'm going to have another baby, and I want to get in as much painting as I can first."

"You're going to have another baby?" Lynnie says, staring.

"We're going to have hundreds of babies," Ross says, putting his arms around Claire from behind. "We're going to have hundreds and hundreds of babies."

Afterward, Lynnie would become heavy and slow whenever she even thought of the time when Frank was sick. Their room was desolate while he was in the hospital; when he returned she felt how cramped it had always been before. Frank was testy all the time then, and cried easily. Her family deserved their troubles, she thought. Other people looked down on them, looked down and looked down, and then when they got tired of it they went back to their own business. But her family — and she — were the same whether anyone was looking or not.

Isobel's mother stops Lynnie on the sidewalk to ask after Frank. The special, kind voice she uses makes Lynnie's skin jump now. How could she ever have thought she adored Isobel's mother? Lynnie wonders, shuddering with an old, sugared hatred.

At night Lynnie can see Isobel in her room, brushing her hair, or sometimes even curled up against her big white pillows, reading. Has Isobel seen Ross and Claire that day? Lynnie always wonders. Did they talk about anything in particular? What did they do?

At school, Isobel sends her display of cheery waves and smiles in Lynnie's direction, and it is as though Ross and Claire had never existed. But once in a while she and Isobel meet on the sidewalk, and then they stop to talk in their ordinary way, without any smiles or fuss at all. "Claire's in a good mood," Isobel tells Lynnie one afternoon. "She loves being pregnant."

Pregnant. What a word. "How's Ross?" Lynnie says.

"He's all right." Isobel shrugs. "He's got an assistant now, some student of his. Mary Katherine. She's always around."

Lynnie feels herself beginning to blush. "Don't you like him?"

"I like him." Isobel shrugs again. "He lends me books."

"Oh." Lynnie looks at Isobel wonderingly. "What books?" she says without thinking.

"Just books he tells me to read," Isobel says.

"Oh," Lynnie says.

It is spring when Lynnie returns to the stone house. She is hugged and exclaimed over, and Emily and Bo perform for her, but she looks around as though it were she who had just come out of a long illness. The big, smooth toys, the wonderful picture books no longer inspire her longing, or even her interest.

"We've missed you," Claire says. Lynnie rests her head against the window frame, and the pale hills outside wobble.

But Claire has asked Isobel to sit for a portrait, so Isobel is at the stone house all the time now. The house is full of people — Lynnie upstairs with Emily and Bo, and Ross in his study with Mary Katherine, and Isobel and Claire in the big room among Claire's canvases.

In the afternoons they all gather in the kitchen. Sometimes Mary Katherine's boyfriend, Derek, joins them and watches Mary Katherine with large, mournful eyes while she smokes cigarette after cigarette and talks cleverly with Ross about his work. "Doesn't he drive you crazy?" Mary Katherine says once to Claire. "He's so opinionated."

"Is he?" Claire says, smiling.

"Oh, Claire," Mary Katherine says. "I wish I were like you. You're *serene*. And you can *do* everything. You can paint, you can cook . . ."

"Claire can do everything," Ross says. "Claire can paint, Claire can cook, Claire can fix a carburetor . . ."

"What a useful person to be married to," Mary Katherine says.

Claire laughs, but Derek looks up at Mary Katherine unhappily.

"*I* can't do anything," Mary Katherine says. "I'm hopeless. Aren't I, Ross?"

"Hopeless," Ross says, and Lynnie's eyes cloud mysteriously. "Truly hopeless."

Now and again Ross asks Isobel's opinion about something he has given her to read. She looks straight ahead as she answers, as though she were remembering, and Ross nods soberly. Once Lynnie sees Ross look at Mary Katherine during Isobel's recitation. For a moment Mary Katherine looks back at him from narrow gray eyes, then makes her red mouth into an O from which blossoms a series of wavering smoke rings.

One day in April, when several students have dropped by, the temperature plummets and the sky turns into a white, billowing cloth that hides the trees and farmhouses. "We'd better go now," one of the students says, "or we'll be snowed in forever."

"Can you give me and Lynnie a lift?" Isobel asks. "We're on bikes."

"Stay for the show," Ross says to her. "It's going to be sensational up here."

"Coming?" the student says to Isobel. "Staying? Well, O.K., then." Lynnie sees the student raise her eyebrows to Mary Katherine before, holding her coat closed, she goes out with her friends into the blowing wildness.

"We should go, too," Derek says to Mary Katherine.

"Why?" Mary Katherine says. "We've got four-wheel drive."

"Stick around," Ross says. "If you feel like it." Mary Katherine stares at him for a moment, but he goes to the door, squinting into the swarming snow where the students are disappearing. Behind him a silence has fallen.

"Yes," Claire says suddenly. "Everybody stay. There's plenty of food — we could live for months. Besides, I want to celebrate. I finished Isobel today."

Isobel frowns. "You finished?"

"With your part, at least," Claire says. "The rest I can do on my own. So you're liberated. And we should have a magnificent ceremonial dinner, don't you think, everybody? For the snow." She stands, her hands together as though she has just clapped, looking at each of them in turn. Claire has a fever, Lynnie thinks.

"Why not?" Mary Katherine says. She closes her eyes. "We can give you two a ride home later, Isobel."

Bo and Emily are put to bed, and Lynnie, Isobel, Ross, Claire, Mary Katherine, and Derek set about making dinner. Although night has come, the kitchen glimmers with the snow's busy whiteness.

Ross opens a bottle of wine and everyone except Claire drinks. "This is delicious!" Lynnie says, dazed with happiness, and the others smile at her as though she has said something original and charming.

Even when they must chop and measure, no one turns on the lights. Claire finds candles, and Lynnie holds her glass up near a flame. A clear patch of red shivers on the wall. "Feel," Claire says, taking Lynnie's hand and putting it against her hard, round stomach, and Lynnie feels the baby kick.

"Why are we whispering?" Ross whispers, and then laughs. Claire moves vaporously within the globe of smeary candlelight.

Claire and Derek make a fire in the huge fireplace while Ross gets out the heavy, deep-colored Mexican dishes and opens another bottle of wine. "Ross," Claire says. But Ross fills the glasses again.

Lynnie wanders out into the big room to look at Claire's portrait of Isobel. Isobel stares back from the painting, not at her. At what? Staring out, Isobel recedes, drowning, into the darkness behind her.

What a meal they have produced! Chickens and platters of vegetables and a marvelously silly-looking peaked and scroll-rimmed pie. They sit at the big table eating quietly and appreciatively while the fire snaps and breathes. Outside, the brilliant white earth curves against a black sky, and black shadows of the snow-laden trees and telephone wires lie across it; there is light everywhere — a great white moon, and stars flung out, winking.

Derek leans back in his chair, closing his eyes and letting one arm fall around Mary Katherine's chair. She casts a ruminating, regretful glance over him; when she looks away again it is as though he has been covered with a sheet.

Isobel gets up from the table and stretches. A silence falls around her like petals. She goes to the rug in front of the fire and lies down, her hair fanning out around her. Lynnie follows groggily and curls up on one of the sofas.

"That was perfect," Claire says. "Ideal. And now I'm going upstairs." She burns feverishly for a moment as she pauses in the doorway, but then subsides into her usual smoky softness.

"Goodnight," Lynnie calls, and for full seconds after Claire has disappeared from view the others stare at the tingling darkness where she was.

Ross pushes his chair back from the table and walks over to the rug where Isobel lies. "Who's for a walk?" he says, looking down at her.

Mary Katherine stubs out a cigarette. "Come on," Ross says, prodding Isobel with his foot. Isobel looks at his foot, then away.

Ross is standing just inches from Lynnie; she can feel his outline — a little extra density of air.

"Derek," Mary Katherine says softly. "It's time to go. Lynnie? Isobel?"

"I can run the girls home later," Ross says.

"Right," Mary Katherine says after a moment. She goes to the closet for her coat.

"Come on, you two," Ross says. "Up. Isobel? This is not going to last —" He gestures toward the window. "It's tonight only. Out of the cave, lazy little bears. Into the refreshing night."

Ross reaches a hand down to Isobel. She considers it, then looks up at him. "I hate to be refreshed," she says, still looking at him, and shifts slightly on the rug.

"I don't believe this," Mary Katherine says quietly.

Lynnie sits up. The stars move back, then forward. The snow flashes, pitching her almost off balance. "Wait, wait," Isobel says, scrambling to her feet as Mary Katherine goes to the door. "We're coming."

In the car Derek makes a joke, but no one laughs. Next to Lynnie, Isobel sits in a burnished silence. Branches support a canopy of snow over them as they drive out onto the old highway. Three cars are parked in front of the motel. They are covered with snow; no tire tracks are visible. All the motel windows are dark except one, where a faint aureole escapes from behind the curtain. Isobel breathes — just a feather of a sigh — and leans back against the seat.

Lynnie wakes up roughly, crying out as though she were being dragged through a screen of sleep into the day. Frank is no longer in his bed, and the room is bright. Lynnie sits up, shivering, exhausted from the night, and sees that the sun is already turning the snow to a glaze.

"You got in late enough," Lynnie's mother says when Lynnie comes downstairs.

"I tried not to wake you," Lynnie says.

"I can imagine," her mother says. "You were knocking things over left and right. I suppose those people gave you plenty to drink."

"I wasn't drunk, Mother," Lynnie says.

"No," her mother says. "Good. Well, I don't want you staying late with those people again. You can leave that sort of thing to Isobel. She looked fairly steady on her feet last night going up the drive."

Lynnie looks at her mother.

"I wonder what Isobel's parents think," Lynnie's mother says.

"Isobel's parents trust her, Mother," Lynnie says.

"Well, that's *their* problem, isn't it?" her mother says.

Isobel has stopped coming to the stone house, and her portrait leans against the wall, untouched since she left. But one day, at the beginning of summer, she goes along with Lynnie to see the new baby.

"He's strange, isn't he?" Claire says as Isobel picks him up. "They're always so strange at the beginning — much easier to believe a stork brings them. Did a stork bring you, Willie? A stork?"

Through the window they can see Ross outside, working, and Lynnie listens to the rhythmic striking of his spade and the earth sliding off it in a little pile of sound. "We're planting a lilac," she hears Claire say. Claire's voice slides, silvery, through the gold day, and Ross looks up, shading his eyes.

The sun melts into the sky. Lynnie hears Claire and Isobel talking behind the chinking of the spade, but then once, when there should be the spade, there is no sound, and Lynnie looks up to see Ross taking off his shirt. When had Claire and Isobel stopped talking?

Isobel stands up, transferring Willie to Lynnie.

"Don't go," Claire commands quietly.

"No . . ." Isobel says. Her voice is sleepy, puzzled, and she sits back down.

The room is silent again, but then the door bangs and Ross comes in, holding his crumpled shirt. "Hello, everyone," he says, going to the sink to slap cold water against his face. "Hello, Isobel." He tosses back dripping hair.

"Hello," Isobel says.

Lynnie looks up at Claire, but Claire's eyes are half closed as she gazes down at her long, graceful hands lying on the table. "Yes," Claire says, although no one has spoken.

"Ross," Isobel says, standing, "I brought back your book." She hands Ross a small, faded book with gold on the edges of the pages.

He takes the book and looks at it for a moment, at the shape of it in his hand. "Ah," he says. "Maybe I'll find something else for you one of these days."

"Mm," Isobel says, pushing her hair back.

Willie makes a little smacking sound, and the others look at him.

"When's good to drop things by?" Ross says.

"Anytime," Isobel says. "Sometime." She pivots childishly on one foot. "Saturdays are all right."

Claire puts her hands against her eyes, against her forehead. "Would anybody like iced tea?" she asks.

"Not I," Isobel says. "I have to go."

The students have left town for the summer — even Derek. At least, Lynnie has not seen him since the night it snowed. And Mary Katherine herself is hardly in evidence. She comes over once in a while, but when she finishes her work, instead of sitting around the kitchen, she leaves.

Lynnie might be alone in the house, except for Bo and Emily. Claire is so quiet now, sealed off in a life with Willie, that sometimes Lynnie doesn't realize that she is standing right there. And when Lynnie and the children are outside, the children seem to disappear into the net of gold light. They seem far away from her — little motes — and barely audible; the quiet from the house muffles their voices.

Ross is frequently out, doing one thing and another, and his smiles for Lynnie have become terribly kind — self-deprecating and sudden, as though she had become, overnight, fragile or precious. Now that Isobel has finally gone away, Ross and Claire seem to have gone with her; her absence is a vacuum into which they have disappeared. Day after day, nothing changes. Day after day, the sky sheds gold, and nothing changes. The house is saturated with absences.

Now Lynnie sees Isobel only as she streaks by in the little green car she has been given for her sixteenth birthday, or from the window in her room at night before she draws the curtain. One Saturday afternoon when Lynnie is outside with her brothers, Ross pulls up across the street. He waves to Lynnie as he walks up Isobel's drive and knocks on the door. Lynnie watches as Isobel opens the door and accepts a book he holds out to her. Ross disappears inside. A few minutes later he re-emerges, waves again to Lynnie, and drives off.

These days Lynnie's mother is more irritable than usual. There have been rumors of layoffs at the plant. Once, when Lynnie is watching TV with her, they see Isobel's father drive up across the street. "Look at that fat bastard," Lynnie's mother says. "Now, there's a man who knows how to run a tight ship."

Even years and years later, just the thought of the school building could still call up Lynnie's dread, from that summer, of going back to school. Still, there is some relief in finally having to do it, and by the third or fourth day Lynnie finds she is comforted by the distant roaring of the corridors and the familiar faces that at last sight were the faces of strangers.

One afternoon the first week, she sees Cissy Haddad looking in her direction, and she waves shyly. But then she realizes that Cissy is staring at something else. She turns around and there is Isobel, looking back at Cissy. Nothing reflects from Isobel's flat green eyes.

"Isobel —" Lynnie says.

"Hello, Lynnie," Isobel says slowly, and only then seems to see her. Lynnie turns back in confusion to Cissy, but Cissy is gone.

"Do you want a ride?" Isobel asks, looking straight ahead. "I've got my car."

"How was your summer?" Isobel asks on the way home.

"All right, " Lynnie says. The sky is a deep, open blue again. Soon the leaves will change. "I was sorry you weren't around the stone house."

"Thank you, Lynnie," Isobel says seriously, and Lynnie remembers the way Cissy had been staring at Isobel. "That means a lot to me."

Lynnie's mother looks up when Lynnie comes into the house. "Hanging around with Isobel again?" she says. "I thought she'd dropped you."

Lynnie stands up very straight. "Isobel's my friend," she says.

"Isobel is not your friend," her mother says. "I want you to understand that."

On Saturday, Lynnie goes back to her room after breakfast, and lies down in her unmade bed. Outside it is muggy and hot. She has homework to do, and chores, but she can't force herself to get up. The sounds of the television, and of her brothers playing outside, wash over her.

A car door slams, and Lynnie gets up to look out the window — maybe Isobel is going somewhere and will want company.

But it is not Isobel. It is Ross. Lynnie watches as Ross goes up Isobel's front walk and knocks on the door. The sound of brass on brass echoes up to Lynnie's room.

Isobel's car is in the driveway, but her mother's and father's are gone. Lynnie watches as Isobel appears at the front door and lets Ross in, and then as dim shapes spread in Isobel's room.

Lynnie returns to her bed and lies there. The room bears down on her, and the noise; one of her brothers is crying. She turns violently into the pillow, clenched and stiff, and for a while she tries to cry, but every effort is false, and unsatisfactory. At certain moments she can feel her heart beating rapidly.

Later, when she gets up again, Ross's car is gone. She turns back to the roiling ocean of sheets on her own bed, and reaches out, anticipating a wave rising to her, but it is enragingly inert. She grabs the unresisting top sheet and tries to hurl it to the floor, but it folds around her before it falls, slack and disgusting. The bottom sheet comes loose more satisfyingly, tearing away from the mattress and streaming into her arms like clouds, but a tiny sound bores into the clamor in her ears, and she wheels around to see Frank standing in the doorway with his hand on the knob. He looks at her, breathing uncomfortably through his mouth, before he turns away, closing the door behind him.

That night Lynnie's mother sits in front of the television in the dark, like a priestess. The cold, pale light flattens out her face, and craterlike shadows collect around her eyes, her mouth, in the hollows of her cheeks. "And what do you think of your employer visiting Isobel?" she says.

Across the street, Isobel's window blazes. "He lends Isobel books," Lynnie says.

"I see," her mother says. "Quite the little scholar."

The next day, Lynnie rides her bicycle to the stone house to say that she will not be working there any longer. Pedaling with all her strength, she is not even aware of reaching the edge of town, though afterward she can see every branch of the birchwood along the old highway as it flashes by, every cinder block of the motel, even the paint peeling from its sign.

Claire stands in the doorway while Lynnie talks loudly, trying to make herself heard through the static engulfing her. She has too much homework, she tries to explain; she is sorry, but her mother needs her. Her bicycle lies where she dropped it in her frenzy to get to the door, one wheel still spinning, and while she talks she sees dim forms shifting behind Isobel's window, a brief tumbling of entwined bodies on the damp leaves under the birches, the sad, washed light inside the old motel, where a plain chest of drawers with a mirror above it stands against the wall. In the mirror is a double bed with a blue cover on which Ross lies, staring up at the ceiling.

"Yes . . ." Claire is saying, and she materializes in front of Lynnie. "I understand . . ." From inside, behind Claire, comes the sound of Ross whistling.

It is the following week that Isobel leaves. Lynnie watches from her window as Isobel and her mother and father load up her father's car and get into it. They are taking a trip, Lynnie thinks; they are just taking a trip, but still she runs down the stairs as fast as she can, and then, as the car pulls out into the street, Isobel twists around in the back seat. Her face is waxy, with an unhealthy glow, and her hair ripples out around her. Lynnie raises her hand, perhaps imperceptibly, but in any case Isobel only looks.

So nothing has to be explained to Lynnie the next day or the next or the next, when Isobel does not appear at school. And she is not puzzled by the groups of girls who huddle in the corridor whispering, or by Cissy Haddad's strange, tight greetings, or by the rumor, which begins to circulate almost immediately, of an anonymous letter to Isobel's parents.

And when, one day soon after Isobel's departure, Isobel's mother passes her on the sidewalk with nothing beyond a rapid glance of distaste, Lynnie sees in an instant what Isobel's mother must always have seen until now: an impassive, solid, limp-haired child, an inconveniently frequent visitor, breathing noisily, hungry for a smile — a negligible girl, utterly unlike her own daughter. And then Lynnie sees Isobel, vanishing brightly all over again as she looks back from her father's car, pressing into Lynnie's safekeeping everything that should have vanished along with her.

Separation

FROM ANTAEUS

THE SOCIAL WORKER said: "I think he needs a group experience."

Not looking at JoAnn, handing a piece of paper with a black design JoAnn saw later was the steeple of a church. Ascension Play School.

"It's no trip for you," the social worker said to JoAnn. "See that building there, behind the Episcopal church. They wrote to us, saying they're offering a scholarship to any child of ours who might benefit from a group experience."

Child of *ours?*
    Of *yours?*
    No one's but mine.

She put her hand over her mouth, to keep back something. Sickness? Bad words that would cause trouble later on? Words that would be put down in the file. She knew their ways. This Mrs. Pratt was not the first of them, she'd had a lot of them in towns over the years.

The game was shut your mouth.
    The game was shut your mouth and keep it shut.
    The game was shut your mouth and give them what they wanted.

Town after town. Arriving. Making your way to the county seat, the hall, the metal desks, the forms to be filled out, the bad lights with their buzzing noises, and the questions.

Name?

Her husband's. Not an out-of-wedlock child. Her son. Hers, but everything all right before the law. The husband, not abandoning, but driven off. Pushed out. No room for him, he knew it, and was sorry, but he knew. One day: "Well, I'll be shoving off."

"All right."

A night she stayed up, when the baby had the croup. Her husband saw her happiness. He saw how happy she was, after the steaming shower and the rush outside to the cold air, after all this, the easy, even breathing. And her humming. Song after song.

"Well, I'll be shoving off."

"All right."

Rubbing the boy's wet head with a dry towel. Wet from the steam she'd set up in the bathroom. His hair that smelled like bread. She put her lips to it, and breathed it in. His easy breath, the wet smell of his hair. And looked up at the father, at the husband, sorry for him, but it was nothing, he was right to leave, there wasn't any place for him.

Humming, his damp head and his easy breathing. Happy, happy. All I want.

He needs a group experience.

All I have ever wanted.

Her childhood: blocks of muteness. Of silence because what was there to say. Neglect, they called it. She was kept alive. Fed. Clothed. She saw now that could not have been so easy. The flow of meals, sweaters, jackets, in the summer short-sleeved shirts and shorts, a bathing suit, washed hair, injections that were law. She felt sorry for her mother, whom she barely could remember now. She had trouble calling up the faces of the past.

Her memory: the outline of a head, a black line surrounding nothing. The faces blank. Unharmful ghosts, but nothing, nothing to her. And of course no help.

It was why she didn't like the television. All the filled-in faces. She wanted, sometimes, to ask people about their memories. Do you remember people when you are away from them? The faces? At what point do they come alive?

Even her husband's face grown ghostly.

But she never said these things. She kept to herself. Smiling, quiet, clean. She and her son.

Never causing trouble.

Keeping things up.

Arriving on time for the social worker.

The clinic.

The dentist, who said it was all right if she sat on the chair and he sat on her lap to be examined. Otherwise he'll scream.

Fine, then, Mrs. Verbeck. Just keep it up. Keep him away from sugar snacks. Fresh fruit. Apples or carrot sticks. Water rather than soda or other sweetened drinks.

Yes, thank you. Yes.

You've done a good job. Not one cavity. You floss his teeth?

I will.

We'll show you how. Miss Havenick, the hygienist, will show you.

"Let's open our mouth, Billy."

Not yours. His.

And mine.

She wanted to phone the call-in radio and ask one of the doctors.

Are the faces of people empty to other people as they are to me?

Except his face. The one face I have always known.

At night while he slept she sat on a stool beside him just to learn his face. So that she never would forget.

An angry baby. Happy only in her arms.

He doesn't take to strangers. Thanks, no, I can manage. Thanks.

Did anyone look at her face? In the shadowy childhood, family of shadow, furniture the part of it that she remembered most. The green couch. The red chair.

Did anyone look at my face?

He needs a group experience.

*

But we are happiest alone.

But never say it. She knew what people thought. Children need other children. They believe that, everyone believes it.

Only I do not believe it.

Only he and I.

Happy, happy in the studio apartment, in the trailer, in the basement rented in the rotting house. Happy in the supermarket, laundromat, bank where we stand on line to cash the check from welfare. Singing, eating meals we love, the walks we take, bringing back leaves, pine cones. Puzzles we do in silence, cartoon shows we watch.

She wanted to say to them: "We're very happy."

She never said these things. She moved.

Five towns. Five different states.

He needs a group experience.

This time she thinks they may be right. Now he is four years old. Next year, no hope.

No hope. No hope.

All I have ever wanted.

On the first day of school, she dresses him. She didn't dare to buy new clothes for school. She puts on him the clothes that he has worn all summer. Black jeans with an elastic waist. An orange short-sleeved shirt with a design of a bear on the left breast pocket. White socks, his old red sneakers he is proud of. Velcro. He can do them himself.

The teacher says: "He's never had a group experience?"

"No, just with me."

"Maybe, then, for the first few days you can stay with him. For a little while. Until he adjusts to the group situation."

She sees the other mothers bought their boys and girls new clothes. And for themselves. She parks the car behind the church and waits till they have all gone in the little building, like a hut, built for the children. All the other mothers know each other. Like each other. And the children.

There is no one that we know.

The teacher is standing at the door. "Good morning Jessica, Kate, Michael, Daniel, Jason, Alison."
    "And here comes Billy."

Children are playing on the swings and slides.
    Children are playing in the sandbox.
    Girls are pretending to cook at the toy stove, using toy pots and spoons and dishes.
    Boys are in the corner making a house of large blocks, then shoving it down, building it, knocking it down, fighting, building.

Billy hides his face in her shoulder.
    "I won't leave you."
    "Maybe tomorrow," says the teacher. "After he gets more used to the group, you'll feel that you can leave after a while."

The teacher's pants are elastic-waisted, like the children's pants. She wears blue eye shadow, her fingernails are pink as shells. She is wearing sandals with thin straps. She is wearing stockings underneath the sandals. JoAnn wonders: Maybe they are socks that only look like stockings. Maybe they stop.

At night he says: "Don't take me back there."
    "All right," she says. Later she says: "I made a mistake. We have to go."

The second day of school he will not look at anybody. When the teacher puts her hand on his shoulder to ask if he sees anything he might like to play with, he pushes her hand away and looks at her with rage. "No one said you could touch me." He hides his eyes. He grinds his eyes into his mother's shoulder blade.
    She's proud that he can speak up for himself. But she is frightened. Now what will they do?

*

In the playground, he lets her push him on a swing. She lights a cigarette. The other mothers don't approve, although they try to smile. They tell her about their children, who had problems getting used to school.

"My oldest was like that. Till Christmas."

No one is like us. No one is like he is.

One morning he says he's tired. She tells him he doesn't have to go to school. She keeps him home for three days. Both of them are happy.

But the next day it's worse in school. Only one of the mothers smiles at her. She says: "You know, maybe Billy's finding the group too large. Maybe he could just come over to our house. Daniel's used to the group. If they made friends, maybe that would help Billy in the group."

"Thank you," JoAnn says. "But we're so busy."

The social worker says: "You're not working on this separation."

Everything has been reported. The social worker takes it as a bad sign that JoAnn refused the other mother's invitation. Which she knows about.

"If I were you," she says, ". . . or maybe some counseling. For both your sakes.

JoAnn is terrified. She tells the other mother she would like to come. The other mother writes her name and address down on a piece of paper torn from a pad in the shape of an apple with a bite out of it. It says "Debi — 35 Ranch Road." And in parentheses "Dan's mom."

For this, she buys her son new clothes.

He never cries anymore. Nobody can make him do anything he doesn't want to. His eyes are bright green stones. No one can make him do anything. This makes her feel she has done right.

The morning that they are going to the house they take a bath together. They laugh, they soap each other's backs. Lately she sees him looking at her sex a second longer than he ought to, and his eyes get hard and angry when he sees she sees. She knows they will not bathe together much longer after this year. But this year. Yes.

Debi, the mother, has to look several places for an ashtray. JoAnn hasn't realized there are no ashtrays until she has already lit up. They are both embarrassed. Debi says, "Somehow most of the people I know quit." She goes through her cabinets and then finds one from a hotel in Canada. "We stole in on our honeymoon," she says, and laughs.

Billy knows his mother doesn't want him to play with Danny. She knows he knows. But she can feel his bones grow lively on her lap; she feels his body straining toward the other children. Danny and his sisters, Gillian and Lisa. And the toys. The house is full of toys. Trucks, cars, blocks, toy dinosaurs are scattered all over the wooden floors. But the house is so big it still looks neat with all the toys all over. The house is too big, too light. The house frightens JoAnn. She holds Billy tighter on her lap. He doesn't move, although she knows he wants to. And she knows he must.

"Look at the truck," she says. "Should we go over and look at that truck?"

Debi jumps out of her chair, runs over to the children.

"Let's show Billy the truck. See Danny's truck, Billy?" She gets down on her knees. "Look how the back goes down like this."

JoAnn doesn't know whether or not to go down on her knees with Debi and the other children. She stands back. Billy looks up at her. His fingers itch to touch the truck. She sees it. She gives him a little push on the shoulders. "Go play," she says. She lights another cigarette and puts the match in the heart-shaped ashtray she has carried with her.

Billy isn't playing with the other children. He is playing alongside them. Danny and his sisters are pretending to make dinner out of clay. They don't talk to Billy; they don't invite him to play with them; they leave him alone, and he seems happy with the truck. She sees he has forgotten her. For him she is nowhere in the room.

Debi says, "Let's go into the kitchen and relax. They're fine without us."

JoAnn feels the house will spread out and the floor disappear. She will be standing alone in air. The house has no edges; the walls are not real walls. Who could be safe here?

In the kitchen in a row below the ceiling there are darker-painted leaves. She tells Debi she likes them.

"I did them myself. I'm kind of a crafts freak. Are you into crafts?"

JoAnn says she always wanted to do ceramics.

"I do ceramics Thursday nights," says Debi. She brings a cookie jar shaped like a bear to the table. "I made this last month," she says. "And while you're at it, have one." She offers JoAnn the open jar. "I made them for the kids, but if you won't tell I won't."

The cookies frighten JoAnn. The raisins, and the walnuts and the oatmeal that will not dissolve against her tongue.

"If you want, there's room in our ceramics class on Thursdays. I think it's important to have your own interests, at least for me. Get away, do something that's not connected to the kids. Get away from them and let them get away from you."

JoAnn begins to cough. She feels she cannot breathe. The walls of the big room are thinning. She is alone in freezing air. Her ribs press against her thin lungs. Debi says: "You okay, JoAnn?"

"I smoke too much. This year, I'm really going to quit. I've said it before, but now, this year I'm really going to do it."

They hear a child scream. They run into the living room. Danny is crying.

"He hit me with the truck."

"Did you hit him with the truck?" JoAnn says. "Tell Danny you're sorry."

Billy looks at them all with his bright eyes. Except at her. He does not look at his mother. He knows she doesn't want him to apologize. He knows that she is glad he did it. He did it for her. She knows this.

"We've got to be going," says JoAnn, picking Billy up. He presses the truck to him. "Put the truck down," she says.

He doesn't look at anyone.

"Don't go," says Debi. "Really, they were doing great. All kids get into things like that. They were doing great for a long time."

"We've got to go," JoAnn says, looking in the pocket of her plaid wool jacket for the keys. "Billy, give Danny back his truck."

"Danny, can Billy borrow the truck till school tomorrow?" Debi asks.

JoAnn pulls the truck from her son's grip.

"Thanks, but he doesn't need it," she says, smiling, handing back the truck. "It isn't his."

The truck falls from her hand. It makes a hard sound on the wooden floor. Hearing the sound, Danny begins to cry again.

"Let's try it again," says Debi. "They were really doing great there for a while."

JoAnn smiles, holding Billy more tightly. "Sure thing," she says.

At night, while he sleeps and she sits on the stool beside his bed to watch, she thinks of him in the room with the other children. Him forgetting. She thinks of him pushing the truck back and forth on the floor beside the other children, thinks of the walls thinning out, and her thin lungs that cannot enclose the breath she needs to live.

Alone. Alone.
All I have ever wanted.

In the morning he says: "You should have let me take that truck."

She says: "Do you want to go back to that house?"

"I want the truck."

"Danny's a nice boy, isn't he?"

He says: "Are you going to leave me alone today?"

"I don't know," she says. "I'll see."

When they arrive, the teacher says: "I think Billy's ready for a regular day today. I think the time's come definitely."

She doesn't look at JoAnn when she says this. She takes Billy's jacket off and hangs it on his hook below his name. She does not let go of his hand. "Billy, I heard you played with Danny yesterday. That's so terrific. He brought in the truck today, for you to play with while you're here."

The teacher leads him into the class, closing the door behind her so JoAnn can't see them. So that he cannot look back.

She stands in the hall. Her hands are freezing. She pulls the fake fleece collar of her plaid coat around her ears. Her heart is solid and will not pump blood. She walks into the parking lot. She gets into her car and starts it. She does not know where she will get her air, how she will breathe. The engine stalls. She pumps the gas pedal and starts the car again.

And then she hears him. He is calling. He is running toward the car. She sees that he has put his coat on by himself. She sees him standing at the car door, opening it, getting in beside her.

She can breathe, the air is warm and helpful for her breathing. They are driving, singing. They are happy.

    She says to him: "Let's pack up all our things. Let's find another place, a better place to live in."

Happy, singing.

He will leave me soon enough.

ELIZABETH GRAVER

The Body Shop

FROM THE SOUTHERN REVIEW

MY MOTHER HAD ME sort the eyes. Blue in the biggest box, green in the middle, brown in the smallest box. She had me organize the hands: good, slightly damaged, very damaged, child's, woman's, or — that rare thing — man's. I screwed in legs, stood on an inverted bucket and dabbed paint at chipped neck joints.

"Get behind the ears, Simon," she told me as I stroked on paint. "Between the fingers, in the cracks." She mixed the sample flesh tones on an artist's palette, adding purples, greens — garish colors I couldn't imagine would transform into skin. And yet everything grew younger around my mother — the sallow became rich, the chipped became whole. Dull painted eyes were cut out with a razor and replaced with lambent glass ones; suddenly it was hard to stare back. Ten years old, I spent my afternoons tracing the facets of the body. Later, when I began to encounter real flesh, the girls and women seemed off to me for a long time, too wide, too soft, all excess, evasion, and shifting eyes.

My mother had lovers. Businessmen, usually, but sometimes artists, and they were mad for her, all of them, arriving at the shop to steal a moment from her day, standing in a corner while she shone lights on her dummies and tested colors, her black hair cut short around her head like a boy's, her long hands splashed with paint. We couldn't stop watching her, my mother's lovers and I, perhaps because she rarely looked back. To me she barked commands in shorthand:

"Mrs. Revere at three — invoice, Simon. Spot check on wedding dress. Where is that goddamn polish? I told you, baby, polish on the blue shelf, would you just *try?*"

To the lover in the corner she said little, but as she passed by with a wig or a coffee can full of paintbrushes, she would run a finger along the underside of his wrist or tap him, and then me, on the chin. A movie, dinner, the theater, they would offer, but she didn't like to leave me alone at night; the Adelsteins had had a break-in two years ago, and if Pammy hadn't hidden behind winter coats in the closet, everyone agreed she would have been stabbed or raped. Sometimes my mother invited the lover to the apartment. We sat then, the three of us, in the living room littered with lace ends and plastic fingernails. She grew quiet, thoughtful. She made me tell stories: "Tell him about the teacher who passed his gallstone around in class." "Tell the one about the frog and Mrs. Booth."

On first telling, when I was alone with my mother, I had delivered the stories with great aplomb. We had laughed until we choked, doubled over the workbench, calming ourselves with deep breaths and then meeting each other's eyes and starting up again. In front of my mother's lovers, my stories came out cold and thin.

"There's just this biology teacher, Mr. Rodman," I would say, and my mother would squint and tuck in her chin, knowing I'd started out all wrong. After a while I did it on purpose, tired of my role as dancing monkey, tired of the men's tight smiles and coughed-up laughs. Eventually, when my mother clapped her hands or yawned, I would be allowed to leave to do my homework. Nobody much wanted to talk anyway. Either she would usher the man down the front hall then, saying she had to make an early start tomorrow, or else they would go into her bedroom and shut the door. Through the crack underneath her door would seep a nearly total silence; only a sneeze or a brief, amputated bark of laughter ever reached my ears.

"Sweet, that man," she would say absently in the morning, or "Jesus, Simon lovey, I'm sorry I made you a boy. What a bunch of boors."

Then she would take out a marking pencil and give me a lesson, scribbling hurried, slanted letters on scraps of pattern paper. There were boors and there were bores and boars, just as there were holes and wholes, whiches and witches, friezes and freezes, nights and knights. Sometimes, my mother said, a talented person could beat the odds and be a boring boor.

The men never stayed overnight, for my mother had her own

sense of propriety which surfaced now and then, and she must have thought I would get bad ideas. Also she needed her sleep. The business was growing, truckloads of tired mannequins arriving each week for face-lifts, special assignments for fashion shows, wedding parties, state gala events. We still shopped carefully, accustomed to a life of thrift, but my mother was making a way for herself in the world, making a way for me.

I liked the special orders best. They were the ones we got to dress, their skin tones calibrated to their outfits — tan beauties for the bathing suit sale, a ruddy Mrs. Santa, a pair of feverish children on skates. Only the fanciest stores demanded our services; the others couldn't afford our prices, didn't see the need for the refurbishment of their aging mannequins, for our special artistic touch. My mother could do anything, take a Basic — a female, stripped-down, unpainted base — and round it out with papier mâché, clay, and wire until it was a buxom, sparkling Mrs. Claus, one eye lowered in a wink. She didn't much like the stock or seasonal, preferring the stately or exotic, real challenges, one-timers: Count Dracula, Humpty Dumpty, the young bride made to stand in the center of a fiftieth wedding anniversary gala wearing a dress long outgrown by its owner. We pasted the aging scalloped wedding photo over the workbench, and my mother made studied improvements — longer lashes, a smaller waist, little buds of nipples to show ever-so-faintly through the delicate fabric of the dress. When the plump and wealthy client stopped by each week to see how her former self was shaping up, my mother would steer her by the arm into the lovers' corner and tell her to stay quiet so we could concentrate.

With the increasing amount of money the shop was bringing in, she started a college fund, bought me educational toys, sent money to orphans in Israel and to help my alcoholic father in California — which was also like giving to a charity, she said. But chemistry sets and hand-carved chessboards gathered dust at home, for I worked in the shop after school each day, the way she had in her father's tailor shop. "Rich, lazy boys are terrible creatures," she would tell me, but really she couldn't hold on to hired help, nobody up to her standards, nobody trained, the way I was, from birth. My toys, stacked up in corners, became resting places for piles of fabric and skeins of colored yarn.

We worked hard, barely pausing for dinner. Each day I took the subway home from school, bought a candy bar for myself and one for my mother, and came directly to the store. In the evening, when the neighborhood turned dangerous, we lowered the metal grille over the shop window, fastened the police lock, and pulled down the green shade. Unless she had a man friend calling at our apartment down the street, we waited until our stomachs started rumbling too loudly to be ignored and then ate standing in the shop, Chinese food from the Magic Lantern next door. The dummies stood like naked female sentries, throwing confident, curved shadows about the room. At eight I began my homework while she kept on. We gave names, sometimes, to the ones we had been working on for a while. Miss Bridie for the wedding dress girl, Amber and Coffee-Tea-Or-Me for the wispy bathing suit twins, Mr. Baby-They're-Playing-Our-Song for the debonair tanned gentleman in a white suit. As deadlines approached, the names got shortened: "Wrap up Mr. Baby, Simon. Put another coat on Coffee's lips."

One day she named a handsome dummy Frank, after my father, and kissed it on the forehead, and it came to me that she still loved him, that the checks and the long phone conversations in which she told him to get himself to a doctor — to get himself on unemployment, or would he like a ticket east? — were for herself as much as for him, probably more. I wouldn't refer to the mannequin as Frank, but called it by its official name: Invoice 304. I didn't want a father, didn't see the need. I was not unhappy — not after school, not on the weekends. At school I felt out of place and often missed my mother, but in order to leave the classroom behind, I had only to smell the turpentine on my shirt cuff or stare at my hands covered with nail polish, dots of paint, scabs of glue like a peeling second skin.

The last week in February I celebrated my eleventh birthday. Two days later, in what I took as nature's belated gift, class was dismissed early because of an approaching blizzard. The sky was gray and bloated, and though we had been instructed to go straight home, some boys were running off to play games in a vacant lot a block from school. For a moment I considered joining them, but I wasn't good at games, and besides, I pictured my mother's surprise at seeing me early, how I would come in the back way and sneak up behind her with a mannequin arm, tickle her neck and hear her scratchy laugh. I took the subway. By the time I had emerged from the dark tunnels, it had begun to snow. I ate my candy bar as I walked to the workshop, licking off the snowflakes as they dotted the chocolate with white spots.

When I got to the back door, I opened it carefully, then moved easily through the dark storeroom to the box of ladies' arms and separated one from the rest, sliding it out inch by inch so as not to clank. I sucked in my breath, tense with anticipation of my small joke, how the moment would approach and arrive, and then we would laugh about it afterwards, reenacting it, until it became one of our nurtured private memories, one of the stories which fell flat before any but our own ears. As I crept toward the front workroom, I heard voices, hers and someone else's, a customer's.

"How many again?" she said, and he answered, "Hundreds for you, you do such a beautiful job. How do you get them so beautiful? Almost as pretty as you."

"Sweat," my mother said. "Sweat and broken nails." I paused, knowing not to interrupt her with a customer, hoping she would mention my name: My son Simon helps every day after school. I couldn't do it without him.

"The thing is," said the man's voice, and by now I was leaning behind the doorway and could see the back of his dark suit, his bald head rimmed with a neat line of white hair. "The thing is we have the people in Queens who usually do it. For a good price, too."

"What people?" said my mother. "You're talking a shoddy paint job. Nobody does this the way I do."

"No," said the man. "No, probably not."

And then he was leaning toward her and whispering something in her ear, so that I wondered if I had been spotted and found out. My mother backed off, said, "Oh, for God's sake. This is a business I run here."

"Yes," said the man. "I know."

"Well, then?" said my mother.

And the man said, "For years I've had nobody, but I run a good and decent business."

"Me too, I run a good and decent business," said my mother, and he shrugged and started to walk off. My mother looked over toward the storeroom as if she were staring straight at me, and then she whispered something to herself, untied her apron, and lifted it over her head. She lowered her chin and began to unbutton her workshirt, then turned so the man could unfasten her brassiere, which he did with calm, efficient hands. She turned again and drew him to her, the back of his head disappearing from my sight as he lowered his face to her chest.

"This is it," she said.

I dropped the arm with a clatter, turned to run. As I swiveled around I caught a glimpse of my mother's hands flashing toward me through the air.

"Simon!" she called, but I ran through the dark storeroom and out into the snow, and though I stood there for a minute catching my breath, half expecting her to show up at the back door, only silence issued from the building. As I started down the street trying to push the picture of my mother from my mind, other pictures came to me — the teenage couple in our neighborhood who rode a motorcycle, how the girl pressed up behind the boy, put her chin on his shoulder and slid her hands into the waistband of his jeans. My father — the way, when I was almost too young to remember, he would call me in some mornings and let me crawl into bed with them, between their large bodies smelling of sleep. Then we would be sandwiches — pastrami, egg, roast beef. I would be the meat, and my parents, hugging each other around my skinny body, would be the bread, kissing and tickling my stomach and the back of my neck until I laughed so hard that once I actually wet the bed. I wasn't sure if I really remembered this, or if my mother had told it to me. Sometimes I doubted I'd ever had a father at all.

There were other things I was more sure of — the noises which came from my mother's room when she had guests there at night, the pride I felt at school Open House when she was prettier than all the other mothers, a red scarf in her hair. I knew how to link the tiny metal catches on the tops of her dresses to close the collar, how to apply a thin, even coat of fingernail polish to the run on her stocking, how to scratch her back or her chin for her when her hands were covered with paint. My mother prided herself on being up-front, and yet when I saw her there with the white-haired man, I had a queasy feeling that I knew nothing about her, about anything, the whole world operating in secret exchanges behind my back — even this mother who allowed her son no secrets, who scrubbed and questioned and drew out my insides until so much was on the surface that I wondered if anything could be left inside.

"I hate you," I muttered, turning down a residential side street, a cluster of cats scrambling out of my path. The snow was slippery, already turning brown. The vocabulary words we were learning that week in school began to run through my head like a dull song: procrastinate, nonchalant, efficient, hypocrite. That was the one I wanted, and balancing on someone's front stoop, I said it: "Hypocrite." I would say it again when I saw her, sneer if she didn't know what it meant. For she wasn't so smart, my mother, after all, and I was getting smarter every day.

When I got too cold, I went back to the store, back to the workroom, tiptoeing in case he was still there, but he was gone. My mother had put on her apron and begun to mix colors again.

"Simon," she said, and I kicked at the side of a work table with my boot. "I've asked you not to come in when I have a customer. You're home early, huh? Because of the snow?"

I looked at the ceiling.

"Can you believe how much it's snowing?" she asked. I stared at a web of cracks from a leak we'd had. "Maybe you can stay home tomorrow. It takes them forever to clear the roads."

My voice sounded inside my head, then came out. "Who was he?"

"Who was he? He was — he was just a man. Just a very important man who runs the period fashion show at the opera. They read our ad in the paper."

I took a deep breath. My mother looked a bit twisted to me, bent out of shape, as if someone had taken her apart and put her back together again slightly out of whack. Then I realized that she had buttoned her workshirt wrong, so that it hung crooked across her chest.

"Your shirt's a mess —" I said, pointing.

"Oh." She looked down and began redoing the buttons. "Yes. Thank you." I stood with the snow melting off my boots in a slick puddle and watched her hands.

"Well," she said when she had finished buttoning. "He gave us a big account, baby. You feel like helping? I'm all ready to get down to work."

I shook my head, and she sighed and stepped toward me, but I backed away.

"What, are you mad at me, Simon? If you are, just say so. Are you, huh?"

I shook my head again.

"Oh, come on, honey," she said, and I could feel something stretching out, growing taut and panicked in her voice. "Let's just forget it, okay?"

I nodded, but we both knew I didn't mean it, and I could tell how badly she wanted me to open my mouth and say anything at all. I pictured a silver zipper on my mouth, closing it like stitches, sealing it from her. I kicked at the bench again and felt my mouth twist into a scowl. She pushed aside the palette she had been mixing on so that a glob of paint fell like a bird dropping to the floor. She bent down and began attacking the paint spot with a sponge.

"Okay fine," said my mother. "Go play baseball. Go play with the other kids."

As she scrubbed, she began to hum a cheerful tune. I started to back toward the front door, pledged to silence, but the zipper on my mouth gave way, and I found myself whispering, "Shut up bitch, shut up bitch," under my breath. My mother straightened up, came after me.

"What did you say?"

"Nothing."

She grabbed my jacket collar, dug her nails into my neck. "What did you say, Simon?"

"Bye. I said bye." I had begun to cry, trying to squirm away from her.

My mother peered down at me, and in the narrowed slits of her eyes I saw a pure and concentrated disdain which made her hands tense up and her lips and the bridge of her nose grow tight and pale.

"Don't you ever lie to me," she said. "Do you hear me? Don't you ever, ever lie to your mother, you little bastard!"

"What I said," I told her, twisting out of her hold, "was 'shut up bitch.' " I yelled it as she leaned over me, directly into her ear. "Bitch!" I tried to think of the vocabulary word I had used before, but it had slipped away.

My mother grabbed me again, slapped me hard across the

cheek, and then she was pressing me to her apron, which smelled of turpentine, touching her mouth to my hair.

"Oh Jesus, baby," she said, and her torso shook so that I wondered if she had begun to laugh or cry. She rocked me, but I held myself rigid. "Some pair we are, the bitch and the bastard. What do you think the Adelsteins would say to that?"

I shrugged, and she let go of me, patted me on the behind.

"Wow," she said. "I've never seen you get so mad. You've got quite a temper under there, huh? That's good. You're going to need it in this world."

And I felt her swiftly take it from me — my small arsenal of playground obscenities, my temper — felt it change under her stamp of approval until it became flat and useless, no longer mine. Bitch, I thought, but the word sounded dull, like a rusty blade.

"We've got nothing but each other, kiddo, whether you like it or not," she said. "I love you to death. You have the afternoon off. Live it up, because tomorrow we get going on the costume show, if you still want to help."

As I started out the door, she called, "Simon," and I turned.

"I don't expect *you* to be perfect," she said, and I thought of how many times that week she had made me redo the fingernail polish on a hand because I'd smeared the edges, or botched the color slightly, or let a brushstroke show.

"Okay, I expect a lot of you," she added, reading my mind. "But just to try your best, is all. No more."

I pictured her guiding the old man's mouth to her breast like a baby's, waving her hands as she saw me standing there. I bit down on my lip and turned again to leave.

"I *do* try my best," my mother called, and for the first time in my memory, I thought she really was about to cry.

"You try raising a kid and running this lousy business," she said, and she gasped and let her jaw drop as if the air had turned to water and she couldn't breathe. As she reached out her hand to steady herself, the emergency medical number 911 flashed across my brain, but then she was standing straight again, dry-eyed, drawing in slow breaths.

"I — I was dizzy. I guess I'm a little upset," she said after a moment, then sighed. "Would you come and give your old ma a hug?" So I went and held her and thought how she wasn't so tall — I was catching up — and she wasn't as pretty as she used to be —

all the little lines on her neck and around her eyes. But still somehow I didn't want to leave her for a neighborhood full of strange
kids and games I hardly knew how to play.

"How many?" I asked her, and she said, "It's a windfall, sweetie.
Ninety-five women, twenty kids, ten men. It'll be gorgeous, in
the lobby of the opera hall. Spring tones, and the supply budget
is enormous. They want a Queen Victoria, and Mary What's-her-
name — Queen of —"

"Scots."

"Just testing. The royalty in the center, and then the hand-
maidens in a circle, and the children on the stairs going up."

Her eyes were shining; she had begun to wave her hands. We
would have to clear out work space, bring in the barrels to mix
uniform lots of flesh paint. We would have to organize ourselves.

"It's snowing," I said. "Nobody plays baseball in the snow."

And my mother took my hand as if she'd known that all along
and led me to the musty storeroom to gather parts.

Twice a week I went to see my mother at the King David Residence for Jewish Elders, a stately nursing home where she sat
with her one leg, the other gone to gangrene below the knee a
few years back, and cancer running races through her remaining
bones. Saturdays, I brought my daughter, Rebecca, nine years
old and a beauty, although she didn't quite know it yet. In my
mother's private room we perched among fabric scraps and ribbons, and my mother gave Rebecca gifts — a feathered hat, a ten-
dollar bill with "For My Treasure" written in block letters on the
portico of the United States Treasury, a piece of lace to weave
through her braid. Rebecca was in the best schools, doing well;
my mother was receiving top-notch care. Still, they found much
to complain about. The man who fit her prosthesis kept feeling
up her thigh, said my mother, and when I motioned at my
daughter, she said, "Oh shush, Simon. Why not teach her early
what to watch out for? With her looks, they'll be all over her like
flies."

Rebecca complained that she didn't win the singing prize at
school, though she was sure she had the best voice.

"Of course you do," said her grandmother. "The judges must
be deaf."

The two of them criticized the food, the smell of disinfectant.

They bitched. As they grew more animated, their displeasure became a sort of cockeyed joy; their nostrils flared, they made wide paths with their hands. I watched. When Rebecca went down the hall to beg Jell-O off the nurses, my mother gestured for me to come closer, put her hand on my knee, and asked me how Kimberly was.

"Would you just ask your granddaughter, Ma," I said. "You know I'm no expert."

For three years I'd been divorced, and for three years she'd asked me how Kimberly was as often as she dared, usually once or twice a month.

"When you pick your daughter up and drop her off, you must see something," she said, and I wondered what she expected from me, expected from this ex-wife of mine whom she could never get along with, both of them too fiery to make a proper mix, and myself placed between them like a piece of shade. Weekends when I dropped my daughter off and picked her up, I got no further than the corner. When, rarely, Kimberly called me, it was because she was, in her words, so lonely she could die, just jilted, or because the harp concert she gave got a lousy review, or because Rebecca had expressed interest again in moving in with me.

Then my ex-wife and I met in parks and cafés and soothed each other with the familiar odd gesture — hair smoothed away from a forehead, a squeezed hand, a slipped-in kiss. Or rather I soothed her. Staying angry was beyond me, though I had my ways and tempted my daughter to the apartment with expensive stereo equipment, a lack of regulations, an overabundance of her favorite food. I had fixed it up since the days I'd lived there as a boy, knocked down walls, installed a skylight. The neighborhood was growing gentrified. I had painted Rebecca's room, formerly the sewing room, a rose faux-marble. My own room I left white.

My mother said, "I just don't want you to be alone. Is there someone else?"

I shook my head no. Only the business — the decorative art, marbleizing, and trompe l'oeil jobs I did in luxury apartments, restaurants, and hotels — so much more than I could keep up with, an excess of money, of clients. I had become quite skilled at painting, though I still could not paint people — only flora, fauna, imitation stone. A few months earlier, I had been featured in a slick magazine with a picture of the lake I painted onto the floor of the Restaurant des Cygnes. I showed the article to my mother, and she held it up to the light, her eyesight weak.

"Yes," she said. "Yes. Fine. Lovely. You'd better make the clients take off their shoes when they go in there, or it'll be ruined in no time."

"There are mirrored paths," I said. "I'll take you there sometime for dinner." And she blew air out of her mouth with a whistling sound and gestured dismissively at her false leg.

She asked me if I needed money, for Rebecca, her school, for myself, a treat. "No," I said. "I'm fine." Always the same thing.

"I'd slip that prosthesis man a check," she said, "if he'd only keep his hands to himself."

I looked away, and she said, "You don't believe me, Simon. Have I ever lied to you? He must be a sick man, maybe on drugs or something, the way his hands shake."

I didn't want to think about it, so I went down the hall to retrieve Rebecca, and then we wheeled my mother to the flagstone patio and sat staring at the small pond. The stooped and hobbled residents were everywhere; my mother waved and called to them by name. Most of them adored her, for her charm, her wit. The old men left gifts outside her door, and each week she took the objects from a drawer and tried to give them to Rebecca or me — chocolates, a deck of cards, a faded Rosh Hashanah card.

"Their children give them presents," she said, "and they give the presents to me, and then what am I supposed to do?"

Some people at the residence disliked my mother, jealous, she said, of the son who visited twice a week, and the fact that she had gotten her money from her own hard work, not from the sweat of others or her husband's pocket, and because her granddaughter was the loveliest one around. Rebecca skipped on the lawn, balanced with extended arms on the edge of the concrete pond, and I called out to her to be careful or she'd fall.

"Leave her be," said my mother. I called out again, louder this time, and Rebecca turned, lost her balance, and plunged one sneakered foot and a blue-jeaned leg into the shallow pond. "Oh shit!" she yelled, then clamped her hand over her mouth as the old people stared. My daughter went to her grandmother's room, where she knew how to find things. When she joined us again, she was wearing a striped skirt of my mother's, down to her ankles and held up with a sash, and peach silk Chinese bedroom slippers laced with gold thread. She pranced in front of us and made a face.

"Oh no you don't! You put that dry sneaker back on your left foot to leave me one clean slipper," said my mother. "But thank you for falling so conveniently. What do I need with the right one anyway?"

We drove to the Botanical Gardens and took a walk. Pushing the wheelchair through so much cultivated green, I found myself dizzied by the pollen, by the soft earth which gave way beneath my feet, the garden mazes of shaped hedges and flowering trees.

My mother pointed things out to us: gardenia, flowering maple, bachelor buttons, clematis, weeping cherry tree. Rebecca remembered them from last time, though she never quite seemed to be listening. She anticipated answers, pointed and ran in circles, recited names back. I followed in my head, but they were too quick for me — another world altogether out there with all those green and growing things. I ran through names of pigments in my mind as I saw the colors in the unfamiliar flowers: alizarin crimson, cerulean blue, rose madder, burnt umber, venetian red.

"Poppy," said Rebecca, and crouched in its center like a spider, I saw lampblack.

Half listening to their talk, I made a mental list of decorative painting methods: stipling, combing, dragging, mottling, pouncing, rag-rolling, tuffbacking, decoupage, frottage. Most of it I had taught myself. I rested my hand on my mother's head, stroked her hair, still so soft. She closed her hand around mine, and we stopped for an instant while Rebecca ran on ahead.

"Hi," I said to my mother.

"Baby," she said.

Such a secret, juvenile pleasure I took in the fact that my mother did not know the shoptalk of my trade.

This morning she died, my mother. It was bound to happen sometime. I know that, I tell myself that: just as everybody has a mother, everybody's mother dies. We are having a cold spell; inside, the air is static, crackling with heat. My daughter, who is with me for the weekend, sits quietly as I tell her, then goes to her room and shuts the door. I leave her there in the apartment where I grew up and go for a walk on the winter streets. Krugel's is having a fur sale. The women in the window are naked underneath their minks, the joints of their wrists showing, their eyes flat and dull as slate. I have not kept up the mannequin business, though I still get calls from ex-clients now and then: a nativity scene, a pair of lovers, a fife and drum corps. I say no.

If I were my mother, I could replace her body part by part — a plastic leg, a glass eye, skin mixed from a slew of gaudy colors, hair tinted with a supple brush. I could mix and match, scrape and barter, make do. But I am not my mother, and loss comes to me whole and unwieldy, as awkward as the bulky man in the overcoat who looks out at me from the shop window, eyes level with the fur-clad women's jointed waists. What, I wonder, have I become? What has she made of me with such careful pruning, such close directives, such proximity to all she knew as true? A stringy knot of reproach begins to tie itself in my gut that she has not done better, made more of me, made me more — a woman of her talent, energy, and skill. I have not come out feeling particularly grown, though I do feel old. I expect myself to be smaller, wish myself smaller, but the man I see is overweight, no youngster, brow furrowed, chin weak, face clouded by the condensation of the cold.

"You're a details person, is what you are," my mother told me when I was a boy. "You go ahead with the lashes and fingernails and leave the rest to me."

I think for a moment about her money piled on top of my own, what a rich man I have just become, how, if I liked, I could never work another day in my life, how I could stay by my daughter's side. I think of my mother watching Rebecca by the water, telling me to leave the child be. What, I wonder, would she have done if I had been the one playing on the edge, and still a clumsy boy? I was not that sort of child. It is not a good idea, I realize, to go home just now; I should learn to leave my daughter to herself and her salty grief.

I begin to walk, and the windows are full of bodies, most of them poorly rendered, awkwardly posed in the evening light. I cannot look without correcting, patching a joint here, a chip there until I reach the end of the street. A details person, said my mother, but already the details begin to slide from me. I am not sure where to go from here, so I turn and make my way slowly back on the other side. My thoughts are critical — I see only the shoddiness, the carelessness, the way a woman's arm in the window is bent as if she broke it, her foot curved as if caught in a lifelong cramp.

What I cannot do, my weak point, is create a perfect window world, the figures poised like bits of grace, their mouths on speech's threshold, their eyes on the edge of sight. It is not that it cannot be done — I've seen it — but I cannot do it myself. For a moment I imagine bribing the Krugel's security guard to let me into the window; I would bring along a palette, some tubes of paint, some glass eyes. Then I would do my best to transform the fur-clad women into graceful, happy creatures — I'd bend their arms into motion and provide them with new eyes. But my daughter is home alone, and these days in the city a security guard would probably shoot me in the head. Anyway, they are nothing but mannequins, and I am nothing but a heavy man in an overcoat, growing colder and colder as I walk along until my lungs hurt from the mere act of breathing, and I can think of nothing but getting warm.

SIRI HUSTVEDT

Houdini

FROM FICTION

IN THE END they put me in the hospital. That was after all the
other treatments had failed. The Inderal, the Cafergot, the Mel-
laril, the Elavil, the little white inhaling box, and the famous Fish
cocktail. Every day I took the test and swallowed enormous pills
of Thorazine at regular intervals. That was where I met Mrs. O.
She was in bed 3. I was in bed 2, and Mrs. M. was in bed 4. Bed 1
was empty.

As a migraineur, I had low status. Admittedly I was a bad case:
I had had pain in my head for seven months almost without res-
pite. Sometimes it was mild, sometimes brutal. My bowels were
racked. I peed too much. I was supernaturally tired. I saw black
holes and tiny rings of light; my jaw tingled; my hands and feet
were ice-cold; I was always nauseated. My body had become the
meeting place for ridiculous symptoms, but what I had was still a
headache and headaches had little clout on the neurology ward.
The day I arrived, the fat nurse said, "She's one of Dr. Fish's,"
and after that they pretty much left me alone. They changed my
bed and filled my water pitcher, but they rarely spoke to me. They
seemed suspicious. And I didn't demand further attention, because I was guilty. It was clear to me that I had made the headache, created the monster myself, and just because I couldn't get
rid of the damned thing didn't mean I wasn't to blame. Besides,
speaking was difficult. I had to do it through a cocoon of Thorazine. The distance between the place where the words originated — somewhere deep within the headache — and where they
had to go — out into the room — seemed insurmountable. In the

beginning I was a quiet patient. It wasn't until later, after the incidents with Mrs. O., that one of the nurses called me a troublemaker.

Every morning Dr. Fish would poke his head into the room and wave, and I would wave back and smile. But I knew he was disgusted. Dr. Fish was a man who liked successes. He liked them so much that before I landed in the hospital he told me that I was improving when I was not, and now that I was so conspicuously unimproved, he shunned me. My person had become the sign of his failure, a recalcitrant body, a taunt to his medical prowess. Our relationship had been false from the start. I now believe that this dishonesty was rooted in Dr. Fish's method of interrogating his patients. He used a tape recorder. Had he actually recorded his patients' speech, this approach might have been harmless, but as it was, the only voice on those tapes was Dr. Fish's. When I arrived for my first appointment, he greeted me warmly, invited me to sit in a beautiful leather chair, asked me how I was feeling, and encouraged me to describe my symptoms. I told him that I had a painful head as usual, and was about to launch into the story of my headache when he grabbed a microphone from his desk and spoke loudly into it: "Iris Vegan. Case number 63912. Tuesday, September 2, 1980." Then he nodded toward me and smiled, a signal to continue. I had prepared notes about my headache on index cards and looked down at them to orient myself.

"It started last June," I said. "I was walking home from the library on Broadway, and I remember that the street looked different to me, very clear and beautiful, and I felt incredibly happy. I even said to myself, 'I've never been happier than I am now.' "

"Yes," he said, and fingered his bald head.

I could see that Dr. Fish was restless, and although I wanted to explain that the feeling of completeness, of perfection, was essential to the story, I rushed on. "But as soon as I stepped inside my apartment, I felt a tug on my left arm, just as if someone had yanked it hard. I lost my balance and fell down. I was so dizzy and sick to my stomach that I didn't get up for a long time. While I was sitting there on the floor, I saw lights, hundreds of bright sparks that filled up half the room, and after they disappeared, I saw a big, ragged hole in the wall. That hole scared me to death, and the strange thing was that I didn't experience it as a problem

with my vision. I really thought that a part of the wall was missing. I don't know how long it lasted, but after the hole was gone,
the pain started."

Dr. Fish picked up the microphone. "The patient suffered a
scintillating and a negative scotoma."

This ferocious editing had a peculiar effect on me. As the interview continued, I mumbled, coughed, forgot words, and lost
track of what I was saying. Before I was sent to Dr. Fish, who was
known in New York as "The Headache Czar," I had tried to tell
my story to six less famous physicians, and each time I had lost
my tongue. I felt that if only I could articulate my illness in all its
aspects, I might give a trained ear the clue that would make me
well, but my words were always inadequate. And most of what I
said was of no use to Dr. Fish either. He let it pass like so much
irrelevance, interrupting me now and then for a curt synopsis.
"The patient says that vomiting has on occasion relieved her pain."

Every week I went to Dr. Fish, and every week I looked better
to him, less pale, less drawn, less tired. He interrupted me more
frequently and summarized my complaints in an increasingly op-
timistic light. I couldn't see or feel these changes myself, but Dr.
Fish was confident, and I half believed him. The truth is that I
participated in the deception. I was studying for my oral exams
then, and I was desperate for the treatments to work. If they didn't,
I would fail. Of the 647 works on my list, 233 novels, plays, stories, and poems were still only titles to me. I had to know them
by May 15. Every day I sat in the library, staring at a great work
of literature that I couldn't read. My head was in the way, a stubborn obfuscating cloud at best, an excruciating lump at worst.
Measuring the degrees of my pain became an obsession. When
my head lightened, I was jubilant. The pills are helping, I would
think. But when it seemed to hurt more, I despaired. Mountains
of books were piled on my desk, and as the days passed, the very
sight of them threw me into a panic. Nevertheless, I pretended
to be well. It was a point of pride. With Dr. Fish I was always
cheerful. I joked about my nerves. I smiled even when the headache raged, and I had to hide my trembling hands by clasping
them tightly together. Concealing illness from a physician is absurd, but I couldn't bear to be seen for what I was — a person
going to pieces.

Then in January I was suddenly worse. I couldn't get out of

bed. I threw up my pills and was leaden with exhaustion, but sleeping seemed only to aggravate the pain. After a week of unabated wretchedness, I dragged myself to Dr. Fish's office for my appointment and blubbered shamelessly in his leather chair. He told me to check into Mount Olympus Hospital the following morning.

I seldom left the room. All its particulars became familiar to me: the tiny flaws and marks on the white wall adjacent to my bed, the long narrow cut in the Formica surface of my night table, the frayed edge of my blue blanket. And I spent hours looking at Mrs. O.'s bed curtain. One of its rings was broken; this disturbed the symmetry of the fabric's folds, and when the curtain was drawn there was a sag in the upper right corner. I can still see it perfectly. My senses were oddly acute during that time. I wasn't always able to open my eyes to the room's fluorescent glare, but when I could, I saw its contents with remarkable clarity. Every sound on the ward vibrated through me; my nerves were as resonant as a tuning fork. The smells of antiseptic, urine, and hospital food were often so pungent that I hid my nose in the pillow. But at the same time my body was impossibly heavy, and even lifting an arm required a huge effort. It was a curious state. I felt like a turtle hundreds of years old, its soft inner body encased in a stone shell. It was never clear to me whether the things I saw, heard, smelled, and felt were distorted or I was merely hypersensitive. At any rate, things were not the same. I can't say what was behind it — whether it was the drug, the headache, or my state of mind. Probably it was all of these, but while I was there, lying in that bed, the world changed. Mrs. O. had a lot to do with it. She was the secret — the paralysis and the frenzy — but I didn't understand that until the very end.

Mrs. M. was a woman who took charge. She had instituted a hierarchy in the room according to illness. In her view, she suffered on a higher plane than either I or Mrs. O. did. She had a nervous disorder that made walking difficult, but her "mind" was unaffected, and she reminded us of this repeatedly. "Thank God, I haven't lost my marbles. That's the worst. As long as you've got your wits about you, you won't shame yourself." I ranked a distant second on Mrs. M.'s scale of maladies. She quickly surmised that my ailment, unlike hers, was psychosomatic, or as she bluntly put it, "There's nothing really wrong with you, is there? It's all in your head." Nevertheless, my neurasthenia rated far above the affliction of poor Mrs. O. Mrs. M. referred to her neighbor on the left simply as "the loony." Mrs. M. was supposed to practice walking but disliked it and walked only when the nurses insisted, and then she screamed at the disobedient limbs, "Move, damn you! Move, you idiots!" She much preferred sitting up in bed and talking. She went at it full tilt, babbling without pause, the bleached curls of her permanent trembling as she shook her head for emphasis. Her chief subject was money. "How do you expect me to get any service around here without something to grease the wheels, for Christ's sake? Green. I need green." Mrs. M. did get attention. I'm quite sure she bribed the nurses. They fussed over her far more then they did over Mrs. O. or me, and once, early in the morning, I witnessed a transaction. Mrs. M. dug under the corner of her mattress and pressed something into the fat nurse's hand. I suspect she paid them not to make her walk, because she did very little walking while I was there. She talked. She talked all day — to the doctors, to the nurses, to me, to her daughter on the phone, to no one, to anyone, about money, about Mrs. O., and every word clanked and rang in my sore head. "Look at the loony, will you? She eats like a dog. Yesterday lunch she ate Jell-O with her hands. She had gravy in her nose. Why did they put me in here? They should keep people like that separate, out of the way. I can't stand to look at it anymore. It'll cost me. It always costs me. I've got to get a different room — a private room, maybe, with curtains, real curtains, not these cheap shades." When she wanted to count her money (this occurred at least once a day), Mrs. M. would remain seated on the bed but would pull the sheet over her entire body to hide the procedure, and I would hear her muttering the numbers to herself — "Twenty, forty, sixty, seventy, seventy-five, seventy-eight, seventy-eight dollars and sixty-two cents." When she spoke to her daughter, she always said that she had "no dough," but Mrs. M. seemed to have bills and coins hidden everywhere — in her bed, on her person — and whenever she moved, she rustled and jangled.

Mrs. M. meant to dominate, to fill up the room with herself, but despite her incessant chatter and her bulk (she was a fleshy woman with jowls and a substantial bosom), it was the small and silent Mrs. O. who took up space. She was a delicate woman in her late seventies, the victim of some nervous catastrophe. That event or series of events had left her incoherent. What remained was a fragmented being, a person shattered into a thousand pieces, but those bits of Mrs. O. inhabited the room like a crowd of invisible demons.

When I first saw her, she was lying motionless in bed, a frail corpselike figure, but when I walked past her, she sat up with surprising energy and pointed at me. I looked at Mrs. O. with her extended arm and finger, her face alert as if she were waiting for me to respond. It was only when I turned my head away that she let her arm drop. I have no idea why she did it. It was an act typical of her only in the sense that it was unpredictable. One never knew what Mrs. O. would do next, and it was this quality that made life in the room precarious.

Mrs. O. was a conundrum to everyone, and thus the object of rumor, gossip, and speculation. Like most people confined to an institution, she had been divested of a past life. She was born old and in her hospital gown. I asked about her. I wanted to know who she had been and where she had lived. No one knew. Yet the ward buzzed with stories of her mischief. The very first afternoon of my stay, I overheard two nurses talking outside the door. I'm certain one told the other that Mrs. O. had bitten a doctor. There was some mention of "bathroom nastiness" as well. Mrs. M. swore that Mrs. O. was violent and, moreover, that she was hatching a plot. "She's got something up her sleeve, mind you, and it isn't pretty." Later that same day, an orderly named Washington, one of the few people besides Mrs. M. with whom I ever had a real conversation, said that when Mrs. O. first arrived she had spent one disastrous night roaming the corridors. He hadn't worked that shift, but a friend of his had caught up with Mrs. O. in the maternity ward at four in the morning. She was standing outside the nursery with her nose pressed to the glass. "Just looking at the babies, all quiet and thoughtful-like." But later that day, various acts of sabotage were uncovered: the contents of a garbage can strewn in a stairwell, bed linens and towels ripped off the shelves in a hall closet and thrown to the floor, a missing food cart found in the shower stall of a bathroom. They were all blamed on Mrs. O. But how could she have wandered the halls without being seen? Washington couldn't understand it. Mrs. M. adamantly maintained that Mrs. O. was capable of disguising herself in a staff uniform and sneaking about the halls unnoticed. "The loony's crafty as hell," she said. But Washington had a different opinion. "How could that itsy-bitsy old lady lift one of those giant trash cans?"

The next morning a neurologist came to visit Mrs. O. He was a young doctor, vigorous and handsome. I noticed that his face and arms were deeply tanned. He strode over to her, sat down on the edge of her bed, and drew the curtain around the two of them. He greeted her in a friendly way, something on the order of "And how are we doing today?" There was no response. I heard stirring in the sheets, a few muffled grunts, and then nothing. Seconds later, the doctor flung back the curtain and hurried out the door. He looked stricken. When I leaned over to look at Mrs. O., she was smiling broadly, and it was then that she reminded me of someone I knew or had known. I tried to dredge up the lost face and name, but they resisted me. This uncanny sense of familiarity subsided very quickly, but it left a residue, a doubt that stayed with me. What had spawned that moment of recognition? Was it really something in her expression or was it something inside me? In any case, I began to watch Mrs. O. more closely.

The residents made daily rounds to give us the test. It was an unnecessary ritual, but I supposed they needed the practice. It consisted of a series of questions followed by some mild pinpricking. Frankly, Mrs. M. and I both enjoyed it. The test punctuated our day, and it was pleasant to be quizzed by those rosy young men in their white coats. Mrs. M. even primped for the occasion. She would pinch her cheeks and pat her curls when she saw a likely candidate coming through the door and was visibly disappointed when the resident turned out to be female. Mrs. O., on the other hand, was usually cantankerous. There were a couple of days when she lay passively in her bed, smiling meekly and nodding as the questions were posed to her one by one; but more often she rebelled, and when an examiner approached her, she would bat and kick at him furiously, letting out one high-pitched shriek after another. More awful, however, were the days when Mrs. O. was eager to take the test. It always began with the question "What is your name?" Mrs. O.'s face would contort into a look of profound bewilderment. She would squint as she searched, desperate to extract the correct words from her unyielding brain. Then, as she clenched her jaw, her face would grow red from effort. It seemed that she thought she could press out the name only if she pushed hard enough. With each subsequent question, her straining increased. "Where are you now? What season is it? What is today's date? What is this object?" the doctor would say, waving a pencil in her face. By the time he was pricking her thigh with a needle and asking, "Can you feel this?" Mrs. O. was exhausted and miserable. And despite the fact that she couldn't reply to a single preliminary question, she felt the pinpricks. One day she looked up at the resident and said in a tired, plaintive voice, "Why on earth are you doing that to me?"

The fact was that Mrs. O. wasn't one person, she was many people, and no one knew who might turn up from one moment to another. This plurality gave the room an air of constant expectation. I found myself charting the course of Mrs. O.'s lunacy as if it were my calling. Every morning Mrs. O.'s husband arrived for his daily visit. The climate of this morning encounter was often indicative of Mrs. O.'s persona for that day, and I always tried to be awake for it. He was tall and stooped, a man of clean, pressed suits and many ties. As Mrs. M. expressed it, he was "nicely pulled together." The person Mrs. O. had once been could be seen in him and in the things he brought her: a pale blue quilted robe with silk ribbons at the neck and waist; a small, immaculate toilet bag with pink flowers; a shiny brass travel clock. When he arrived, he would walk slowly to her bed, place his offering of the day on the windowsill, sit down beside her, and take her hand in his. He did this without fail and regardless of her reception of him. One day he would find a stone in the bed, a body so pale and rigid that it might have been dead; on another, a flapping, writhing screwball who laughed so hard that she choked on her own saliva. Or he might find her ruminating, her old face solemn with concentration. He took it all very well, witnessing his wife's metamorphoses with remarkable composure. I saw him excited only once. It happened in the early part of my stay. He had taken her hand, and I saw her turn toward him. Her face was completely transformed. The change was unmistakable. She knew him.

He grabbed his wife's wrists and stared into her face. "Eleanor! Eleanor!" he called out to her, but she had already lapsed into forgetfulness. He hunched over in his chair, and I saw his back quiver.

When Dr. Fish said, "I'm going to put you in the hospital," I had felt immense relief. They'll take care of me, I thought, I'll get well at last. And when I'm out, I'll read and read. But I didn't rest in the hospital. Although my movements had been slowed by the drug, my brain raced, and I was breathing poorly, in little cramped gusts. Fragments of the books I was supposed to know came and went in my miserable head. I had memorized the first scene of *King Lear* and tried to recall it, but it had vanished. It was all nothing then, nothing and more nothing. I worried about the books I didn't know and the money I didn't have, money to pay for what my university insurance wouldn't cover: twenty percent of the bill. My headache would turn my parents into debtors, and there was nothing I could do. I was frozen in a hospital bed; it was impossible to know for how long. I had read once about an eighteenth-century English noblewoman who had suffered from a headache for more than twenty years. I began to imagine that I would never get well, that I would die as a neurological footnote: "There is one reported case of a woman who was ill with migraine for fifty-two years. See Glower, 'Vascular migraine syndrome,' *JAMA* 1498, p. 43." My parents called often. I lied, telling them I felt better. When friends called, I told them not to come. A few insisted, and they came with flowers and chocolates. During these visits I always felt less pain, but after them I was worse. I read the change as a further sign of my neurosis, and it depressed me. Stephen called, almost a year after we had parted ways. A mutual friend had told him I was in the hospital. He said he was coming to see me, and I didn't tell him not to come. "Tuesday," he said, "I'll be there Tuesday at two o'clock."

During the day I was able to restrain my growing alarm, but at night I entered a state of dread. This feeling was intensified by the fact that they tied Mrs. O. down at night. They did it after we had been given our medication, and after the overhead lights had been turned off. The procedure required three people, two to hold the patient down and one to secure the straps to the bed.

The nurses called the device a "posy." When on, this canvas fetter resembled an elaborate and tortuous undergarment that took on a life of its own and sprouted appendages to foil the wearer. Getting Mrs. O. into this gruesome outfit was no small matter. She screamed, bit, clawed, and once as she fought she said over and over, "What is it? What is this thing?" After they had left the room, she would begin the struggle to free herself. She shook the metal bars at the sides of her bed. She shook them grunting rhythmically and without pause. She was indefatigable, an engine of determination. I don't know how long she kept it up, but it seemed to go on and on. It was the sound of the night for me, and I never slept until I was sure that she had given up. I watched and waited, because even in those first days before she had done anything to me, I was expectant.

I can't remember what day of the week it was, but on the morning of the first incident, Mrs. O., who had uttered perhaps twenty words since I had first seen her, began to speak. It was a rambling, even idiotic monologue, but it had the tantalizing quality of an unfinished story.

"Where's my old Peter? I put him away, and now I can't find him. Oh, the songs I used to know, Lucy, every word by heart, every note as clear as day, and he used to tell me I sang like an angel. It was an open-and-shut case. They drowned him sure as if they'd held his head underwater with their own hands, and not a single one of them went to jail. The last mean trick, I tell you. He wasn't right in the head, and they took advantage. I can't forget the two of them. They looked all pale and kind of stiff in their good clothes by the grave. Dirt poor, but decent as they come. And that dead boy was all they had." Mrs. O. clicked her tongue. "A sad, sad story." She shook her head. "Tell me the one about the lady on the hill, Eddie. You know, the one where she puts a cold hand on the back of his neck three nights in a row." I heard her humming a tune to herself, something simple and melodic.

About half an hour after the outburst, Mrs. O. turned to me and said loudly, "Don't just lie there, stupid! Do something!"

"Are you speaking to me?" I said.

"Of course I'm speaking to you. Who else would I be speaking to?"

Mrs. O.'s lucidity left me speechless. I looked at her face and

saw something cruel in it, like the guilty smile of a child torment-
ing another.

I didn't answer her, and she seemed to forget me very soon.
She wrung her sheet between her hands and bit at it distractedly.
Within minutes she was asleep on her back, her eyelids still partially open, and I could see the watery blue of one iris from my
bed. I dozed too, but was awakened by a small sharp pain in my
back. I turned and saw Mrs. O. standing over me. She was moving her thumb and index finger together like an angry crab. She
reached out and pinched my cheek hard. I jolted backward and
had an urge to slap her, but my arm was reluctant, too heavy to
comply.

"Get up, get up, sleepyhead!" she chanted to me, and grinned,
displaying a row of small discolored teeth. She bent over me again,
waving those fingers in my face.

"Go away! Go away!" I heard my voice crack hysterically as I
protected my face with my hands.

A nurse appeared. "Relax," she said to me. "She's not going to
kill you. Up to your old tricks, are you, Ellie? Back to bed with
you."

Mrs. O. smiled meekly, took the nurse's hand, and was led back
to her corner of the room.

After that, I was reluctant to sleep. I have since asked myself
why the pinching seemed so terrible. Her transgression had been
minor, after all; the pinches hadn't really hurt. Perhaps it was
that she had come too close, that my bed had lost its boundaries,
and that once that invisible threshold had been crossed, I no longer
felt safe. She would be back, I knew it. The chant "Get up, get
up, sleepyhead!" resounded like an annoying jingle in my brain.
Why was she pestering me? She never interfered with Mrs. M. I
was her victim. Why? Was it because I did in fact know her from
somewhere, and that she, in her own jumbled way, remembered
me? It was impossible. I began to worry that I was not only nervous but mad, one step away from an asylum. Mrs. M. stopped
talking about getting another room. Mrs. O.'s attentions to me
were far too amusing. "She's got it in for you, kiddo," she told
me. "Who knows what the crafty little bugger will do next?"

Two days later there was another incident. Again it happened
while I slept. Sleep was irresistible to me then, and as hard as I

tried to fight it, I couldn't keep myself awake all day. It began as a dream that took place in the bed where I slept. In the dream, I woke and saw a body lying next to me, a warm, strangely wet body of a woman. I lifted her arm but it fell lifelessly to the sheet. This person is dead, I thought. I've got to get her out of here. But then I felt arms around my throat and something heavy on my face. I need air, I thought, and an erotic sensation coursed through me. I opened my eyes. Mrs. O. was in bed with me. Her skinny arms were around me in a suffocating embrace. She was kissing me. I pushed her away hard.

Mrs. M.'s voice came from behind her curtain. "For Christ's sake, what's happened now?"

"She's in my bed." I bit my hand to keep back a sob.

Mrs. O. was crumpled up at the end of the bed. Her gown was untied and had fallen over a bony shoulder. She looked at me, her small wrinkled face wet with tears. A doctor was at the door.

"What's going on here?" he said.

"She climbed into my bed while I was asleep. It's unbearable, just unbearable. Please, move her somewhere else. I can't stay here with her."

He looked at me and squinted, as if I were very far away. "We're making arrangements to have her moved, but we're too crowded right now. As soon as a bed opens up, we'll get her out of here. She's really quite harmless, you know." He smiled and pushed his hand over his balding head. "I'll make sure someone keeps an eye on her."

I didn't mention the kiss to anyone. It was too bizarre, too unlikely.

After the kiss, nothing happened for three days. It may have been that the staff was keeping a closer watch on Mrs. O. and she knew it, but I'm not sure. In all events, she was less active, more prone to phases of immobility and blankness. Those mornings when her husband sat with her, I wondered what he would think if he knew that his wife had crawled into my bed and molested me. The kiss, always entangled in the dream, became a physical memory that shuddered through me without warning. The heavy moist corpse and the withered old woman who had pressed herself upon me, her tongue in my mouth, left their fitful traces, and I was helpless against them. My pain had ballooned: it filled my whole head and seemed to enlarge my skull as it grew. I was all head then, a female Humpty-Dumpty with four useless limbs. And I worried. I worried all day and most of the night. I worried about my head, about my exams, about Mrs. O., about Stephen's upcoming visit, and I worried about worrying. Anxiety fed my pain, but I didn't know how to stop it.

I looked terrible, and whenever I spoke, I panted and blew and embarrassed myself. Even Dr. Fish appeared concerned. He commented on my pallor and was clearly surprised that someone he had drugged so thoroughly was breathing like a steam engine. I was cold too, and I couldn't get warm. One afternoon a nurse brought me a pair of circulation socks. They were long affairs made of a white fabric like girdle material. They had no toes. I never knew the reason for this curious omission, but I wore them faithfully throughout my internment and still have them in a drawer, souvenirs of a time when my blood moved too slowly.

I fell in a world of only liminal consciousness. Always at sleep's border, I had to fight to remain awake. Mrs. M.'s patter took on a distant quality, as if she were speaking to me from another room. From time to time I heard coins jingling. She's counting her money, I thought. But my ears had started playing tricks on me then, and it may have been nothing. Twice I heard my mother call my name. These auditory hallucinations were clear and loud. Her voice was there in the room, and the moment I heard it, I wanted to answer her, but instead, I marveled at that inner voice and wondered if it weren't another indication of encroaching madness. I was overcome too by loneliness, by a sense that I was shut inside a body that was going its own way. I've done it, I thought, I've created this huge, bad head, summoned the voice of my mother, dreamed up dead bodies, and generally caused my own disintegration, but how can I undo it all? I'm a ghost. Mrs. O.'s lady ghost — or perhaps she's mine, a revenant come to tell me something — my own half-naked little spirit braying in the wilderness.

The night before Stephen's visit, Mrs. O. broke out. My recollection of this event is confused, and I can't trust it. I know that they strapped her in as usual and that as soon as they left her, she began to writhe and shake just as she did every night. My pain had reached its zenith; it seared through the Thorazine and I

lost all control of my breathing. I gulped and wheezed. I heard
Mrs. O. rocking the bars behind her curtain, yet the noise seemed
to be coming from within my own head. She groaned. I whimpered, but I wanted to howl in the dark as a wounded dog, to
lose myself in an orgy of screaming. Instead, I gagged myself on
the sheet. Mrs. M. spoke to me, but I couldn't hear what she was
saying — something about "the racket." I pressed my fingers
against my temples. My nerves are erupting, I thought. Then I
heard a loud noise, something being torn. I recall moving my
fingers to my ears, as if that gesture could tell where the noise
had originated. The curtain across the room billowed, and then
Mrs. O. was on the floor, her arms outstretched, her mouth wide
open. It was much larger than seemed possible, a monstrous
gaping hole in her face. I looked at her in the dim light of the
room, her gown hanging like a rag from her shoulders, and I felt
a violent jab in my chest, as if the wind had been kicked out of
me. I tried to call out, but my voice was tiny, an inaudible squeak.
I heard Mrs. M. bellow, "She's out! She's out!" Mrs. O. turned
her back to me and headed for the door. I saw her flat, wrinkled
buttocks as she ran stiff-kneed from the room.

The next morning, Mrs. M. christened her "Houdini." The
name change signaled a shift in Mrs. M's opinion of her as well:
contempt was now mingled with respect. "Houdini's got spunk!"
she said to me. "Tie her up, chain her, send her to the bottom
of the East River in a trunk, and she'll find a way out. By God,
she's got spunk!" "Spunk" was the wrong word. Mrs. O. had will,
a profound, unspeakable will. I don't understand what I saw
that night or why I felt knocked breathless. But the image of
that midget body as it stood in triumph on the floor, and that
mouth, that terrible mouth, is now rooted in me and I can't turn
away from it. It's still frightening, and yet I find it irresistible.
I have a need to conjure it again and again, to go on looking
into it.

But that morning, the morning after it happened, I tried to
forget it. It was too recent, and I was a knot of misery. My headache had eased some. It always did with daylight, but my scalp
was so tender that even the pressure of the pillow was irritating,
and my arms and legs hummed with a peculiar energy, as if they
were electrified. There's more, I thought, there's going to be more.
Mrs. O. had been sedated, and she slept during her husband's

visit and for several hours afterward. I could see her through a
gap in her curtain — a shrunken body in the sheets. Mrs. M. slept,
too. I waited for Stephen. At one-thirty, I sat up in bed very slowly,
found my mirror in a drawer, and tried to do something with my
face. My hands shook. I was white, and there were black pits under my eyes. Now I've lost my looks too, I thought. I managed to
comb my hair, rouge my cheeks, and put on a robe. Mrs. M., who
had just awakened, looked at me and said, "Must be a man." Stephen was forty minutes late. He was always late. He appeared at
the door looking elegant, his long coat draped over an arm. He
presented me with a small paper bag. In it were two books: a new
translation of selected poems by Leopardi and a volume of poems
call *Unearth* by an American poet I had never heard of. I thanked
him. He was garrulous and distant. He must have been startled
by my appearance but said nothing. I wished he had. I spoke to
him without gasping and felt proud of my control, but my eyes
were sensitive to the light, and I had to squint at him during our
conversation. The impression I made was apparently worse than
I thought, because at one point he looked at me and said, "How
did this happen?" There was incredulity in his voice. "Iris, you've
got to pull yourself together."

I studied his face and impeccable white shirt. He's a foreigner,
I thought. He has nothing to do with me. Perhaps I had loved
him for that, for his bouts of astonishing coldness when he detected weakness in others. I disgust him, I thought. It was probably the first time during my entire stay in the hospital that I truly
forgot Mrs. O., but as I looked at Stephen, I saw her behind him,
still in bed but awake and erect. Her blue eyes shone and she
leaned toward me. I didn't answer Stephen. Instead, I looked at
Mrs. O. I looked into her eyes and she met my gaze. She saw me.
Stephen turned in his chair.

"Who is that?" he said.

"It's Mrs. O.," I said.

"What's she doing?"

"I don't know."

"Why are you looking at her like that?"

"Be quiet," I said. "She's going to speak."

He smiled then. I don't know why he did it, but I saw his
expression in the corner of my eye and remembered his sweetness all at once, but it was Mrs. O. who held me, not Stephen.

She had crawled forward to the edge of her bed and was holding the frame with her hands.

"What's the matter with her?" he said.

"Shut up," I said.

Mrs. M. answered. "She's out of her head, but she's got something for your girlfriend."

Stephen said nothing.

Mrs. O. opened her mouth. At first there was no sound, but then a noise came from deep in her throat and she began to call out, her eyes fixed on mine. "Eleanor!" she said. It was a short, urgent cry. "Eleanor!"

"By God, she's remembered her name!" said Mrs. M. "That tops it all. Bring on the interns! Let's have the test! The first question, please!"

"Don't," I said to Mrs. M., and surprisingly, she held her tongue.

Mrs. O. was calling me. I knew it. We were both kneeling at that point and facing each other. "Why are you calling me?" I said.

"Eleanor! Eleanor!" she repeated. Her face looked desperate.

Stephen had his hand on my shoulder. He was pulling me back. "Iris, what are you doing?"

His distaste was palpable. Although he cultivated ideas that embraced the perverse and forbidden, Stephen was squeamish, and his adventures were strictly of the fashionable, literary sort. I saw him recoil. He gave me a look of disbelief.

"You can leave if you want to," I said.

"Eleanor!" cried Mrs. O. It was the same tone her husband had used when calling out to her.

Stephen had stood up. He touched my arm. "Do you want me to leave?" he said.

I did not look at him. "Yes." I said it very softly.

My eyes burned in the light. I saw Mrs. O.'s pinched little face. She's calling me, I thought. She's calling me. I leaned over the end of the bed and called back. "I'm here!" I called her as if she were far away, and as the sound of my voice came from me, it was as if a wind had blown through my body, opening my lungs and throat. I called out again, "I'm here!"

Two nurses responded to the commotion. I heard Stephen say "Excuse me" as he went out the door. Mrs. M. was busy explaining, but I didn't listen. The truth was that I was indifferent to all of them. It didn't matter to me that I had made a scene. The exchange absorbed me totally. I called out again and kept my eyes on Mrs. O. Her small frame trembled as she stared at me. A nurse had her by the arm, but she managed to wriggle free. She was listening. I could see it. Her head was cocked and her face had a pensive look on it. Her thin white hair was sticking up in wild tufts. She hugged herself and rocked. She had stopped calling.

A nurse tugged at my elbow. "You're getting her all riled up," she said.

But Mrs. O. was still, very still. She lay on her back with her eyes open, but they didn't move, and her passive features seemed alien for the first time. She doesn't look like anyone I know at all, I thought. I lay back and closed my eyes.

The nurse scolded me. "It's been one thing after another with you two. I really believe that you've egged her on. You're a troublemaker, that's what you are. You should know better than to get her crazy. Imagine, toying with a half-wit. You've gone too far!" I heard her march out of the room. I didn't open my eyes. I began to breathe very deeply and slowly, and I counted each breath. I counted for a long time.

That afternoon, Dr. Fish sent a psychiatrist to my bed. He spoke to me kindly in a low voice, and he had a white beard that I found reassuring. He didn't ask about Mrs. O. until the very end. Instead, he inquired about my studies, my parents, my friends. He wanted to know when my headache started and what my other symptoms were. He touched on the subject of my love life with great delicacy and registered my response that it was nonexistent with half a nod. I tried to speak in good sentences and to enunciate clearly. My head hurt, but my breathing was much improved, and I think I convinced him that I was sane. When he finally asked me why I had been screaming at Mrs. O., I told him very honestly that I didn't know, but that at the time it had seemed important to do so, and that I hadn't been screaming but calling. He didn't seem at all shocked by this answer, and before he left he patted my hand. I think I would have enjoyed my talk with him had I not worried about what the conversation was going to cost. He looked expensive to me, and I kept wondering if his sympathy was covered by my insurance.

A calm overtook my body that evening. The headache sat firmly in my skull, but I felt less nauseated and the vibrations in my limbs had vanished. I ate every bite of my bad dinner and fell asleep very early. They had to wake me for my pill, and I never heard them tie Mrs. O. down. I slept like a person in a coma and woke with difficulty the next morning. I remember that I had to push myself toward consciousness and that I had a sense of moving my arms in water and propelling myself to the surface. I was too drowsy to focus properly and at first I didn't notice that she was gone, but when I finally roused myself, I saw that Mrs. O. was not in her bed. The bed was freshly made, her belongings had disappeared, and the curtain was pulled neatly to one side.

"Where is she?" I asked Mrs. M.

"Beats me," she said. "She's not here. That's all I know, and the nurses aren't saying beans. I got the same line every time I asked: 'It's none of your business.' " Mrs. M. lent her voice a nasal, officious tone. "And when I think of all I've done for those tight-assed cows and what I've had to put up with. No offense, but between you and Houdini, it's been a circus. I'll tell you what I think. Old Houdini had the last laugh. She did her disappearing act. Poof!" Mrs. M. snapped her fingers. "She vanished into thin air."

I looked at the empty bed. Since then, I've often puzzled over Mrs. O.'s disappearance. Perhaps Mrs. M. lied to me. She may have seen them move the old lady while I slept. Mrs. O. could have had a stroke or seizure in the middle of the night. She could have died and been taken to the morgue. But I didn't consider these possibilities at the time. I was simply amazed by her absence. Had I not been so sure that my memories were real, I might have thought that she was my invention, a character I had blown to life for my own purposes. As I reflected, I felt a tiny spasm in my arm — the first sign of the crisis. It came fast, a brief but violent nerve storm, a quake in my system so powerful that even while it was happening, a part of me regarded it with awe. My arm moved again; it actually jumped on the sheet. I felt a surge of nausea and dizziness. I dragged myself from the bed and lurched past Mrs. M. to the bathroom. I vomited. My intestines cramped horribly, and then my bowels fell out of me. The paroxysm seemed to send all my internal organs into the toilet. I steadied myself on the sink and looked at my hideous face in the mirror. "You're a ridiculous person, Iris," I said, "a ridiculous person." I saw my head move in the glass. It felt smaller, lighter.

"Are you okay in there?" It was Mrs. M. "Should I get the nurse?"

"No," I said. "I'm all right."

I used my shoulder to push open the heavy bathroom door and then walked slowly across the room, clutching the back of my gown so that it wouldn't fly open. I sat down on the edge of the bed and remained sitting there for a long time. The light seemed unusually dim to me, and I looked out the window toward the stone-gray wall of another building. It was dark outside, and large snowflakes were falling steadily.

"It's snowing," I said.

"Of course it is," said Mrs. M. "It's been snowing for days."

MIKHAIL IOSSEL

Bologoye

FROM BOULEVARD

MY BEST FRIEND is afraid of his father-in-law. "I love my wife, but her father is my father-in-law!"

"That's a shame," I say, pausing in front of the newsstand.

He pulls at my sleeve. "Come on, you've already read those! I respect my wife, but her father hates me!"

I laugh. He frowns: "What's so funny?"

"Gorbachev has made the front page of *Pravda!*"

He sighs. "I couldn't care less about my wife, but her father is dangerous!"

"Everyone is dangerous," I point out.

"That's true," he says. "But I don't have to share an apartment with everyone. Not everyone is an unpredictable nut."

"Everyone is a nut," I say.

"That's true," he says. "But I'm not afraid of other nuts. Other nuts age gracefully. Other nuts don't scream 'GET OUT!' when I walk into their room hoping to watch some TV."

"Don't walk into his room," I suggest.

"I don't!" he says.

"You're exaggerating," I say.

It's Saturday, the best time of the week. Fresh from the weekly downtown bathhouse, we walk along Liteiny Prospekt, past the beer bar and the KGB Headquarters, to the Kolkhoz Market. One of our bathhouse friends is throwing a party nearby and we have to buy a hunk of lamb. Vodka has been getting harder to find since they started closing down the liquor stores late last May, but our bathhouse friend's relative works in a big restaurant and can always sell us a dozen bottles from his home stock. Now, as we approach the market, the bottles are already rolling lazily in the bathtub under the streams of cold tap water, waiting.

"Tell your father-in-law to be patient," I suggest. "Talk to him. Let him know that you care. Tell him that soon scientists will re-program his genetic code — God, this is silly! — and he won't have to die. Tell him to quit smoking and drinking and wait."

"He doesn't drink, he doesn't smoke," my best friend says.

"Threaten him. Tell him that you're going to write a letter to his Party Committee."

"He's not a member of the Party."

"You're exaggerating," I say.

It's fall, but it feels like spring. A minute ago clouds were all over the Leningrad sky; now the sky is clean blue. We buy two glasses of diluted beer from the market beerstand.

"What lousy beer!" he says, blowing off the heavy foam.

I agree: "The worst."

He smiles contentedly. "Yesterday I was buying beer near my house. There was a line. There was a bum with no money in the line, begging for a glass of beer. He kept repeating: 'I'm not ask-ing you for a marble palace with fountains, just buy me a glass of beer!' I bought him a glass of beer. He said: 'You've just made me the happiest man alive!' Two hours later, when I came down-stairs for a glass of beer, he was still there, saying: 'I'm not asking you for a glass of vodka, just buy me a glass of beer!' I bought him a glass of beer, to see if he would recognize me. He didn't. He said: 'You've just made me the happiest man alive!' People are so miserable!" He chuckles.

"See that man in the pink overcoat? He's been listening to us!" I say loudly. The man in dirty pink glances at me, peels himself off the beerstand, and walks away. He is drunk. We look at each other, smiling.

I leave the party on Sunday night and get into a cab. Thinking that I'm too drunk to notice, the driver intends to take me home along the right bank of the Neva — a five-ruble trick. "I'm watching you!" I tell him with a laugh. He pouts. I stumble and stagger my way upstairs. "I stumble, but I rarely fall," as my girl-friend often says — usually out of context. Now I'm home.

*

Late next morning, warily hungover, I gulp down a teapot of stale
water and cautiously open my door. I hear hurried steps downstairs. They become inaudible and are followed by the sigh and
shudder of the entrance door as someone bursts out. None of
today's newspapers are left at the newsstand below — no *Pravda,*
no *Leningrad Pravda,* no *Izvestiya;* only old magazines. I go back
up through the dark doorway, to the second-story set of plywood
mailboxes along the green wall. I pause, looking around, holding
my breath, before dipping my fingers through the wide crack between the upper plank and the rough edge of the front casing,
deep into the innards of a mailbox. There are several accessible
boxes in the set, but some of them don't interest me. I know which
box has a copy of *Pravda,* and two others — *Izvestiya* and *Leningrad Pravda.* I have to act quickly, but the heartwarming feeling
of discovering the thin sheet under my fingertips makes me linger, as always, enjoying the danger — more imaginary than real,
yet still sweet.

Back up in my room, I sit at the table, preparing to read. Every
time I open a newspaper, a part of me hopes for something extraordinary to have happened overnight, as if the newspaper
would, indeed, print something truly extraordinary; something
extraordinarily true. I close my eyes, I hold my breath, knowing
that in a moment, when I take a glance at the headlines, the suspense will be gone and the hope — pleasantly ridiculous — will
vanish: the borders are not going to be proclaimed open; the KGB
will not have been disbanded; who am I fooling? I'm sitting in
my chair, waiting.

Every time I read a newspaper, recognizing with experience
the real meaning of each word that has been omitted, replacing
the newspaper's firm noes with my own timid yeses, the world's
activity takes me aback; it makes me feel sad: while I was asleep,
people were being born and killed, speeches were being delivered, men and women were falling in love and making love . . .
while I was asleep.

I fold the newspapers.

I hear steps behind my door. It could be a caretaker with a
subpoena from the district commandant's office or a voluntary
people's militia patrol checking their list of politically unstable
locals. I'm not home. All my friends know that I never open the
door without first having been contacted on the phone. All my

close friends know the secret code of ringing my doorbell: two short rings, one long one, one short one. I'm nobody's fool. I wait, but nothing happens and I begin to dial the number of a friend of mine who works at the Moskovsky train station ticket office. My best friend and I are going to Moscow tomorrow, for a day — to get away from Leningrad. I keep getting busy signals, then she picks up the phone. "A tough order on such short notice, honey," she says. I promise her a box of chocolates, a bottle of champagne, and seven rubles. "Seven? Why seven? Why not six or eight?" she asks, intrigued. We agree on ten.

I open my door and, a box of chocolates in my bag, leave to pick up the tickets. Champagne shouldn't be a problem: Leningrad alcoholics don't drink it; it puts them off, they respect it too much, they don't appreciate the idea of bubbles.

When I get back home five hours later, there's the word SCUM scribbled on my door with white chalk. I look around, ready to run. I hold my breath. I wipe off the chalk with my sleeve.

I go downstairs, to the fourth floor, and find the same inscription on one of the doors down there. I go upstairs, to the sixth floor: all the doors are clean. I go all the way down, to the first floor, and find one of the doors there also marked by some nut. These things happen. I return to my room.

Whenever I walk in from the outside, my room always makes my heart leap with joy. It's dusty, it's a mess, but it's mine. When I walk in from the outside and latch and lock the door, looking at the books on the shelves, the pictures on the walls, the papers and the typewriter on the table, the empty bottles in the corner, a porcelain figurine of a ballerina on top of the old TV, I feel that I have finally arrived. I feel safe and strong. A moment before I was outside, in open space, and now I'm in here, unhurried. When the phone starts to ring, I can pick it up or not. I can read a paper instead.

The phone rings. I pick it up and say in a changed, low voice, as I always do when I am not sure who is calling (which I never am): "Speaking." It's my mother. She sounds urgent: "I need to see you."

"Do you want me to come over?" I ask. She lives five blocks down the street.

"No. We'll meet outside."

"Mother, it's cold and dark outside!"

"So?" she says.

"So do you want to come over?"

She sighs impatiently. "Don't be stupid. It's important. We can't talk inside. Do you understand?"

Instantly concerned, I laugh good-naturedly: "Oh Mom, you don't seriously believe that both our places are . . ."

"Shut up!" she exclaims, frightened.

"All right, all right, you do believe it! All right! I'll meet you in five minutes." We hang up.

I meet her in five minutes; she is close to tears. Late last night someone called her on the phone and told her that her son had just been run over by a truck. She dropped the phone on the floor. When she picked it back up, the caller laughed and said that it was a joke. However, he added, today's joke is often tomorrow's reality. "What do you want from me?" she asked. "Nothing. I'm a friend and I would hate to see you upset," he said, hanging up.

I'm scared. I laugh and hug her: "Mother, the world is full of nasty nuts! He didn't even know your name, or mine. Believe me, it's not worth your tears!"

"I don't believe you," she says, dabbing her eyes with a handkerchief. "They are after you, can't you see? I don't know why, but they are, and I even know why, and I'm scared!"

"Let's go up to my place and get drunk!" I suggest. Whenever I'm with her, I feel strong and wise — simply because she is not.

"Promise me that you'll stop doing whatever they want you to stop doing!" she says.

"Give me some more time," I ask her. "Things are now changing everywhere."

"No they are not!" she says.

"Not yet," I admit.

"I'm scared, I'm scared!" she says. I want to say: "So am I!"

I say: "I have some good wine and beer up in my room!"

"You're lying," she says.

"I'm not!" I lie angrily.

"Stop being an alcoholic! Please!" she screams suddenly. Compared to her, everyone is an alcoholic.

"You're overreacting," I say.

Late at night, after the late news on TV, I go to bed, leaving on the flickering TV and the lights; that way, I feel safe, as if someone were watching me and I were not alone. I don't like falling asleep. If I don't wake up in the morning, the lights in my room, seen from the street, would let whoever might be worried by my nonexistence — my mother, my best friend, my girlfriend — know that something was wrong, and then they would break in and find me. My worst fear is not that I'm going to die in my sleep, but that no one would know that I was dead. I imagine what I must look like now: a grown-up man, lying in bed with the lights on, healthy and thinking about being dead. I start to laugh cautiously. Then I imagine myself lying in bed and laughing at the picture of myself lying in bed and laughing, and I start to laugh louder. My left-side neighbor bangs his fist against the wall: "Young man! Let me sleep! Do you know what time it is?" He never protests when I have a noisy bunch of friends over late at night. His irritated, reassuring voice makes me wonder how could I have possibly felt forgotten and forlorn a moment ago. It reminds me of an old joke — two men are drinking wine late at night; one man asks the other, in whose room they're drinking, "What's that huge piece of wood doing on your bed?"

"That's my late-night clock," the other man says.

"How so?"

"Watch this." He grabs it and brings it hard against the wall. Immediately comes the neighbor's muffled groan: "For Christ's sake! Are you out of your mind? It's three-thirty in the morning!"

I laugh again, this time louder. My neighbor slams the wall with his fist.

Next morning I decide against going downstairs for the newspapers. Soon I hear steps outside. I tiptoe to the door and hold my breath. I press my eye against the keyhole. I can see the midsection of a man moving cautiously around outside my door. If he starts writing on it, I'll unlatch it, unlock it, and throw it open. He'll slouch heavily against the elevator door, moaning, covering his face, swaying like a Hasid in prayer. "Comrade, did I hurt you?" I'll exclaim, rushing to him, kneeling by his side. "Did I break your nose? Let me see! It's okay, it's happened to me!"

It has. Once, when I was in high school, three friends of mine were waiting for me outside, unaware that I had a habit of tiredly pressing my forehead against the door before pushing it open. They knew that it was me coming out, but they didn't know that it was my face they were hitting when they jokingly kicked the door back shut with the trained feet of soccer players. A heavy wooden plank across the door broke my nose and I fell like a sack of flour. Then, still unconscious, I jumped to my feet and sprinted off. They caught up with me, grabbed my hands, and led me away from the marshy wasteland surrounding the school building to my grandmother's. She wasn't home. I came to and saw my face in the mirror, which my friends were trying in vain to cover from me with their bodies. The nose crossed my face like an angry red thunderbolt.

"You were saying things when we dragged you to your grand-mother's!" my friends told me later.

"I was unconscious!" I pointed out to them.

"You kept saying: 'Oh God, a minute ago everything was fine! Oh God, a minute ago everything was good!' " they told me.

"You're exaggerating," I said.

The man steps in front of the neighbor's door. I hear the sound of chalk against dry wood. Then he turns around and hurries down the stairs. I open my door and step out to follow him. Now, in the street, I can see his back. He is middle-aged and shorter than me. He doesn't know that I'm watching him. He drops into the doorway across the court. I wait outside.

After a minute, he walks back out. Glancing around, he doesn't see me: I'm hidden behind the kindergarten fence. He walks off and I follow him for fifteen minutes as he methodically steps into every second doorway along his route. Then I grow impatient and decide to confront him. Maybe I won't even hit him; maybe I'll just slap him on the shoulder from behind: "Hi, scum!" Then suddenly his walk changes: it becomes leisurely. He deviates from the pattern of doorways, takes off his hat and smoothes his skimpy hair. He is now going home from work. I wait until he disappears in his doorway, two blocks away from mine, and then follow him inside. I hear a door up on the third floor being slammed shut. I'm good at locating the sources of sounds, and when I'm on the third floor, I know which door is his. Uncertain, I stand in front of it. Then I pull a piece of paper and a pencil out of my pocket.

Leaning against his door, I write: "I'LL BE WATCHING YOUR EVERY STEP!" I leave the note on his doormat and go back to my room.

I want to take a shower before the trip to Moscow, but there's no water in the hissing rusty bathroom pipes. These things happen. I pack my bag, get into a cab, and go to my girlfriend's place. She's not home. I take a shower, then she returns from work, we make love, and I take a shower again and leave for the Moskovsky train station.

There are four clear days ahead of me — a day in Moscow, three days in Leningrad. I am a night guard at a public park on the outskirts of Leningrad once a week, and my next shift is on Sunday. I'm supposed to be there every other night, but my boss doesn't mind my being absent for a week: partly because I pay him ten rubles from my monthly salary — eighty rubles, which can buy twelve bottles of cheap vodka, or could, when vodka was easy to find — and also because a public park doesn't need to be guarded at night anyway.

My best friend and I meet five minutes before the departure. We love trains. We've spent years on the railroad. Late at night, when you're both tired and alert, nothing depends on you, nothing is expected of you, except accepting the roadbed, which unfolds over dark terrain. You wake up to a rusty plateau under the rain and three trees. You wake up the next morning to see the same. You can travel for days without ever seeing anything else. Water is boiling on the stove, the coals smell like hot iron, the trainman is drunk, three unshaven men in your compartment are sipping wine and playing cards while you're reading a slow novel on the upper bunk and thinking pleasant and forgettable thoughts.

The train leaves at midnight, to a brass-band rendition of "The Great City's Hymn" on the station radio. It's a Red Arrow train, plush and comfortable, a Soviet version of the Orient Express.

There are two other passengers in our compartment, and we can't drink, although we bought some wine for the trip. Drinking has been strictly prohibited on the railroad ever since they started their anti-alcohol campaign late last May; for drinking one might end up getting unseated in the middle of nowhere.

All we can do is talk. We look out the window and see the

succession of dark hills nearby and strings of bright unblinking lights in the distance. We walk out of our compartment to the only place where we can't be found, at least for a while — the rocking space between the two cars. We quickly down two bottles of wine. Soon the other two passengers go to bed, falling asleep in the blue shade of tiny overhead lamps, and we can finish the rest of our wine. Halfway through the journey, the train makes a stop in Bologoye. I start remembering my first trips to Moscow, when I was five or six and used to spend as much time in Moscow as in Leningrad. My grandmother had lived most of her life in Moscow, but her daughter — my mother — lived in Leningrad, and Grandmother had to make a choice between the two cities. Whenever she went back to Moscow for a visit, which happened once every three months, she would take me along. Each time it genuinely surprised me that people could actually go to bed and fall asleep on the train, as if they were not going to Moscow and that night were no different from other nights. My grandmother would fall asleep, too. One night I slipped out of the compartment into the empty corridor. Halfway through the journey, the train made a stop in Bologoye. I looked at the building behind the station office. High above, in the only illuminated window, I saw a man in a white shirt. He was looking outside and seemed young and pensive. I liked the idea of he and I being the only two nonsleepers in the world. It occurred to me that I would never see him again. I waved to him, bouncing up and down. He didn't see me. I was just about to get off the train, while my grandmother was asleep, when the train pulled out.

"Show me that building," my best friend says.

"I haven't been able to find it since," I say guiltily. "But I'm sure it was there when I saw it."

"If you had actually gotten off the train, it would've made a nice story," he says.

We discuss the trains for a while. Then we fall asleep. Three hours later we are in Moscow; thirty hours later we are back in Leningrad.

When I arrive at my doorway, two old women, who always sit on the bench by the outer wall of the building, giggle and nod: "Young man!"

I stop: "What's up, ladies?"

"No, nothing!" they say, giggling.

"What's that, citizens?"

"No, nothing!" they say.

There are wet spots on the steps by the elevator. There's a note on my doormat: "YOU'VE FLOODED OUR APARTMENTS, YOU IRRESPONSIBLE MAN!"

The floor in my room is soaking wet. Water stands in lakes on the tiled floor in the bathroom. I try the shower: no water in the pipes, but the shower handle is turned on. I realize what's happened: discovering that there was no water before my trip to Moscow, I hurried to my girlfriend's, forgetting that the shower handle had been turned on. Later that night, the water started pouring into the tub.

I rush downstairs, to the fourth floor. All four flooded tenants silently step out of the doors.

I've destroyed their apartments. The ceilings have fallen down, the plaster on the walls is cracked, and the chairs stand in the water over the carpets.

They tried to break into my place, the tenants tell me, but the door wouldn't give — I grin sheepishly, proudly: "Of course not!" — and they called the superintendent's office instead. The water supply had been cut off, but it was too late. I keep nodding mournfully, until my neck starts to ache.

Strangely enough, the worst damage has been done to the third-floor apartment, not the one on the fourth floor. The third-floor tenant, an old woman, shows me a heavy piece of ceiling that nearly killed her in her sleep. "I was sleeping, and this thing nearly killed me: it landed on the pillow an inch from my face!"

I weigh it in my hands: it is heavy. The thought that I might have become an unknowing murderer while sitting in a train to Moscow makes me shiver. "It almost killed me!" she repeats, as if unable to comprehend the idea of being dead.

"You're exaggerating," I say.

An hour later the four tenants and I are sitting around the table in my room. They intend to sue me. I suggest a more pragmatic approach. I have a friend who can repaint their apartments for a small fee, and I'm willing to pay the damages, I say, but if we get the court officials involved, it will take the four of them years before they see my money.

"Obviously, you're not planning on being around here for years," the second-floor tenant observes ironically. He's an old bald man.

"What do you mean?" I ask. I know what he means.

He purses his lips. "Obviously, someone in this room is planning on leaving this country soon. Am I wrong?" He is right. How did he know?

There is a pause. "That's none of your business, comrade!" I say heatedly. I'm supposed to look indignant.

He shakes his head. "I've been a member of the Party since 1938, a veteran of the war, and let me tell you: back in those days, we knew how to treat a traitor!" There's another awkward pause in the room. Poor old jerk!

"So it's you we have to be thankful to now that we're up the creek without a paddle, comrade revolutionary?" says a first-floor tenant, an old woman in thick glasses. He waves hopelessly.

"Three hundred rubles," I say. "Total."

They start arguing. Everyone claims that his apartment has suffered a greater damage. "Five hundred!" the old man says.

"You shouldn't be thinking about money!" a fourth-floor tenant points out to him. "You should be thinking about the world revolution!"

"This is neither here nor there," I say.

"Five hundred!" he repeats adamantly. We agree on four.

I have no idea where to get four hundred rubles. I'll have to stop eating. I'll have to stop drinking. I'll have to stop riding around in cabs.

I'll have to sell most of my books.

I start mopping up the floor. I had been meaning to have it washed for years; now it doesn't need washing. It's clean. I pick up a dozen books from the floor. They are wet, their pages glued together. They can't be sold.

Suddenly I feel an attack of nausea, cold sweat popping up on my forehead. It's inexplicable, and I start to panic: what is it? What if I have some kind of cancer? I rush to the bathroom and bend over the sink, trying to throw up. I can't. My heart is pounding, my eyes go blind, bloodshot. I stagger off, thinking: "So this is how it happens!" I collapse on the bed and fall asleep.

I'm awakened by the ringing of the phone. I don't awaken easily. The phone rings with impatient authority.

"Is Comrade Litovtsev home?" asks an official female voice.

"He's not home," I say in a changed voice.

"Comrade Litovtsev, please stop fooling, will you?" the woman says with sudden chumminess.

"Who's speaking?" I ask angrily.

"You men!" she says playfully. "Comrade Litovtsev, according to my records, we've talked twenty times over the last ten years, both on the phone and otherwise. That's one-third of your life! How many women have you known longer?"

"I'm hanging up now!" I say, but I don't. I know who she is. I feel numb.

"This is Inspector Zvereva from the District Office of Visas. Comrade Litovtsev, where have you been? I called you yesterday."

"I'm around, I'm around," I say.

"Congratulations! You've been granted an exit permit! You must leave in a month . . . Are you there?"

"I'm here," I say.

"Congratulations! You've been granted . . ."

"Oh, cut it out, comrade!"

She is silent for a moment. Then her voice becomes business-like.

"You have to come to our office early next week, with six photographs of yourself, six by nine centimeters, without a hat. You will be given a list of signatures to obtain from various organizations and hospitals. Then you'll have to go to Moscow to complete the paperwork."

"Damn it, inspector, I've just returned from Moscow!" I say.

"We know," she says, hanging up.

I return to bed and fall back asleep.

In the morning, I'm awakened by the phone. It rings every fifteen minutes. I take a cab to my girlfriend's place. She doesn't have a phone. No one knows that I'm here. I sit around, reading her newspapers: an earthquake in Mexico; a tornado in the American Midwest; a strike in France; new disarmament initiatives coming from Moscow; a housewife from Byelorussia has found a gigantic mushroom in her garden. Then my girlfriend

comes home from work. We drink wine; I tell her that I'm leaving soon. "For how long?" she asks. "Forever, honey," I say, feeling like being cruel. Why? Maybe because the harsher the words,
the less attention she is going to pay to them. She nods. She puts
her glass down on the table and starts shivering. I look at her;
she doesn't look at me. "Stop it!" I say. "Please." She keeps shivering. "Will you cut it out?" She shakes her head. "You're overreacting," I say.

We go to bed, determined to make love with the final tenderness of imminent and irreversible separation, but our minds are
too preoccupied with that finality, and we end up drinking more
wine instead. We sit at the table, looking outside.

I leave early in the morning. It's Saturday, bathhouse day. I
try to get a cab, but there are none in the quiet streets of my girlfriend's neighborhood. Usually it's easier in Leningrad to get a
ride from a "privateer," the owner of a private car, but there are
not many of those either on Saturday mornings, and I wave my
hand in vain until, almost an hour later, a tan Zhiguli pulls up at
the curb. I climb into the back seat and tell the driver my desti-
nation. He nods and switches on the morning music.

As we approach my part of Leningrad, he glances at me in the
mirror: "Leaving, Litovtsev? That's not good. Normally I don't
drive traitors around in my car."

"Here we are!" I say, startled.

"My personal opinion is that you belong in jail," he says pen-
sively. "What do you think?"

"I didn't know you people have to work weekends!" I say.

He shrugs: "It's okay."

We pass by the neighborhood where our family lived for years,
since I was eight. Then, when I was eighteen, we moved out. That
was long before I got my own place to live.

"I don't think you have instructions to hassle me, do you?" I
ask. Not that I expect him to say, "You bet I do."

"I'm just a driver," he says.

We proceed in silence. Then he turns to me: "I'm going to miss
you. Are you going to miss me?"

I shrug. "You're too cute."

"You've already had all the happiness in life that you were entitled to," he says pompously. Poor pompous ass.

He pulls up in front of the bathhouse. I offer him three rubles. He shakes his head. I climb out of the car.

"Have a good bath!" he says.

I walk in; then I turn around: smiling, he's following me. "Are you coming too?" I ask.

"Are you coming too?" he asks.

I laugh. He frowns: "What's so funny?"

"I've never seen a naked plainclothesman before!" I explain.

He sighs. "Don't be naive. Of course you have!"

My best friend and I slip out of the bathhouse an hour before the end of the session. We keep looking back nervously, but the man is nowhere in sight. We've shaken him off. We look at each other, smiling.

Late at night, in my best friend's house, I knock on the door to his father-in-law's room. I have a bottle of vodka in my hand. My best friend tries to pull me away from the door.

There's no answer. I walk in. His father-in-law turns from the window. I hold out the bottle in my hand. He shakes his head. I take a gulp.

"I have some good and some bad news for you," I say, smiling encouragingly. "The bad news is that our sun will only continue to shine for five billion more years; after that it will brighten for a while and then it will dim and the solar system will become dark and cold, and if we manage to survive until then, we'll still have to die. The good news is that, chances are, by that time mankind will have discovered a way to do without the sun. Don't give up hope!"

He continues staring at me, probably thinking: "Who the hell is this?" Then he turns back to the window.

I take another gulp, shrug, and leave. When I reach the first floor, I can hear sounds in the doorway: the shuffling of invisible feet, silent voices. I open the first-floor window, step onto the sill, and jump out. I land on my feet; then I fall on my knees. I've injured my leg. Limping, I turn the street corner and look back up, at the bright second-floor window. He's standing there, looking out. I grin and wave. He turns away. My leg hurts. I stop a cab. "I don't care if you know me!" I warn the driver.

He looks at me and yawns. "Flash the cash, pal!"

He has to take me home along the right bank of the Neva, because it's late and all the big drawbridges are being thrown open.
I have time to think: what if I arrive at my door and find it omi-
nously, darkly ajar? Should I just walk in? Or what if there's
something scribbled on my door, and when I start wiping it off
someone jumps me from behind?

But nothing happens. My doorway is quiet; my door is clean
and locked. I fish for the keys in my pocket. I can't find them. I
must have lost them when jumping from the window. It occurs
to me that my morning driver could have stolen them from my
pocket when we were in the bathhouse.

There's a strip of light under my door. I sit down on the stairs.
It's three-thirty in the morning. I hear the front door downstairs.
Then I hear steps. I get up and thrust my shoulder against my
door. It won't give in. I hit it, and then I hit it again. I sit down
on the stairs. Then I get up and hit it again. Then I hit it again.

People step out of their doors upstairs and downstairs, screaming, "Let us sleep!" I break in.

My heart leaps with joy. I sit at the table, reading the old newspapers, thinking about those who have left before me. They were
bitter. Suspecting that after they left, their apartments would be
turned over to the District Department of Visas, some of them
would peel off wallpaper in the living room and bore a hole in
the wall, where they would conceal a fresh egg. Then they would
cover the hole with a plaster slab and wallpaper.

I will do no such thing. Maybe I'll put a note under the doormat: "I'LL BE WATCHING YOUR EVERY STEP!" or "I'LL BE
BACK!" — it will add suspense to their lives, even though I know
that I won't be back. It's easy to become sentimental at this hour.

Soon it starts to look like morning outside. Leaving my broken
door open, I go downstairs, to the newsstand.

DAVID JAUSS

Glossolalia

FROM SHENANDOAH

THAT WINTER, like every winter before it, my father woke early each day and turned up the thermostat so the house would be warm by the time my mother and I got out of bed. Sometimes I'd hear the furnace kick in and the shower come on down the hall and I'd wake just long enough to be angry that he'd wakened me. But usually I slept until my mother had finished making our breakfast. By then, my father was already at Goodyear, opening the service bay for the customers who had to drop their cars off before going to work themselves. Sitting in the sunny kitchen, warmed by the heat from the register and the smell of my mother's coffee, I never thought about him dressing in the cold dark or shoveling out the driveway by porchlight. If I thought of him at all, it was only to feel glad he was not there. In those days my father and I fought a lot, though probably not much more than most fathers and sons. I was sixteen then, a tough age. And he was forty, an age I've since learned is even tougher.

But that winter I was too concerned with my own problems to think about my father's. I was a skinny, unathletic, sorrowful boy who had few friends, and I was in love with Molly Rasmussen, one of the prettiest girls in Glencoe and the daughter of a man who had stopped my father on Main Street that fall, called him a "goddamned debt-dodger," and threatened to break his face. My father had bought a used Ford Galaxie from Mr. Rasmussen's lot, but he hadn't been able to make the payments and eventually Mr. Rasmussen repossessed it. Without a second car my mother couldn't get to work — she had taken a job at the school lunchroom, scooping out servings of mashed potatoes and green beans — so we drove our aging Chevy to Minneapolis, where no one knew my father, and bought a rust-pitted yellow Studebaker. A few days later Molly Rasmussen passed me in the hall at school and said, "I see you've got a new car," then laughed. I was so mortified I hurried into a restroom, locked myself in a stall, and stood there for several minutes, breathing hard. Even after the bell rang for the next class, I didn't move. I was furious at my father. I blamed him for the fact that Molly despised me, just as I had for some time blamed him for everything else that was wrong with my life — my gawky looks, my discount-store clothes, my lack of friends.

That night, and others like it, I lay in bed and imagined who I'd be if my mother had married someone handsome and popular like Dick Moore, the PE teacher, or Smiley Swenson, who drove stock cars at the county fair, or even Mr. Rasmussen. Years before, my mother had told me how she met my father. A girl who worked with her at Woolworth's had asked her if she wanted to go out with a friend of her boyfriend's, an army man just back from the war. My mother had never agreed to a blind date before, or dated an older man, but for some reason this time she said yes. Lying there, I thought about that fateful moment. It seemed so fragile — she could as easily have said no and changed everything — and I wished, then, that she had said no, I wished she'd said she didn't date strangers or she already had a date or she was going out of town — anything to alter the chance conjunction that would eventually produce me.

I know now that there was something suicidal about my desire to undo my parentage, but then I knew only that I wanted to be someone else. And I blamed my father for that wish. If I'd had a different father, I reasoned, I would be better-looking, happier, more popular. When I looked in the mirror and saw my father's thin face, his rust-red hair, down-turned mouth, and bulging Adam's apple, I didn't know who I hated more, him or me. That winter I began parting my hair on the right instead of the left, as my father did, and whenever the house was empty I worked on changing my voice, practicing the inflections and accents of my classmates' fathers as if they were clues to a new life. I even practiced one's walk, another's crooked smile, a third's wink. I did not think, then, that my father knew how I felt about him, but now that I have a son of my own, a son almost as old as I was then, I know different.

If I had known what my father was going through that winter, maybe I wouldn't have treated him so badly. But I didn't know anything until the January morning of his breakdown. I woke that morning to the sound of voices downstairs in the kitchen. At first I thought the sound was the wind rasping in the bare branches of the cottonwood outside my window, then I thought it was the radio. But after I lay there a moment I recognized my parents' voices. I couldn't tell what they were saying, but I knew they were arguing. They'd been arguing more than usual lately, and I hated it — not so much because I wanted them to be happy, though I did, but because I knew they'd take their anger out on me, snapping at me, telling me to chew with my mouth closed, asking me who gave me permission to put my feet up on the coffee table, ordering me to clean my room. I buried one ear in my pillow and covered the other with my blankets, but I could still hear them. They sounded distant, yet somehow close, like the sea crashing in a shell held to the ear. But after a while I couldn't hear even the muffled sound of their voices, and I sat up in the bars of gray light slanting through the blinds and listened to the quiet. I didn't know what was worse: their arguments or their silences. I sat there, barely breathing, waiting for some noise.

Finally I heard the back door bang shut and, a moment later, the Chevy cough to life. Only then did I dare get out of bed. Crossing to the window, I lowered one of the slats in the blinds with a finger and saw, in the dim light, the driveway drifted shut with snow. Then my father came out of the garage and began shoveling, scooping the snow furiously and flinging it over his shoulder, as if each shovelful were a continuation of the argument. I couldn't see his face, but I knew that it was red and that he was probably cursing under his breath. As he shoveled, the wind scuffed the drifts around him, swirling the snow into his eyes, but he didn't stop or set his back to the wind. He just kept shoveling fiercely, and suddenly it occurred to me that he might have a heart attack, just as my friend Rob's father had the winter before. For an instant I saw him slump over his shovel, then collapse face-first into the snow. As soon as this thought came to me,

I did my best to make myself think it arose from love and terror, but even then I knew part of me wished his death, and that knowledge went through me like a chill.

I lowered the slat on the blinds and got back into bed. The house was quiet but not peaceful. I knew that somewhere in the silence my mother was crying and I thought about going to comfort her, but I didn't. After a while I heard my father rev the engine and back the Chevy down the driveway. Still I didn't get up. And when my mother finally came to tell me it was time to get ready, her eyes and nose red and puffy, I told her I wasn't feeling well and wanted to stay home. Normally, she would have felt my forehead and cross-examined me about my symptoms, but that day I knew she'd be too upset to bother. "Okay, Danny," she said. "Call me if you think you need to see a doctor." And that was it. She shut my door and a few minutes later I heard the whine of the Studebaker's cold engine, and then she was gone.

It wasn't long after my mother left that my father came home. I was lying on the couch in the living room, trying to figure out the hidden puzzle on "Concentration," when I heard a car pull into the driveway. At first I thought my mother had changed her mind and come back to take me to school. But then the back door sprang open and I heard him. It was a sound I had never heard before and since have heard only in my dreams, a sound that will make me sit up in the thick dark, my eyes open to nothing and my breath panting. I don't know how to explain it, other than to say it was a kind of crazy language, like speaking in tongues. It sounded as if he was crying and talking at the same time, and in some strange way his words had become half-sobs and his sobs something more than words — or words turned inside out, so that only their emotion and not their meaning came through. It scared me. I knew something terrible had happened, and I didn't know what to do. I wanted to go to him and ask him what was wrong, but I didn't dare. I switched off the sound on the TV so he wouldn't know I was home and sat there staring at Hugh Downs's smiling face. But then I couldn't stand it anymore and I got up and ran down the hall to the kitchen. There, in the middle of the room, wearing his Goodyear jacket and workclothes, was my father. He was on his hands and knees, his head hanging as though it were too heavy to support, and he was rocking back and forth

and babbling in a rhythmical stutter. It's funny, but the first thing
I thought when I saw him like that was the way he used to let me
ride on his back, when I was little, bucking and neighing like a
horse. And as soon as I thought it, I felt my heart lurch in my
chest. "Dad?" I said. "What's wrong?" But he didn't hear me. I
went over to him then. "Dad?" I said again and touched him on
the shoulder. He jerked at the touch and looked up at me, his
lips moving but no sounds coming out of them now. His forehead was knotted and his eyes were red, almost raw-looking. He
swallowed hard and for the first time spoke words I could recognize, though I did not understand them until years later, when
I was myself a father.

"Danny," he said. "Save me."

Before I could finish dialing the school lunchroom's number, my
mother pulled into the driveway. Looking out the window, I saw
her jump out of the car and run up the slick sidewalk, her camel-
colored overcoat open and flapping in the wind. For a moment I
was confused. Had I already called and told her what had happened? How much time had passed since I found my father on
the kitchen floor? A minute? An hour? Then I realized someone
else must have told her something was wrong.

She burst in the back door then and called out, "Bill? Bill? Are
you here?"

"Mom," I said, "Dad's —" and then I didn't know how to finish
the sentence.

She came in the kitchen without stopping to remove her ga-
loshes. "Oh, Bill," she said when she saw us, "are you all right?"

My father was sitting at the kitchen table now, his hands fluttering in his lap. A few moments before, I had helped him to his
feet and, draping his arm over my shoulders, led him to the table
like a wounded man.

"Helen," he said. "It's you." He said it like he hadn't seen her
for years.

My mother went over and knelt beside him. "I'm so sorry," she
said, but whether that statement was born of sorrow over something she had said or done or whether she just simply and guilt-
lessly wished he weren't suffering, I never knew. Taking his hands
in hers, she added, "There's nothing to worry about. Every-

thing's going to be fine." Then she turned to me. Her brown hair was wind-blown, and her face was so pale the smudges of rouge on her cheeks looked like bruises. "Danny, I want you to leave us alone for a few minutes."

I looked at her red-rimmed eyes and tight lips. "Okay," I said, and went back to the living room. There, I sat on the sagging couch and stared at the television, the contestants' mouths moving wordlessly, their laughs eerily silent. I could hear my parents talking, their steady murmur broken from time to time by my father sobbing and my mother saying "Bill" over and over, in the tone mothers use to calm their babies, but I couldn't hear enough of what they said to know what had happened. And I didn't want to know, either. I wanted them to be as silent as the people on the TV, I wanted all the words to stop, all the crying.

I lay down and closed my eyes, trying to drive the picture of my father on the kitchen floor out of my head. My heart was beating so hard I could feel my pulse tick in my throat. I was worried about my father, but I was also angry that he was acting so strange. It didn't seem fair that I had to have a father like that. I'd never seen anybody else's father act that way, not even in a movie.

Outside, the wind shook the evergreens, and every now and then a gust would rattle the windowpane. I lay there a long time, listening to the wind, until my heart stopped beating so hard.

Some time later, my mother came into the room and sat on the edge of the chair under the sunburst mirror. Her forehead was creased, and there were black mascara streaks on her cheeks. Leaning toward me, her hands clasped, she asked me how I was feeling.

"What do you mean?" I wasn't sure if she was asking if I was still feeling sick or if she meant something else.

She bit her lip. "I just wanted to tell you not to worry," she said. "Everything's going to be all right." Her breath snagged on the last word, and I could hear her swallowing.

"What's wrong?" I asked.

She opened her mouth, as if she were about to answer, but suddenly her eyes began to tear. "We'll talk about it later," she said. "After the doctor's come. Just don't worry, okay? I'll explain everything."

"The doctor?" I said.

"I'll explain later," she answered.

Then she left and I didn't hear anything more until ten or fifteen minutes had passed and the doorbell rang. My mother ran to the door and opened it, and I heard her say, "Thank you for coming so quickly" and "He's in the kitchen." As they hurried down the hall past the living room, I caught a glimpse of Dr. Lewis and his black leather bag. It had been years since the doctors in our town, small as it was, made house calls, so I knew now that my father's problem was something truly serious. The word *emergency* came into my mind, and though I tried to push it out, it kept coming back.

For the next half-hour or so, I stayed in the living room, listening to the droning sound of Dr. Lewis and my parents talking. I still didn't know what had happened or why. All I knew was that my father was somebody else now, somebody I didn't know. I tried to reconcile the father who used to read to me at night when my mother was too tired, the man who patiently taught me how to measure and cut plywood for a birdhouse, even the man whose cheeks twitched when he was angry at me and whose silences were suffocating, with the man I had just seen crouched like an animal on the kitchen floor babbling some incomprehensible language. But I couldn't. And though I felt sorry for him and his suffering, I felt as much shame as sympathy. *This is your father,* I told myself. *This is you when you're older.*

It wasn't until after Dr. Lewis had left and my father had taken the tranquilizers and gone upstairs to bed that my mother came back into the living room, sat down on the couch beside me, and told me what had happened. "Your father," she began, and her voice cracked. Then she controlled herself and said, "Your father has been fired from his job."

I looked at her. "Is that it?" I said. "That's what all this fuss is about?" I couldn't believe he'd put us through all this for something so unimportant. All he had to do was get a new job. What was the big deal?

"Let me explain," my mother said. "He was fired some time ago. Eight days ago, to be exact. But he hadn't said anything to me about it, and he just kept on getting up and going down to work every morning, like nothing had happened. And every day

Mr. Siverhus told him to leave, and after arguing a while, he'd go. Then he'd spend the rest of the day driving around until quitting time, when he'd finally come home. But Mr. Siverhus got fed up and changed the locks, and when your father came to work today he couldn't get in. He tried all three entrances, and when he found his key didn't work in any of them, well, he threw a trash barrel through the showroom window and went inside."

She paused for a moment, I think to see how I was taking this. I was trying to picture my father throwing a barrel through that huge, expensive window. It wasn't easy to imagine. Even at his most angry, he had never been violent. He had never even threatened to hit me or my mother. But now he'd broken a window, and the law.

My mother went on. "Then when he was inside, he found that Mr. Siverhus had changed the lock on his office too, so he kicked the door in. When Mr. Siverhus came to work, he found your dad sitting at his desk, going over service accounts." Her lips started to tremble. "He could have called the police," she said, "but he called me instead. We owe him for that."

That's the story my mother told me. Though I was to find out later that she hadn't told me the entire truth, she had told me enough of it to make me realize that my father had gone crazy. Something in him — whatever slender idea or feeling it is that connects us to the world and makes us feel a part of it — had broken, and he was not in the world anymore, he was outside it, horribly outside it, and could not get back in no matter how he tried. Somehow I knew this, even then. And I wondered if someday the same thing would happen to me.

The rest of that day, I stayed downstairs, watching TV or reading *Sports Illustrated* or *Life,* while my father slept or rested. My mother sat beside his bed, reading her ladies' magazines while he slept and talking to him whenever he woke, and every now and then she came downstairs to tell me he was doing fine. She spoke as if he had some temporary fever, some twenty-four-hour virus, that would be gone by morning.

But the next morning, a Saturday, my father was still not himself. He didn't feel like coming down for breakfast, so she made him scrambled eggs, sausage, and toast and took it up to him on a tray. He hadn't eaten since the previous morning, but when she came back down a while later all the food was still on the tray. She didn't say anything about the untouched meal; she just said my father wanted to talk to me.

"I can't," I said. "I'm eating." I had one sausage patty and a few bites of scrambled egg left on my plate.

"Not this minute," she said. "When you're done."

I looked out the window. It had been snowing all morning, and the evergreens in the back yard looked like flocked Christmas trees waiting for strings of colored lights. Some sparrows were flying in and out of the branches, chirping, and others were lined up on the crossbars of the clothesline poles, their feathers fluffed out and blowing in the wind.

"I'm supposed to meet Rob at his house," I lied. "I'll be late."

"Danny," she said, in a way that warned me not to make her say any more.

"All right," I said, and I shoved my plate aside and got up. "But I don't have much time."

Upstairs, I stopped at my father's closed door. Normally I would have walked right in, but that day I felt I should knock. I felt as if I were visiting a stranger. Even his room — I didn't think of it as belonging to my mother anymore — seemed strange, somehow separate from the rest of the house.

When I knocked, my father said, "Is that you, Danny?" and I stepped inside. All the blinds were shut, and the dim air smelled like a thick, musty mixture of hair tonic and Aqua Velva. My father was sitting on the edge of his unmade bed, wearing his old brown robe, nubbled from years of washings, and maroon corduroy slippers. His face was blotchy, and his eyes were dark and pouched.

"Mom said you wanted to talk to me," I said.

He touched a spot next to him on the unmade bed. "Here. Sit down."

I didn't move. "I've got to go to Rob's," I said.

He cleared his throat and looked away. For a moment we were silent, and I could hear the heat register ticking.

"I just wanted to tell you to take good care of your mother," he said then.

I shifted my weight from one foot to the other. "What do you mean?"

He looked back at me, his gaze steady and empty, and I wondered how much of the way he was that moment was his medication and how much himself. "She needs someone to take care of her. That's all."

"What about you? Aren't you going to take care of her anymore?"

He cleared his throat again. "If I can."

"I don't get it," I said. "Why are you doing this to us? What's going on?"

"Nothing's going on," he answered. "That's the problem. Not a thing is going on."

"I don't know what you mean. I don't like it when you say things I can't understand."

"I don't like it either," he said. Then: "That wasn't me yesterday. I want you to know that."

"It sure looked like you. If it wasn't you, who was it then?"

He stood up and walked across the carpet to the window. But he didn't open the blinds; he just stood there, his back to me. "It's all right for you to be mad," he said.

"I'm not mad."

"Don't lie."

"I'm not lying. I just like my father to use the English language when he talks to me, that's all."

For a long moment he was quiet. It seemed almost as if he'd forgotten I was in the room. Then he said, "My grandmother used to tell me there were exactly as many stars in the sky as there were people. If someone was born, there'd be a new star in the sky that night, and you could find it if you looked hard enough. And if someone died, you'd see that person's star fall."

"What are you talking about?" I asked.

"People," he answered. "Stars."

Then he just stood there, staring at the blinds. I wondered if he was seeing stars there, or his grandmother, or what. And all of a sudden I felt my eyes start to sting. I was surprised — a moment before I'd been so angry, but now I was almost crying.

I tried to swallow, but I couldn't. I wanted to know what was wrong, so I could know how to feel about it; I wanted to be sad or angry, either one, but not both at the same time. "What *happened?*" I finally said. "*Tell* me."

He turned, but I wasn't sure he'd heard me, because he didn't answer for a long time. And when he did, he seemed to be answering some other question, one I hadn't asked.

"I was so arrogant," he said. "I thought my life would work out."

I stood there looking at him. "I don't understand."

"I hope you never do," he said. "I hope to God you never do."

"Quit talking like that."

"Like what?"

"Like you're so *smart* and everything. Like you're above all of this when it's you that's causing it all."

He looked down at the floor and shook his head slowly.

"Well?" I said. "Aren't you going to say something?"

He looked up. "You're a good boy, Danny. I'm proud of you. I wish I could be a better father to you."

I hesitate now to say what I said next. But then I didn't hesitate.

"So do I," I said bitterly. "So the hell do I." And I turned to leave.

"Danny, wait," my father said.

But I didn't wait. And when I shut the door, I shut it hard.

Two days later, after he took to fits of weeping and laughing, we drove my father to the VA hospital in Minneapolis. Dr. Lewis had already called the hospital and made arrangements for his admission, so we were quickly escorted to his room on the seventh floor, where the psychiatric patients were kept. I had expected the psych ward to be a dreary, prisonlike place with barred doors and gray, windowless walls, but if anything, it was cheerier than the rest of the hospital. There were sky-blue walls in the hallway, hung here and there with watercolor landscapes the patients had painted, and sunny yellow walls in the rooms, and there was a brightly lit lounge with a TV, card tables, and shelf full of board games, and even a crafts center where the patients could do decoupage, leatherwork, mosaics, and macramé. And the patients we saw looked so normal that I almost wondered whether we were in the right place. Most of them were older, probably veterans of the First World War, but a few were my father's age or younger. The old ones were the friendliest, nodding their bald heads or waving their liver-spotted hands as we passed, but even those who only looked at us seemed pleasant or, at the least, not hostile.

I was relieved by what I saw, but evidently my father was not, for his eyes still had the quicksilver shimmer of fear they'd had all during the drive from Glencoe. He sat stiffly in the wheelchair and looked at the floor passing between his feet as the big-boned nurse pushed him down the hall toward his room.

We were lucky, the nurse told us, chatting away in a strange accent, which I later learned was Czech. There had been only one private room left, and my father had gotten it. And it had a *lovely* view of the hospital grounds. Sometimes she herself would stand in front of that window and watch the snow fall on the birches and park benches. It was such a beautiful sight. She asked my father if that didn't sound nice, but he didn't answer.

Then she wheeled him into the room and parked the chair beside the white, starched-looking bed. My father hadn't wanted to sit in the chair when we checked him in at the admissions desk, but now he didn't show any desire to get out of it.

"Well, what do you think of your room, Mr. Conroy?" the nurse asked. My mother stood beside her, a handkerchief squeezed in her hand.

My father looked at the chrome railing on the bed, the stainless steel tray beside it, and the plastic-sealed water glasses on the tray. Then he looked at my mother and me.

"I suppose it's where I should be," he said.

During the five weeks my father was in the hospital, my mother drive to Minneapolis twice a week to visit him. Despite her urgings, I refused to go with her. I wanted to forget about my father, to erase him from my life. But I didn't tell her that. I told her I couldn't stand to see him in that awful place, and she felt sorry for me and let me stay home. But almost every time she came back, she'd have a gift for me from him: a postcard of Minnehaha Falls decoupaged onto a walnut plaque, a leather billfold with my initials burned into the cover, a belt decorated with tur-

quoise and white beads. And a request: would I come see him
that weekend? But I never went.

Glencoe was a small town, and like all small towns it was devoted to gossip. I knew my classmates had heard about my father — many of them had probably even driven past Goodyear
to see the broken window the way they'd drive past a body shop
to see a car that had been totaled — but only Rob and a couple of
other friends said anything. When they asked what had happened, I told them what Dr. Lewis had told me, that my father
was just overworked and exhausted. They didn't believe me any
more than I believed Dr. Lewis, but they pretended to accept that
explanation. I wasn't sure if I liked them more for that pretense,
or less.

It took a couple of weeks for the gossip to reach me. One day
during lunch Rob told me that Todd Knutson, whose father was
a mechanic at Goodyear, was telling everybody my father had
been fired for embezzling. "I know it's a dirty lie," Rob kept saying, "but some kids think he's telling the truth, so you'd better do
something."

"Like what?" I said.

"Tell them the truth. Set the record straight."

I looked at my friend's earnest, acne-scarred face. As soon as
he'd told me the rumor, I'd known it was true, and in my heart I
had already convicted my father. But I didn't want my best friend
to know that. Perhaps I was worried that he would turn against
me too and I'd be even more alone.

"You bet I will," I said. "I'll make him eat those words."

But I had no intention of defending my father. I was already
planning to go see Mr. Siverhus right after school and ask him,
straight out, for the truth, so I could confront my father with the
evidence and shame him the way he had shamed me. I was furious with him for making me even more of an outcast than I had
been — I was the son of a *criminal* now — and I wanted to make
him pay for it. All during my afternoon classes, I imagined going
to see him at the hospital and telling him I knew his secret. He'd
deny it at first, I was sure, but as soon as he saw I knew everything, he'd confess. He'd beg my forgiveness, swearing he'd never
do anything to embarrass me or my mother again, but nothing
he would say would make any difference — I'd just turn and walk

away. And if I were called into court to testify against him, I'd
take the stand and swear to tell the whole truth and nothing but
the truth, my eyes steady on him all the while, watching him sit
there beside his lawyer, his head hung, speechless.

I was angry at my mother too, because she hadn't told me the
whole truth. But I didn't realize until that afternoon, when I drove
down to Goodyear to see Mr. Siverhus, just how much she hadn't
told me.

Mr. Siverhus was a tall, silver-haired man who looked more
like a banker than the manager of a tire store. He was wearing a
starched white shirt, a blue-and-gray-striped tie with a silver tie
tack, and iridescent sharkskin trousers, and when he shook my
hand he smiled so hard his crow's feet almost hid his pale watery
eyes. He led me into his small but meticulous office, closing the
door on the smell of grease and the noise of impact wrenches
removing lugs from wheels, and I blurted out my question before either of us even sat down.

"Who told you that?" he asked.

"My mother," I answered. I figured he wouldn't try to lie to
me if he thought my mother had already told me the truth. Then
I asked him again: "Is it true?" But Mr. Siverhus didn't answer
right away. Instead, he gestured toward a chair opposite his gray
metal desk and waited until I sat in it. Then he pushed some
carefully stacked papers aside, sat on the edge of the desk, and
asked me how my father was doing. I didn't really know — my
mother kept saying he was getting better all the time, but I wasn't
sure I could believe her. Still, I said, "Fine."

He nodded. "I'm glad to hear that," he said. "I'm really terribly
sorry about everything that's happened. I hope you and your
mother know that."

He wanted me to say something, but I didn't. Standing up, he
wandered over to the gray file cabinet and looked out the window at the showroom, where the new tires and batteries were on
display. He sighed, and I knew he didn't want to be having this
conversation.

"What your mother told you is true," he said then. "Bill was
taking money. Not much, you understand, but enough that it soon
became obvious we had a problem. After some investigating, we

found out he was the one. I couldn't have been more surprised.
Your father had been a loyal and hardworking employee for
years — we never would have put him in charge of the service
department otherwise — and he was the last person I would have
expected to be stealing from us. But when we confronted him
with it, he admitted it. He'd been having trouble meeting his
mortgage payments, he said, and in a weak moment he'd taken
some money and, later on, a little more. He seemed genuinely
sorry about it and he swore he'd pay back every cent, so we gave
him another chance."

"But he did it again, didn't he?" I said.

I don't know if Mr. Siverhus noticed the anger shaking my voice
or not. He just looked at me and let out a slow breath. "Yes," he
said sadly. "He did. And so I had to fire him. I told him we wouldn't
prosecute if he returned the money, and he promised he would."

Then he went behind his desk and sat down heavily in his chair.
"I hope you understand."

"I'm not blaming you," I said. "You didn't do anything wrong."

He leaned over the desk toward me. "I appreciate that," he
said. "You don't know how badly I've felt about all of this. I keep
thinking that maybe I should have handled it differently. I don't
know, when I think that he might have taken his life because of
this, well, I —"

"Taken his life?" I interrupted.

Mr. Siverhus sat back in his chair. "Your mother didn't tell you?"

I shook my head and closed my eyes for a second. I felt as if
something had broken loose in my chest and risen into my throat,
making it hard to breathe, to think.

"I assumed you knew," he said. "I'm sorry, I shouldn't have
said anything."

"Tell me," I said.

"I think you'd better talk to your mother about this, Danny. I
don't think I should be the one to tell you."

"I need to know," I said.

Mr. Siverhus looked at me for a long moment. Then he said,
"Very well. But you have to realize that your father was under a
lot of stress. I'm sure that by the time he gets out of the hospital,
he'll be back to normal, and you won't ever have to worry about
him getting like that again."

I nodded. I didn't believe him, but I wanted him to go on.

Mr. Siverhus took a deep breath and let it out slowly. "When I came to work that morning and found your father in his office, he had a gun in his hand. A revolver. At first I thought he was going to shoot me. But then he put it up to his own head. I tell you, I was scared. 'Bill,' I said, 'that's not the answer.' And then I just kept talking. It took me ten or fifteen minutes to get him to put the gun down. Then he left, and that's when I called your mother."

I must have had a strange look on my face, because the next thing he said was, "Are you all right?"

I nodded, but I wasn't all right. I felt woozy, as if I'd just discovered another world inside this one, a world that made this one false. I wanted to leave, but I wasn't sure I could stand up. Then I did.

"Thank you, Mr. Siverhus," I said, and reached out to shake his hand. I wanted to say more, but there was nothing to say. I turned and left.

Outside in the parking lot, I stood beside the Chevy, looking at the new showroom window and breathing in the cold. I was thinking how, only a few months before, I had been looking through my father's dresser for his old army uniform, which I wanted to wear to Rob's Halloween party, and I'd found the revolver tucked under his dress khakis in the bottom drawer. My father had always been full of warnings — don't mow the lawn barefoot, never go swimming in a river, always drive defensively — but he had never even mentioned he owned this gun, much less warned me not to touch it. I wondered why, and I held the gun up to the light, as if I could somehow see through it to an understanding of its meaning. But I couldn't — or at least I refused to believe that I could — and I put it back exactly where I found it and never mentioned it to anyone.

Now, standing there in the bitter cold, I saw my father sitting at a desk that was no longer his and holding that same gun to his head. And I realized that if he had killed himself with it, the police would have found my fingerprints on its black handle.

I didn't tell my mother what I had learned from Mr. Siverhus, and I didn't tell anyone else either. After dinner that night I went straight to my room and stayed there. I wanted to be alone, to figure things out, but the more I thought, the more I didn't know what to think. I wondered if it was starting already, if I was already going crazy like my father, because I wasn't sure who I was or what I felt. It had been a long time since I'd prayed, but that night I prayed that when I woke the next day everything would make sense again.

But the next morning I was still in a daze. Everything seemed so false, so disconnected from the real world I had glimpsed the day before, that I felt disoriented, almost dizzy. At school, the chatter of my classmates sounded as meaningless as my father's babble, and everything I saw seemed out of focus, distorted, the way things do just before you faint. Walking down the hall, I saw Todd Knutson standing by his locker, talking with Bonnie Kahlstrom, a friend of Molly Rasmussen's, and suddenly I found myself walking up to them. I didn't know what I was going to say or do, I hadn't planned anything, and when I shoved Todd against his locker, it surprised me as much as it did him.

"I hope you're happy now," I said to him. "My father *died* last night." I'm not sure I can explain it now, but in a way I believed what I was saying, and my voice shook with a genuine grief.

Todd slowly lowered his fists. "What?" he said, and looked quickly at Bonnie's startled, open face.

"He had *cancer*," I said, biting down on the word to keep my mind from whirling. "A tumor on his brain. That's why he did the things he did, taking that money and breaking that window and everything. He couldn't help it."

And then my grief was too much for me, and I turned and strode down the hall, tears coming into my eyes. As soon as I was around the corner and out of their sight, I broke into a run. Only then did I come back into the world and wonder what I had done.

That afternoon, my mother appeared at the door of my algebra class in her blue uniform and black hair net. At first I thought she was going to embarrass me by waving at me, as she often did when she happened to pass one of my classrooms, but then I saw the look on her face. "Excuse me, Mr. Laughlin," she said grimly, "I'm sorry to interrupt your class, but I need to speak with my son for a moment."

Mr. Laughlin turned his dour face from the blackboard, his stick of chalk suspended in mid-calculation, and said, "Certainly, Mrs. Conroy. I hope there's nothing the matter."

"No," she said. "It's nothing to worry about."

But out in the hall, she slapped my face hard.

"How *dare* you say your father is dead," she said through clenched teeth. Her gray eyes were flinty and narrow.

"I didn't," I answered.

She raised her hand and slapped me again, even harder this time.

"Don't you lie to me, Daniel."

I started to cry. "Well, I wish he *was*," I said. "I wish he was dead, so all of this could be over."

My mother raised her hand again, but then she let it fall. She didn't have enough left in her to hit me again. "Go," she said. "Get away from me. I can't bear to look at you another minute."

I went back into the classroom and sat down. I felt awful about hurting my mother, but not so awful that I wasn't worried whether my classmates had heard her slap me or noticed my burning cheek. I saw them looking at me and shaking their heads, heard them whispering and laughing under their breath, and I felt humiliation rise in me like nausea. I stood up, my head roiling, and asked if I could be excused.

Mr. Laughlin looked at me. Then, without even asking what was wrong, he wrote out a pass to the nurse's office and handed it to me. As I left the room, I heard him say to the class, "That's enough. If I hear one more remark . . ."

Later, lying on a cot in the nurse's office, my hands folded over my chest, I closed my eyes and imagined I was dead, and my parents and classmates were kneeling before my open coffin, their heads bowed in mourning.

After that day, my mother scheduled meetings for me with Father Ondahl, our priest, and Mr. Jenseth, the school counselor. She said she hoped they could help me through this difficult time, then added, "Obviously, I can't." I saw Father Ondahl two or three times, and as soon as I assured him that I still had my faith, though I did not, he said I'd be better off just seeing Mr. Jenseth from then on. I saw Mr. Jenseth three times a week for the next month, then once a week for the rest of the school year. I'm not sure how these meetings helped, or even if they did. All I know is that, in time, my feelings about my father, and about myself, changed.

My mother continued her visits to my father, but she no longer asked me to go along with her, and when she came home from seeing him, she waited until I asked before she'd tell me how he was. I wondered whether she'd told him I was seeing a counselor, and why, but I didn't dare ask. And I wondered if she'd ever forgive me for my terrible lie.

Then one day, without telling me beforehand, she returned from Minneapolis with my father. "Danny," she called, and I came out of the living room and saw them in the entryway. My father was stamping the snow off his black wingtips, and he had his suitcase in one hand and a watercolor of our house in the other, the windows yellow with light and a thin swirl of gray smoke rising from the red brick chimney. He looked pale and even thinner than I remembered. I was so surprised to see him, all I could say was, "You're home."

"That's right," he said, and put down the suitcase and painting. "The old man's back." Then he tried to smile, but it came out more like a wince. I knew he wanted me to hug him and say how happy I was to see him, and part of me wanted to do that, too. But I didn't. I just shook his hand as I would have an uncle's or a stranger's, then picked up the painting and looked at it.

"This is nice," I said. "Real nice."

"I'm glad you like it," he answered.

And then we just stood there until my mother said, "Well, let's get you unpacked, dear, and then we can all sit down and talk."

Despite everything that had happened, our life together after that winter was relatively peaceful. My father got a job at Firestone, and though for years he barely made enough to meet expenses, eventually he worked his way up to assistant manager and earned a good living. He occasionally lost his temper and succumbed to self-pity as he always had, but for the rest of his life he was as normal and sane as anybody. Perhaps Dr. Lewis had been right after all, and all my father had needed was a good rest. In any case, by the time I was grown and married myself, his breakdown seemed a strange and impossible dream and I wondered, as I watched him play with my infant son, if I hadn't imagined some of it. It amazed me that a life could break so utterly, then mend itself.

But of course it had not mended entirely, as my life had also not mended entirely. There was a barrier between us, the thin but impenetrable memory of what we had been to each other that winter. I was never sure just how much he knew about the way I'd felt about him then, or even whether my mother had told him my lie about his death, but I knew he was aware that I hadn't been a good son. Perhaps the barrier between us could have been broken with a single word — the word "love" or its synonym "forgive" — but as if by mutual pact we never spoke of that difficult winter or its consequences.

Only once did we come close to discussing it. He and my mother had come to visit me and my family in Minneapolis, and we had just finished our Sunday dinner. Caroline and my mother were clearing the table, Sam was playing on the kitchen floor with the dump truck my parents had bought him for his birthday, and my father and I were sitting in the living room watching "60 Minutes." The black pastor of a Pentecostal church in Texas was talking to Morley Safer about "the Spirit that descends on us and inhabits us." Then the camera cut to a black woman standing in the midst of a clapping congregation, her eyes tightly closed and her face glowing with sweat as she rocked back and forth, speaking the incoherent language of angels or demons. Her syllables rose and fell, then mounted in a syntax of spiraling rapture until finally, overcome by the voice that had spoken through her, she sank to her knees, trembling, her eyes open and glistening. The congregation clapped harder then, some of them leaping and dancing as if their bodies were lifted by the collapse of hers, and they yelled, "Praise God!" and "Praise the Lord God Almighty!"

I glanced at my father, who sat watching this with a blank face, and wondered what he was thinking. Then, when the camera moved to another Pentecostal minister discussing a transcript of the woman's speech, a transcript which he claimed contained variations on ancient Hebrew and Aramaic words she couldn't possibly have known, I turned to him and asked, in a hesitant way, whether he wanted to keep watching or switch channels.

My father's milky blue eyes looked blurred, as if he were looking at something a long way off, and he cleared his throat before he spoke. "It's up to you," he said. "Do you want to watch it?"

I paused. Then I said, "No" and got up to change the channel.

Perhaps if I had said yes, we might have talked about that terrible day he put a gun to his head and I could have told him what I had since grown to realize — that I loved him. That I had always loved him, though behind his back, without letting him know it. And, in a way, behind my back too. But I didn't say yes, and in the seven years that remained of his life, we never came as close to ending the winter that was always, for us, an unspoken but living part of our present.

That night, though, unable to sleep, I got up and went into my son's room. Standing there in the wan glow of his night light, I listened to him breathe for a while, then quietly took down the railing we'd put on his bed to keep him from rolling off and hurting himself. I sat on the edge of his bed and began to stroke his soft, reddish blond hair. At first he didn't wake, but his forehead wrinkled and he mumbled a little dream-sound.

I am not a religious man. I believe, as my father must have, the day he asked me to save him, that our children are our only salvation, their love our only redemption. And that night, when my son woke, frightened by the dark figure leaning over him, and started to cry, I picked him up and rocked him in my arms, comforting him as I would after a nightmare. "Don't worry," I told him over and over, until the words sounded as incomprehensible to me as they must have to him, "it's only a dream. Everything's going to be all right. Don't worry."

LEONARD MICHAELS

Viva la Tropicana

FROM ZYZZYVA

BEFORE WORLD WAR II, Cuba was known for sugar and sex, but there was also a popular beach with sand imported from Florida, and grand hotels like the Nacional where you could get a room with a harbor view for ten dollars, and there were gambling casinos organized by our glamorous gangsters whose faces appeared in *Life* magazine, among them Meyer Lansky and my uncle-by-marriage, Zev Lurie, a young man who could multiply giant numbers in his head and crack open a padlock with his hands. *Habañeros,* however, celebrated him for his dancing — rhumba, mambo, cha-cha — rhythms heard nightly in New York, Miami, Cuba, Mexico, Central America, and much of South America, where Zev toured as an exhibition dancer before he went to Cuba and caught the fancy of big shots in the mob.

The first time I heard mambo, I was in a Chevy Bel Aire, driving from Manhattan to Brooklyn with Zev's son, my cousin Chester. We'd just been graduated from high school and were going to a party. To save me the subway ride, Chester came to pick me up. He wore alligator shoes, like Zev's dancing shoes, and a chain bracelet of heavy silver, with a name tag, on his left wrist. It was a high school fashion, like penny loafers and bobby socks. Chester had spent time in Cuba, but mainly he lived with his mother in Brooklyn and hardly ever saw his father. Uncle Zev, I believe, didn't love Chester too much, or not enough. This accounts for an eccentric, showy element in his personality, which distinguished him in high school as a charming ass, irresistible to girls, obnoxious to boys. As we drove, he flicked on the radio. The DJ,

Symphony Sid, began talking to us, his voice full of knowing, in the manner of New York. He said we could catch Tito Puente this Wednesday at the Palladium, home of Latin music, 53rd and Broadway. Then Symphony Sid played a tune by Puente called "Ran Kan Kan."

Chester pulled the Chevy to the curb, cut the motor, and turned the volume way up. "You know what this is?" I shrugged, already afraid Chester was about to do something show-offy. He lunged out of the car and began to dance, his alligators flashing on the asphalt. "Cuban mambo," he cried, pressing his right palm to his belly, showing me the source of the music, and how it streams downward through your hips and legs into your feet. He danced as if he had a woman in his arms, or the music itself was a magnificent woman, like Abbe Lane or Rita Hayworth, with mammalian heat and substance, as required by the era. Chester's every motion displayed her with formal yet fiery adoration. His spine was straight, shoulders level, and his head aristocratically erect, the posture of flamenco dancers, but the way he moved was more fluid and had different hesitations. "This is Cuba, baby. *Ritmo caliente.*" He looked very macho. I could see why girls liked him.

I envied his talent and succumbed to his love of this music and dancing, in which I saw the shadow of Uncle Zev, greater dancer and friend of gangsters, who moved in a greater life, far away in the elegant casinos of Havana, where beautiful women and dangerous men took their nightly pleasure. I began yearning to go to Cuba, but over thirty years would pass before I had the chance. America was almost continuously at war or on the verge of war, and there was the revolution in Cuba. Then, in 1987, I was invited to a film festival in Havana. I'd be in the American contingent, which included film directors, screenwriters, photographers, and journalists.

The night before I left, I received a phone call from Uncle Zev, who for the past twenty years had lived in Brooklyn with his wife, Frances, my mother's sister. I lived in Berkeley.

"You're going to Havana."

"How did you know?"

"I know."

In this way, with his old-fashioned gangsterish manner, he intimidated me.

"I need a favor," he said.

"Of course. Anything."

"There's a woman in Havana. Consuelo Delacruz. I am saying this once, which is already too much, so listen. Go to Consuelo. Identify yourself. Get down on your knees. Then say . . ."

"I think you said get down on my knees."

"Say that your Uncle Zev continues to worship the ground she walks. Say he kisses her feet. Get a pencil and paper and I'll tell you how to say it in Spanish."

"I already feel guilty. Chester and I used to be close. We went to high school together."

"Chester is in the construction business. A Manhattan contractor. Last month was very bad. He made two hundred fifty thousand. You think he gives a shit about human feelings? I'm telling you about undying love in the heart of an old man. Are you a sensitive writer or what?"

"Should I kiss her feet, assuming I find her?"

"She works at the Tropicana. I'll fill in the background. Listen."

In a few minutes he'd told me a long story . . .

Zev worked in Havana from the late forties to the mid-sixties. When Fidel made his triumphant progress through the streets, with Che Guevara and Celia Sanchez, a doctor and the daughter of a doctor, Zev stood in the delirious crowds, trying to figure out what to do with his life. Not political, he was indifferent to the revolution, except that it cost him his job, but he was madly in love with Consuelo Delacruz, who refused to leave Cuba with him. To struggle with English, in a Brooklyn grocery store, would be an insufferable humiliation. Besides, Zev was married.

He lingered in Havana, doing this and that, and didn't leave until obliged to do so by the revolutionary government. In 1966, the Ministry of Economics unearthed ledgers in the Hotel Capri, where George Raft once had the penthouse suite, and discovered Zev's initials beside certain figures, again and again, right up to New Year's Eve, 1959, suggesting that he had been in possession of great sums of gambling money, not only from the Capri, but from the Nacional and Tropicana, too. The revolution wanted it. He showed them a receipt, the same he'd shown the mob, proving he'd turned over the money to Batista before his flight to the Dominican Republic. In a fit of moral disgust, Fidel personally ordered Zev's expulsion. He said, "I wanted only to burn the money in your face."

Zev had been a runner between the casinos and Batista's officers. On the night Batista fled, Zev rushed with conga drums on his shoulders down O'Reilly Street to the docks and then into a receiving shed. Two soldiers emerged from behind crates, took the drums, which contained over a million dollars, and gave Zev a photo of Batista. This was the receipt. Across the eyes of the photo, Batista always signed his mother's name. The photo was signed, but across the mouth, not the eyes. Zev understood that the soldiers, whom he'd never seen before, intended to hand the money over to the revolution and thereby escape Fidel's tribunals and the firing squad. Neither here nor there, as far as Zev was concerned. He had to present the authentic receipt to parties who also had firing squads. Zev laughed. "I see it's over with Batista, eh, amigos?" The soldiers laughed, too, and Zev broke the neck of one with a forearm blow and disemboweled the other with a knife even as their laughter resonated in the shed. Searching their uniform pockets, he found the authentic receipt. He spent that night with Consuelo, in her apartment, brooding.

"Return the money, or give it to the revolution."

"The soldiers are in a crate at the bottom of the harbor. I have the receipt. The money is for you and the child."

"Nobody will need money anymore. What child do you mean?"

Now, 1987, considering the economic misfortunes of the revolution, Zev figured Consuelo would be glad to have the money, but he wanted her to come to the States. I was to explain this to Consuelo, reading from the Spanish dictated to me by Zev over the phone. She knew about the money. She didn't know what Zev had done with it.

That night in Havana, twenty-eight years ago, lying in the arms of Consuelo, Zev made a plan — to be put into effect only if he continued to love Consuelo. "I am a realistic person. Feelings die," he said. Seven years later, a few weeks before Zev was deported, his child was born. He was still in love with Consuelo.

From the pattern of whorls in the tiny thumbprint, Zev worked out a formula. It translated into a graph. This graph described the proportionate distance between peaks and valleys along the

shaft of a key that opened a bank box in Zurich. The original
key was destroyed. To reconstruct it, Zev's child — now twenty-
one years old — had to supply the thumbprint. That's how Zev
planned it in 1959. Only one person in the world, his Cuban love
child, could lay hands on the money. Zev had waited seven years
in Cuba and loved Consuelo. He'd waited over twenty years away
from her. He loved her no less. The old man cried himself to
sleep at night.

On December 22, at ten P.M. I walked into the Tropicana and
began looking for Consuelo Delacruz to tell her that she and the
child were rich in dollars and the undying love of my uncle, Zev
Lurie. I imagined he was at that moment huddled in a heavy wool
coat, his face bent against the blades of winter, hustling through
freezing New York streets from his office to his limousine. My
heart went out to him. I was delivering warmth to the lonely winter of his life and I was glad. He'd confessed to me. I felt honored, grateful. I valued his intimacy.

I passed through an entranceway of pointed arches, then a
lobby, and entered the largest outdoor nightclub in the world.
Tiers of white tablecloths, in a great sweep of concentric circles,
descended toward a vast curved stage. There were trees all about,
tall palms and flamboyants, the towering walls of a natural cathedral open to the nighttime sky. I went to a table near the edge of
the stage. A waiter approached. I pulled out my notebook and
asked, *"Donde puedo encontrar Consuelo Delacruz?"*

"Ron y Coca-Cola," he said.

Music started, lights began flashing, dancers appeared onstage.

I raised my voice. *"Consuelo Delacruz. Ella trabaja aquí."*

"Cuba libre?"

"O.K.," I shouted. He left. Was I reading incorrectly? Mis-
pronouncing? I'd try again when the drink came.

The Marxian adage "Nothing can stop the course of history"
is incontestable, but here was the Tropicana, in a Havana suburb, the creation of fifties architecture, airy and geometrical,
and, on its stage, just as in the prerevolutionary days, the garish,
glitzy artificiality of Las Vegas tits-and-ass dance routines.

At the next table, two men in identical white shirts, with pale,
expressionless robot heads, from East Germany, were sipping
beer. Beyond them, on platforms built high in the air, on either

side of the stage, appeared an orchestra, chorus, and dancers, performing in the trees, with the fantastic sensationalism of show-biz Americana. *Viva la Tropicana!* I said to myself, and looked about for my waiter and my drink. It was coming to me in the hand of a tall, slender black woman, very handsome, about fifty or so. I got right down on my knees and started reading the Spanish in my notebook. When I glanced up, she was half smil-ing, her eyes softly inquisitive.

"Zev?"

I nodded. She set the drink on the table, tugged me to my feet, kissed me, and pulled me after her along the aisle that curved with the stage front, and then behind it into darkness tangled with wires. We stopped only to gape at each other, to see what couldn't be said. She asked fifteen questions. Spanish is the fast-est language in the world. Cuban Spanish is even faster, but if she'd spoken with the slow lips of death, I'd have understood none of it. She continued to hold my hand, hers quivering with eager-ness to know what I couldn't tell her. Gradually, she made out in my eyes no hope, no Spanish.

"*Norteamericano?* Brook-leen?"

Then, more strongly, she pulled me after her through the dark and around behind the stage into an alley, like another part of the city, no longer the Tropicana, and pulled me toward two near-naked women, their heads glorified by mountains of feathers, their bodices all spangles. They practiced dance steps together, not noticing our approach until Consuelo thrust me in front of one of them. To me she said, "*La niña*, Zeva." To her she said, "*Tu padre lo mandó. Anda hablar con él. Hablale.*" *La niña* looked from her mother to me, then just at me, fixing me with large dark eyes rich in incomprehension. Words came, as if experimentally. "You are from Zev?"

"He sent me to see your mother."

She was Chester's half-sister, Zev's love child, my cousin. I had to tell this to myself, review the facts, before saying, "I am your cousin." She told this to her mother who, while she'd had no trouble kissing me earlier, seemed now to show faint reserve, though she smiled and said, "Ah." Zeva stepped toward me. In a sweetly formal way, she kissed my cheek, whispering, "Did he send us money?" I whispered, too. "More than you can imagine."

After the last show, I waited for them at the front gate. Zeva emerged wearing blue jeans, a white T-shirt, and sandals. She looked like an American college student. Consuelo had gone ahead to get their car, an old Chevy, like the one Chester drove years ago, but very rusted, battered, and loud. We drove along the Malecón, where waves smashed against the sea wall, stood high in the air, and collapsed along the sidewalk and onto the avenue. Facing the ocean were rows of old, grim, suffering buildings, arcades and baroque ornamentation, much decayed, and very beautiful in decay. I had glimpses of Arabic tile work and the complicated glass of chandeliers hanging amid clotheslines in rooms where the rich once lived. We turned right, passing through a large square, then along empty streets with hardly any lights. The Chevy sounded very loud, echoing in the darkness, because there were no other sounds, no voices, no music, and nobody about.

This was the Old Town, where Zeva and Consuelo had an apartment in a three-story building with a much broken facade,elaborate mortar work along the balconies fallen away, iron railings loose in their moorings, and tall windows eaten up by water and fungus. The apartment was long and very narrow, with a linoleum floor throughout. Lights hung from the ceiling by naked wires. Chests and tables were loaded with porcelain figurines, ashtrays, framed photos, and innumerable bright little cheap glass nameless things, like junkshop memorabilia. We sat in the kitchen at an oval Formica-topped table. The surface was imitation gray marble with an aluminum border. The pipe legs were also aluminum. Right out of the fifties. In an L.A. antique shop, it would sell for about a thousand bucks — with the four chairs. Zeva looked at her hands when I finished the story and said, "Which one?"

"Aren't they the same?"

"Maybe only one is good. I could give you impressions of both thumbs, or I could cut them off and you bring them to him."

"He wants all of you," I said.

Consuelo, respectful of our deliberations, waited for us to conclude. Zeva told her where we stood. Then an argument started. I couldn't understand it, but it touched old disagreements. Zeva wanted to go to the States. Consuelo didn't. Consuelo rose, stood with arms folded across her chest, looking down at us. Then, from her angry rigidity, she bent abruptly and hugged me. She did the same with Zeva, then walked off down the narrow hall to a bedroom. Zeva said, "She's tired. She's going to sleep. You stay here tonight. She wants you to. I'll fix a bed for you by the windows, or take my room. I won't be able to sleep, anyway. This is terrible. Terrible. I don't know Zev, but he must be a thoughtless man. How could he do this to me? To us? We have lived for years with promises. This apartment is ours. Almost ours. We are buying it slowly. Now you bring new promises from him. She wants to tell the authorities. It won't be too good for you. I'm sure you'll be detained. Come, I'll show you."

I followed her to the window.

The street was empty except for a man at the corner, ordinary-looking, wearing a hat, brim pulled down front and back.

"The police?"

"They will want to know what we talked about."

"We're cousins. We talked about Zev. You told me about yourself, how you learned English. How did you learn English?"

"I don't really know."

"You don't?"

"After Zev was thrown out, my mother was in ill favor. She lost her job at the Tropicana. They gave it back to her later, but for years she did other work, mainly cooking and cleaning for the family of a diplomat. She took me with her every day. I played with their children. They spoke English. I spoke English. When they switched to Spanish, so did I. There were also other languages. The family had lived in different countries. I spoke maybe five languages. It was all language to me and I never knew which I was speaking."

"You don't speak a child's English."

"I studied it later in school. If you speak one language as a child, then another, you are left with a child's knowledge of the first. Like changing lovers."

"Have you changed many lovers?"

"I can count them on one thumb, but I imagine you grow and mature with the next lover, and the next. With the first you are always a child. I wanted to be in the foreign service, so I studied English. I would like to travel. I'm good at languages, but I'm a little too black, a little too much like a woman. Opportunities didn't come my way. My mother says Zev speaks nine languages. She refuses to admit she understands a word of English."

"Zev still loves her."

"She obliged him to speak to her in Spanish. If a man loves you, she says, he must prove it every day. When Zev spoke to her, always in Spanish, he reminded himself of what he felt for my mother. She's a real Cuban, very warm and loving, but when she tells me what Zev did to Batista's soldiers, there is no pity in her voice. I ask her why not. She says, Your father is a man."

The man in the street lit a cigarette and glanced up; the flare of the match revealed his eyes. I waved to him. He looked away.

She said, "Americans think anything can be made into some joke. Do you like rice and beans? If not, you may have to learn."

We stood near each other, easy in our nearness, familial. It wasn't an American feeling. My cousin was very attractive, but I had no trouble with that. I put my arm around her shoulder. She leaned against me, as if we'd grown up together, two Latin kids, always touching. "I like rice and beans," I said.

I wasn't detained in Cuba. Nothing was done to me; nobody asked questions. On the last night of the film festival, I was invited to a grand dinner, with hundreds of others, at the Palacio de la Revolución. Long tables in parallel lines, with wide aisles between them, were laid out with Cuban foods. Guests walked the length of the tables, loading their plates, then returned for more. At the end, they served cakes and excellent Cuban ice cream. Without announcement, Fidel appeared and the crowd swarmed toward him, surrounding him, but this was an elegant crowd of well-dressed people, and they felt the necessity of leaving him a little space in front. I couldn't approach closely, but I could see his head and shoulders, the top of his green army uniform, his beard and intense black eyes. He was the tallest man in the hall, perhaps six-foot-five. His head was large, leonine, heroic, bending slightly toward those who asked questions, listening with utter seriousness. I saw a monument, not simply the man called Fidel, but the living monument of himself. He seemed, in that instant, while talking to a man in the crowd, to be talking beyond that man to me. "Of course," he said, "we would publish the works of Kierkegaard. If somebody came to me with the manuscript, say, of his great work, *Either/Or,* I would think it is worth a million dollars."

When my plane landed in Miami, I went to a phone and called
Zev. It was five A.M., but he'd said to phone him the moment I
arrived. I was sure he'd want to hear from me. Besides, I was too
excited to wait. As soon as he said hello, I began telling him I'd
met Consuelo, and I told him about his brilliant daughter, Zeva,
how she spoke several languages, how well she danced, though
I'd seen her only as a spangled figure among others, all bur-
dened by colorful feathers. "Zev, why didn't you say the baby was
a girl?"

"I couldn't remember for sure."

"Oh, come on."

"When you get a little older, the differences between boys and
girls matter less."

I told him Fidel is willing to let them go to the States, but with
conditions. *Either* the million dollars is returned to the revolution, *or* Zev's women never leave. "It's up to you."

"He spoke to you personally?"

"Not exactly. It was indirect, but we were in the same room. I'd
been followed by the police. He certainly knew who I was."

"Right, right. Well, I have the bank and the number, but only
Zeva can open the box. The key is her thumb. Wait in Miami. I'll
catch a plane this afternoon. Stay with my friend Sam Halpert. I
want you to call him, but listen carefully. When you hang up,
look around, look at the people. Look good. Then take a walk.
Make four or five turns like you're lost, you don't know the airport. Don't go into toilets. Stay in plain sight. Then find another
phone and call Sam — Sam Halpert — and then look around
again. You'll recognize the one who's following you. Describe the
guy to Sam. Whatever he tells you, do it."

"Zev, you're scaring me."

"I'll see you soon."

The phone went dead as I shouted, "Wait a minute." I dialed
him again. What the hell did he think I was, a person with nothing to do but hang around Miami? The phone rang at his end.
Nobody answered. Too damn bad. Zev would fly here for nothing. I slammed down the receiver and started toward my San
Francisco flight, so angry that I forgot to look around at the faces,
but there were none, anyhow, just a man lying on a bench with a
Miami Herald covering his face, sleeping.

I didn't notice him.

I didn't notice his white shoes, either.

Blind with feeling, I thrust along the passageways where slender neon tubes of pastel light floated, a modernistic touch, suggesting a chemical bloodstream fed the airport's extremities. My big leather shoulder bag slammed against my hip, my breathing was loud. I talked to myself, finishing the conversation with Zev, telling him he was my favorite uncle. I'd admired and loved him since I was a kid, but . . . I owed him a lot, nevertheless . . . I'd never forget that he paid my college fees, still . . . that he pulled strings in New York to get me summer jobs, and, when my high school sweetheart became pregnant, Zev found us the doctor in New Jersey and paid for the operation. Then I stopped raving and let myself wonder if maybe it wasn't anger that I felt but fear.

The philosophers say nothing in the mind is inaccessible to the mind. They are wrong. The mind is promiscuous. It collects more than you can ever possibly know. *It* — not me — had seen white shoes, and taken in the man on his back, sleeping under the newspaper. Minutes after the phone call, as I stood at a coffee counter, still tumultuous, I saw white shoes dangling from legs on either side of a stool and I remembered — I'd seen them before — remembered what I didn't know I knew. I remembered the newspaper, too, which the man was now reading.

I left my coffee untasted on the counter, went to a phone, trying to be efficient, though hurried and frightened. I dialed Information, then Sam Halpert. Not once did I glance back at White Shoes, but I'd have bet a million dollars his eyes were set high in his head, which I'd seen as a blondish blur, complexion pocked and gullied from cheek to neck, as if he'd been washing in acid. Somebody picked up the phone, and, without any hello, said, "Can you hear me good?"

I said, "Yes. Sam Halpert?"

"Start laughing."

"I have nothing to laugh at, Mr. Halpert."

"This is a hilarious phone call, if somebody is watching you."

I laughed, laughed.

"Don't overdo it, kid. What does he look like?"

"Blond. Ha, ha, ha. Maybe six feet tall. Late twenties. Your average white trash." The expression surprised me. It came flying out of fear, as if to strike the man. "Ha, ha, ha. Blue-and-white

Hawaiian shirt, white slacks, white shoes with pointed toes. Ha, ha, ha. I'm scared out of my mind."

"I want you to talk to me. Move your mouth, shake your head, laugh. Then hang up and go look for a taxi. Don't run. Don't dawdle. Don't get ideas about calling a cop. Tell the taxi driver to go to Bayside, and to drop you at the flags."

"The flags?"

"You'll see like a park, flags at the entrance. An aisle of flags. Walk through the flags. There's shops on either side. Go straight, straight, straight till you're standing on a concrete ledge facing the bay. Below the ledge you'll see a parapet. Go down to it and walk right. Repeat what I said."

"Taxi to Bayside. Aisle of flags."

"Laugh."

"Ha, ha, ha. Through flags to water, down to parapet, walk right. Ha, ha, ha, ha, ha."

"The taxi will cost maybe fifteen bucks. You got fifteen bucks?"

"Yes. What if you're not there? It isn't even six A.M. I'll be alone, Mr. Halpert. Wouldn't it be advisable to wait a few hours until there are people in the streets? Ha, ha."

"Am I here?"

"Yes."

"I'll be there."

"But wouldn't it be advisable . . ."

"I gave you the best advice you'll ever get." He hung up.

Another outrage. Zev had told Sam Halpert to expect my call. He'd known this would happen. I wasn't living my own life. Walking, talking, laughing, but it wasn't me. There was no trouble getting a cab. Maybe Zev had arranged that, too. I was driving through Miami followed by a creep.

Minutes later, I dragged my shoulder bag out of the back seat of the taxi, paid the driver. He abandoned me in the tremendous and brilliant emptiness of a business center, tall new buildings amid older ones alongside the park and Bayside, a mall built at the edge of Biscayne Bay. The aisle of flags marked a wide bleak walk into the mall. I was entering it when I heard a car door slam. I turned, saw a taxi and the blue-and-white shirt moving free of it. I thought to drop my bag and run, but I wasn't supposed to know I was being followed. It wasn't advisable.

The water lay before me, black but for the lights of slow-moving boats way out and city lights skimming the surface, defining the shore. Where concrete ended and became a ledge, I saw the parapet, wide enough for two men walking side by side. A stairway took me down. I walked right, doing everything right. Below, water slapped listlessly at the wall. It didn't give a damn about me. There was nobody in sight along the parapet, but after a few yards I saw a man up ahead descending a stair toward a small dock, taller than the blond, wearing a Windbreaker, jeans, and tennis shoes. He stopped to light a cigar, all very casual. A local yachtsman. He started toward me along the wall to my right. I had to keep to the water side, which unnerved me, though there was room to pass each other easily. He walked in a loose, loping, athletic way, slightly tipped forward. I assumed he was Sam Halpert, but maybe he wasn't Sam Halpert. As we drew close, he looked for my eyes and said, "Good morning, kid," and passed me. Then I heard a cry, and turned. The blond in the Hawaiian shirt, kicking and flailing, sailed off the parapet through the air.

The tall man, his arm thrust out with the shove he'd given the blond, flicked his cigar into the water. The flying blond, having hit with a great splash, thrashed toward the wall, slapping at its ·slimy face, seeking a fingerhold. There was none. He couldn't drag himself out. Halpert came toward me. "Forget him. Let's go."

The blond thrashed in the water, mouth a black O closing, going under, then bobbing up, opening to an O again, as if swallowing a pipe, his eyes wild with lights of fear.

"He's drowning," I said.

"You kidding? This is Miami. Everybody here is a fish. Let's go." He began tugging at my arm. I pulled it away.

"That man is drowning, Mr. Halpert."

"Call me Sam."

"You and Zev have your ways and I have mine, Sam."

That instant, a chunk of concrete broke from the wall above my head, leaving a hole big as a grapefruit, and I heard the gunshot — much louder than I'd have expected — and I saw the blond go under again, black booming steel in hand.

Sam said, "I'll hold your bag, kid. Jump in after him."

We took off along the parapet as I yelled back at the water, "Drown, fucker. I hope you drown."

Sam drove, sometimes stopping at stop signs, sometimes not. I wasn't concerned. Little concerned me. The shot missed my head and left me with a sense of my potential for instant nothingness. The blond face lingered in memory, mouth and eyes wide open, begging life to enter, aware it was drowning, but I couldn't feel for his terror, too much awed by myself being alive, strangely humiliated, but alive.

We cut through residential areas heavy with the sweetness of flowers. I lay back against the seat. A dark sensuous weight of air and silence lingered before morning, neither dark really nor yet morning, and I took in solemn banyan trees beginning to emerge, hulking, elephantine, streaming tendrils, and I saw white houses set back from the road.

"I could go Dixie Highway," said Sam, "but I figured you'd want to look at the neighborhoods. Ever been to Miami?"

"No."

"You'd never guess how little it costs me to live here."

"Probably not."

"I don't live like the dancing man. Never stops, that guy. I told him I play tennis on the local courts. He says, 'You don't own a court?'"

"That's Zev."

"Not in the mood to talk? You can't believe Sam is blabbing."

"I can't believe it."

"We'll talk later. No hurry. It's beginning the way Zev figured. Fidel made his move. Now we make ours, and play it through to the end. Fidel never quits. Blood of the conquistadors."

"What if he drowned?"

"Fidel is a great swimmer."

"I mean White Trash."

"What I'm about to say is not an insult, but you're an asshole."

"Do you carry a gun, Sam?"

"Am I an American?"

"I keep seeing his face go under."

"A face like that should go under. You told him to drown. Don't you say what you mean?"

"You sound like my girlfriend, Sonny. She expects to see me

tomorrow, but I'll be in Miami. She'll say, 'If you wanted to be here, you'd be here. Don't you say what you mean?'"

"She talks like that to you? Let me ask you a question, man to man. Is the screwing you get worth the screwing you get?"

"Yes."

He laughed. "We have different needs."

"What do I smell?"

"Mango. We're passing an orchard."

"I don't see it."

"Most of the trees have been cut down. Beautiful trees. I love mango. Very good for your digestion. Do you know the death rate in Florida is higher than the birthrate, but the population is growing. Five thousand new residents a week. They need houses. Goodbye mangos. There's money around to build a lot of houses."

"Drogas?"

"I don't know from *drogas.* Ask your uncle. He owns a bank in Miami. I'm just his lawyer."

"I'm dying to sleep, but I'm afraid I'll dream. That guy's face. I'm still watching it."

"It could have been him watching you. You never saw a man die. Don't worry. You came to the right city."

"I'm flying out of here."

"I know what you mean. It's a rude introduction to the life, but Zev needs you. There's my house. You sleep. Later, we'll talk. Work things out."

"Why does Zev need me?"

"There's a hundred guys who would kill for Zev."

"Like you?"

"Like me."

"So why me?"

"You're family, people he trusts."

"He's got a son."

"Zev wouldn't want Chester to do it. The kid is too eager to please. He's a crook. He'll see chances for himself, lose sight of the goal. Anyhow, Zev doesn't want to owe him anything. We talked about you for a long time before you got that call. You're not a crook. There's nothing you want. You're perfect."

"For what?"

"We'll talk later."

We were in the driveway to Sam's house, parked beside a wood fence about seven feet high.

"I want to go home."

"You want to be with your girlfriend, what's her name. I know how you feel. Hungry?"

"I couldn't eat. I haven't slept for two or three nights, partying in Havana. Then this. I expected to sleep on the flight to San Francisco, but look where I am. Where the hell am I?"

"South Miami, at the edge of Dade County. It's good you're sleepy. That's an animal feeling. You're going to like it here. Hey, do you like mud wrestling? We got that in Miami Beach. We'll go tonight. What do you say? Twenty-five naked girls wrestling in the mud. It'll take your mind off your problems. Tell me, kid, what's not to like in Miami?"

"I must be out of my mind, feeling depressed in Miami."

Sam's house, a stucco box with a flat roof, had a red tile floor in the living room and very little furniture — rattan couch, rattan chairs, a coffee table, and a dining room table. No curtains, no rugs. A bachelor's house. Some full-page cartoons, cut from magazines, were pasted to a wall in the living room, perhaps hiding cracks in the Sheetrock. There was a kitchen, dining room, and two bedrooms.

He showed me into one of the bedrooms. I dropped my shoulder bag, took off my clothes, and lay down on a thick foam mat on a plywood base. It felt good, but I could have slept on the ground. I didn't wash, didn't want to move. I sprawled on my back beneath a light wool cover, in my underwear, and shut my eyes.

Sam began making phone calls in the living room, beyond the wall, door shut, but I heard every word. It was early, too early for phone calls. He talked to an international operator, then people overseas, in different time zones, making hotel reservations. Somebody was going to travel "overseas." Beautiful word. It named a feeling. Sorrow at not going home. I missed Sonny and thought again of the man's face, drowning.

Sorrow attached to the face more strongly than would a feeling in waking life; weepy pressure, as if I were about to cry, but I was tired and into dreaminess. I never act out in dreams. Doing nothing, I've come, not even touching the woman. Sonny once said she'd come during a lecture, toppling out of her chair, moaning. I teased her. She said men have impoverished lives. So much they don't feel. How much did a man need? My feelings reduced to her. She was wearing her black leather miniskirt, sitting in the front row, naked legs crossed. She leaned over the armrest where it expanded into a table for her notebook and uncrossed her legs. The flash of her underpants shocked the professor, made him brilliant, made her go toppling out of her chair. Seeing her taken like that, we came together, she on the floor, me in South Miami, loving her feelings, but, in the bowels of sleep, Sonny on the floor, ravished, unconscious, it wasn't her. It was Zeva. How an innocent moment becomes another, which is depraved, I don't know. Sam's voice returned to me, saying, "Don't worry, kid, you'll see her again."

I felt light without opening my eyes — the way an amoeba sees — through skin. I knew it was afternoon.

"Was I talking in my sleep?"

He stood beside the bed. Sam. No dream. I hadn't yet seen him in natural light — tall with dark little close-together eyes and the sloping shoulders of an athlete, holding a glass of orange juice in a long hand. "I never met Zev's kid," he said. "She got to you. Have some orange juice from my trees. Zev calls her 'it.' The poor bastard doesn't even let himself call her a her. He's been dying twenty years, telling nobody. Did you fuck her?"

"I didn't hear you say that." I sat up and took the juice from his hand. "I told her what I was supposed to, that's all. About the money. Then we just talked. I liked her a lot and felt very happy for Zev. I didn't know what's what. I still don't."

"This has nothing to do with money. Let's go eat. I'll tell you what's what." He put my bag in his car. Apparently I wasn't coming back.

I recognized neighborhoods we'd driven through earlier in the semidarkness. Then we were near the center of town and out of Sam's car, walking through the funereal lobby of a hotel. Somebody was shoving a vacuum cleaner across the rug. It droned, abdominal and despairing in the shadowy cave of the lobby. A buffet had been set up in the dining room. We loaded trays, took a table in a corner beside a long window, light filtering through gauzy white curtains, bathing us in a smoky glow; its quality came to me, as had odors in the night air, mixtures of perfumed decay, but the light wasn't as palpable. It stirred different nerves, like desert light, with holy intimations. Sam and I ate in silence, soldiers on a lonely mission. Coffee was served.

Sam looked to see if I was ready to listen. I avoided his look, but felt its pressure. He would talk, tell me what's what, whether or not I was receptive. There was no forgetting what had happened, trying to enjoy sensations of light, as if I had time for the mere luxury of being alive.

He said, "This is about women and power, kid. They need each other, like Samson and Delilah, or Zeus and Leda. In Cuba, Fidel is known as the Bull. A force of nature, you know what I mean? Like he told Khrushchev to grow balls — bomb New York, vaporize Washington? What a guy."

Sam had shoved a man into Miami Bay and been indifferent. Now he leaned toward me, grinning, glee in his eyes, loving the great destroyer. He expected me to relish the idea of Fidel. I could only nod, which wasn't enough for him, but he continued to lean toward me, grinning, urging me to feel something in myself that wasn't there.

"When Fidel was in the mountains, there was a shortage of women. What did he do? He didn't do anything. They came to him."

"They came to him?"

"Naturally. But some didn't go because they wanted to fuck a god. They were sent. You think this is incredible? See it. The afternoon is hot. You can hardly breathe. Mosquitos cover your skin like hair. Fidel and the others have just returned from patrol. They squat in a clearing in the woods, too tired to worry about Batista's police. A woman steps out of the woods. She doesn't say a word. She's gorgeous. The men wait for Fidel to acknowledge her. What does he do? He does nothing. He's Fidel. So she goes to him and stands until she feels that her claim on his *cojones* is not inconsistent with his revolutionary principles. 'Are you the only one?' he asks, thinking of his men. She says her colleagues wait in the woods. He nods to his men. They go into the woods. Listen, kid, it is the common practice. The shah of Iran had high-class whores sent to him from Paris, and he couldn't always get it on, let alone up. Fidel never paid a cent. Women wanted to go.

Their motivation was basic to the universe, like the law of gravity. Every woman wants to fuck a god. No exceptions. Here is where Zev comes in."

"I can guess."

"You're a quick study." He looked pleased and disappointed at once. "Go ahead. Guess."

"Zev was already in the business."

"You and me will have conversations at a high level, but you look like you tasted something distasteful, not familiar to your mind."

"I thought Zev's business had to do with gambling. I never asked what else."

Sam shook his head, then blinked and rubbed his eyes, as if he'd developed a tic. He was trying too hard. This wasn't exactly the conversation he'd expected. I felt dim regret. He was doing his job. He wanted to come through for Zev, but I wasn't listening to him in the right spirit.

"Your uncle was in the business," he said quietly, no longer working on me. "Gambling, drugs, whores — so what? He's diversified since Cuba, but he's still in the business. You see in the newspapers how a cabinet official is getting off a plane in Berlin with fifteen advisers wearing suits and ties. To you they look important. Compared to Zev, they are errand boys. You will never see Zev stepping off a plane in Berlin, Beijing, Dakar, or Teheran on anybody's business but his own. Before the government types get on their planes, they phone Zev, ask if he's free for lunch. Maybe he'll give them some phone numbers in Helsinki. Sure, they're going to talk about arms control, but there's talk and there's talk, and nobody ever talks to anybody except in bed. Departments of the CIA and KGB are run by whores, many of them supplied by Cherchez La, Zev's international information service. For you, he got on a plane. He'll be at the airport in a little while."

"All right, he's big, he's important. He came to America as an immigrant kid. Life was tough. He made his way. It's the common story. I didn't ever want to know everything. He's been good to me. Look, Sam, I get your point. I believe you. But it makes no difference. I don't care how important he is. I don't admire his line of work, and I don't think he's flying down here for me."

"Why not? It's been a long time since he's seen you. Remember what you said when I asked if you fucked Zeva? You said, 'I didn't hear you, Sam,' or something like that." His tone was melancholy and nostalgic, as if he'd referred to the distant past.

"I remember. So do you. You have an ear for facts. What are you getting at now? Are you setting me up for something? I don't like the feeling, Sam."

His ears — I hadn't noticed until that instant — protruded slightly; long and batlike; fact-catchers. He dipped his head, in a tiny, sheepish, oriental bow, to concede the point.

"When I was a boy, I knew the statistics for every player in the major leagues. I could name the capital of every country in the world. I love facts. Do you know, in the state of Florida, you're never more than sixty miles from water? Don't get so excited. You feel strongly for the Cuban bitch. I approve. You want to protect her honor. Maybe you have Latin blood. Maybe you'd die for *la familia*. But right now you're suffering from culture shock." He stabbed the tabletop with his fingertip. "Here, you're in America, not Berkeley. Miami is America and I'm trying to tell you something. I don't think you can hear me. Let me — please — tell you something. In the human brain there are two major centers. One is for sex, the other is for aggression. They lie side by side. Cut the links between them and a natural human person becomes a fucking liberal. Somebody cut your links?"

"What the hell are you talking about?"

"Cesar Chavez says, 'Don't eat grapes,' so you don't eat grapes?"

"Damn right I don't. You've got my number. Is it all right to change the subject now, or do you intend to finish the story?"

He sighed, rubbed his eyes again. As though much discouraged, he continued. His voice went flat and thick.

"The rest is obvious. Some women were sent by Zev. When they came down from the mountains, Zev put them on airplanes to places like Zurich, Caracas, Stockholm. Different ambassadors helped him. The same later, after the revolution. The women still live in distant places with their sons. We call these women Vessels. The sons we call Potentates."

"That's very poetic."

"Everything is in Zeva's thumb."

"That sure isn't what I told her. I feel like a liar. Fidel knows about his *familia?*"

"He has received photographs. He sees boys becoming young

men. No question who is the father. Fidel is prepotent, you know what I mean? It's a technical fact."

"What do you mean?"

"If the stud is prepotent, it doesn't matter what the woman looks like. Fidel's baby grows up big, handsome, smart, with a memory for detail. It talks when it's six months old and never stops. By the time it's six years old, it's kicking ass. No kid on the block can handle it. Beat it with a baseball club and it comes off the floor fighting. You follow me? I'm talking about a hero."

"Sounds like a pit bull."

"Fidel is no longer young. The revolution no longer feels to him like his personal expression. He finds himself looking at the photos. He cares. He needs these sons. He is ready to deal. That guy in the water bothers you, but we had to send a strong message. No other way. He was dead before he left Havana. Or you were dead."

"Zev risked my life to send a message?"

"It was the first stage of our negotiations. The last is when the Potentates go to Havana, and Zev's women leave."

"What about his daughters? He had none?"

"Sure he did. There's one right in Havana. He sends her Christmas presents. That's a fact. But he'll bargain only for Potentates. Zev wants you to find them. You won't talk to reporters, won't sell the story, won't make deals on the side with the Vessels, or subcontract with other operatives. You won't even think about that kind of shit. We'll have Zeva in a couple of days and you two will fly to Zurich. You go to the bank and open the box. You'll find cash and bank books in the names of the Vessels. Give the bank books to the manager. He'll show you the status of each account along with addresses in different cities. With the cash you and Zeva play while you find the Potentates and put them on planes to Havana. You have a month. After that Zeva's passport is invalid. If she isn't back in Havana, Consuelo is dead."

"I can imagine us playing. How many sons?"

"Some Vessels miscarried, and some, like I told you, had daughters. Of twenty-eight babies, fifteen sons."

"Zev wants me to find fifteen men I never saw in my life, who could be anywhere in the world, and put them on planes to Havana?"

"They won't be so hard to find. They look like him. Maybe a couple are dead. There could be a few it wouldn't be wise to send to Fidel. You have to study them; use good judgment. Figure, eleven. Maybe less. Look, Consuelo is already in jail. You understand? It's under way."

"What if they won't go?" I said, panic in my heart. "Not everybody is like me."

This was like agreeing that I might go. Unthinkable, but I'd said the words. Not everyone is like me, including me, but I'd been shoved over the edge with news about Consuelo. Sam picked up the implicit agreement. As if the main issue were settled, his mood changed. Encouraged, he said, "Tell a guy in France or Norway he's won a free trip to Cuba, and you think he won't go? Miami is full of European tourists and Latin Americans. Not only drug barons. We've also got former dictators and their dependents who are to a high degree scumbags. They drive around in fancy cars, wearing gold chains and no shirts. Like the guy who lives across from me. He parks on my grass. I asked him nicely not to do it, but he keeps on doing it."

"Must be a scumbag."

"I've been feeding broken-glass hamburgers to his watchdog."

"Sam, I have an idea. You and Zev write letters to the Potentates and stick plane tickets to Havana in the letters. I'll help."

"We don't know who they are. And maybe you're right, some won't go. We'll tell you how to encourage them."

"You think I'm a travel agent."

"That could be your cover — a business card, official papers, home office in Miami, secretaries answering the phone."

I detected in Sam's long narrow face, broken by the glint of small dark eyes, an *idea* of me passing across his features like a breeze across a lake. It touched the strong nose, the sensuous droop of his lower lip. But it wasn't me. He saw the travel agent. There'd been a flash of intenser concentration on my presence, like an animal fixed in his gunsight stare, through which I could see Zev's stare, his invincible determination of how things will be; and I saw that I had nothing to say about it, only to behave as Zev assumed I would, because I wasn't a crook and there was nothing I wanted.

I said, "There are chores I have to do in Berkeley. Not very

important, but they're my life, such as it is. Otherwise, I'd leave
for Zurich this minute. What the hell. Why not? Zev is my favorite uncle. I owe him plenty."

"What do you have to do? I mean *have to do*. Like pay some
bills?"

"That's right. Like pay some bills. Telephone, gas, electric . . ."

"Like pick up your car at the dealership?"

"Yes, as a matter of fact."

"The new clutch was five hundred and seventeen bucks. We
paid. The car is sitting outside your place. Your landlady will drive
it around the block every couple of days. Your other bills are also
paid. As for your girlfriend's birthday present . . ."

"Oh God."

"You forgot, didn't you? Don't even know your own fucking
life. Lawyers, accountants, and car mechanics — total strangers —
are living your life. We bought your girlfriend a pair of earrings
at Gump's. Antique jade. They go with her eyes. She'll be pleased.
There is nothing left for you to forget. You're a free man."

"What about my new glasses? They're waiting for me this week
in Berkeley at Dr. Schletter's office."

Sam shoved a brown leather glasses case across the table. I took
out the glasses, tried them on. They seemed correct. He called
for the check.

A free man, I never felt more helpless except in dreams where
I'd want to scream or run and couldn't. I followed him to his car.

"A million bucks to spend traveling around the world with a
beautiful girl, and he worries about his glasses. What a putz. Wait
till Zev hears this. He'll change his mind about Chester."

"No, he won't."

Sam laughed. "He thinks you're perfect."

Zev's plane was a silver twin-engined jet with two pilots. The
first to emerge was a light-skinned black woman. For an instant I
thought she was Zeva. The same size as Zeva with her dancer's
legs, strict posture, aristocratic neck. She wore a one-button jacket
and short tight skirt. High heels forced emphasis into her calves.
The power and shape of her thighs were evident in the skirt,
green-gray cotton, same as the jacket. Her blouse was lavender,
like her shoes. She stood in the door and looked about the tar-
mac. Spotting Sam's car, she called into the plane, no doubt telling Zev we were here.

"Zev's pilot?"

"Also driver, bodyguard, business manager," said Sam. "You want my opinion, she's his sickness. Penelope de Assis. Reminds you of someone?"

"Except for the eyes."

They were mounted on the flared branches of her cheekbones, birds fashioned by a diamond cutter. Fifty feet away, I could tell they were blue.

"Where did Zev find her?"

"In Rio, dancing in the street for tourists. She was eight years old, shaking her ass to a conga drum. She's been with him fifteen years. She signs his checks, kid, so be polite. Her name, let me repeat, is Penelope. Don't call her Penny. Don't suppose any other familiarity is allowed. She's the one who fixed your life in Berkeley."

"Nobody knew about the glasses except me and Dr. Schletter."

"She saw a photo in a writer's magazine. You're at the typewriter working on a screenplay, but she could tell you weren't reading the type, so she phoned every optometrist within a mile of your house, to ask if your glasses were ready. Your girlfriend was easier. Penelope needed only her license plate number."

"How does she feel being a surrogate daughter?"

"She feels that Penelope de Assis — nobody else — is the daughter of the yid from Odessa, Zev Golenpolsky Lurie. That's how Zev once wanted it. Now he wants a little distance — room for the other women, you know what I mean? Is it too much to want? Penelope says no, no, no. She'd love to have a sister. She'd love to kill her."

"Let's push Penelope into the bay."

"Try it. I've seen her kick out a man's teeth. There's Zev."

He was coming down the steps from the plane, Penelope, at the bottom, watching. I saw his age in Penelope's tension — as if braced to save him should he lose his balance — and also in his slowness and caution. He glared at her, despising her concern or his dependency. The cossack-yellow hair was still yellow, straight, thick as honey and brushed back flat in the old fashion, appropriate to a dancing dandy. When he looked toward us and grinned, terrific peasant teeth appeared in the square, heavily structured Russky head, built for hard blows. He wore a black linen suit, pink shirt, gray tie. He carried nothing. I hadn't seen him for over twenty years — our dealings were by phone, me asking for favors until he asked — not that I'd understood — for my life. He looked much as I remembered. Sam and I got out of the car. Zev came toward us. Then I could see more indications of age — seams in his neck and a downward pull about the wide, heavy mouth — but still, in his sixties, Zev could pass for a younger man, even here in the Miami sunlight through which he approached with a strong step, the blue-eyed Penelope de Assis at his side.

He embraced me, then shoved me back, arm's length, his hands lingering on my shoulders.

I said, "You betrayed me, Uncle Zev."

He shook his head, sighing. His words came slowly, with the weariness of ancient disappointment.

"You did me a favor unknowingly. Is that what you call betrayal?"

"Yes."

"I'm sorry that's how you feel, but I can understand. I won't ask more of you. Say 'No, Uncle Zev. You ask for too much,' and I will walk right back into that airplane and there will be no hard feelings."

His green-and-yellow flecked eyes stayed strictly on mine as he extended his left hand toward Penelope, palm upward. "You have a reservation on the next flight to San Francisco. It leaves in two hours and forty-five minutes."

Penelope put an air-ticket envelope into his palm. He rattled it in my face.

"Say no. Use this ticket. You fly first class. Say it — 'No, Uncle Zev. I feel deeply how much this means to you, but my answer is no.' A chauffeured car will meet you in San Francisco and drive you home. Phone your girlfriend. Take her to dinner at Jack's. It's on me."

"Uncle Zev, give me a chance to —"

"I'm still talking. Should you say yes, I have also made a reservation for you at my hotel in Key Biscayne. They're holding a bay-view suite. A speedboat is at your disposal. It's got a thousand horses. Penelope will drive you to the hotel and buy you decent clothes in the shop. To these old eyes, the way you're dressed, you look like a piece of shit."

"Uncle Zev, please, this isn't about clothes and speedboats."

"You got something better in your miserable life? What? Writing a screenplay? It's digging a ditch. They make a movie, the ditch becomes a sewer." He squeezed my shoulder. "Soft as a fairy."

"All right, enough." I snatched the ticket out of his hand and tore it in half. My freedom had been compromised by neediness and favors, but the trouble was deeper — in the chemistry. I stared at the epicanthic folds that lay on his tigerish, Genghis Khan eyes, the grainy texture of his heavy skin, the yellow hair — each of the billion strands an expression of his soul — and I was hypnotized by the force, the mystery of his particular being, which I couldn't reconcile with the idea that he was a son of a bitch. Penelope took the torn ticket from me and slipped it into her jacket pocket. Frugal.

"All right, what?"

"Introduce me to your daughter."

Having said "daughter," I glanced at her. There was no gratitude in her face. If she felt anything, it looked like anger. Maybe Sam hadn't told me enough. Zev's voice, now low and harsh, as if I'd kicked him in the groin, said, "Penelope de Assis, meet my nephew."

We shook hands. She said, "I'd like to talk to you."

"Listen to her," said Zev. "She knows more about you than you. Sam and I must have a short conference in the plane. We'll meet you later at the hotel and go to dinner. You'll be there. I like a Spanish restaurant on Calle Ocho. You know it, Sam?"

"The Malaga."

Zev snapped his fingers. "Correct." Turning to me, he said, "Afterwards, we'll go dancing. What do you say?"

"What's the difference?"

"Truer words were never spoken. Buy clothes. Look good. Take a ride in the speedboat. Penelope, show my nephew how to live." Sam handed Penelope the keys to his car.

Driving to Key Biscayne, Penelope concentrated on the road and, it seemed, didn't want to speak. I figured I knew why. She'd witnessed my confrontation with Zev and decided she had nothing, after all, to say to me. With an apologetic and resentful tone — coming out of an irrational need to be polite and make her approve of me — I began to apologize for causing her trouble, though I was more sinned against than sinning — "I had no idea of the complications in my Cuba trip. I didn't even know you existed until a few minutes ago" — when she grunted and swung her arm, like a backstroke in tennis, banging my jaw with the heel of her fist. Blindly, reflexively, my hands flew up, catching the next blow on my wrists. The car swerved left and right as she overcorrected, hitting the brakes, tearing gravel. We stopped. A fiend with searing cold blue eyes screamed at me:

"Why didn't you just say no and get the fuck out of here?"

Then she stiffened, pressing herself back against the seat, and breathed deeply. A hundred cars and trucks passed before she restarted the engine, reentered traffic. We sped on to Key Biscayne.

My jaw was hot. I wanted to touch it, but I sat like a dummy, not looking at her legs, the skirt awry, pulled up to her crotch. Dummy or not, I was alert and feverish. Only she and I existed in Miami. Pray, I told myself, for patience. Be silent, strong, clean of heart. You don't know what's going on. A wrong word and she might drive into a palm tree.

As we pulled into the hotel grounds, she said she would go to the shop, buy some clothes, bring them to me. "You will keep whatever you like. I'll return the rest." She would choose the clothes alone. Her tone was cold and curt. No talk of styles, colors, materials. She didn't ask for my sizes. Go to my suite, sit in the bar, take a walk about the grounds, look at the trees, flowers, shore birds, or ride in the speedboat. If I preferred, she would ride with me later. "I assume you'll want me," she said matter-of-factly, without the coyness or arrogance of a good-looking woman, or any apparent suspicion that I might prefer to strangle her. The boat ride didn't matter to her one way or the other. Please myself. She'd see me in an hour.

I went to my suite, lay down on a couch, got right up and looked out the window. Looked, didn't see, lay down again, shut my eyes, waited, waited, waited. There was a knock at the door. Penelope came in with jackets, shirts, pants, socks, shoes, and bathing trunks. She dropped everything on the couch, smiling faintly, as if amused by the colors and variety. I was glad to see this other face. It was possible almost to like her. But, far more important, despite her volatile personality, I was oppressed by desire. "Try this on," she said, holding up a jacket. I took it from her.

With Penelope looking, I stood before a mirror staring at my reflection. The clothes were horrible and exciting, too gorgeous, flashy, expensive-looking, designed. Penelope said, "That looks good. Return these shirts. Keep the two jackets. I like those shoes." She tossed clothes onto the couch, one pile to return, the other to keep. I was proud when she liked something, embarrassed when she didn't. Putting clothes on, taking them off, I began to sweat. It was hard work; her eyes on me. I said, "I can't stand this anymore."

"Let's go for the boat ride. I'll meet you at the dock in fifteen minutes." She snapped up the clothes to be returned. The door shut behind her. I waited ten minutes, opened the door, and walked out to the dock.

She was at the wheel of a speedboat, standing barefoot, in a black bikini and black sunglasses, not watching for me, just standing there, waiting. I climbed in and stood beside her, holding on to a rail. She turned on the engines and maneuvered slowly into the bay.

The Miami skyline was suspended in the enormous trance of late afternoon as we picked up speed heading into the heart of space. Then she cut the motor and the choppy, pummeling flight gave way to stillness and silence. Stillness and silence, deep and abrupt as when passing through the door of a cathedral into sanctified vacancy, but this was towering air above vast waters.

I wondered, as I often had, why falling in love is so important to everybody — since the invention of the feeling — but, in the ambient grandeur, sense became sensation, and I entered a zone of blood, exceedingly alert, no thoughts. An airliner, lifting slowly above the city, seemed motionless, like our drifting boat in the quiet afternoon. Penelope wasn't in any hurry to talk. Neither was I. I waited as if for a degree of darkness to descend and make words. Lights went on here and there among faraway buildings, and a moon appeared. Penelope removed her sunglasses. "Please forgive me for what happened earlier. I know what you think of me," she said.

"I've forgotten the business in the car."

"That's good of you, but I would do it again. What I'm thinking about, really, is that Sam told you I'm jealous and afraid I'll be shoved out in the cold, didn't he?"

"He didn't say that."

"Yes, he did. I know the man. He had to say it. Perhaps you don't listen carefully. He takes the simplest view of everything. That's what makes him useful to Zev and also dangerous. Well, he's wrong about me. I've no reason to be jealous or afraid. See that one and that one." She pointed to a cluster of tall buildings. "I own them. I own buildings in New York and Los Angeles, too, and a ranch in New Mexico and a chain of car washes. Except for my brains and my ass, everything I own cometh from Zev Lurie. But I am the owner. And there is always more, more, more. Zev puts a paper in front of me and says, 'Sign.' I sign."

"Why does he do that?"

"So he won't be responsible for anything. Nobody can sue him, he says, and take his property. But I believe he wants only to feel young. Like a baby. Irresponsible. Property makes you age. So he's still a baby and I'm five hundred years old — I own so much. Do you know why I'm telling you this?"

"No."

"Guess."

"Your heart is broken."

"You're less stupid than I thought. What's she like?"

"You could be friends."

"What makes you think so?"

"She's very, very nice, but what's wonderful is . . ."

Penelope was wrong. I'm very stupid. I've said very stupid things. I've lost sleep thinking about them. In a rush of pity — sympathy, affection, hope — I said the most stupid thing ever. Her hands whitened on the wheel. Tendons stood forth in her neck. Her eyes were huge, shining with pain.

"What do you mean she looks exactly like me?"

"I don't mean anything. I am too enthusiastic. I exaggerated a trivial coincidence." I was almost shouting, as if to crush her anger before it gained momentum.

"What do you mean, coincidence? What the hell do you mean? This face? This neck? These arms and legs? What? She has these breasts?" She tore off the top of her bikini and pulled down the pants, flung the pieces at her feet, screaming, "This is me. This is me, not her."

There wasn't a lot more to see, seeing her naked. She was less modest than a three-year-old. Desire fled.

"I'm sorry," I said, stooping to pick up the bikini pieces at her lovely narrow feet; from there on up, trembling stone flesh. I slipped the bikini top over her head. She didn't do the rest, just let it hang like a rag necklace. Down on one knee, I held the bottom for her to step into it. She did. I drew it up her legs. We stood face to face.

Desire returned in a rush.

I looked away with a cry, looked back, kissed her, and — to my embarrassment — she merely said, "What's that noise?"

I let her go instantly and listened.

There was a bumping like my heart against the boat, though duller and trailing hollow reverberations along the bottom, irregular and persistent. We leaned over the side, peering into the water. "Must be a flashlight in the console," she whispered, as if someone were around to hear us. We didn't need the light. Sliding into view from beneath the boat, bobbing and bumping against the side, came the head and the gaping, glossy, moon-foiled eyes of White Trash, mouth open as if to suck the world. His right arm was gone, the stump stringy and red.

Penelope groaned, "Sharks," as a smooth gray snout, tiny eyes and undershot maw, burst from below and took White Trash's head away in a quick shake and a noise like tearing silk, then a slither, an arcing plunge into oblivion. I grabbed my neck, gagging as if it had happened to me. Penelope staggered to the wheel.

Engines coughed, grumbled, propellers took purchase on the bay. We lurched between white plumes lifting on either side like wings, as we raced toward the lights of Key Biscayne, me yelling against the rage of the engines. "I know him, I know him. That's White Trash," I yelled, as if it were a great boast, my claim to a life of action. I yelled the whole story, how he followed me from the airport, how he ended in the bay, and then, having spent myself, I said, "I make trouble for everybody, don't I?"

She laughed. "Not the sharks." In a sweetly bemused tone, she added, "I hope you haven't made us late for dinner."

It occurred to me she was joking. I answered seriously, "You're going too fast and I don't want dinner. I don't want new clothes. I don't want speedboats. Zev can go to hell with his property. I don't want any of it — not even you. Tell him that. No, I'll tell him myself. I see what you're all doing and I don't want any of it. NOT EVEN YOU."

"Don't say that." Her voice was low, faintly reproachful. She slowed the boat. "I was only teasing, because I'm turned on. Aren't you? Don't bullshit me about your fine character. Tell me the truth."

What I felt of exhilarating horror diffused into a generalized vibrancy. "I could fuck a sea gull," I said with eerie tenderness, never more depraved or truthful.

"It's nothing personal?"

The speedboat drifted. Her eyes were strange diamonds, their authority not to be denied.

That night, sharks feasted in the fateful bay, and I loved her and loved the loving of her, which seemed very obvious, perhaps too obvious. She said, "What keeps you from loving me?"

Occasional clouds crossed the moon and were bleached to a glow.

Did she expect an answer?

I though of Zev and Sam. The desk clerk would say I had gone for a speedboat ride with Penelope and never returned. Zev would be alarmed.

The enveloping night came down like a swirl of black camellias, except for stars and moon and the electric syllables of the Miami skyline singing cheerily against the blackness.

Penelope lay in my arms.

I hadn't forgotten what she said.

Gradually and gradually, it came to me that Zev wasn't alarmed. Not at all. My providential uncle hadn't gone to the hotel. If he'd bothered to phone the hotel desk, it was to confirm what he supposed.

However my life swerved, it answered to his remote determinations even as the fragrant waters of Penelope opened to me in widening circles like the Red Sea for Moses.

She said, "Do you like my body?"

"Can't you tell?"

"Why don't you say it?"

"I see that you aren't a monster."

"How sweet of you. But what if I were?"

"It would be a hard test."

"Then you don't love me."

"Not like that. You aren't my child."

"I'm young."

"Make me young."

It was better the second time. I was better, less eager, and her body spoke to mine in easy dreamy pleasure that seemed to rise from the very navel of the cosmos, flowing through her into me.

Holding my face, looking into my eyes, she said, "Your turn."

"No."

"Didn't you say that you wanted everything?"

"No."

"Can I give you something? How about a building?"

"No."

"Then take them all."

"That's nice of you, but I'm not a landlord."

"Not one little building? Tell you what, I'll give you five percent of one. You claim depreciation and never pay taxes again in your life. Spend the money on me."

"Who are you?"

"You're being cruel."

Labor and spin, yet everything returns from whence it came in the night. I found myself thinking, yeah yeah, in the manner of Uncle Zev — so who was I falling in love with? A mulatto from Rio — arms, legs — who? Aside from the delicate sweetness of her breathing, who?

The ogling moon hung upon my question. I kissed her neck, which answered me little.

Zev found her dancing in the street.

Now he had visions of a lonely deathbed in Brooklyn, wanting flesh of his flesh beside him.

"It's nothing personal?" she'd wittily said.

I licked her ears, then she put her tongue in my mouth. Dark, delicate scholarship.

I wondered if there would be another time. There wouldn't ever be everything, or enough, but there could be more. She lay on her back, eyes shut. She didn't have to see. I was there, like the night, completely given to her. I sat up and looked around.

A white star burned on the water, as if it were the *more* I had in mind. It was far away, growing bigger and brighter, an immense dazzling. Then it came toward us, shooting lights, searching the bay. I realized it was no star, but some kind of ship, brighter than the stars, too bright to see in detail. Penelope sensed my tension, and sat up, too. We watched it approach.

"Good or bad?" she whispered.

I made out a high sharp prow and three tall masts strung with lights, a great steaming funnel among them, everything blazing white, beautiful as the Taj Mahal. Then I heard the doon-doon throb of conga drums and the sinuous elegance of a Latin flute. With the schooner almost upon us, I read, painted on the side, *El Señor.*

Two men at the stern leaned over a rail. One was Sam. The other was Zev. Zev shouted, "We've been looking for you two all over the bay. Come aboard. We're going to Cuba." He said it the Spanish way, "Cooba," shouting again, "Cooba." He and Sam laughed as powerful lights spun around our speedboat in crazily hilarious blinding celebration.

Penelope stood up and waved and laughed with them, marveling at the schooner, long and high and glacial, shining on the black water. "Isn't Zev certifiably insane?" she said, an awestruck child in her voice, very plaintive and adoring. She didn't care, but I covered her with my shirt anyway.

LORRIE MOORE

Willing

FROM THE NEW YORKER

IN HER LAST PICTURE the camera had lingered at the hip, the naked hip, and even though it wasn't her hip, she acquired a reputation for being willing.

"You have the body," studio heads told her over lunch at Chasen's.

She looked away. "Habeas corpus," she said, not smiling.

"Pardon me?" A hip that knew Latin. Christ.

"Nothing," she said. They smiled at her and dropped names. *Scorsese, Brando.* Work was all playtime to them, playtime with gel in their hair. At times Sidra felt bad that it *wasn't* her hip. It should have been her hip. A mediocre picture, a picture queasy with pornography: movies like these, she knew, eroticized the unavailable. The doctored and false. The stand-in. Unwittingly, she had participated. Let a hip come between. A false, unavailable, anonymous hip. She herself was true as a goddam dairy product, available as lunch whenever.

But she was pushing forty.

She began to linger in juice bars. Sit for entire afternoons in places called I Love Juicy or Orange-U-Sweet. She drank juice and smoked a cigarette now and then. She'd been taken seriously — once — she knew that. Projects had been discussed: Nina. Portia. Mother Courage with makeup. Now her hands trembled too much, even drinking juice, *especially* drinking juice, a Vantage wobbling between her fingers like a compass dial. She was sent scripts in which she was supposed to say lines she would never say, not wear clothes she would never not wear. She began to get obscene phone calls, and postcards signed "Oh, yeah, baby." Her boyfriend, a director with a growing reputation for expensive flops, a man who twice a week glowered at her Fancy Sunburst guppy and told it to get a job, became a Catholic and went back to his wife.

"Just when we were working out the bumps and chops and rocks," Sidra said. Then she wept.

"I know," he said. "I know."

And so she left Hollywood. Phoned her agent and apologized. Went home to Chicago, rented a room by the week at the Days Inn, drank sherry and grew a little plump. She let her life get dull, dull but with Hostess cakes. There were moments, moments bristling with deadness, when she looked out at her life and went *"What?"* Or worse, feeling interrupted and tired, "Wha-?" It had taken on the shape of a terrible mistake. She hadn't been given the proper tools to make a real life with, she decided, that was it. She'd been given a can of gravy and a hairbrush and told, "There you go." She'd stood there for years, blinking and befuddled, brushing the can with the brush.

Still, she was a minor movie star, once nominated for a major award. Mail came to her indirectly. A notice. A bill. A Thanksgiving card. But there was never a party, a dinner, an opening, an iced tea. One of the problems with people in Chicago, she remembered, was that they were never lonely at the same time. Their sadnesses occurred in isolation, lurched and spazzed, sent them spinning fizzily back into empty, padded corners, disconnected and alone.

She watched cable and ordered in a lot from a pizza place. A life of obscurity and radical calm. She rented a piano and practiced scales. She invested in the stock market. She wrote down her dreams in the morning to locate clues about what to trade. *Disney,* her dreams said once. *St. Jude Medical.* She made a little extra money. The words *cash cow* nestled in the side of her mouth like a cud. She got obsessed. She tried to be original — not a good thing with stocks — and she began to lose. When a stock went down, she bought more of it, to catch it on the way back up. She got confused. She took to staring out the window at Lake Michigan, the rippled slate of it like a blackboard gone bad.

"Sidra, *what* are you doing there?" shrieked her friend Tommy long distance over the phone. "What are you? You're living in some state that borders on North Dakota!" He was a screenwriter in Santa Monica. Once, a long time ago and depressed on Xtasy, they had slept together. He was gay, but they had liked each other very much.

"Maybe I'll get married," she said. She didn't mind Chicago. She thought of it as a cross between London and Queens, with a dash of Cleveland.

"Oh, *please,*" he shrieked again. "What are you *really* doing?"

"Listening to seashore and self-esteem tapes," she said. She blew air into the mouthpiece of the phone.

"Sounds like dust on the needle," he said. "Maybe you should get the squawking-crickets tape. Have you *heard* the squawking-crickets tape?"

"I got a bad perm today," she said. "When I was only halfway through with the rod part, the building the salon's in had a blackout. There were men drilling out front who'd struck a cable."

"How awful for you," he said. She could hear him tapping his fingers. He had made himself the make-believe author of a make-believe book of essays called *One Man's Opinion,* and when he was bored or inspired he quoted from it. She waited. "I was once in a rock band called Bad Perm," he said instead.

"Get out." she laughed.

His voice went hushed and worried. "What *are* you *doing* there?" he asked again.

Her room was a corner room where a piano was allowed. It was L-shaped, like a life veering off suddenly to become something else. It had a couch and two maple dressers, and was never as neat as she might have wanted it. She always had the DO NOT DISTURB sign on when the maids came by, and so things got a little out of hand. Wispy clumps of dust and hair, the size of small heads, bumped around in the corners. Smudges began to darken the moldings and cloud the mirrors. The bathroom faucet dripped, and, too tired to phone anyone, she tied a string around the end of it, guiding the drip quietly into the drain so that it wouldn't bother her anymore. Her only plant, facing east in the window, hung over the popcorn popper and dried to a brown crunch. On the ledge, a jack-o'-lantern she had carved for Halloween had rotted, melted, frozen, and now looked like a collapsed basketball — one she might have been saving for sentimental reasons, one from the Big Game! The man who brought her room-service breakfast each morning — two poached eggs and a pot of coffee — reported her to the assistant manager, and she received a written warning slid under the door.

On Fridays she visited her parents in Elmhurst. It was still hard for her father to look her in the eyes. He was seventy now. Ten years ago he had gone to the first movie she had ever been in, had seen her remove her clothes and dive into a pool. The movie was rated P.G., but he never went to another one. Her mother went to all of them and searched later for encouraging things to say. Even something small. She refused to lie. "I liked the way you said the line about leaving home, your eyes wide and your hands fussing with your dress buttons," she wrote. "That red dress was so becoming. You should wear bright colors!"

"My father takes naps a lot when I visit," she said to Tommy.

"Naps?"

"I embarrass him. He thinks I'm a whore hippie. A hippie whore."

"That's ridiculous. You're the most sexually conservative person I know."

"Yeah, well."

Her mother always greeted her warmly, puddle-eyed. These days she was reading thin paperback books by a man named Robert Valleys, a man who said that after observing all the suffering in the world — war, starvation, greed — he had discovered the cure: hugs.

Hugs, hugs, hugs, hugs, hugs.

Her mother believed him. She squeezed so long and hard that Sidra, like an infant or a lover, became lost in the feel and smell of her — her sweet, dry skin, the gray peach-fuzz on her neck. "I'm so glad you left that den of iniquity," her mother said softly.

But Sidra still got phone calls from the den. At night, sometimes, the director phoned from a phone booth, desiring to be forgiven as well as to direct. "I think of all the things you might be thinking, and I say, *Oh, Christ.* I mean, do you think the things I sometimes think you do?"

"Of course," said Sidra. "Of course I think those things."

"*Of course! Of course* is a term that has no place in this conversation!"

When Tommy phoned she often felt a pleasure so sudden and flooding it startled her.

"God, I'm so glad it's you!"

"You have no right to abandon American filmmaking this way!"
he would say, and she would laugh loudly, for minutes without
stopping. She was starting to have two speeds: Coma and Hysteria. Two meals: breakfast and popcorn. Two friends: Charlotte
Peveril and Tommy. She could hear the clink of his bourbon glass.
"You are too gifted a person to be living in a state that borders
on North Dakota."

"Iowa."

"Holy bejesus, it's worse than I thought. I'll bet they say that
there. I'll bet they say 'bejesus.' "

"I live downtown. They don't say that here."

"Are you anywhere near Champaign-Urbana?"

"No."

"I went there once. I thought from its name that it would be
a different kind of place. I kept saying to myself: champagne,
ur*bah*na, *champagne*, ur*bah*na! Champagne! Urbana!" He sighed.
"It was just this thing in the middle of a field. I went to a Chinese restaurant there and ordered my entire dinner with *extra*
MSG."

"I'm in Chicago. It's not so bad."

"Not so bad. There are no movie people there. Sidra, what about
your *acting talent?*"

"I have no acting talent."

"Hello?"

"You heard me."

"Yes, but for a minute there I thought maybe you had that dizziness thing again, that inner-ear imbalance."

"Talent. I don't have *talent*. I have willingness. What *talent?*" As
a kid she always told the raunchiest jokes. As an adult she could
rip open a bone in herself and speak out of it. Simple, clear. There
was never anything to stop her. Why was there never anything to
stop her? "I can stretch out the neck of a sweater to point at a
freckle on my shoulder. Anyone who didn't get enough attention
in nursery school can do that. Talent is something else."

"Excuse me, O.K.? I'm only a screenwriter. But someone's got
you thinking you went from serious actress to aging bimbo. That's
ridiculous. You just have to weather things a little. Besides, as I
say in *One Man's Opinion*, willing yourself to do a thing is brave,
and the very essence of talent."

Sidra looked at her hands, already chapped and honeycombed with bad weather, bad soap, bad life. She needed to listen to the crickets tape. "But I *don't* will myself," she said. "I'm just already willing."

She began to go to blues bars at night. Sometimes she called Charlotte Peveril, her one friend left from high school.

"Siddy, how are you?" In Chicago, "Sidra" was thought of as a hillbilly name. But in L.A. people had thought it was beautiful and assumed she'd made it up.

"I'm fine. Let's go get drunk and listen to music."

Sometimes she just went by herself.

"Don't I know you from the movies?" a man might ask at one of the breaks, smiling, leering in a twinkly way.

"Maybe," she'd say, and he would look suddenly panicked and back away.

One night a handsome man in a poncho, a bad poncho — though was there such a thing as a good poncho, asked Charlotte — sat down next to her with an extra glass of beer. "You look like you should be in the movies," he said. Sidra nodded wearily. "But I don't go to the movies. So if you *were* in the movies, I would never have gotten to set my eyes on you."

She turned her gaze from his poncho to her sherry, then back. Perhaps he had spent some time in Mexico or Peru. "What do you do?"

"I'm an auto mechanic." He looked at her carefully. "My name's Walter. Walt." He pushed the beer her way. "The drinks here are O.K. as long as you don't ask them to mix anything. Just don't ask them to mix anything!"

She picked it up and took a sip. There was something about him she liked: something earthy beneath the act. In L.A. beneath the act you got nougat or Styrofoam or glass. Her mouth was lined with sherry. Her lips shone with beer. "What's the last movie you saw?" she asked him.

"The last movie I saw. Let's see." He was thinking, and she could tell he wasn't good at it. She watched with curiosity the folded-in mouth, the tilted head: at last, a guy who didn't go to the movies. His eyes rolled back like the casters on a clerk's chair, searching. "You know what I saw?"

"No. What?" She was getting drunk.

"It was this cartoon movie." Animation. She felt relieved. At least it wasn't one of those bad art movies starring what's-her-name. "A man is asleep having a dream about a beautiful little country full of little people." He sat back, looked around the room, as if that were all.

"And?" She was going to have to push and pull with this guy.

"And?" he repeated. He leaned forward again. "And one day the people realize that they are only creatures in this man's dream. Dream people! And if the man wakes up, they will no longer exist!"

Now she hoped he wouldn't go on. She had changed her mind a little.

"So they all get together at a town meeting and devise a plan," he continued. Perhaps the band would be back soon. "They will burst into the man's bedroom and bring him back to a padded, insulated room in the town — the town of his own dream — and there they will keep watch over him. And they do just that. Forever and ever, everyone guarding him carefully, but nervously, making sure he never wakes up." He smiled. "I forgot what the name of it was."

"And he never wakes up."

"Nope." He grinned at her. She liked him. She could tell he could tell. He took a sip of his beer. He looked around the bar, then back at her. "Is this a great country, or what?" he said.

She smiled at him, with longing. "Where do you live," she asked, "and how do I get there?"

"I met a man," she told Tommy on the phone. "His name is Walter."

"A forced relationship. You're in a state of stress — you're in a *syndrome,* I can tell. You're going to force this romance. What does he do?"

"Something with cars." She sighed. "I want to sleep with someone. When I'm sleeping with someone, I'm less obsessed with the mail."

"But perhaps you should just be alone, be by yourself for a while."

"Like you've ever been alone," said Sidra. "I mean, have you *ever* been alone?"

"I've been alone."

"Yeah, and for how long?"

"Hours," said Tommy. He sighed. "At least it felt like hours."

"Right," she said, "so don't go talking to me again about inner resources."

"O.K. So I sold the mineral rights to my body years ago, but, hey, at least *I* got good money for mine."

"I got *some* money," said Sidra. "I got some."

Walter leaned her against his parked car. His mouth was slightly lopsided, paisley-shaped, his lips anneloid and full, and he kissed her hard. There was something numb and on hold in her. There were small dark pits of annihilation she discovered in her soul, in the loosening fist of it, and she threw herself into them, falling. She went home with him, slept with him. She told him who she was. A minor movie star once nominated for a major award. She told him she lived at the Days Inn. He had been there once, to the top, for a drink. But he did not seem to know her name.

"Never thought I'd sleep with a movie star," he did say. "I suppose that's every man's dream." He laughed — lightly, nervously.

"Just don't wake up," she said. Then she pulled the covers to her chin.

"Or change the dream," he added seriously. "I mean, in the movie I saw everything is fine until the sleeping guy begins to dream about something else. I don't think he wills it or anything. It just happens."

"You didn't tell me about that part."

"That's right," he said. "You see, the guy starts dreaming about flamingos and then all the little people turn into flamingos and fly away."

"Hmmmm," said Sidra.

"I *think* it was flamingos. I'm not too expert with birds."

"You're *not?*" She was trying to tease him, but it came out wrong, like a lizard with a little hat on.

"To tell you the truth, I really don't think I ever saw a single movie you were in."

"Good." She was drifting, indifferent, no longer paying attention.

He hitched his arm behind his head, wrist to nape. His chest heaved up and down. "I think I may of *heard* of you, though."

Django Reinhardt was on the radio. Sidra listened, carefully. "Astonishing sounds came from that man's hands," she murmured.

Walter tried to kiss her, tried to get her attention back. He wasn't that interested in music, though at times he tried to be. "Astonishing sounds?" he said. "Like this?" He pressed his palms together, making little popping suction noises.

"Yeah," she murmured. But she was elsewhere, letting a dry wind sweep across the plain of her to sleep. "Like that."

He began to realize, soon, that she did not respect him. A bug could sense it. A doorknob could figure it out. She never quite took him seriously. She would talk about films and film directors, then look at him and say, "Oh, never mind." She was part of some other world. A world she no longer liked.

And now she was somewhere else. Another world she no longer liked.

But she was willing. Willing to give it a whirl. Once in a while, though she tried not to, she asked him about children, about having children, about turning kith to kin. How did he feel about all that? It seemed to her that if she was ever going to have a life of children and lawnmowers and grass clippings, it would be best to have it with someone who was not demeaned or trivialized by discussions of them. Did he like those big, fertilized lawns? How about a nice rock garden? How did he feel deep down about those storm windows with the built-in screens?

"Yeah, I like them all right," he would say, and she would nod slyly and drink a little too much. She would try then not to think too strenuously about her Whole Life. She would try to live life one day at a time, like an alcoholic — drink, don't drink, drink. Perhaps she should take drugs.

"I always thought someday I would have a little girl and name her after my grandmother." Sidra sighed, peered wistfully into her sherry.

"What was your grandmother's name?"

Sidra looked at his paisley mouth. "Grandma. Her name was Grandma." Walter laughed in a honking sort of way. "Oh, thank you," murmured Sidra. "Thank you for laughing."

Walter had a subscription to *Autoweek*. He flipped through it in bed. He also liked to read repair manuals for new cars, particularly the Toyotas. He knew a lot about control panels, light-up panels, side panels.

"You're so obviously wrong for each other," said Charlotte over tapas at a tapas bar.

"Hey, please," said Sidra. "I think I'm a little more subtle than that." The thing with tapas bars was that you just kept stuffing things into your mouth. " 'Obviously wrong' is just the beginning. That's where I *always* begin. At 'obviously wrong.' " In theory, she liked the idea of mismatched couples, the wrangling and retangling — like a comedy by Shakespeare.

"I can't imagine you with someone like him. He's just not special." Charlotte had met him only once. But she had heard of him from a girlfriend of hers. He had slept around, she'd said. "Into the pudding" is how she phrased it, and there were some boring stories. "Just don't let him humiliate you. Don't mistake a lack of sophistication for sweetness," she added.

"I'm supposed to wait around for someone special, while every other girl in this town gets to have a life?"

"I don't know, Sidra."

It was true. Men could be with whomever they pleased. But women had to date better, kinder, richer, and bright, bright, bright, or else people got embarrassed. It suggested sexual things. "I'm a very average person," she said desperately, somehow detecting that Charlotte already knew that, knew the deep, dark, wildly obvious secret of that, and how it made Sidra slightly pathetic, unseemly — *inferior,* when you got right down to it. She felt Charlotte studying her face, headlights caught in the stare of a deer. *Guns don't kill people,* thought Sidra. *Deer kill people.*

"Maybe it's that we all used to envy you so much," Charlotte said, a little bitterly. "You were so talented. You got all the lead parts in the plays. You were everyone's dream of what *they* wanted."

Sidra poked around at the appetizer in front of her, gardening it like a patch of land. She was unequal to anyone's wistfulness. She had made too little of her life. Its loneliness shamed her like a crime. "Envy," said Sidra. "That's a lot like hate, isn't it?" Charlotte didn't say anything. Probably she wanted Sidra to change the subject. Sidra stuffed her mouth full of feta cheese and onions, and looked up. "Well, all I can say is, I'm glad to be back." A piece of feta dropped from her lips.

Charlotte looked down at it and smiled. "I know what you mean," she said. She opened her mouth wide and let all the food inside fall out onto the table.

Charlotte could be funny like that. Sidra had forgotten that about her.

Walter had found some of her old movies in the video-rental place. She had a key to his apartment. One night she came over and discovered him asleep in front of *Recluse with Roommate*. It was about a woman named Rose who rarely went out, because when she did she was afraid of people. They seemed like alien life-forms — soulless, joyless, speaking asyntactically. Rose quickly became loosened from reality. Walter had it freeze-framed at the funny part, where the character phones the psych ward to have them come take her away, but they refuse. Sidra lay down next to him and tried to sleep, too, but began to cry a little. He stirred. "What's wrong?" he asked.

"Nothing. You fell asleep. Watching me."

"I was tired," he said.

"I guess so."

"Let me kiss you. Let me find your panels." His eyes were closed. She could be anybody.

"Did you like the beginning part of the movie?" This need in her was new. Frightening. It made her hair curl. When had she ever needed so much?

"It was O.K.," he said.

"So what is this guy, a race-car driver?" asked Tommy.

"No, he's a mechanic."

"Quit him like a music lesson!"

"Like *a music lesson?* What is this, Similes from the Middle Class? *One Man's Opinion?*" She was irritated.

"Sidra. This is not right! You need to go out with someone really smart for a change."

"I've been out with smart. I've been out with someone who had two Ph.D.'s. We spent all of our time in bed with the light on proofreading his vita." She sighed. "Every little thing he'd ever done, every little, little, little. I mean, have you ever seen a vita?"

Tommy sighed, too. He had heard this story of Sidra's before. "Yes," he said. "I thought Patti LuPone was great."

"Besides," she said. "Who says he's not smart?"

The Japanese cars were the most interesting. Though the Americans were getting sexier, trying to keep up with them. *Those Japs!*

"Let's talk about my world," she said.

"What world?"

"Well, something *I'm* interested in. Something where there's something in it for me."

"O.K." He turned and dimmed the lights, romantically. "Got a stock tip for you," he said.

She was horrified, dispirited, interested.

He told her the name of a company somebody at work invested in. AutVis.

"What is it?"

"I don't know. But some guy at work said buy this week. They're going to make some announcement. If I had money, I'd buy."

She bought, the very next morning. A thousand shares. By the afternoon the stock had plummeted ten percent, by the following morning, fifty. She watched the ticker tape go by on the bottom of the TV news channel. She had become the major stockholder. The major stockholder of a dying company! Soon they were going to be calling her, wearily, to ask what she wanted done with the forklift.

"You're a neater eater than I am," Walter said to her, over dinner at the Palmer House.

She looked at him darkly. "What the hell were you thinking of, recommending that stock?" she asked. "How could you be such an irresponsible idiot? She saw it now, how their life would be together. She would yell, then he would yell. He would have an affair, then she would have an affair. And then they would be gone and gone, and they would live in that gone.

"I got the name wrong," he said. "Sorry."

"You what?"

"It wasn't AutVis. It was AutDrive. I kept thinking it was 'Vis,' for 'vision.'"

"'Vis,' for 'vision,'" she repeated.

"I'm not that good with names," confessed Walter. "I do better with concepts."

" 'Concepts,' " she repeated as well.

The concept of Angry Dessert.

The concept of Angry Bills.

The concept of flightless, dodo love.

Outside, there was a watery gust from the direction of the lake. "Chicago," said Walter. "The windy city. Is this the windy city, or what?" He looked at her hopefully, which made her despise him more.

She shook her head. "I don't even know why we're together," she said. "I mean, why are we even together?"

He looked at her hard. "I can't answer that for you!" he yelled. He took two steps back, away from her. "You've got to answer that for yourself!" And he hailed his own cab, got in, and rode away.

She walked back to the Days Inn alone. She played scales soundlessly, on the tops of the piano keys, her thin, jointed fingers lifting and falling quietly like the tines of a music box or the legs of a spider. When she tired, she turned on the television and discovered an old movie she'd been in, a love-murder mystery called *Finishing Touches*. It was the kind of performance she had become, briefly, known for: a patched-together intimacy with the audience, half cartoon, half revelation; a cross between shyness and derision, rudeness and truth. She had not given a damn back then, sort of like now, only then it had been a style, a way of being, not a diagnosis, a demise.

Perhaps she should have a baby.

In the morning, she went to visit her parents in Elmhurst. For winter, they had plastic-wrapped their home — the windows, the doors — so that it looked like a piece of avant-garde art. "Saves on heating bills," they said.

They had taken to discussing her in front of her. "It was a movie, Bob. It was a movie about adventure. Nudity can be art."

"That's not how I saw it! That's not how I saw it at all!" said her father, red-faced, leaving the room. Nap time.

"How are you doing?" asked her mother, with what seemed like concern but was really an opening for something else. She had made tea.

"I'm O.K., really," said Sidra. Everything she said about her-self now sounded like a lie. If she was bad it sounded like a lie, if she was fine — also a lie.

Her mother fiddled with a spoon. "I was envious of you," her mother sighed. "I was always so envious of you! My own daugh-ter!" She was shrieking it, saying it softly at first and then shriek-ing. It was exactly like Sidra's childhood: just when she thought life had become simple again, her mother gave her a new portion of the world to organize.

"I have to go," said Sidra. She had only just gotten there, but she wanted to go. She didn't want to visit her parents anymore. She didn't want to look at their lives.

She went back to the Days Inn and phoned Tommy. He and she understood each other. "I *get* you," he used to say. His child-hood had been full of sisters. He'd spent large portions of it drawing pictures of women in bathing suits — Miss Kenya from Nairobi! — and then asking one of the sisters to pick the most beautiful. If he disagreed, he asked another sister.

The connection was bad, and suddenly she felt too tired. "Dar-ling, are you O.K.?" he said faintly.

"I'm O.K."

"I think I'm hard of hearing," he said.

"I think I'm hard of talking," she said. "I'll phone you tomor-row."

She phoned Walter instead. "I need to see you," she said.

"Oh really?" he said skeptically, and then added, with a sweet-ness he seemed to have grabbed expertly from the air as if it were a fly, "Is this a great country, or what?"

She felt such gratitude to be with him again. "Let's never be apart," she whispered, rubbing his stomach. He had the physical incli-nations of a dog: he liked stomach, ears, excited greetings.

"Fine by me," he said.

"Tomorrow let's go out to dinner somewhere really expensive. My treat."

"Uh," said Walter, "tomorrow's no good."

"Oh."

"How about Sunday?"

"What's wrong with tomorrow?"

"I've got . . . Well, I've gotta work and I'll be tired, first of all."

"What's second of all?"

"I'm getting together with this woman I know."

"Oh?"

"It's no big deal. It's nothing. It's not a date or anything."

"Who is she?"

"Someone whose car I fixed. Loose mountings in the exhaust system. She wants to get together and talk about it some more. You know, women are afraid of getting taken advantage of."

"Really."

"Yeah, well, so Sunday would be better."

"Is she attractive?"

Walter scrinched up his face and made a sound of unenthusiasm. "Enh," he said, and placed his hand laterally in the air, rotating it up and down a little.

Before he left in the morning, she said, "Just don't sleep with her."

"*Sidra,*" he said, scolding her for lack of trust or for attempted supervision, she wasn't sure which.

That night he didn't come home. She phoned and phoned and then drank a six-pack and fell asleep. In the morning she phoned again. Finally, at eleven o'clock he answered.

She hung up.

At eleven-thirty her phone rang. "Hi," he said, cheerfully. He was in a good mood.

"So, where were you all night?" asked Sidra. This was what she had become. She felt shorter and squatter, and badly coiffed.

There was some silence. "What do you mean?" he said cautiously.

"You know what I mean."

More silence. "Look, I didn't call this morning to get into a heavy conversation."

"Well, then," said Sidra, "you certainly called the wrong number." She slammed the phone down.

She spent the day furious and trembling and sad. She felt like a cross between Anna Karenina and Amy Liverhaus, who used to shout from the seventh-grade cloakroom, "I just don't feel *appreciated.*" She walked over to Marshall Field's to buy new makeup.

"You're much more of a cream beige than an ivory," said the young woman working the cosmetics counter.

But Sidra clutched at the ivory. "People are always telling me that," she said, "and it makes me very cross."

She phoned him later that night and he was there. "We need to talk," she said.

"I want my key back," he said.

"Look. Can you just come over here so that we can talk?"

He arrived bearing flowers — white roses and irises. They seemed wilted and ironic; she leaned them against the wall in an empty glass, no water.

"All right, I admit," he said. "I went out on a date. But I'm not saying I slept with her."

She could feel, for the first time, the promiscuity in him. It was a heat, a creature, a tenant twin. "I already know you slept with her."

"How can you know that?"

"Get a life! What am I, an idiot?" She glared at him and tried not to cry. She hadn't loved him enough, and he had sensed it. She hadn't really loved him at all, not really.

But she had liked him a lot!

So it still seemed unfair. A bone in her opened up, gleaming and pale, and she held it to the light and spoke from it. "I want to know one thing." She paused, not really for effect, but it had one. "Did you have oral sex?"

He looked stunned. "What kind of question is that? I don't have to answer a question like that."

"*You don't have to answer a question like that.* You don't have any rights here!" she began to yell. She was dehydrated. "You're the one who did this. Now I want the truth. I just want to know. Yes or no!"

He threw his gloves across the room.

"Yes or no," she said.

He flung himself onto the couch, pounded the cushion with his fist, placed an arm up over his eyes.

"Yes or no," she repeated.

He breathed deeply into his shirtsleeve.

"Yes or no."

"Yes," he said.

She sat down on the piano bench. Something dark and coagu-
lated moved through her, up from the feet. Something light and
breathing escaped through her head: the house of her, plastic-
wrapped, burned down to tar. She heard him give a moan, and
some fleeing hope in her, surrounded but alive on the roof, said
perhaps he would beg for forgiveness. Promise to be a new man.
She might find him attractive as a new, begging man. Though at
some point he would have to stop begging. He would just have
to be normal. And then she would dislike him again.

He stayed on the sofa, did not move to comfort or be comforted, and the darkness in her cleaned her out, hollowed her
like an acid or a wind.

"I don't know what to do," she said, something palsied in her
voice. She felt cheated of all the simple things — the radical calm
of obscurity, of routine, of blah domestic bliss. "I don't want to
go back to L.A." She began to stroke the tops of the piano keys,
pushing against one and finding it broken — thudding and
pitchless, shiny and mocking like an opened bone. She hated, hated
her life. Perhaps she had always hated it.

He sat up on the sofa, looked distraught and false — his face
badly arranged. He should practice in a mirror, she thought. He
did not know how to break up with a movie actress. It was boys'
rules: Don't break up with a movie actress. Not in Chicago. If *she*
left *him*, he would be able to explain it better, to himself, in the
future, to anyone who asked. His voice shifted into something
meant to sound imploring. "I know," was what he said, in a tone
approximating faith, hope, some charity or other. "I know you
might not *want* to."

"For your own good," he was saying. *"Might be willing . . ."* he was
saying. But she was already turning into something else, a bird —
a flamingo, a hawk, a flamingo hawk — and was flying up and
away, but then back again, circling, meanly, with a squint.

He began, suddenly, to cry — loudly, at first, with lots of "oh's,"
then tiredly, as if from a deep sleep, his face buried in the poncho he'd thrown over the couch arm, his body sinking into the
plush of the cushions — a man held hostage by the anxious cast
of his dream.

"What can I do?" he asked. But his dream had now changed,
and she was gone, gone out the window, gone, gone.

ALICE MUNRO

Friend of My Youth

FROM THE NEW YORKER

I USED TO DREAM about my mother, and though the details in the dream varied, the surprise in it was always the same. The dream stopped, I suppose because it was too transparent in its hopefulness, too easy in its forgiveness.

In the dream I would be the age I really was, living the life I was really living, and I would discover that my mother was still alive. (The fact is, she died when I was in my early twenties and she in her early fifties.) Sometimes I would find myself in our old kitchen, where my mother would be rolling out pie crust on the table, or washing the dishes in the battered cream-colored dishpan with the red rim. But other times I would run into her on the street, in places where I would never have expected to see her. She might be walking through a handsome hotel lobby, or lining up in an airport. She would be looking quite well — not exactly youthful, not entirely untouched by the paralyzing disease that held her in its grip for a decade or more before her death, but so much better than I remembered that I would be astonished. Oh, I just have this little tremor in my arm, she would say, and a little stiffness up this side of my face. It is a nuisance but I get around.

I recovered, then, what in waking life I had lost — my mother's liveliness of face and voice before her throat muscles stiffened and a woeful, impersonal mask fastened itself over her features. How could I have forgotten this, I would think in the dream — the casual humor she had, not ironic but merry, the lightness and impatience and confidence. I would say that I was sorry I hadn't been to see her in such a long time — meaning not that I felt guilty but that I was sorry I had kept a bugbear in my mind, instead of this reality — and the strangest, kindest thing of all to me was her matter-of-fact reply.

Oh, well, she said, better late than never. I was sure I'd see you someday.

When my mother was a young woman with a soft, mischievous face and shiny, opaque silk stockings on her plump legs (I have seen a photograph of her, with her pupils), she went to teach at a one-room school, called Grieves' School, in the Ottawa Valley. The school was on a corner of the farm that belonged to the Grieves family — a very good farm for that country. Well-drained fields with none of the Precambrian rock shouldering through the soil, a little willow-edged river running alongside, a sugar-bush, log barns, and a large, unornamented house whose wooden walls had never been painted but were left to weather. And when wood weathers in the Ottawa Valley, my mother said, I do not know why this is, but it never turns gray — it turns black. There must be something in the air, she said. She often spoke of the Ottawa Valley, which was her home — she had grown up about twenty miles away from Grieves' School — in a dogmatic, mystified way, emphasizing things about it that distinguished it from any other place on earth. Houses turn black, maple syrup has a taste no maple syrup produced elsewhere can equal, bears amble within sight of farmhouses. Of course, I was disappointed when I finally got to see this place. It was not a valley at all, if by that you mean a cleft between hills; it was a mixture of flat fields and low rocks and heavy brush and little lakes — a scrambled, disarranged sort of country with no easy harmony about it, not yielding readily to any description.

The log barns and unpainted house, common enough on poor farms, were not in the Grieveses' case a sign of poverty but of policy. They had the money but they did not spend it. That was what people told my mother. The Grieveses worked hard and they were far from ignorant, but they were very backward. They didn't have a car or electricity or a telephone or a tractor. Some people thought this was because they were Cameronians — they were the only people in the school district who were of that religion — but in fact their church, which they themselves always called the Reformed Presbyterian, did not forbid engines or electricity or any inventions of that sort, just card playing, dancing, movies, and, on Sundays, any other activity but the most unavoidable.

My mother could not say who the Cameronians were or why they were called that. Some freak religion from Scotland, she said, from the perch of her obedient and lighthearted Anglicanism. The teacher always boarded with the Grieveses, and my mother was a little daunted at the thought of going to live in that black house with its paralytic Sundays and coal-oil lamps and primitive notions. But she was engaged by that time, she wanted to work on her trousseau instead of running around the country having a good time, and she figured she could get home one Sunday out of three. (On Sundays at the Grieveses' house, you could light a fire for heat but not for cooking, you could not even boil the kettle to make tea, and you were not supposed to write a letter or swat a fly. But it turned out that my mother was exempt from these rules. "No, no," said Flora Grieves, laughing at her. "That doesn't mean you. You must just go on as you're used to doing." And after a while my mother had made friends with Flora to such an extent that she wasn't even going home on the Sundays when she'd planned to.)

Flora and Ellie were the two sisters left of the Grieves family. Ellie was married, to a man called Robert Deal, who lived there and worked the farm but had not changed its name to Deal's in anyone's mind. By the way people spoke, my mother expected the Grieves sisters, and Robert Deal, to be middle-aged at least, but Ellie, the younger sister, was only about thirty, and Flora seven or eight years older. Robert Deal might be in between.

The house was divided in an unexpected way. The married couple didn't live with Flora. At the time of their marriage, she had given them the parlor and the dining room, the front bedrooms and staircase, the winter kitchen. There was no need to decide about the bathroom, because there wasn't one. Flora had the summer kitchen, with its open rafters and uncovered brick walls, the old pantry made into a narrow dining room and sitting room, and the two back bedrooms, one of which was my mother's. The teacher was housed with Flora, in the poorer part of the house. But my mother didn't mind. She immediately preferred

Flora, and Flora's cheerfulness, to the silence and sickroom atmosphere of the front rooms. (In Flora's domain it was not even
true that all amusements were forbidden. She had a crokinole
board — she taught my mother how to play.)

The division had been made, of course, in the expectation that
Robert and Ellie would have a family, and that they would need
the room. This hadn't happened. They had been married for more
than a dozen years and there had not been a live child. Time and
again Ellie had been pregnant, but two babies had been stillborn
and the rest she had miscarried. During my mother's first year
there, Ellie seemed to be staying in bed more and more of the
time, and my mother thought that she must be pregnant again,
but there was no mention of it. Such people would not mention
it. You could not tell from the look of Ellie, when she got up and
walked around, because she showed a stretched and ruined though
slack-chested shape. She carried a sickbed odor, and she fretted
in a childish way about everything. Flora took care of her and did
all the work. She washed the clothes and tidied up the rooms and
cooked the meals served in both sides of the house, and helped
Robert with the milking and separating. She was up before daylight and never seemed to tire. The first spring my mother was
there, a great housecleaning was embarked upon, during which
Flora climbed the ladders herself and carried down the storm
windows, washed and stacked them away, carried all the furniture out of one room after another so that she could scrub the
woodwork and varnish the floors. She washed every dish and glass
that was sitting in the cupboards, supposedly clean already. She
scalded every pot and spoon. Such need and energy possessed
her that she could hardly sleep — my mother would wake up to
the sound of stovepipes being taken down, or the broom, draped
in a dish towel, whacking at the smoky cobwebs. Through the
washed uncurtained windows came a torrent of unmerciful light.
The cleanliness was devastating. My mother slept now on sheets
that had been bleached and starched and that gave her a rash.
Sick Ellie complained daily of the smell of varnish and cleansing
powders. Flora's hands were raw. But her disposition remained
topnotch. Her kerchief and apron and baggy overalls of Robert's
that she donned for the climbing jobs gave her the air of a co-
median — sportive, unpredictable.

My mother called her a whirling dervish.

"You're a regular whirling dervish, Flora," she said, and Flora halted. She wanted to know what was meant. My mother went ahead and explained, though she was a little afraid lest piety should be offended. (Not piety exactly — you could not call it that. Religious strictness.) Of course it wasn't. There was not a trace of nastiness or smug vigilance in Flora's observance of her religion. She had no fear of heathens — she had always lived in the midst of them. She liked the idea of being a dervish, and went to tell her sister.

"Do you know what the teacher says I am?"

Flora and Ellie were both dark-haired, dark-eyed women, tall and narrow-shouldered and long-legged. Ellie was a wreck, of course, but Flora was still superbly straight and graceful. She could look like a queen, my mother said — even riding into town in that cart they had. For church they used a buggy or a cutter, but when they went to town they often had to transport sacks of wool — they kept a few sheep — or produce, to sell, and they had to bring provisions home. The trip of a few miles was not made often. Robert rode in front, to drive the horse — Flora could drive a horse perfectly well, but it must always be the man who drove. Flora would be standing behind, holding on to the sacks. She rode to town and back standing up, keeping an easy balance, wearing her black hat. Almost ridiculous but not quite. A Gypsy queen, my mother thought she looked like, with her black hair and her skin that always looked slightly tanned, and her lithe and bold serenity. Of course, she lacked the gold bangles and the bright clothes. My mother envied her her slenderness, and her cheekbones.

Returning in the fall for her second year, my mother learned what was the matter with Ellie.

"My sister has a growth," Flora said. Nobody then spoke of cancer.

My mother had heard that before. People suspected it. My mother knew many people in the district by that time. She had made particular friends with a young woman who worked in the post office; she was going to be one of my mother's bridesmaids. The story of Flora and Ellie and Robert — or all that people knew of it — had been told in various versions. My mother did not feel that she was listening to gossip, because she was always on the alert for any disparaging remarks about Flora — she would not put up with that. But indeed nobody offered any. Everybody said that Flora had behaved like a saint. Even when she went to extremes, as in dividing up the house — that was like a saint.

Robert had come to work at Grieves' some months before the girls' father died. They knew him already, from church. (Oh, that church, my mother said, having attended it once, out of curiosity — that drear building miles on the other side of town, no organ or piano and plain glass in the windows and a doddery old minister with his hours-long sermon, a man hitting a tuning fork for the singing.) Robert had come out from Scotland and was on his way west. He had stopped with relatives or people he knew, members of the scanty congregation. To earn some money, probably, he came to Grieves'. Soon he and Flora were engaged. They could not go to dances or to card parties like other couples, but they went for long walks. The chaperon — unofficially — was Ellie. Ellie was then a wild tease, a long-haired, impudent, childish girl full of lolloping energy. She would run up hills and smite the mullein stalks with a stick, shouting and prancing and pretending to be a warrior on horseback. That, or the horse itself. This when she was fifteen, sixteen years old. Nobody but Flora could control her, and generally Flora just laughed at her, being too used to her to wonder if she was quite right in the head. They were wonderfully fond of each other. Ellie, with her long skinny body, her long pale face, was like a copy of Flora — the kind of copy you often see in families, in which, because of some carelessness or exaggeration of features or coloring, the handsomeness of one person passes into the plainness, or almost plainness, of another. But Ellie had no jealousy about this. She loved to comb out Flora's hair and pin it up. They had great times, washing each other's hair. Ellie would press her face into Flora's throat, like a colt nuzzling its mother. So when Robert laid claim to Flora, or Flora to him — nobody knew how it was — Ellie had to be included. She didn't show any spite toward Robert, but she pursued and waylaid them on their walks; she sprung on them out of the bushes or sneaked up behind them so softly that she could blow on their necks. People saw her do it. And they heard of her jokes. She had always been terrible for jokes, and some-

times it had gotten her into trouble with her father, but Flora
had protected her. Now she put thistles into Robert's bed. She
set his place at the table with the knife and fork the wrong
way around. She switched the milk pails to give him the old
one with the hole in it. For Flora's sake, maybe, Robert humored
her.

The father had made Flora and Robert set the wedding day a
year ahead, and after he died they did not move it any closer.
Robert went on living in the house. Nobody knew how to speak
to Flora about this being scandalous, or looking scandalous. Flora
would just ask why. Instead of putting the wedding ahead, she
put it back — from next spring to early fall — so that there should
be a full year between it and her father's death. A year from funeral to wedding — that seemed proper to her. She trusted fully
in Robert's patience and in her own purity.

So she might. But in the winter a commotion started. There
was Ellie, vomiting, weeping, running off and hiding in the hay-
mow, howling when they found her and pulled her out, jumping
to the barn floor, running around in circles, rolling in the snow.
Ellie was deranged. Flora had to call the doctor. She told him
that her sister's periods had stopped — could the backup of blood
be driving her wild? Robert had had to catch her and tie her up,
and together he and Flora had put her to bed. She would not
take food, just whipped her head from side to side, howling. It
looked as if she would die speechless. But somehow the truth came
out. Not from the doctor, who could not get close enough to ex-
amine her, with all her thrashing about. Probably, Robert confessed. Flora finally got wind of the truth, through all her high-
mindedness. Now there had to be a wedding, though not the one
that had been planned.

No cake, no new clothes, no wedding trip, no congratulations.
Just a shameful hurry-up visit to the manse. Some people, seeing
the names in the paper, thought the editor must have got the
sisters mixed up. They thought it must be Flora. A hurry-up
wedding for Flora! But no. It was Flora who pressed Robert's
suit — it must have been — and got Ellie out of bed and washed
her and made her presentable. It would have been Flora who
picked one geranium from the window plant and pinned it to
her sister's dress. And Ellie hadn't torn it out. Ellie was meek now,

no longer flailing or crying. She let Flora fix her up, she let herself be married, she was never wild from that day on.

Flora had the house divided. She herself helped Robert build the necessary partitions. The baby was carried full term — nobody even pretended that it was early — but it was born dead after a long, tearing labor. Perhaps Ellie had damaged it when she jumped from the barn beam and rolled in the snow and beat on herself. Even if she hadn't done that, people would have expected something to go wrong, with that child or maybe one that came later. God dealt out punishment for hurry-up marriages — not just Presbyterians but almost everybody else believed that. God rewarded lust with dead babies, idiots, harelips and withered limbs and clubfeet.

In this case the punishment continued. Ellie had one miscarriage after another, then another stillbirth and more miscarriages. She was constantly pregnant, and the pregnancies were full of vomiting fits that lasted for days, headaches, cramps, dizzy spells. The miscarriages were as agonizing as full-term births. Ellie could not do her own work. She walked around holding on to chairs. Her numb silence passed off, and she became a complainer. If anybody came to visit, she would talk about the peculiarities of her headaches or describe her latest fainting fit, or even — in front of men, in front of unmarried girls or children — go into bloody detail about what Flora called her "disappointments." When people changed the subject or dragged the children away, she turned sullen. She demanded new medicine, reviled the doctor, nagged Flora. She accused Flora of washing the dishes with a great clang and clatter, out of spite, of pulling her — Ellie's — hair when she combed it out, of stingily substituting water-and-molasses for her real medicine. No matter what she said, Flora soothed her. Everybody who came into the house had some story of that kind to tell. Flora said, "Where's my little girl, then? Where's my Ellie? This isn't my Ellie, this is some crosspatch got in here in place of her!"

In the winter evenings after she came in from helping Robert with the barn chores, Flora would wash and change her clothes and go next door to read Ellie to sleep. My mother might invite herself along, taking whatever sewing she was doing, on some item of her trousseau. Ellie's bed was set up in the big dining room, where there was a gas lamp over the table. My mother sat on one side of the table, sewing, and Flora sat on the other side, reading aloud. Sometimes Ellie said, "I can't hear you." Or if Flora paused for a little rest Ellie said, "I'm not asleep yet."

What did Flora read? Stories about Scottish life — not classics. Stories about urchins and comic grandmothers. The only title my mother could remember was "Wee MacGregor." She could not follow the stories very well, or laugh when Flora laughed and Ellie gave a whimper, because so much was in Scots dialect or read with that thick accent. She was surprised that Flora could do it — it wasn't the way Flora ordinarily talked, at all.

(But wouldn't it be the way Robert talked? Perhaps that is why my mother never reported anything that Robert said, never had him contributing to the scene. He must have been there, he must have been sitting there in the room. They would only heat the main room of the house. I see him black-haired, heavy-shouldered, with the strength of a plow horse, and the same kind of somber, shackled beauty.)

Then Flora would say, "That's all of that for tonight." She would pick up another book, an old book written by some preacher of their faith. There was in it such stuff as my mother had never heard. What stuff? She couldn't say. All the stuff that was in their monstrous old religion. That put Ellie to sleep, or made her pretend she was asleep, after a couple of pages.

All that configuration of the elect and the damned, my mother must have meant — all the arguments about the illusion and necessity of free will. Doom and slippery redemption. The torturing, defeating, but for some minds irresistible pileup of interlocking and contradictory notions. My mother could resist it. Her faith was easy, her spirits at that time robust. Ideas were not what she was curious about, ever.

But what sort of thing was that, she asked (silently), to read to a dying woman? This was the nearest she got to criticizing Flora.

The answer — that it was the only thing, if you believed it — never seemed to have occurred to her.

By spring a nurse had arrived. That was the way things were done then. People died at home, and a nurse came in to manage it.

The nurse's name was Audrey Atkinson. She was a stout woman

with corsets as stiff as barrel hoops, marcelled hair the color of brass candlesticks, a mouth shaped by lipstick beyond its own stingy outlines. She drove a car into the yard — her own car, a dark-green coupé, shiny and smart. News of Audrey Atkinson and her car spread quickly. Questions were asked. Where did she get the money? Had some rich fool altered his will on her behalf? Had she exercised influence? Or simply helped herself to a stash of bills under the mattress? How was she to be trusted?

Hers was the first car ever to sit in the Grieveses' yard overnight.

Audrey Atkinson said that she had never been called out to tend a case in so primitive a house. It was beyond her, she said, how people could live in such a way.

"It's not that they're poor, even," she said to my mother. "It isn't, is it? That I could understand. Or it's not even their religion. So what is it? They do not care!"

She tried at first to cozy up to my mother, as if they would be natural allies in this benighted place. She spoke as if they were around the same age — both stylish, intelligent women who liked a good time and had modern ideas. She offered to teach my mother to drive the car. She offered her cigarettes. My mother was more tempted by the idea of learning to drive than she was by the cigarettes. But she said no, she would wait for her husband to teach her. Audrey Atkinson raised her pinkish-orange eyebrows at my mother behind Flora's back, and my mother was furious. She disliked the nurse far more than Flora did.

"I knew what she was like and Flora didn't," my mother said. She meant that she caught a whiff of a cheap life, maybe even of drinking establishments and unsavory men, of hard bargains, which Flora was too unworldly to notice.

Flora started into the great housecleaning again. She had the curtains spread out on stretchers, she beat the rugs on the line, she leapt up on the stepladder to attack the dust on the molding. But she was impeded all the time by Nurse Atkinson's complaining.

"I wondered if we could have a little less of the running and clattering," said Nurse Atkinson with offensive politeness. "I only ask for my patient's sake." She always spoke of Ellie as "my patient" and pretended that she was the only one to protect her and compel respect. But she was not so respectful of Ellie herself. "Allee-oop," she would say, dragging the poor creature up on her pillows. And she told Ellie she was not going to stand for fretting and whimpering. "You don't do yourself any good that way," she said. "And you certainly don't make me come any quicker. What you just as well might do is learn to control yourself." She exclaimed at Ellie's bedsores in a scolding way, as if they were a further disgrace of the house. She demanded lotions, ointments, expensive soap — most of them, no doubt, to protect her own skin, which she claimed suffered from the hard water. (How could it be hard? my mother asked her, sticking up for the household when nobody else would. How could it be hard when it came straight from the rain barrel?)

Nurse Atkinson wanted cream, too — she said that they should hold some back, not sell it all to the creamery. She wanted to make nourishing soups and puddings for her patient. She did make puddings, and jellies, from packaged mixes such as had never before entered this house. My mother was convinced that she ate them all herself.

Flora still read to Ellie, but now it was only short bits from the Bible. When she finished and stood up, Ellie tried to cling to her. Ellie wept; sometimes she made ridiculous complaints. She said there was a horned cow outside, trying to get into the room and kill her.

"They often get some kind of idea like that," Nurse Atkinson said. "You mustn't give in to her or she won't let you go day or night. That's what they're like, they only think about themselves. Now, when I'm here alone with her, she behaves herself quite nice. I don't have any trouble at all. But after you been in here I have trouble all over again, because she sees you and she gets upset. You don't want to make my job harder for me, do you? I mean, you brought me here to take charge, didn't you?"

"Ellie, now, Ellie dear, I must go," said Flora, and to the nurse she said, "I understand. I do understand that you have to be in charge and I admire you, I admire you for your work. In your work you have to have so much patience and kindness."

My mother wondered at this — was Flora really so blinded, or did she hope by this undeserved praise to exhort Nurse Atkinson to the patience and kindness that she didn't have? Nurse Atkinson was too thick-skinned and self-approving for any trick like that to work.

"It is a hard job, all right, and not many can do it," she said. "It's not like those nurses in the hospital, where they got everything laid out for them." She had no time for more conversation — she was trying to bring in "Make Believe Ballroom" on her battery radio.

My mother was busy with the final exams and the June exercises at the school. She was getting ready for her wedding, in July. Friends came in cars and whisked her off to the dressmaker's, to parties, to choose the invitations and order the cake. The lilacs came out, the evenings lengthened, the birds were back and nesting, my mother bloomed in everybody's attention, about to set out on the deliciously solemn adventure of marriage. Her dress was to be appliquéd with silk roses, her veil held by a cap of seed pearls. She belonged to the first generation of young women who saved their money and paid for their own weddings — far fancier than their parents could have afforded.

On her last evening, the friend from the post office came to drive her away, with her clothes and her books and the things she had made for her trousseau and the gifts her pupils and others had given her. There was great fuss and laughter about getting everything loaded into the car. Flora came out and helped. This getting married is even more of a nuisance than I thought, said Flora, laughing. She gave my mother a dresser scarf, which she had crocheted, in secret. Nurse Atkinson could not be shut out of an important occasion — she presented a spray bottle of cologne. Flora stood on the slope at the side of the house to wave goodbye. She had been invited to the wedding, but of course she had said she could not come, she could not "go out" at such a time. The last my mother ever saw of her was this solitary, energetically waving figure in her housecleaning apron and bandanna, on the green slope by the black-walled house, in the evening light.

"Well, maybe now she'll get what she should've got the first time round," the friend from the post office said. "Maybe now they'll be able to get married. Is she too old to start a family? How old is she, anyway?"

My mother thought that this was a crude way of talking about

Flora and replied that she didn't know. But she had to admit to herself that she had been thinking the very same thing.

When she was married and settled in her own home, three hundred miles away, my mother got a letter from Flora. Ellie was dead. She had died firm in her faith, Flora said, and grateful for her release. Nurse Atkinson was staying on for a little while, until it was time for her to go off to her next case. This was late in the summer.

News of what happened next did not come from Flora. When she wrote at Christmas she seemed to take for granted that information would have gone ahead of her.

"You have in all probability heard," wrote Flora, "that Robert and Nurse Atkinson have been married. They are living on here, in Robert's part of the house. They are fixing it up to suit themselves. It is very impolite of me to call her Nurse Atkinson, as I see I have done. I ought to have called her Audrey."

Of course, the post-office friend had written, and so had others. It was a great shock and scandal and a matter that excited the district — the wedding as secret and surprising as Robert's first one had been (though surely not for the same reason), Nurse Atkinson permanently installed in the community, Flora losing out for the second time. Nobody had been aware of any courtship, and they asked how the woman could have enticed him. Did she promise children, lying about her age?

The surprises were not to stop with the wedding. The bride got down to business immediately with the "fixing up" that Flora mentioned. In came the electricity and then the telephone. Now Nurse Atkinson — she would always be called Nurse Atkinson — was heard on the party line lambasting painters and paperhangers and delivery services. She was having everything done over. She was buying an electric stove and putting in a bathroom, and who knew where the money was coming from? Was it all hers, got in her deathbed dealings, in shady bequests? Was it Robert's? Was he claiming his share — Ellie's share, left to him and Nurse Atkinson to enjoy themselves with, the shameless pair?

All these improvements took place on one side of the house only. Flora's side remained just as it was. No electric lights there, no fresh wallpaper or new venetian blinds. When the house was

painted on the outside — cream with dark green trim — Flora's
side was left bare. This strange open statement was greeted at
first with pity and disapproval — poor Flora! — then with less
sympathy, as a sign of Flora's stubbornness and eccentricity —
she could buy her own paint and make it look decent — and finally as a joke. People drove out of their way to see it.

There was always a dance given in the schoolhouse for a newly
married couple. A cash collection — called "a purse of money" —
was presented to them. Nurse Atkinson sent out word that she
would not mind seeing this custom followed, even though it happened that the family she had married into was opposed to dancing. Some people thought it would be a disgrace to gratify her, a
slap in the face to Flora. Others were too curious to hold back.
They wanted to see how the newlyweds would behave. Would
Robert dance? What sort of outfit would the bride show up in?
They delayed awhile, but finally the dance was held, and my
mother got her report.

The bride wore the dress she had worn at her wedding, or so
she said. But who would wear such a dress for a wedding at the
manse? More than likely it was bought specially for her appearance at the dance. Pure white satin with a sweetheart neckline,
idiotically youthful. The groom was got up in a new dark blue
suit, and she had stuck a flower in his buttonhole. They were a
sight. Her hair was freshly done to blind the eye with brassy re-
flections, and her face looked as if it would come off on a man's
jacket, should she lay it against his shoulder in the dancing. Of
course she did dance. She danced with every man except the
groom, who sat scrunched into one of the school desks along the
wall. She danced with every man present — they all claimed they
had to do it, it was the custom — and then she dragged Robert
out to receive the money and to thank everybody for their best
wishes. To the ladies in the cloakroom she even hinted that she
was feeling unwell, for the usual newlywed reason. Nobody believed her, and indeed nothing ever came of this hope, if she really
had it. Some of the women thought that she was lying to them
out of malice, insulting them, making them out to be so credu-
lous. But nobody challenged her, nobody was rude to her —
maybe because it was plain that she could summon a rudeness of
her own to knock anybody flat.

Flora was not present at the dance.

"My sister-in-law is not a dancer," said Nurse Atkinson. "She is stuck in the olden times." She invited them to laugh at Flora, whom she always called her sister-in-law, though she had no right to do so.

My mother wrote a letter to Flora, after hearing about all these things. Being removed from the scene, and perhaps in a flurry of importance owing to her own newly married state, she may have lost sight of the kind of person she was writing to. She offered sympathy and showed outrage, and said blunt disparaging things about the woman who had — as my mother saw it — dealt Flora such a blow. Back came a letter from Flora saying that she did not know where my mother had been getting her information, but that it seemed she had misunderstood, or listened to malicious people, or jumped to unjustified conclusions. What happened in Flora's family was nobody else's business, and certainly nobody needed to feel sorry for her or angry on her behalf. Flora said that she was happy and satisfied in her life, as she always had been, and she did not interfere with what others did or wanted, because such things did not concern her. She wished my mother all happiness in her marriage and hoped that she would soon be too busy with her own responsibilities to worry about the lives of people that she used to know.

This well-written letter cut my mother, as she said, to the quick. She and Flora stopped corresponding. My mother did become busy with her own life and finally a prisoner in it.

But she thought about Flora. In later years, when she sometimes talked about the things she might have been, or done, she would say, "If I could have been a writer — I do think I could have been; I could have been a writer — then I would have written the story of Flora's life. And do you know what I would have called it? 'The Maiden Lady.'"

The Maiden Lady. She said these words in a solemn and sentimental tone of voice which I had no use for. I knew, or thought I knew, exactly the value she found in them. The stateliness and mystery. The hint of derision turning to reverence. I was fifteen or sixteen years old by that time, and I believed that I could see into my mother's mind. I could see what she would do with Flora, what she had already done. She would make her into a noble figure, one who accepts defection, treachery, who forgives and stands aside, not once but twice. Never a moment of complaint. Flora goes about her cheerful labors, she cleans the house and shovels out the cow byre, she removes some bloody mess from her sister's bed, and when at last the future seems to open up for her — Ellie will die and Robert will beg forgiveness and Flora will silence him with the proud gift of herself — it is time for Audrey Atkinson to drive into the yard and shut Flora out again, more inexplicably and thoroughly the second time than the first. She must endure the painting of the house, the electric lights, all the prosperous activity next door. "Make Believe Ballroom," "Amos 'n' Andy." No more Scottish or ancient sermons. She must see them drive off to the dance — her old lover and that cold-hearted, stupid, by no means beautiful woman in the white satin wedding dress. She is mocked. (And of course she has made over the farm to Ellie and Robert, of course he has inherited it, and now everything belongs to Audrey Atkinson.) The wicked flourish. But it is all right. It is all right — the elect are veiled in patience and humility and lighted by a certainty that events cannot disturb.

That was what I believed my mother would make of things. In her own plight her notions had turned mystical, and there was sometimes a hush, a solemn thrill in her voice that grated on me, alerted me to what seemed a personal danger. I felt a great fog of platitudes and pieties lurking, and incontestable crippled-mother power, which could capture and choke me. There would be no end to it. I had to keep myself sharp-tongued and cynical, arguing and deflating. Eventually I gave up even that recognition and opposed her in silence.

This is a fancy way of saying that I was no comfort and poor company to her, when she had almost nowhere else to turn.

I had my own ideas about Flora's story. I didn't think that I could have written a novel but that I would write one. I would take a different tack. I saw through my mother's story and put in what she left out. My Flora would be as wrong as hers was right. Rejoicing in the bad turns done to her and in her own forgiveness, spying on the shambles of her sister's life. A Presbyterian witch, reading out of her poisonous book. It takes a rival ruthlessness, the comparatively innocent brutality of the thick-skinned nurse, to drive her back, to flourish in her shade. But she *is* driven

back, the power of sex and ordinary greed drive her back and
shut her up in her own part of the house, with the coal-oil lamps.
She shrinks, she caves in, her bones harden and her joints thicken
and — Oh, this is it, this is it, I see the bare beauty of the ending
I will contrive! — she becomes crippled herself, with arthritis,
hardly able to move. Now Audrey Atkinson comes into her full
power — she demands the whole house. She wants those partitions knocked out which Robert put up with Flora's help when
he married Ellie. She will provide Flora with a room, she will take
care of her. (Audrey Atkinson does not wish to be seen as a monster, and perhaps she really isn't one.) So one day Robert carries
Flora — for the first and last time he carries her in his arms — to
the room that his wife, Audrey, has prepared for her. And once
Flora is settled in her well-lit, well-heated corner, Audrey Atkinson undertakes to clean out the newly vacated rooms — Flora's
rooms. She carries a heap of old books out into the yard. It's spring
again, housecleaning time, the season when Flora herself per-
formed such feats, and now the pale face of Flora appears behind the new net curtains. She has dragged herself from her corner. She sees the light blue sky with its high skidding clouds over
the watery fields, the contending crows, the flooded creeks, the
reddening tree branches. She sees the smoke rise out of the in-
cinerator in the yard, where her books are burning. Those smelly
old books, as Audrey has called them. Words and pages, the om-
inous dark spines. The elect, the damned, the slim hopes, the
mighty torments — up in smoke. There was the ending.

To me the really mysterious person in the story, as my mother
told it, was Robert. He never has a word to say. He got engaged
to Flora. He is walking beside her along the river when Ellie leaps
out at them. He finds Ellie's thistles in his bed. He does the car-
pentry made necessary by his and Ellie's marriage. He listens or
does not listen while Flora reads. Finally he sits scrunched up in
the school desk while his flashy bride dances by with all the men.

So much for his public acts and appearances. But he was the
one who started everything, in secret. He *did it to* Ellie. He did it
to that skinny wild girl at a time when he was engaged to her
sister, and he did it to her again and again when she was nothing
but a poor botched body, a failed childbearer, lying in bed.

He must have done it to Audrey Atkinson, too, but with less
disastrous results.

Those words, *did it to* — the words my mother, no more than Flora, would never bring herself to speak — were simply exciting to me. I didn't feel any decent revulsion or reasonable indignation. I refused the warning. Not even the fate of Ellie could put me off. Not when I thought of that first encounter — the desperation of it, the ripping and striving. I used to sneak longing looks at men, in those days. I admired their wrists and their necks and any bit of their chests a loose button let show, and even their ears and their feet in shoes. I expected nothing reasonable of them, only to be engulfed by their passion. I had similar thoughts about Robert.

What made Flora evil, in my story, was just what made her admirable, in my mother's — her turning away from sex. I fought against everything my mother wanted to tell me on this subject; I despised even the drop in her voice, the gloomy caution, with which she approached it. My mother had grown up in a time and in a place where sex was a dark undertaking for women. She knew that you could die of it. So she honored the decency, the prudery, the frigidity, that might protect you. And I grew up in horror of that very protection, the dainty tyranny that seemed to me to extend to all areas of life, to enforce tea parties and white gloves and all other sorts of tinkling inanities. I favored bad words and a breakthrough, I teased myself with the thought of a man's recklessness and domination. The odd thing is that my mother's ideas were in line with some progressive notions of her times, and mine echoed the notions that were favored in my times. This in spite of the fact that we both believed ourselves independent, and lived in backwaters that did not register such changes. It's as if tendencies that seemed most deeply rooted in our minds, most private and singular, had come in as spores on the prevailing wind, looking for any likely place to land, any welcome.

Not long before she died, but when I was still at home, my mother got a letter from the real Flora. It came from that town near the farm, the town that Flora used to ride to, with Robert, in the cart, holding on to the sacks of wool or potatoes.

Flora wrote that she was no longer living on the farm.

"Robert and Audrey are still there," she wrote. "Robert has some trouble with his back but otherwise he is very well. Audrey has poor circulation and is often short of breath. The doctor says she

must lose weight but none of the diets seem to work. The farm
has been doing very well. They are out of sheep entirely and into
dairy cattle. As you may have heard, the chief thing nowadays is
to get your milk quota from the government and then you are
set. The old stable is all fixed up with milking machines and the
latest modern equipment, it is quite a marvel. When I go out there
to visit I hardly know where I am."

She went on to say that she had been living in town for some
years now, and that she had a job clerking in a store. She must
have said what kind of store this was, but I cannot now remember. She said nothing, of course, about what had led her to this
decision — whether she had in fact been put off her own farm,
or had sold out her share, apparently not to much advantage.
She stressed the fact of her friendliness with Robert and Audrey.
She said her health was good.

"I hear that you have not been so lucky in that way," she wrote.
"I ran into Cleta Barnes, who used to be Cleta Stapleton at the
post office out at home, and she told me that there is some problem with your muscles and she said your speech is affected, too.
This is sad to hear but they can do such wonderful things nowadays so I am hoping that the doctors may be able to help you."

An unsettling letter, leaving so many things out. Nothing in it
about God's will or His role in our afflictions. No mention of
whether Flora still went to that church. I don't think my mother
ever answered. Her fine legible handwriting, her schoolteacher's
writing, had deteriorated, and she had difficulty holding a pen.
She was always beginning letters and not finishing them. I would
find them lying around the house. *My dearest Mary*, they began.
*My darling Ruth, My dear little Joanna (though I realize you are not
little anymore), My dear old friend Cleta, My lovely Margaret.* These
women were friends from her teaching days, her Normal School
days, and from high school. A few were former pupils. I have
friends all over the country, she would say, defiantly. I have dear,
dear friends.

I remember seeing one letter that started out *Friend of my
Youth*. I don't know whom it was to. They were all friends of her
youth. I don't recall one that began with *My dear and most admired
Flora*. I would always look at them, try to read the salutation and
the few sentences she had written, and because I could not bear
to feel sadness I would feel an impatience with the flowery lan-

guage, the direct appeal for love and pity. She would get more
of that, I thought (more from myself, I meant), if she could manage to withdraw, with dignity, instead of reaching out all the time
to cast her stricken shadow.

I had lost interest in Flora by then. I was always thinking of
stories, and by this time I probably had a new one on my mind.

But I have thought of her since. I have wondered what kind of
store. A hardware store or a five-and-ten, where she has to wear
a coverall, or a drugstore, where she is uniformed like a nurse,
or a Ladies' Wear, where she is expected to be genteelly fashionable? She must have had to learn about food blenders or chain
saws, negligees, cosmetics, even condoms. She would have to work
all day under electric lights, and operate a cash register. Would
she get a permanent, paint her nails, put on lipstick? And she
must have found a place to live — a little apartment with a kitch-
enette, overlooking the main street, or a room in a boarding house.
How could she go on being a Cameronian? How could she get to
that out-of-the-way church, unless she managed to buy a car and
learned to drive it? And if she did that she might drive not only
to church but to other places. She might go on holidays. She might
rent a cottage on a lake for a week, learn to swim, visit a city. She
might eat meals in a restaurant, possibly in a restaurant where
drinks were served. She might make friends with women who
were divorced.

She might meet a man. A friend's widowed brother, perhaps.
A man who did not know that she was a Cameronian or what
Cameronians were. Who knew nothing of her story. A man who
had never heard about the partial painting of the house or the
two betrayals, or that it took all her dignity and innocence to keep
her from being a joke. He might want to take her dancing, and
she would have to explain that she could not go. He would be
surprised but not put off — all that Cameronian business might
seem quaint to him, almost charming. So it would to everybody.
She was brought up in some weird religion, people would say.
She lived a long time out on some godforsaken farm. She is a
little bit strange but really quite nice. Nice-looking, too. Especially since she went and got her hair done.

I might go into a store and find her.

No, no. She would be dead a long time now.

But suppose I had gone into a store — perhaps a department

store. I see a place with the brisk atmosphere, the straightfor-
ward displays, the old-fashioned modern look of the fifties. Suppose a tall, handsome woman, nicely turned out, had come to
wait on me, and I had known, somehow, in spite of the sprayed
and puffed hair and the pink or coral lips and fingernails — I
had known that this was Flora. I would have wanted to tell her
that I knew, I knew her story, though we had never met. I imagine myself trying to tell her. (This is a dream now, I understand
it as a dream.) I imagine her listening, with a pleasant composure. But she shakes her head. She smiles at me, and in her smile
there is a degree of mockery, a faint, self-assured malice. Weariness, as well. She is not surprised that I am telling her this, but
she is weary of it, of me and my idea of her, my information, my
notion that I can know anything about her.

Of course it's my mother I'm thinking of, my mother as she
was in those dreams, saying, It's nothing, just this little tremor,
saying with such astonishing lighthearted forgiveness, Oh, I knew
you'd come someday. My mother surprising me, and doing it almost indifferently. Her mask, her fate, and most of her affliction, taken away. How relieved I was, and happy. But I now recall that I was disconcerted as well. I would have to say that I felt
slightly cheated. Yes. Offended, tricked, cheated, by this welcome turnaround, this reprieve. My mother, moving rather carelessly out of her old prison, showing options and powers I never
dreamed she had, changes more than herself. She changes the
bitter lump of love I have carried all this time into a phantom —
something useless and uncalled for, like a phantom pregnancy.

The Cameronians, I have discovered, are or were an uncompro-
mising remnant of the Covenanters — those Scots who in the
seventeenth century bound themselves, with God, to resist prayer
books, bishops, any taint of popery or interference by the king.
Their name comes from Richard Cameron, an outlawed or "field"
preacher, soon cut down. The Cameronians went into battle
singing the Seventy-fourth and the Seventy-eighth Psalms. They
hacked the haughty archbishop of St. Andrews to death on the
highway and rode their horses over his body. One of their min-
isters, in a mood of firm rejoicing at his own hanging, excom-
municated all the other preachers in the world.

JOYCE CAROL OATES

American, Abroad

FROM NORTH AMERICAN REVIEW

IN THE UNMARKED government sedan with the olive-tinted windows, en route to the consul-general's residence in a leafier, less traffic- and bicycle-clogged part of the city, the cultural attaché's wife leaned forward to tell Caroline Carmichael, in a lowered voice, "You won't mention this to anyone tonight, of course, Miss Carmichael — but Mr. Price has been under a good deal of pressure lately. Our office was warned by intelligence that he has been definitely targeted by an Iranian terrorist team. His daughter —" Mr. Price, Norman Price, was the consul-general at whose home Caroline Carmichael would be dining that evening; the occasion of the dinner was, in fact, to honor her, as an American visitor, a "feminist" art historian traveling through Europe under the auspices of a culturally minded United States agency. After thirty-five days of hotels chosen to accommodate the agency's modest per diem and the alarmingly diminished American dollar, and brief, often rackety air flights, and lecture halls mysteriously packed with people or as mysteriously empty, and the usual insomniac and dyspeptic miseries, Caroline Carmichael had begun to think of herself as a seasoned or in any case resigned traveler; a zealous, uncomplaining cultural emissary, as her sponsoring agency surely believed her. But — a terrorist team? Iranian? "Targeted?" The casual remark shocked her; but she managed merely to nod, to nod gravely and with sympathy, as if such a disclosure, such a revelation of the heightened drama of the diplomat's life, were not at all foreign to her, or terrifying.

The cultural attaché, seated up front with the driver, glanced back at his wife, possibly to give warning, but she ignored him, and continued breathlessly, "His daughter Inge — you'll be meeting her tonight — she's visiting them from the States — was followed yesterday for several hours, and there have been other incidents reported. But the Prices didn't want to cancel tonight — so many people, so many *cultural* people, invited by the consulate, are coming. It's an important event, actually. Of course the residence is heavily guarded. Security isn't perfect in this post because there hasn't been trouble since the early seventies, but —" The cultural attaché turned sharply to say, as if this were an old point, and a sore one, "I've put in a request I don't know how many times for a bullet-proof sedan. The consulate has other cars of course, limos, and most of them are equipped, but *this,* the one assigned to our division . . ." His voice trailed off into a bemused silence.

As if in response to this remark, the driver, who did not speak but seemed to comprehend English, began to drive faster; they were rattling over a bridge over one of the wide, placid, usually rain-pocked canals. Caroline Carmichael's heart too accelerated; she stared out at a grim urban landscape of dull brick, rowhouses, tenements, shabby municipal buildings, with here and there signs of "modernization" — cheap high-rise office and apartment buildings, parking garages. Most distracting, and demoralizing — Caroline had arrived in this city only the day before — were the miles of walls, sidewalks, public benches, even trees — enormous dignified elms, oaks, plane trees — defaced by graffiti in wild fluorescent Day-Glo colors. How strange! How ugly! The angry yet idle iconography of youth, seemingly transported from the New York City subway to *this* legendary city — Caroline Carmichael had asked her hosts about it, who does it, and why, why is it tolerated, why isn't it cleaned up, but the answers were rather vague. Youth. The drug culture. "Revolutionaries" without a revolution.

Now she wondered if, out of nowhere, at the next intersection perhaps, or as the driver turned off onto a quieter boulevard, death might come flying at them. Machine-gun fire, a bomb? Caroline Carmichael was of that generation of thoroughly modern, indeed post-modern men and women who expect their deaths to spring from no logical or predictable sequence of events, let alone any ethically coherent algorithm of the soul; why not, then, in the company of such seeming ordinary, good-hearted Americans (the cultural attaché and his wife were both, like Caroline Carmichael, midwesterners: two decades of living abroad had not neutralized their accents), in an automobile of such ordinary dimensions, sudden death by assassination? Misguided political assassination? She laughed uneasily and said, "But you don't think there is any danger, do you? — really?"

Having aroused their guest's alarm, the Bonners were quick now to extinguish it; the wife even patted Caroline's arm. No, they assured her, of course not, there was no real danger — if there were, security would have insisted that the Prices cancel the evening.

"Why do the Iranians want to kill Mr. Price?" Caroline asked.

"Not 'the' Iranians, 'some' Iranians," the cultural attaché said. "In fact, intelligence hasn't been able to learn the name of the terrorist team yet — it must be a small splinter group, only a few men. They can be the most deadly. — They want to kill Mr. Price because he was in Tehran up until the end; he has many Iranian friends in and outside the country."

"They loved him there, him and Georgine both," Mrs. Bonner said passionately.

"I see," said Caroline, though she didn't, quite.

The consul-general's residence was an immense foursquare stone and stucco mansion, painted an improbable, though quite attractive, pale pink; set like a fortress behind fifteen-foot stone walls, with a medieval-looking iron gate and a security booth manned by Marine guards. Caroline Carmichael disliked these young Americans with their blunt shaved heads and purposefully expressionless eyes: in an American embassy in West Germany she had chanced to overhear two of them talking about her, carelessly, rather loudly, having mistaken her for a German woman presumably, for at that moment she'd been alone, and not engaged in conversation with any of her embassy hosts. The brief experience had angered her, yet had made a deeper, more profound impression on her; for she'd felt not only the raw helplessness of being female in a world of men but the helplessness of being perceived as a non-American in a world organized along military lines of power and influence. But tonight the Marine guards were courteous, if mechanical; for Caroline Carmichael had her passport, her identification, her consulate escorts.

Elsewhere in Europe, brought into one or another palatial residence, Caroline Carmichael had several times been informed that the property now belonging to the United States government had once been commandeered by Nazi authorities during World War II; that, indeed, Adolf Hitler himself *had* very likely slept beneath its roof. She waited now for the Bonners to make this remark — it was usually accompanied by an embarrassed laugh — but they did not. Caroline said, looking up at the elegant facade, the graceful portico, "How lovely!" The cultural attaché's wife said, "But Georgine Price would rather live anywhere else."

Fanning the side entrance of the house was a double row of yellow, golden, and pale orange roses, blossoming like an exposed vein of gold in the fading daylight.

A hysterically barking dog, a small terrier with a pink ribbon bouncing from its collar, rushed forward to greet the little party, and had to be restrained by one of the young Marines, as the door swung outward, and Mrs. Price — tall, regal, bony-faced, in a long brocaded gown — welcomed them and ushered them in, all the while chattering at the terrier, which leapt against Caroline Carmichael's legs and licked her hands with a tongue like a wet chamois cloth. "Suzie, be good!" Mrs. Price cried, "— we're all skittish enough tonight without *you*." This was so clear an allusion to the terrorist warning, Caroline supposed it an open secret; though of course she said nothing. She was tonight's guest of honor and meant to acquit herself well.

Mrs. Price, given to lavish gestures, seized Caroline Carmichael's hand and drew it up to her bosom, asking how she was, how she was adjusting to so much travel, not exhausted, they all hoped — "After that perfectly marvelous lecture of yours this afternoon. I learned *so much.*"

She linked her arm through Caroline's and led her sweepingly into the enormous living room, there to endure several vertiginous minutes of introductions, handshakes, studied Old World gallantry, reiterated and perhaps even genuine praise for the afternoon's lecture ("The Iconography of Female Martyrdom in European Art"), and and the repeated offering of glasses of white wine and elaborate appetizers borne on silver trays by uniformed servants. As always in such situations Caroline Carmichael felt sheerly diamagnetic impulses: the wish to be elsewhere, *any-where*; the conviction that, yes, she was in the right place, and deserved her good fortune.

For what after all was the alternative?

Mrs. Price clapped her hands, raised her voice shrilly, "Norman hopes you will all excuse him for being late," then repeated, as if for the benefit of those who had not quite understood, "The consul-general begs your forgiveness, he will be a few minutes late." Mrs. Price was in her mid-sixties, but her manner was youthful, even frenetic; with her widened eyes, her mobile mouth, her graying hair frizzed out electrically about her face, she reminded Caroline Carmichael of John Tenniel's drawing of the Red Queen in Alice's adventures in the looking-glass world. She was gazing at Caroline now with an expression of extreme if muddled solicitude. "Did you say you *were* exhausted, Miss Carmichael? Would you like to lie down for a few minutes upstairs, and rest?" she asked suddenly.

Everyone looked at Caroline Carmichael, awaiting her reply, and Caroline, embarrassed, wondering if she looked so very awful, assured her hostess she wasn't at all exhausted — "I'm really very happy to be here." But Mrs. Price's jittery attention was diverted by new arrivals and a furious spasm of yipping out in the foyer.

Caroline accepted a glass of white wine with a hand that shook just slightly, and found herself in a conversational group that included the insufferable "Parisian cultural critic" who had introduced her that afternoon — the only person they could find, Mr. Bonner rather tactlessly explained, who could do a "creditable job" of introducing Caroline Carmichael to an audience that knew nothing of her work. François was the slender, sinewy, sloe-eyed youngish man's name; he had very white teeth, and a courtly condescending manner. As if to soothe Caroline Carmichael's flurried nerves, he murmured confidentially in her ear, "Please do not worry, Miss Carmichael — your CIA people have everything under control, I am certain." "I'm not worried," Caroline said, startled; she did not want to be drawn into an exchange of confidences, and at such a time.

*

For what seemed like a very long period of time but was probably no more than half an hour the guests in the Prices' living room — there were about fifteen, including a Dutch journalist, a Dutch documentary filmmaker, a German professor and translator, the curator of the city's museum of contemporary art, several members of the United States Consulate and their wives, and a visiting American economist named Zaller who fumbled an unlit pipe in his left hand — talked together animatedly; a neutral observer might have sensed a palpable strain in the atmosphere, a nerved-up giddiness to the air, but might have attributed it to the usual cocktail party excitement. It was nearly time for dinner, but the consul-general had not appeared; Mrs. Price herself was continually disappearing from the gathering, and reappearing, her beringed hands clasped against her bosom, her eyes darting about, mildly glazed over, seeing nothing. A hostess's nightmare, Caroline Carmichael thought. Why don't we all go home? She thought of her own mother, whom she had loved very much, dead now for nearly ten years. She thought of her aging, ailing father, from whom she was estranged; and wondered what sort of telegram the United States government would send him in the event of her sudden death. A stroke victim, Mr. Carmichael decoded the world's myriad hieroglyphics in terms specific to him; his cosmology allowed for nothing so innocently crude as mere accident.

She had a vision, quick, silent, cinematic, of an explosion of fire through the satin-draped windows of the living room; a rolling uncoiling ball of flame that ignited them all in a cataclysmic death. The vision frightened her, yet comforted: for if one had to die, it was surely preferable to die suddenly, and in a sense anonymously, among strangers? Her mother's protracted dying had torn all their hearts and it was likely that her father had never quite recovered from that death, though within a stunning eighteen months he'd remarried — a woman young enough, as the inevitable expression would have it, to be his daughter, but in no way sisterly to his daughter. Mr. Carmichael was professor of philology, emeritus, Oberlin College, formerly a gentleman of authority and cantankerous charm, now a thoroughly routed old man in whom a mild stroke two years before and a subsequent intermittent aphasia had encouraged a true paranoia — a lifelong penchant for imagining others' assessments of him and "plots" in regard to him had now blossomed into a feverish, tireless cycle of fears, recriminations, doubts, pleas for forgiveness, farewell scenes of Shakespearean intensity. For most of my father's life he believed himself Hamlet, Caroline Carmichael told her friends; now he believes himself Lear. Mr. Carmichael had never fully approved of his daughter's choice of a career in its specifics — for was there not something reductive and vulgar about the phenomenon of feminism itself — but he had seemingly wished her well; since his stroke the mere sight of her, the sound of her voice raised in appeal, stirred him to angry tears. His charge seemed to be that she did not love him, or did not love him *enough* — "But what would be 'enough'?" Caroline Carmichael asked the second Mrs. Carmichael, whose pinched smile and ungenerous eyes filled her with foreboding, and was told, in all artless sincerity, "I don't think anything would be enough, Caroline. Maybe you'd better just leave your father alone."

In another part of the world, as through a looking-glass, Caroline Carmichael's twin-self was going through the motions of her routine, domestic life, even as here, in this splendidly if somewhat overly decorated living room, Caroline Carmichael was being ostensibly honored; at home, in her little rented house in a suburb of a large, sprawling, rather featureless midwestern American city, an hour's commute from the state university at which she taught, she was possibly having dinner with friends, or with a male companion (there were two or three extant, rather more friends than admirers, colleagues of hers at the university), though more likely she would be eating alone, in her vague distracted way, as she glanced through her mail or the next day's lecture notes, or made an effort to read one or another of the professional books she invariably agreed to review and was invariably behind in reviewing. The great danger in living alone is that you will read or work while you eat, Caroline Carmichael knew, but, again, the alternate did not appeal; food had not much taste, eaten without company. At home, too, geographical proximity (four hundred sixty-odd miles separated them: a mere day's drive) urged her to think of her father more than she wished to think of him, since such thoughts were to no purpose, and devolved fairly quickly into self-pity.

It was not specifically to flee her father that Caroline Carmichael had agreed to her government's invitation to do an ambitious tour of Western Europe that spring and early summer, but
it had to be confessed that benefits of being "at home" — in any
sense of the term — were not apparent. She read Pavese, and with
satisfaction more than dread underscored the words *Traveling is
a brutality. It forces you to trust strangers and to lose sight of all that
familiar comfort of home and friends. You are constantly off balance.
Nothing is yours except the essential things — air, sleep, dreams, the sun,
the sky — all things tending toward the eternal, or what we imagine of it.*
But that ecstatic flight had not been Caroline Carmichael's experience, for her days were crowded and cacophonous with people: very nice people for the most part, but people nonetheless,
all of them strangers, with smiles, handshakes, special requests,
questions phrased in careful but sometimes perplexing English.
In giddy loops and zigzags Caroline was making her way north,
giving variations of her lecture, meeting with students, teachers,
translators, fellow art historians and feminists, Americans living
abroad; she had begun the tour in Athens and would end it in
Oslo in another twelve days, barring disaster — a sudden physical collapse, a "political" assassination. She was thirty-seven years
old; an attractive woman with level, rather brooding eyes, limp
fine blond-streaked hair, a habit of smiling too quickly, and in-
sincerely; tall, straight-backed, a bit tense; holding herself, as a
former lover had meanly observed, like a bow about to spring an
arrow. Though she was a professionally successful woman — to
the degree that "success" can be measured, without cynicism, in
public, official terms — she harbored nonetheless an adolescent,
romantic hope of meeting, when she traveled, her "fate": recognizing at first sight the individual, or individuals, or scene, or vision, that might give to her journey its unique validity. Otherwise, why leave home?

So she felt disproportionately upset, as if personally insulted,
by *this* fabled city: Amsterdam: a jewel of canals, sixteenth- and
seventeenth-century houses, numberless museums. Its derelic-
tion had begun at the airport; Caroline had seen, on the drive in,
defaced walls and buildings and sidewalks, faded and fresh graffiti side by side, a witless public littering that seemed to proffer a
statement, a cultural critique, but what was the statement? Even

the parks, oases of civic pride in other Western European cities, were here derelict, and sad to see; young people slept sprawled on the grass in midday, or sat on benches, drugged, dazed, utterly vacuous, and seemingly utterly content. It was a nightmare of the welfare state, Caroline Carmichael supposed: a reminder that after all, the fundamental integrity and dignity of the individual could not be assumed. The city was staggering under the financial burden of enormous welfare rolls; there was an army, ever-increasing, of the professionally unemployed; there were squatters' unions, there were even drug users' unions . . . ! Yet Caroline's "The Iconography of Female Martyrdom in European Art" had gone well; it had been surprisingly well attended. No one is so completely alone as the lecturer addressing her audience, Caroline thought, yet this sort of aloneness suited her; excited her; invested her with an eloquent, fiery passion, very much in keeping with the controversial nature of the ideas she presented.

The Parisian critic's introduction, however, had been affable, uninformed, and charmingly condescending; "François" had clearly read nothing of her work, and knew nothing of her, except for a recitation of facts provided him by the consulate. He dwelled upon the fact, which he seemed to find amusing, that Caroline Carmichael was the first woman to receive tenure at her university; the first woman officer of her professional-academic society; the first woman art historian to have been invited to the American Consulate in Amsterdam to speak. In the guise of praising Caroline Carmichael and flattering her American organizers for bringing her here ("for the first time in Professor Carmichael's distinguished career!"), the smiling, dapper little man with his exotically accented English was actually insulting her. But Caroline Carmichael stoically maintained an expression of equanimity, even cheerfulness. She would never betray her feelings, in public. Not even murderous rage could force itself to the surface of her being, in public.

She'd taken the podium from François with a gracious smile, and set about winning over the audience, as she knew she could not fail to do. How perfect Caroline Carmichael would be, she thought, how thoroughly good, kind, courageous, if only she could live out her life in public.

"Your talk was brilliant, Miss Carmichael. *You* were brilliant."
The Prices' twenty-year-old daughter Inge, introduced to Caroline Carmichael by Mrs. Price, grasped her hand fiercely in hers,
as if taking possession; leaned so close, and so urgently, it seemed
for a disconcerting moment she meant to kiss Caroline on the
lips. What an extraordinarily forceful young woman! How completely different from the college-age women Caroline Carmichael taught! An angry light flared up in Inge Price's eyes, as if
in Caroline's defense; her big-boned face — full, fleshy, freckled, warmly pink as if just slapped — loomed large as a moon;
her soft young body was suffused with energy, intent, impu-
dence. At first glance it looked as if she were wearing simply
rags, but there was a logic of sorts, even a slapdash tatterdema-
lion style, to the two or three layers of skirts, the gauzy open-
throated peasant blouse, the shapeless black sweater, or was it a
hand-woven shawl, unraveling down her back. Her hair was long,
frizzed, and knotted, a magnificent copper color, swinging in her
face and in her eyes; her full, soft breasts were loose inside her
clothing; her hips were wide, stolid, fleshy; she reminded Caroline Carmichael of a young Flemish girl in a painting, ruddy with
health, unthinking in beauty. Clearly, her mother was both proud
of and intimidated by Inge, who had swept into the living room
with the intention of helping the servants (with whom, perhaps,
she claimed a spiritual kinship?) but displayed no self-conscious-
ness whatsoever about talking animatedly with the guest of honor
and plying her with questions. Inge was particularly interested in
the iconography of female martyrdom, she told Caroline Carmichael, as it applied to life today and not just to the past; she
wanted to know more about "Inquisitional politics" (of which
Caroline had spoken briefly at the end of her talk) as it applied
to reality and not just to some old art that nobody looks at, or
almost nobody. "How long will you be in Amsterdam? Maybe we
could meet sometime? Maybe tomorrow? As soon as possible —
like, for breakfast?" Inge asked Caroline, breathless, leaning close,
staring at Caroline with her damp, slightly protuberant green eyes.
She exuded a rich mesmerizing scent of something powdery,
heated, not frequently washed; a mustiness of well-worn clothes,
like slept-in bedclothes. Mrs. Price in her brocaded hostess's gown
and scimatar-like jewelry professed a mother's horror, or was it

simply embarrassment — "Why Inge, for heaven's sake, Miss Carmichael is *busy*, I'm sure she has a dozen appointments for tomorrow, interviews —" Caroline Carmichael had taken an unconscious step back from the impertinent young Inge, and now caught her breath, and laughed, rather amazed, startled, smiling — "Why I'm sure we can meet — breakfast would be fine."

So distinct a victory of daughter over mother was this, Inge nudged Mrs. Price and muttered, "O.K., Mother, go *on*, Miss Carmichael and I need to talk," and Mrs. Price shrank away, immediately routed, and Caroline Carmichael continued smiling, continued a bit dazed, for Inge was so striking a young woman, so spectacularly forceful a presence, a ball of flame might have swept into the decorous gathering, contrasting painfully with the older men and women, the majority of them middle-aged, so carefully, even elegantly dressed and groomed. Caroline recalled now having seen this flamboyant young American girl at her lecture that afternoon, she'd been struck by the vehemence with which the girl had nodded, and during the question-and-answer period Inge had ventured a not entirely coherent question about a point Caroline had made on the "enantiomorphic" relationship between asceticism and sadism in religious art of the late medieval, early Renaissance period, a question that was both arrogant and perceptive — for were not "asceticism" and "sadism" both simply patriarchal expressions? — and her loud, self-assertive voice, so distinctly American, caused people in the audience to look at her. Caroline had not known of course that the outspoken young woman was the daughter of the consul-general and Mrs. Price: she'd disappeared after the lecture without coming forward to be introduced.

Now she was talking to Caroline Carmichael in a great rush of words, smiling, smiling a dazzling smile, gripping Caroline's wrist as if they were old, intimate friends, repeating her praise of the lecture, how she'd been blasted by it, it'd blown her mind, some of the slides Caroline had shown, the gouged-out eyes, the martyrs' breasts on trays, the madonna with the greenish sickish skin nursing the spiteful-looking little Jesus, was that German? medieval? or Flemish? or were they all the same, mostly? Inge had dropped out of Bennington in the middle of her sophomore year, she said, and she didn't intend to return, or maybe

she would, but not right now; she wasn't going to succumb
to parental pressure — "You can't imagine what it's like! I'm
a foreign service brat, my daddy is the *biggest* deal anywhere
he's posted, and the hell of it is, Caroline," she said, drawing near
to murmur in Caroline Carmichael's ear, "he's a dear sweet noble
man and I love him, he's a saint practically, like everybody says.
And Mommy too in case she has misled you. She's *too weird*. But
they're both good people, they're ready to die, just about, doing
their duty, representing the United States fucking foreign policy, my daddy was almost killed already two times I know about
and other times I'm not supposed to know about. They're *good*
people, that's all. I love them, they're crazy, it's weird! They're
not *evil*. You quoted the feminist, I forgot her name, she was one
of the suffragist pioneers I guess, she said 'women don't have
enough evil in them' — ?"

Caroline Carmichael laughed with pleasure, since this remark
was one that had made a strong impression on her when, years
before, she'd first come upon it. "Rebecca West said that. But she
was speaking of the women of Great Britain, a certain caste of
women, in 1912 —"

Inge nodded vehemently but must not have been listening, for
she said, leaning close to Caroline Carmichael again, her eyes humid and dilated, a marvelous pellucid green like a child's marble,
"Have you been introduced to that guy with the pipe over there,
standing over there by the door, 'Peter Zaller'? — He's CIA, but
'analysis' as they call it, not 'covert.'" She snorted with indignation and turned her lower lip inside out in a razzing derisory
gesture. "Like he doesn't know what a dirty war is, or a friendly
assassination!" Caroline glanced over at the fairly ordinary-ap-
pearing gentleman in question, asked what "analysis" was; but
Inge's interest in Mr. Zaller had already consumed itself. She returned to her earlier, more passionate topic of Caroline Carmichael's lecture — images of severed hands, severed heads, ma-
donnas as martyrs, the ecstasy of death — maybe Caroline could
provide her with a list of books to read, paintings to look up, the
names of the most important radical feminists back in the States?
And when could they meet? *Could* they meet tomorrow? Sometime in the midmorning, at Caroline's hotel? Which hotel was it?
"All the hours between your lecture and now," the breathless

young woman said, fixing her eyes on Caroline's in a way that was both annoying and flattering, "I was just walking mainly, by the canals, though they don't like me to because of — some problem they're having with security — and all that while can you guess what I was thinking?"

She stared at Caroline Carmichael so intently, Caroline felt a stab of simple fear. "Yes — ?"

"I want to be you."

The remark hung in the air as if uttered but not received: for Caroline Carmichael was quite nonplussed by it.

Then Mrs. Price returned, the consul-general in tow, for at last Mr. Price had come home — a tall white-haired gentleman with sad eyes, a rather ashen skin, a handsome courtly mouth. "Miss Carmichael! How good to meet you! And how terribly sorry I am for being late!" he exclaimed, quite as if he meant it; as if he'd been hurrying, these hours, simply to meet *her*. It was the diplomatic style par excellence, and Caroline Carmichael, not at all deceived, was nonetheless charmed. She shook hands with him — his hand was warm, dry, reassuring, strong. As they talked she noticed, to her mild regret — or was it sheer relief — that Inge Price was slipping away. At last it was time for dinner.

During this stately meal Caroline Carmichael was distracted by the appearance, at regular, almost predictable intervals, of Inge, who was helping the two uniformed servants serve the food; emerging like a sunburst through the swinging door that led to the kitchen pantry, tray in her hands, lower lip caught in her teeth. Her waist-long coppery hair gleamed with static electricity; she'd tied a crimson sash tight around her waist, ethnic-style, as if to emphasize her full, shapely, exuberant young body. Approaching Caroline Carmichael — Inge had made certain, it seemed, that she, and not the others, served Caroline's and Mr. Price's end of the table — she smiled like a clever child. Clearly the girl was enjoying her handmaiden role, and had played it before: "helping out" with her parents' social obligations. She appeared too to be on companionable terms with the household staff. How striking she is, Caroline thought, trying not to stare. And how perverse, her imagining she would want to be *me*.

Nonetheless it was flattering. In her mind Caroline Carmi-

chael rapidly catalogued the titles and names she would provide
Inge with in the morning. Yes, and she must remember to get
Inge's address so that she could mail her paperback copies of her
own two books.

The consul-general, seated at the head of the table, with Caroline Carmichael to his right, showed none of the distracted-
ness one might be excused for showing if one were purportedly
on a terrorist "target list" but engaged his guest of honor in polite, even quite animated conversation, inquiring after Caroline's
background, her work, her impressions of Europe and of her
foreign service hosts thus far — and what did she think of Amsterdam? "It's a beautiful city," Caroline said, then, faltering a
bit, "— except for the neglect." "Ah yes indeed," Mr. Price murmured, smiling, "— the 'neglect.' " At the far end of the sump-
tuously set table, barely visible beyond the many-branched can-
delabrum, Mrs. Price kept up an exclamatory hostess's dialogue
with guests, punctuated by peals of girlish laughter. The food
was Middle Eastern, Iranian in fact, rich and delicious and altogether new to Caroline Carmichael; the wines too were delicious,
and seemed to be going rapidly to her head. Inge appeared
through the swinging door, this time to collect the first-course
dishes; there was an innocence in her head-on plunging manner.
She smiled in Caroline Carmichael's direction.

Caroline's heart lifted in simple happiness. She said to Mr. Price,
"How lovely this is! — all of this! the room, the table! What fascinating lives you all must lead!"

Norman Price looked at Caroline Carmichael and smiled, po-
litely at first, then with more animation. "Yes, do you know," he
said, considering, "— all in all, that's so. I have had nearly forty
years of it — Georgine and I, both — and, yes, that's so: fascinating."

The Prices had been posted in the USSR, in Western Africa, in
Iran, in Japan, in Germany, and again in Iran, and Norway; their
foreign posts had alternated with posts in Washington, but they
had always preferred to live abroad, even with the difficulties of
bringing up children. Mr. Price had learned the languages of each
of the countries in which he had lived, he'd learned as much as
possible about their histories and cultures, and, yes, he said, in
reply to a question of Caroline's, Iran remained their favorite

country, by far — "We miss it terribly, still, to this day, Georgine and I both." Before the revolution, when Mr. Price had been deputy chief of mission in Tehran, the Iranians they had known — "Not the shah and his associates, but the others" — were wonderfully sensitive, well-educated people, superior people, educators, intellectuals, doctors, scientists, artists. What a tragedy had befallen them! A tragedy, really, for the world! Caroline said awkwardly, "You must have been very upset, when —" Mr. Price said, smiling, " 'Upset' isn't a word allowed in a diplomat's vocabulary, Miss Carmichael." He was breathing not quickly but deeply; in that instant he looked his age, and rather hunted. Caroline saw that he had drained his wineglass and was staring at the dregs.

Later, midway in the meal, Mr. Price seemed to regain his interest in Caroline Carmichael, and asked her about her parents — were they still living? She told him about her father; but only minimally, stressing his accomplishments, his long and productive and seemingly happy professional life. For that is how she meant to remember him after all. For that is how she *would* remember him. Mr. Price's father, he told her, smiling fondly, nostalgically, had been a jack-of-all-trades, even, as a young man, a semiprofessional boxer, boxing in clubs, possibly not quite legal clubs, in the metropolitan New York area. "Sometimes he just boxed for wristwatches," Mr. Price said. "I have an old snapshot of him with a half-dozen wristwatches on each arm." "Really!" Caroline Carmichael exclaimed. Her eyes filled with tears of sentiment as if the snapshot — sepia-tinted, much wrinkled — were before her. Glancing up, she saw Inge Price just emerging through the swinging door, bearing an enormous cut-glass salad bowl in her arms.

After the salad course was served Mr. Price said, "I see you've made my daughter's acquaintance, Miss Carmichael," and Caroline murmured a vague assent. In a neutral voice Mr. Price said, "Our youngest daughter is a fiercely independent young woman. Perhaps because she has always been the baby of the family — there are eighteen years separating her and our eldest, Robert. She left Bennington, for instance, without informing us — or the college — and went 'backpacking' in Canada. For a while." He paused, shaking his head, sighing. Caroline could not determine whether his tone was wry or troubled. Careful to show no inordinate curiosity, she asked a few questions about Inge Price, what was Inge interested in studying, how had she responded to being brought up in a series of foreign countries, how long was she visiting him and Mrs. Price here in Amsterdam? "Ah, not long, I hope?" Mr. Price said. "— Amsterdam is dangerous." Seeing Caroline's look of inquiry, he amended, "I mean for young people. Young people without work and resources who have a special penchant for" — he paused to select the perfect word — "drift."

Drift! Caroline Carmichael, whose life was so much a matter of schedules, timetables, deadlines, and obligations, thought the idea uniquely appealing.

Elsewhere at the long table were conversations of a more abstract, less personal nature, and to one or another of these the consul-general and Caroline Carmichael now sought to attach themselves, for it was uncommon for two people to talk together so exclusively at so formal a gathering — talk of air, water, and soil pollution ("East Germany is the most criminal, but France is not far behind"), and of AIDS in Europe (*"We* will not make the mistake the United States is making — refusing to distribute free needles to narcotics addicts"), and of World War II memories, still distressingly fresh ("The Dutch were starving and living like animals well into 1945, when most of the rest of Europe was liberated"). There was talk, even, though it was brief and rather vague, of the CIA and its recent actions, that very day headlined in the *International Herald Tribune,* in Central America, and Peter Zaller gained the attention of the table by saying in an aggrieved voice, "What no one seems to realize, even otherwise well-informed people, is that Central Intelligence is primarily concerned with analysis — only three percent of the staff is engaged in covert operations." "And there is no direct link between the two?" the German professor asked skeptically. "There is very little communication," Mr. Zaller said. "Then perhaps there should be more communication," the German professor said. It was time for coffee to be served; Mr. Zaller, unlit pipe still in hand, like a talisman, slipped away from the table — to make a telephone call, Caroline wondered, or simply to use the guest bathroom? — and Mrs. Price said gaily, "It's so enormously thoughtful of Peter, I *adore* that man, he refrains from smoking that ghastly pipe of his in company." Thus conversation shifted to smoking, and those at the table who had once smoked and no longer did declared themselves, and those who continued to smoke but wished they could break the habit declared themselves, and those who smoked and were adamant in their intentions to continue to smoke declared themselves, and Mrs. Price, scarcely listening, with the euphoria of a hostess who has feared the worst for her dinner and has seemingly been spared, called out shrilly, "Everything in moderation, my father always said! Vices not excepted!" And now the German professor, whose name was Fredrich, a plump stolid bespectacled man of late middle age who taught American literature at the University of Mainz and who was an old friend of the Prices', entertained the table by telling of how he had participated in World War II for "approximately fifteen minutes": aged eighteen, he had been parachuted into Allied occupied territory in France in 1943, was taken prisoner at once, and spent the remainder of the war in a POW camp in Galesburg, Illinois. "Galesburg!" Caroline Carmichael exclaimed unthinkingly. "I was born in Galesburg!" Fredrich smiled at her, showing broad discolored teeth. "But long after my time there, Miss Carmichael, surely!" he said gallantly.

And then the alarm went off.

A piercingly loud, shrill noise, more substantial than a whistle, not quite a siren — and Caroline Carmichael thought, almost calmly, Now it is going to happen.

Suddenly the Prices and the consulate people were all efficiency: quick and brisk and methodical, as if this very scene had been rehearsed countless times. Georgine Price, from whom one might have expected hysteria, was immediately mobilized, rising from her chair to push open French doors at her rear and helping to usher out onto the terrace, and from there down a short flight of stone steps to the grass, her frightened guests. Like the others, Caroline Carmichael turned docile at once, for there was no time for panic, and, like a grammar school student in a fire drill, acquiesced to the consul-general's lowered, wonderfully authoritative voice: "This way, please. Out these doors. Inge? — come along. Here. Out here. Yes. Step right along." Caroline Carmichael stood shivering in the grass, breathing in the fresh chill damp night air that smelled of roses, or so she imagined,

hugging herself as if to forestall an attack of convulsive shuddering. She felt it in her bowels more powerfully than elsewhere, the
shock of it, the irony, that the very possibility with which she had
been toying for hours — of suffering chaos, of being attacked and
murdered by faceless strangers — had been no idle anecdotal
fantasy after all.

The residence had been activated into a state of emergency
within seconds. Every window blazed with light; spotlights in the
shrubbery had switched on, exposing the pink stone and stucco
mansion like a rather garish movie set; there were men's voices,
the sounds of heavy footsteps. The high-pitched wailing continued. Caroline Carmichael wondered: was the residence under
siege? Had shots already been fired? Was a bomb about to deto-
nate? She backed off in the grass, choked with emotion. She did
not want to die. She was terrified of dying. Overhead the night
sky was very black, numberless winking stars scrambled her vision, she thought of her father who was a lonely frightened dying
old man trapped inside the frail encasement of his skull. If she
survived, she thought, she would fly home at once and beg his
forgiveness. For he was quite right: she hadn't ever loved him
enough.

A hand closed about hers, with a hard little squeeze. Inge whispered in her ear, "Don't worry! Daddy won't let anything happen to us!"

The alarm stopped abruptly. Mr. Price, who had evidently
reentered the house, appeared now in the doorway, cupping his
hands to his mouth to call out, with a joviality that sounded un-
forced, "Sorry! False alarm! It was only the smoke detector!"

"I'm so terribly sorry, and so terribly embarrassed," Peter Zaller
said, red-faced, sweating with shame, but they told him not to be
sorry and not to be embarrassed in the slightest — they much
preferred him and his pipe, after all, to the real thing. "But I feel
like such a damned fool," he said. Mrs. Price laughed wildly and,
seizing one of her guest's hands simply because the woman was
seated close by, said, "No, no, *no. We* are the fools. The damned
detectors are too *sensitive!*"

The brief remainder of the evening passed in this way, convivial, a bit giddy, and Caroline Carmichael thought how comi-

cal, life, how fundamentally silly and farcical, yes, and anecdotal, finally — it would make a perfect little story after all, that a formal dinner party in her honor at the consul-general's residence in Amsterdam had been routed, the guests thrown into terror for their lives, because a man had crept off to smoke his outlawed pipe in a bathroom, *and who was this individual but an officer of the CIA?*

As if on cue, the dinner party dissolved promptly at 11 P.M. Before Caroline left, driven back by the Bonners to her little hotel near the Stedelijk Museum, she made a date with Inge Price for 9 A.M. the next morning in the coffee shop of her hotel. ("I'll be there! — and I can take you to some museums afterward!" Inge said.) Mr. Price shook Caroline's hand in farewell and seemed genuinely sorry she was leaving Amsterdam in two days — "I so much enjoyed our conversation, Miss Carmichael." As if they had indeed come through a siege together, Mrs. Price warmly embraced Caroline, and complained hoarsely in her ear, "How I wish my daughter could take a tutorial course with someone like you, Miss Carmichael! — by mail, if no other way! It would do her a world of good to use her brains for once. All Inge seems to do is waste time, court disaster — she's forever taking up strays — lame ducks —" The consul-general laid a hand on his wife's arm and said gently, "Georgine, dear, Miss Carmichael's car is waiting." The frenzied terrier Suzie, thrown into a seemingly permanent state of excitation by the alarm and the evacuation of the house, was yipping wildly, her toenails clicking on the marble foyer floor and her damp cold busy little nose poking about against Caroline Carmichael's knees.

Outside, a Marine guard stood by the opened rear door of the sedan, stony-faced with fury, or contempt, or simple boredom.

And in the morning, though Caroline Carmichael waited patiently in the coffee shop of her hotel well past 10 A.M., sipping coffee, adding to the list of names and titles she'd devised for Inge Price, the young woman failed to appear. Caroline's little table overlooked the street, where movements — traffic, pedestrians, bicyclists — continually drew her attention. But Inge failed to appear, nor did she telephone.

Caroline had a small breakfast, hard rolls and jam, a glass of rather synthetic orange juice, left a note for Inge with the proprietress ("I'll be upstairs in my room until 11 — please come right up: 302"), went back to her room telling herself that in the event Inge had not arrived by 11:00 she would go out, to the Stedelijk Museum in fact. And possibly, since it was so close, the Van Gogh Museum as well.

So she sat in her cramped, rather dour little room, telling herself now that she wasn't waiting exactly, she was simply reading, for she had always intended to read *The Diary of Anne Frank* and with the Frank house only a few miles away from where she was, what more fitting opportunity? And so engrossing was the book, so beautifully and tragically modulated the young girl's voice, it was nearly 11:30 when she checked the time. Out of nervousness — the aftermath, no doubt, of the previous evening's bad scare, and the intervening night's insomnia — she had not been able to read the Frank diary in chronological sequence; fearing the accumulation of suspense and tension, she'd been skipping about, and in a sort of numbed horror she read, near the end, *I am saying goodbye to you before our death. Dear Father: I am saying goodbye to you. We are so anxious to live, but all is lost — we are not allowed! I am so afraid of this death, because little children are thrown into graves alive. Goodbye forever.*

I kiss you.

Caroline Carmichael snatched up her trench coat and umbrella and hurried out. Walking in the rain, beneath the slanted umbrella, dodging bicyclists who came hurtling at her, she told herself it was nothing, her hurt and disappointment were nothing, think of true disappointment, true hurt, true terrorism and terror, think of Anne Frank and the millions of others, children tossed living into graves, think of anyone and anything other than Caroline Carmichael, thirty-seven years old, alone, walking blindly in the rain in a city the color of pewter, telling herself *strays, lame ducks, what else did you expect!*

I want to be you.

She spent an absorbed ninety minutes in the Stedelijk Museum, might have had lunch in the stylish café but returned to her hotel just in case, for what if Inge Price, breathless, apologetic, hair in her eyes, had arrived in her absence. . . . Though she could see that her mailbox was empty save for her oversized key, Caroline Carmichael nonetheless asked the desk clerk if there were any messages for her. No messages, she was told.

So she wrote out a message herself for Inge, for the desk clerk to give her should she arrive, and went out again in the rain, and had lunch alone in a crowded neighborhood restaurant, not an expensive and certainly not an elegant place by the look of it, but, the American dollar being so low, expensive enough. As if to spite her own mean-spirited inclination, she left a generous tip. Then she went to the Van Gogh Museum, though this was, in a sense, out of spite, for of all museums the Van Gogh was surely the one Inge Price would have liked to take her to — what more appropriate, for two Americans visiting Amsterdam? At 3:00 P.M. she was scheduled for an interview in the coffee shop of her hotel, so she returned, and quite enjoyed, or appeared to enjoy, the well-informed and provocative questions put to her by the young Dutch woman journalist, and if she was hurt, indeed dismayed and bewildered, by Inge Price's failure to contact her, she gave no sign.

She left the hotel again, desperate to be in the open air. No matter the perpetual rain, the graffiti scrawls that assaulted the eye. The Dutch flew by on their grim high-seated and -handled old bicycles, unpainted bicycles, and the Dutch faces pale and grim-looking, pale hard plain-pewter faces, sexless, with strong bones. She would telephone the consulate in the morning, before she left for the airport, she would leave a message for Inge Price, some sort of brisk matter-of-fact message, she'd mail the list of names and titles to the girl too, for why not be generous in the face of another's rudeness. She had made up her mind to continue with her tour — on to Hamburg, to Copenhagen, to Stockholm, to Oslo. She would not return home to her father only to be rebuffed another time, the very thought was absurd and sentimental, serving no purpose. Caroline Carmichael was of all things purposeful.

"I am an American," she thought, "— at least." She was walking by an open-air flower market, the rain had turned to mere drizzle, she folded up her umbrella and carried it under her arm. The thought, conceived in meanness, blossomed in her heart; and so transformed her face that, for several blocks, passers-by glanced at her, some of them fellow Americans perhaps, with faint quizzical stares, half-smiles, almost of recognition.

FRANCINE PROSE

Dog Stories

FROM SPECIAL REPORT—FICTION

SO OFTEN, AT WEDDINGS, one kisses and hugs the bride and groom and then stands there dumbstruck, grinning with dread. But to-day the guests congratulate Christine and John and immediately ask Christine, "How's your leg?" If Christine's leg didn't hurt, she might almost feel thankful that a dog bit her a few days ago and gave her guests something to say.

Hardly anyone waits for an answer. They can see for them-selves that Christine is wearing a bandage but limping only slight-ly. They rush on with the conversation, asking, "What happened, exactly?" though nearly all of them live nearby, and nearly all of them know.

By now Christine can tell the story and at the same time scan the lawn to see who has come and who hasn't, to make sure some-one is in charge of the champagne and the icy tubs of oysters, and to look for Stevie, her nine-year-old son. Stevie is where she knows he will be — watching the party from the edge, slouched, meditatively chewing his hand. The white tuxedo he picked out himself, at the antique store where Christine bought her thirties lawn dress, hangs on him like a zoot suit.

Many of the wedding guests wear elegant vintage clothes, or costly new ones designed to look vintage: peplums, organza, cab-bage roses, white suits, and Panama hats; it is late afternoon, mid-July and unseasonably hot, so that quite a few of the guests look, like the garden, bleached of color and slightly blown. For a mo-ment Christine wishes they'd held the wedding in June, when the irises and the peonies were in bloom; then she remembers it wasn't till May that they made up their minds to get married.

At first she tries to vary the dog-bite story from telling to telling — to keep herself interested, and for John's sake; John has had to listen to this thirty times. But finally she gives up. She says: "I stopped at a barn sale near Lenox. I was crossing the road. A big black dog, some kind of shepherd-Labrador mix, came charging out of nowhere and sunk its teeth in my leg. I screamed — I think I screamed. A woman came out of a barn and called the dog. It backed off right away."

Even as she tells it, Christine knows: despite its suddenness, its randomness, the actually getting bitten, it isn't much of a story. It lacks what a good dog story needs, that extra dimension of the undoglike and bizarre. She and John used to have a terrific dog story about their collie, Alexander — a story they told happily for a few years, they got bored with and told reluctantly when party talk turned to dog stories. At some point they had agreed that telling dog stories marked a real conversational low, and from then on they were self-conscious, embarrassed to tell theirs. That was even before Alexander died.

Yet today, as they greet their guests and the talk drifts from Christine's bite to dogs in general, Christine realizes that she now has another dog story. She tells it, she cannot avoid it, and the guests respond with escalating dog stories: dumb dogs, tricky dogs, lucky dogs with windfall inheritances, mean dogs that bite. From time to time John or Christine senses that the other is on the verge of telling the story about Alexander. Although they are both quite willing to hear it, both are relieved when the other holds back. Christine feels that this — thinking of the story and knowing the other is also thinking of it and not telling it — connects them more strongly than the ceremony about to take place.

Perhaps her dog-bite story would be livelier if she added some of the details that, for laziness and other private reasons, she has decided to leave out. She can't talk about the woman, the dog's owner, without hearing that edge of shrill complaint and nasty gossip about how awful strangers can be; your own wedding seems like a funny place to be sounding like that.

When the woman got hold of the dog, she had stayed there, a few feet away, not moving. The dog got quiet instantly — that in itself seemed weird. The woman said, "You scared of dogs?" Christine's leg didn't really hurt yet, but her heart was pounding. "We used to have a dog," she said. The woman cut her off. "They always know when you're scared," she said. Only then did she drag the dog away. "Don't move," she told Christine. She came back with a bottle of alcohol. It could have been kerosene, yet Christine let her splash it on her leg. The pain made Christine's knees go rubbery. She turned and did a stumbling, terrible little dance toward the car. Probably the woman was right to yell after her, "Hey, you shouldn't drive!"

Nearly all the wedding guests know that Christine is pregnant; it's part of the sympathy her dog-bite story evokes and why everyone winces when she tells it. Men tend to ask about the dog: what's being done, has it bitten anyone before? The women ask about Stevie. Everyone is relieved to hear that Stevie was home with John. It isn't just his having been spared the sight of his mother being hurt, but that most of the guests have seen Stevie around dogs — any dog except Alexander. It's really quite a performance. He simply turns to stone. It has taken Christine years not to smile apologetically as she pulls Stevie off to the car.

All week the house has been full of visiting friends, teenagers hired to help out, carpenters converting part of the barn into a studio for Christine. It is her wedding present from John, for which she feels so grateful that she refrains from mentioning that the construction should have been finished weeks ago. And no wonder. All but one of the carpenters were on a perpetual coffee break at her kitchen table, smoking Camels and flirting with the catering girls, though the one the girls liked was the other one, the handsome one, Robert, who was never at the table but out working in the barn.

Christine began taking refuge in the studio, watching Robert work. A few days ago, she invited Robert to the wedding. Now she looks for him and sees him, standing not far from Stevie.

Standing on her good leg, Christine leans her weight against John. "Sit down," he says. "Take it easy." He has been saying this since she got pregnant, more often since the bite. But if she greets the guests sitting, she will just have to talk about that. She tells herself that none of it — the adrenaline, the tetanus shot, the pain — has in fact been harmful. She wants desperately to protect the baby, though in the beginning she argued against having it. John said he understood, but she had to remember: Stevie was a baby for so long, but it won't be like that again.

No one here has ever met Stevie's dad, who went back to Philadelphia when Stevie was fifteen months old. One thing Christine likes about being settled is that she got tired of explaining. Describing how Stevie's dad left right after learning that something was really wrong with Stevie, she was often uncertain about how angry or self-righteous or sympathetic she was supposed to sound.

When Stevie was two she had moved here to the country, found a rented house and a woman to watch him while she supported them substitute-teaching art. Evenings, she would have long, loud conversations from across the house with Stevie, who couldn't yet sit up. That was when she met John. John has a small construction company; he built the house they live in. When Christine and Stevie moved in, she quit teaching, put Stevie in a special day program in Pittsfield, and was able to paint full time. Stevie loves John, and signs of Christine and John's success are everywhere: the house, the garden, the nail-polish-red Ferrari that Annette, Christine's art dealer, has just this moment driven up from New York.

Annette wears white pedal pushers and an enormous white man's shirt; her leopard high heels sink into the lawn so that pulling them out gives her walk a funny bounce. She plows through a circle surrounding Christine and John, first hugs, then briskly shakes hands with them both, then looks down at Christine's bandage and says, "I hope they crucified Rin Tin Tin." Christine wonders how literally Annette means this; she remembers a recent art piece, some sort of ecological statement involving a crucified stuffed coyote.

"It's under observation," says Christine. "The doctor called the town sheriff —"

"Observation!" Annette says. "At the end of a loaded gun. Well, I don't know. Why would anyone want a dog? Remember when Wegman's dog got lost and he put up signs on the lampposts and of course the signs got recognized and taken down — they're worth fortunes now."

"Did he ever find the dog?" John asks.

"Of course not," says Annette.

"That's fabulous," says John. Christine has often noticed how quickly Annette makes people sound like her, use her words —

even John, who likes Annette, but not for the reasons Annette thinks. He isn't fooled by her asking him for business advice; he knows she has a perfectly good high-powered accountant of her own.

Annette wedges herself between John and Christine, leans toward Christine, and says, "Let's see the new studio."

But John and Christine are watching a tall man with Donahue-platinum hair bounding toward them across the lawn. It's the minister, Hal Koch. "Like in the soft drink," he said when they went to see him in his study; Christine thought he must say that often, a good man guiding strangers in their choice between a soda and a dirty word. She'd wanted to go to a justice of the peace, elope without leaving town. But John wants something more formal, guests and God as witnesses that now she is really his. John has a religious streak, inherited no doubt from his mother, a wraithlike woman in an orange dress and wooden yoga beads, now edging timidly toward Stevie.

Without even registering Annette, Hal Koch shakes hands with John, then Christine. He says, "Terrific place!" Within a few seconds he is questioning John about construction costs. John answers patiently, though Christine can tell it is driving him mad; it is a measure of his sweetness and patience that he will not even let himself catch her eye. In fact she likes it that this sort of talk can take place, that people know John, respect him, know what to say. Christine had been grateful for this in Hal Koch's study, because while John and the minister were quietly talking about John's business, Stevie was switching the overhead light on and off as fast as he could.

When Stevie finally stopped, Hal had said, "He's a beautiful kid."

"I've learned a lot from him," John said. "I feel like I'm privileged to know him."

This is how John stands up for Stevie, by telling the truth: there is more to Stevie than anyone suspects. But there is also the way John says "know him" and a funny thing he does with his eyes; she has seen him do it so many times and never figured out how exactly he tells people without a word that Stevie isn't his. Everyone seems to catch on, even Hal Koch, who redirected his compliment to Christine. It isn't that John is disowning Stevie, distancing himself beyond ill luck or faulty genes. He just wants extra credit. And really he deserves it. People who admire John for taking on Stevie can't imagine what that means. It's partly why this wedding — why John and Christine's life — makes the guests feel so good that a little dog bite can't touch it.

John and Christine and the minister walk over to the rose arbor. Everyone gathers round. The guests have nearly fallen silent when John holds up his hand and walks over and gets Stevie and pulls him under the arbor with them. He leans Stevie back against his stomach and joins his arms in a *V* down Stevie's chest. Stevie looks pleased. A wave of emotion rises up from the guests, a tide of pleasure and sympathy. And suddenly Christine hates them. It's not that she doesn't value their kindness but that she will scream if one more person, however genuinely, wishes her well.

Of course her nerves are raw: three months pregnant, the heat, the nonstop achy drumbeat of blood in her leg — and on top of that, getting married. She is glad that the service is short, the barebones civil ceremony, glad that it all goes by very fast and in a kind of fog. In his study, Hal Koch had asked if they wanted a prayer or a poem — he said lots of couples chose poems. He put this question to Christine, though the wedding was John's idea. Christine said, "How about the Twenty-third Psalm?" and there had been a funny moment when the two men fell silent and looked at her until she laughed and said, "Joke."

With evening, the perfumy scent of the tall white lilies fills the entire garden. This is the worst time of year. It used to be taken for granted that people go crazy around midsummer night and stay up all night in the grip of unruly dreams and desires. All day the sun gives the world a hallucinatory buckle, and even in the evening after a shower, heat seems to keep shimmering behind your eyes like the ocean's roll after a voyage. No one could look at the trees and the flowers and not know that this is their peak.

The air is humid and sweet, and the green of the grass is the brightest it has been all day. Christine feels suddenly dizzy. She's sure she can get away with a glass of white wine, but a few of the guests seem less certain, and before they move on to the lemon tarragon chicken and spinach salad, their glances stray accusingly toward her glass. John helps Stevie fill his plate. Christine sees Robert walking across the lawn toward the studio. There is something she wants to tell him: the reason she'd stopped at that barn sale was that they were selling a work sink she knew would be perfect for the studio. Maybe if the sink is still there, Robert could drive by and look at it.

Inside the studio, Robert leans against a sawhorse, slowly smoking a joint. He holds it out to Christine, and though she knows it is madness getting stoned at your wedding, with all its social obligations, and probably terrible for the baby, she takes it, takes a drag. Soon she feels uncomfortable standing, looks around for something to lean on, and nearly backs into the table saw before Robert points and yells, "Yo!"

"That's all I need," says Christine. "A little something to match the dog tooth marks in my leg."

"It's strange about weddings," says Robert. "I've noticed. People tend to get seriously accident-prone. One of my brothers got married with his arm in a sling, and a cousin got married in a neck brace."

"At the same time?" asks Christine. "What happened?"

"Different times." Robert laughs. "I don't know. My brother was hunting, fell out of a tree. The cousin I think was in a car wreck. How's your leg?"

"Fine," Christine says, and then for some reason says, "Really? Really, it hurts."

Robert says, "I'll take a look at it for you." His voice has in it an unmistakable flirty edge, and Christine is pleasantly shocked, not so much by the sexual suggestion — which he can only make because he is younger and working for her and this is her wedding day and nothing can possibly come of it — as by the intimacy of his daring to joke about so serious a subject as her dog bite. In some ways it presumes more, makes some bolder claim than John's unfailing solicitousness, and by distracting her, works better to reassure her and dull the pain. She fears that Robert will ask what happened exactly and that she'll get halfway through the story and stop. But what he says is, "Was that the barn sale out on 7, a couple houses past the Carvel?"

"That's the one," Christine says.

"I stopped there," says Robert. "Believe it or not. They were selling a work sink — big slabs of bluestone, copper fixtures, enormous, you could see it from the road. It will be great for this place. It was only a hundred and twenty-five bucks. If you guys don't want to pay for it, we can call it a wedding present from me. This must have been after you were there. There was no sign of a dog. I'm going back with some friends this week to help load it onto the pickup . . ."

Robert rattles on, clearly worried about spending John's money, and so doesn't see Christine's eyes fill with tears. One thing she'd thought as she stopped at the sale was how good the sink would look in the studio, and the other — she knew this and blamed herself at the moment the dog ran toward her and even thought this was *why* she was getting bitten — was the pleasure of telling Robert she'd found it; they had been talking a lot about sinks. This is another part of the story she's told no one. She feels as if she has been caught in some dreadful O. Henry plot, some "Gift of the Magi" sort of thing, except that couple were newlyweds and in it together and on their way up. The implications of this happening to her and Robert are in every way less simple.

All week, she has been saying that she fears the finishing of the studio because it means she must start working again. But that, she realizes now, isn't the reason at all. She feels as if just telling Robert that she too stopped for the sink would add up to more than it is, to some sort of declaration, an irrevocable act — though most likely he would just see it as your ordinary, everyday be-lieve-it-or-not.

"Thank you," she says. Even this comes out more heartfelt than she'd planned. She is so uncertain of what to say next that she's almost relieved when Annette walks in.

"What a space!" Annette says. "God, I could fit my whole loft in that corner."

"Robert built most of it," Christine says and is instantly sorry. Annette wheels on Robert with that fleeting but intense curios-ity — part affected, part sincere — that art-world people seem to have for anyone who actually does anything. As Annette looks at Robert, Christine wishes she'd given her the lightning studio tour, once around and out the door — she might not have even *seen* him. But isn't this what Christine wants, some version of the ap-preciation she desires when Annette comes to look at her work?

Robert looks directly at Annette and smiles. Annette gives him her three-second downtown grin, but so good-humoredly and with such invitation that a familiar wave of jealousy, loneliness, and embarrassment overcomes Christine. But why should she feel that way now? She, after all, is the bride. Her being the bride is probably why Robert sees no disloyalty in turning so easily from her to Annette.

"How *are* you?" Annette asks Christine, meaning — it's clear from her tone — the pregnancy, not the bite. She's trying hard to focus, to not let her sudden interest in Robert make her exclude Christine. But she is only making things worse, making Christine feel damaged, out of the running, like some guy with a war wound in a Hemingway novel.

"All right," Christine says. "The dog bite didn't help."

"God," Annette says. "I just remembered. That's what happened to Jo-Jo the Dog Boy's mother. She got bitten by a dog when she was pregnant. Remember Jo-Jo the Dog Boy?"

"I sure do," Robert says. "Poor guy. The real-life Chewy-Chewbacca." Both he and Annette seem pleased to have found this bit of trivia knowledge in common.

"Great," says Christine. "Thanks a lot. That's just what I need to hear."

"Chris*tine,*" says Annette. "No one believes that stuff anymore."

"What are we talking about?" Robert says. The fact of Christine's pregnancy seems to have just dawned on him. "Double congratulations!" he says. "I wondered why you guys would bother getting married after all this time." He can't resist looking at Christine's belly. That he feels free to do this — and that he hadn't known, though she'd assumed that everyone knew — reminds Christine of what it's like to be pregnant: a secret for so long, and even when it is obvious, still a secret — all those secret shifts and movements no one else can feel. Suddenly she is stung with envy, though not of Robert and Annette or their lives — which, she tells herself, lack everything she treasures most about her own life. It is something else entirely. She feels that her life is closing down; it has always been closed down.

It takes a while for the audio to come back. When it does, Annette is saying, "People say dogs are smart. It's something people say. People who never had dogs. I say, compared to what? Cats?

In my experience dogs are very, very dumb. When I was growing up in Anchorage, the family across from us had a dog team they'd let pull the kids down the hill in front of their house, and one day the dogs pulled the sled and three kids right in the path of a snowplow. Brilliant."

"Jesus," Robert says. And a moment later, "You grew up in Anchorage?"

"Some dogs are smart," says Christine. "Alexander."

"Well," says Annette. "Alexander. Christine's dog."

"What kind of dog was he?" Robert asks.

"A romantic," Annette says.

Robert looks quizzically at Christine. And now there is no way for Christine not to say it, not to tell the story she has been thinking about all day: "Alexander fell in love. With a female collie down in Sheffield. He met her when we left him there with friends, one weekend we went away. The female lived up the road from our friends. She was in heat when we picked Alexander up, so we took her home with us, but she kept running away. So we brought her back to Sheffield and the next day Alexander disappeared. He'd never run away before. We thought he was dead. And two days later our friends called to say he'd showed up at the collie family's house."

"Sheffield's fifteen miles away," Robert says.

"Fourteen point five," Christine says. "We clocked it." She remembers watching the odometer on John's pickup, proud of their dog and jubilant that he was not only alive but in love. How eager they had been to fuse their lives then, for Stevie to be John's child, Alexander to be Christine's dog. But Alexander was never really — as Annette just called him — Christine's dog. She still misses him, but it is John who took him to the vet when she was down in the city, John who, without ever saying much, has grieved.

She remembers the night they went to get Alexander from the collie family: the family lived in a tiny house, a cabin, the dogs were inside, stuck together, everyone was laughing, jumping out of their way, it was impossible to talk, but even so it seemed wrong to separate them. They left Alexander there until the female went out of heat and he was ready to come home.

Robert and Annette are waiting for more, but Christine has nothing to say. She is sorry she told the story. She thinks she has told it at the wrong time, to the wrong people, for entirely the wrong reasons, and for a moment it seems likely that she will never tell it again. And what good can come from telling a story about a dog that was more capable of passion than its owners may ever be? She gives Annette and Robert a little wave. Then she goes outside.

The light is almost gone. The guests have finished their food and are sitting at the tables, talking quietly. On each table is a lighted candle inside a paper bag. The muted lights are at once festive and unbearably sad. Christine looks around for Stevie, whom — after a scary minute or two — she spots in the field behind the house. She had been searching for the white suit, but Stevie has changed his outfit. He has borrowed someone's black silk jacket with a map of Guam on the back; it comes nearly down to his knees. On his head is an enormous set of stereo headphones, and instead of shoes he wears his winter moon-boots, silver Mylar that catches the light, thick soles that raise him inches off the ground. He is stalking fireflies in the high grass, lifting his legs very high, like a deer.

Christine is watching so intently that she jumps when John comes up beside her. They stand in easy silence for a few moments and then John says, "It doesn't feel different, does it? Being married. It feels exactly the same."

At first Christine doesn't answer, but keeps on watching Stevie, who is moving his head oddly, again like a deer, as if he is tracking fireflies not by looking for light but by listening.

John's face, in silhouette, strains forward. Staring across the dark lawn, he is trying very deliberately not to seem as if he is waiting for her to reply.

"It's fine," Christine tells him. "Nothing's changed. We've always been married," she says.

JOHN UPDIKE

A Sandstone Farmhouse

FROM THE NEW YORKER

JOEY'S FIRST GLIMPSE of the house was cloudy in his memory, like an old photo mottled by mildew. During the Second World War, his family owned no car, and renting one, for their infrequent excursions out of the compact brick city where his father worked, embarrassed the twelve-year-old boy to the point that he didn't see clearly through the windows, or was not conscious of much beyond his internal struggle not to be carsick. He fought the swaying, jiggling motion, which was mixed with the warm confluent smells of rubber floor mat and petroleum combustion, and the patient pale veiny look of his father's hand on the gearshift knob. Farm country, miles of it, poured past. Depressing, monotonous fields moved up and down beneath their hazy burden of crops. A winding asphalt highway climbed a hill, passed a lumpy stone church, then settled into a flat stretch where they slowed to turn left down a dirt washboard road that shook the car sickeningly. Not a building in sight. No sign of civilization but telephone poles carrying a single wire. Another turn, right this time, down an even smaller dirt road, and they stopped, and in the sudden flood of fresh air as Joey opened the car door, the green of the grass rose waxy and bright to greet his giddiness, his nausea. In his cloudy memory, they went up to the house and there were people in it, farm people, wearing cotton and thick muddy shoes, shyly trying to get out of their way, like animals. There was a front porch, he remembered that much. With a banister upheld by boards jigsawed into an ornamental shape, and a secret space underneath, of weeds and pebbly dirt. A space where chickens could scratch and dogs could lie and pant during hot weather, the kind of space that is friendly and inviting to a boy of the age he was just outgrowing.

By the time they had bought the house with its surrounding eighty acres and moved in, he was thirteen, and the front porch had vanished, leaving a space between the front of the house and the cement walk where they eventually planted crocuses and tulips and erected a grape arbor. Joey as an adult could not remember how or when it had happened, their tearing down the rotten old porch. Pieces of it remained in the barn — segments of banister with the ornamental balusters cut of inch-thick pine. Once he even took a baluster home with him, back to New York City, as some kind of memento, or sample of folk art. The pattern held a circle in the center, a circle with a hole, between two shapes jigsawed into the wood, one like an arrow and one like a fish. Different-colored flakes fell dryly from it, brittle layers of old-time lead paint. The object, not quite of art, rested sideways on the black marble mantel of his apartment for a while, then found its way to the back of a closet, with broken squash rackets and college textbooks and table lamps that might someday be made to glow again. Like his mother, he had trouble throwing anything away.

If he and his father and grandfather had torn the porch down themselves, he would have remembered so heroic a labor, as he did the smashing of the lath-and-plaster partition that separated the two small parlors downstairs, making one big living room, or the tearing out of the big stone kitchen fireplace and its chimney, right up into the attic. Joey remembered swinging the great stones out the attic window, he and his grandfather pushing, trying not to pinch their fingers, while his father, his face white with the effort, held the rope of a makeshift pulley rigged over a rafter. Once clear of the sill, the heavy stones fell with a ghostly slowness, seen from above, and accumulated into a kind of mountain it became Joey's summer job to clear away. He learned a valuable lesson, that first summer on the farm, while he turned fourteen: even if you manage to wrestle only one stone into the wheelbarrow and sweatily, staggeringly trundle it down to the swampy area this side of the springhouse, eventually the entire mountain will be taken away. On the same principle, an invisible giant, removing only one day at a time, will eventually dispose of an entire life.

When, over forty years later, his mother died, and the at last uninhabited house yielded up its long-buried treasures, he came upon a photograph of her at the age of ten, posing in front of the porch. Someone in pencil, in a flowing handwriting not his mother's — hers was tiny, and cramped, and back-slanted — had marked on the back "Taken August 1914. Enlarged August 1917." Someone had loved this snapshot enough to have it enlarged and mounted on thick gray cardboard: who?

His mother, wearing a low-waisted dress, dark stockings, and black shoes with big, thick heels, her hair done up in a long braid that hangs over one shoulder, is holding the collar of a young medium-sized dog, part collie. Both the child and the dog are looking straight into the camera with similar half-smiles and wide-spaced, trusting eyes. They are standing on a cement walk that is still there, uncracked; behind them the porch balusters repeat their simple artful pattern and a small rosebush blooms. The long-dead dog, the recently dead human female look identically happy. Joey would hardly have recognized his mother but for the thick abundance of her hair — a chestless cheerful little girl in old woman's shoes. Beyond the edge of the barn to her right, ghostly in the enlargement, are fences and trees of which no trace remains and, just barely visible, an entire building that has vanished — a tobacco shed, perhaps. The lawn is edged around the walk, and the fences look trim. This was the private paradise, then, to which she attempted to return, buying back the old sandstone farmhouse that her parents, feeling full enough of tobacco profits to retire, had sold while she was innocently off at normal school. Precocious, she had been skipped, and was sent off at the age of twelve, and hated it, hated it all, including the hour-long trolley ride to Kutztown. The swaying, the ozone, the drunk men who sat down beside her made her sick.

She loved the old house; she loved the *idea* of it. For most of her life, except for the twenty years of exile in her young womanhood, when she went to normal school, then to college, and married a man she met there, and traveled with him until the Depression cost him his traveling job, and bore him a son, in the heart of the Depression, while they were all living with her parents in the brick city house — except for these twenty years, she happily inhabited an idea. The sandstone house was built, her fond research discovered, in 1812. In that era, teams of masons and stonelayers roamed the countryside, erecting these Pennsylvania farmhouses on principles of an elegant simplicity. Their ground plan was square, set square to the compass. The south face basked in the maximum of sunshine; the east windows framed the sunrise, and the west the sunset. The cornerstones were cut at a slightly acute angle, to emphasize the edge. The stout scaffolding was rooted in holes in the thirty-inch walls as they rose, and these holes were plugged with stones four inches square as the masonry was pointed, and the scaffolding dismantled, from the top down. In the mortar, lime from the lime kiln was mixed with sand from creek beds, to match the stones. Though the size of the stones raised and fitted into place was prodigious, the real feats of leverage occurred in the quarrying. Sandstone exposed in an outcropping was rendered useless by weather, but underneath the earth the sound stone slept, to be painstakingly split by star drills and wedges and "feathers" of steel, and then hauled out by teams of horses, on wagons or sleds. Sometimes the wagons shattered under the load of a single great stone. But this vast hauling and lifting continued, a tidal movement like that of the glaciers which here and there had deposited huge moraines, acres frightening in their sheer stoniness, in the middle of the forests — heaped-up depths of boulders in which no tree could take root, barren geological deposits fascinating and bewildering to nineteenth-century minds, so eager to see God's hand everywhere.

For sensitive, asthmatic Joey, removed from a brick semidetached city house where he had felt snug, where he could hear through his bedroom walls the neighbors stirring as he awoke, and the milk being delivered on the porch, and the trolley cars clanging at the corner a block away, the silent thickness of stones just behind the old plaster and wallpaper, and the rough hearths and fireplaces visible within the country house, seemed to harbor nature's damp and cold. A sullen held breath dwelled in the walls. The summer's heat brought swarms of wasps, millipedes, carpenter ants, and silverfish out from the crannies. That first winter in the house, before an oil furnace was installed in the basement, a kerosene-burning stove in the living room provided the only heat. Joey remembered the stove clearly; it was painted chocolate brown, and stood on little bent legs on an asbestos sheet papered with imitation wood grain. He spent days huddled in blankets next to this stove, on a grease-spotted sofa that had been brought close. With his constant cold, he missed days of school, and hated to, for it was warm at school, and there was running water, and flush toilets. And girls in long pleated skirts and fuzzy sweaters and bobby socks, who belonged to the modern era, to civilization. He clung to civilization by reading; huddled in the brown stove's aura of coal oil, he read anything — P. G. Wode-house, Ellery Queen, John Dickson Carr, Thorne Smith — that savored of cities and took him out of this damp, cold little stone house.

His mother remembered that first winter with rueful pleasure, as a set of tribulations blithely overcome. "It was really very hard, I suppose, on everybody — you were *so* sick, and your father had to struggle so to get to work in that old Chevrolet that was all we could afford, and for my parents it was a terrible defeat, to come back to the farm when they had gotten away; they would hide together in the corner just like children — but I was so happy to be here I hardly noticed. The movers had broken the large pane of glass in the front door, and for some reason that whole first winter we never managed to replace it; we lived with a sheet of cardboard wedged over the hole. It's incredible that we sur-vived." And she would laugh gaily, remembering. "We tried to light fires in the living-room fireplace, but all the wood the Schel-lenbargers had left us in the basement was moldy elm, and that fireplace never did draw well, even when the swifts' nests weren't plugging it up. Smoke leaks out into the room, I've never under-stood why. If you look up the flue with a flashlight, the stone-work has a twist."

Joey seemed to remember, though, waking upstairs and put-ting his feet onto the bare wood floor and grabbing his school clothes and hurrying in his pajamas down the narrow stairs — the treads worn in two troughs by generations of footsteps, the nailheads protruding and shiny and dangerous — to dress in front of the fireplace, where logs were crackling. The freezing upstairs air would lick at his skin like flame, like the endless conversations between his mother and her parents, incessant flowing exchanges that would ripple into quarrel and chuckle back again into calm while he focused, when he was home, into the pages of his book. His grandfather had a beautiful, patient, elocutionary voice; his grandmother spoke little, in guttural responses. His mother, unlike most adults, hadn't parted from her parents, and clung to them with old tales and grievances, like someone adding up the same set of figures day after day and always expecting a different answer. As Joey huddled by the stove, heated conversations were in his ears as the smell of coal oil was in his nostrils, but always, those five years (only five!) that he lived in the sandstone house with four adults, his attention was aimed elsewhere — on schoolwork, on the future. He tried to ignore what was around him. The house, even when plumbing and central heating and a telephone were installed, and new wallpaper made the repainted rooms pretty, embarrassed him.

He was never more embarrassed than in that summer before they moved in, before they owned even the erratic old Chevrolet. Several times, his mother made him travel with her by bus out to the farm they already owned. She had a vision of a windbreak of pines rimming the big field, along the road, and she and Joey carried seedlings in boxes, and shovels, and pruners, and a watering can — all this humiliating apparatus dragged onto a city bus by a red-faced middle-aged woman and a skinny boy with ears that stuck out and dungarees that were too short. His mother wore a checked shirt like a man's and a straw sun hat and a pair of light-blue overalls with a bib; she looked like a farmer in a Hollywood musical comedy. There was no space inside the bus for the shovels; the driver had to store them in the luggage compartment and then stop and get out in the middle of nowhere to hand the tools over. It was a relief when the bus, headed south toward Washington, D.C., disappeared around a bend in the highway.

Joey and his mother walked down the dirt washboard road in the heat, carrying their equipment. He had never been so humiliated, so ridiculous, and vowed never to be again. He couldn't blame his mother, he still needed her too much, so he blamed the place — its hazy, buggy fields, its clouds of blowing pollen that made him sneeze and his eyes water, its little sandstone house like a cube of brown sugar melting in the heat, in a little dip of hillside beneath an overgrown, half-dead apple orchard. All through noon and into the afternoon they cleared little spaces at the edge of the field, where the Schellenbargers' last crop of field corn was pushing up in limp green rows, and cut away burdock and poison ivy and honeysuckle, and dug holes, and set in each hole a little six-inch puff of pine tree, and sprinkled water over the socket of sandy red earth. Moving a few paces farther on to plant the next tree, Joey could no longer see the last one amid the weeds and wild grass. The work seemed hopeless. Yet when the afternoon breeze came up, he felt a purity of silence — perhaps one car an hour passed, the people staring at this woman and boy in clothes neither country nor city — that didn't exist in his beloved street of semidetached houses. And there was a kind of heroism to his periodic trudge, with the empty sprinkling can, the half-mile along the edge of the cornfields to the empty house, with its rusty iron pump on the back porch, and then the long haul back, the sloshing can as heavy as a stone.

He felt heroic to himself. Space for heroism existed out here. He was determined to impress his mother — to win her back, since here on this farm he for the first time encountered something she apparently loved as much as she loved him.

At last, the weeds threw feathery long shadows upon one another and the tiny pines were all planted in the hopeless roadside jungle and it was time to walk back up the dusty washboard road to wait for the bus from Washington to round the corner. Having gone and come so far, the bus could be as much as an hour late, and their eyes would sting, staring down the gray highway for it, and his stomach would sink at the thought that they had missed it and were stranded. But not even this possibility daunted him, for he had forged a mood of defiant collusion in which he was numbed to humiliation and played a role both stoic and comic, costarring with his heavy mother in her straw sun hat and his lanky, sharp-faced sidekicks, the clippers and the shovel. Years later, he could even laugh with her about it, those awkward hot trips to plant a line of trees most of which never thrived, choked by thistles and bindweed or severed by a too zealous mower. Yet a few of the pines, perhaps six or seven, did live to tower along the road bank — shaggy-headed apparitions taller than a ship's mast, swaying in the wind. By this time, the dirt road was macadamized and hummed with traffic, and the bus route to Washington had long ago been abandoned as unprofitable.

Five years after the September when they had moved, Joey went to college and, essentially, never returned. He married in his senior year, and after graduation moved to New York City. Another of his mother's visions, along with that of the farm as paradise, was of him as a poet; he fulfilled this heroic task as best he could, by going to work for an ad agency and devoting himself to the search for the arresting phrase and image, on the edge of the indecent, that incites people to buy — that gives them permission, from the mythic world above, to buy. The business was like poetry in that you needed only a few lucky hits, and he had his share, and couldn't complain. He never again had to get on a bus with a shovel.

The numbers attached to the years and decades slowly changed, and with them the numbers in his bank account and on his apartment building. His first marriage took place in three different apartments, his turbulent second in four, his short-lived third in only one, and now he wondered if women had not quite been his thing all along. He had always felt most at ease, come to think of it, in the company of men, especially those who reminded him of his father. But it was the AIDS-conscious eighties by then, and his hair had passed through gray into virtual white, and he found the personalities of young men an effective barrier to thinking about their bodies, and he was content to share his life with his books, his CDs (compact disks, certificates of deposit), his modest little art collection mixed of watery commercialism and icy minimalism. On the other side of the white walls of his apartment he could hear the mumble and thump of his neighbors, and he liked that. He was home.

Three hours away, his widowed mother lived alone in the sandstone house. Joey had been the first to depart, and then a few years later his grandfather died, suddenly, with a stroke like a thunderclap, and then, after a bedridden year, his grandmother. This created an extra room upstairs, so Joey and his first wife and young children, when they came to visit in the sixties, no longer had to camp out downstairs, on cots and the sofa spotted by the peanut-butter crackers he used to eat when sick and consigned to reading the days away. The upstairs had two real bedrooms, to which the doors could be closed, and a kind of hall-way beside the head of the stairs where he had slept for five years, listening to the four adults rustle and snore and creak while girls and prayers and the beginnings of poems all ran together in his brain. His grandfather, on his way downstairs in the early morn-ing, would ruffle the hair on the sleeping boy's head, and the gathering sounds of family breakfast, as Joey's grandmother and parents followed, would rise under him with the smell of toast, a doughy warmth of life rising beneath the cold bare floorboards.

There was a fourth room, a small room in the northwest cor-ner, where his mother had once been born, in a long agony of labor — a rural calvary, as Joey imagined it, with flickering lamps and steaming kettles and ministering cousins arriving by horse and buggy — that shaped her relations with her own mother into, it seemed, a ferocious apology, a futile undying adhesion in an attempt to make amends. She nursed her mother in the old woman's long paralyzed agony of dying, but not always patiently, or tenderly, and when the ordeal at last was over she was left with additional cause for self-blame, more sorry images. "I spent my whole life," she concluded, "trying to please my mother, and never did."

Joey would ask, irritated by these pat surges of self-dramatiza-tion, "Did she ever say so?"

"No, but you knew her. She never said anything."

"Unlike *my* mother," he said, with an ironic pretense of gal-lantry.

She heard the irony. "Yes, I inherited Pop's gift of gab," she said. "It's been a curse, really. If you talk enough, you don't feel you have to *do* anything."

This fourth room had become the bathroom, with a tub but no shower, a basin but no cabinet. Toothpaste, sun lotion, hand creams, razors, dental floss, slivers of soap thriftily stuck together all accumulated on the deep sill overlooking the blackening shin-gles of the back-porch roof. After his father died, in the early seventies, the house gradually lost the power to purge itself of accumulation. Their occupancy, which had begun with removal of the porch and the chimney stones, now silted the attic and cel-lar and windowsills full with souvenirs of his mother's lengthen-ing residence. On the theory that it would save the wild birds from being eaten, she had fed a stray cat that came to the back porch;

this cat then became several, and the several became as many as forty. The kitchen became choked with stacked cases of cat food, and a site in the woods, at the end of a path overgrown with raspberry canes, became a mountain of empty cat-food cans. Tin Mountain, Joey's children called it. Magazines and junk mail and church pamphlets sat around on tables and chairs waiting to be bundled and taken to the barn, to wait there for the Boy Scouts' next paper drive. Photographs of Joey and his children, Christmas cards and valentines from relations and neighbors, piled up on available spaces like a kind of moss. Even the table where his mother ate had room eventually for only one plate and cup and saucer, her own. The house was clogging up, Joey felt, much as her heart — coronary angiography had revealed — was plugging with arteriosclerosis, and her weakly pumped lungs were filling with water.

His arrivals, as the years went on, seemed to accumulate. He would park his car by the barn and pick his way across the line of steppingstones that in the decades since they were laid (even Granny, stiff and bent over, helping with the crowbar) had been silted over by the sandy soil and its crabgrass. On the back porch there would be a puddle of cats and kittens mewing to be fed. Entering the back door with his suitcase was like stepping into a quicksand smelling of cat food and damp cardboard. His mother saved, in separate sections of the floor, the plastic bags the supermarket bagged her groceries in, and slippery stacks of mail-order catalogues, and a bucketful of maddeningly snarled baling twine, to make bundles for the barn with. He recognized in this accumulation a superstition he had to fight within himself — the belief that everything has value. The birds in the trees, the sunflower at the edge of the orchard, the clumsily pasted-up valentine received years ago from a distant grandchild — all have a worth that might at any moment be called into account. It was a way of saying that one's own life was infinitely precious.

There would be a peck of a kiss at the door, and he would carry the suitcase upstairs, past the whirling, nipping mongrel bitch, who was thrilled to have a man in the house. The guest room had been his parents' old room. When she became a widow, his mother had moved into her parents' old room, closer to the room in which she had been born. The move was part, Joey felt, of an obscure religious system that had nothing to do with Christianity. He remembered how, in a surprising rite of that system, his parents, the day after his grandmother died, took her stained, urine-soaked mattress outdoors and burned it, down near the stones he had dumped, darkening the sky all morning with the smoke.

Here, in this guest room, at night, without a wife to distract and comfort him, he would begin to fight for his breath. The bed sagged so that his back hurt. The pillow felt heavy and dense. The sandstone hearth of the never-used fireplace in the room would emit an outdoor dampness. Birds and bats and mice would stir in the porous walls, and his mother's motions would make her bed beyond the thin wall creak. Was she awake, or asleep? He could relax deeply only in the early morning, when the dog would wake her, scrabbling on the bare boards with her claws, and the two of them would slowly, noisily head downstairs, and the can opener would rhythmically begin to chew through the first installment of cat-food cans.

The guest room for some reason had no curtains; in the dead of the night the moon burned on the wide sills as if calling to him, calling him back to a phase his whole adult life had been an effort to obliterate. The asthma, the effect of inner tightening and complication, wasn't so bad, usually, the first two nights; he might manage five or six hours of sleep each if he could then get away, back to cozy, salubrious New York. But on long holiday weekends he would struggle through the whole third night with the accumulated house dust and pollen in his lungs, and the damp hard pillow, and the obdurate moonlight, so accusatory in its white silence.

He was aware of his mother and himself, lying each in bed, as survivors of the larger party that had once occupied this house. It was as if, on a snowy pass, they had killed and eaten the others, and now one of the two remaining must perish next. She, too, in her eighties, had breathing problems, and slept with her head up on two pillows. One night she woke him with the soft words, "Joey. I'm not doing so well. Put on your daddy's old overcoat and come downstairs with me."

He was awake, his head clear as moonlight, in an instant. "Shall we call the hospital?"

"No, I just need to sit up. You know which overcoat, it hangs at the foot of the stairs."

It had hung there for years, one of those curious comforting rags his father would acquire in thrift shops or outlet stores. Joey had often seen it on him, in the last year of the old man's life, when his legs turned white and phlebitic and his nose turned blue with poor circulation and his eyes sank deeper and deeper into his head and his deafness worsened. But to the end his father had held his head high, and took a lively interest in the world. Once a social-science teacher, he continued to read fat history books, and wrote Joey, in one of his rare letters, in his patient, legible schoolteacher's hand, that being deaf made it easier for him to concentrate.

Joey wondered why his mother was being so insistent about the coat, but obediently put it on. It had a fuzziness unusual in dark overcoats, and was big for him, since his father had been bigger than he. She was right; once it was on, over his pajamas, he became a child again, and calm, and trusting. They went downstairs and turned up the thermostat and sat in the dark living room together, he on the sofa and she in her television-watching chair, and he watched her struggle for breath, in little sudden shuddering gasps like the desperate heaves of a bird caught in the chimney.

"Do you hurt?" he asked.

She had little breath for speaking, and shook her head no, and her head underwent again the convulsion, as if trying to keep above water. "It's like," she gasped, "a squeezing."

"Sure you wouldn't like to drive to the hospital?"

A vigorous headshake again. "What can they do, but torture you?"

So he sat there, in his father's overcoat, fighting sleepiness, wondering if his mother would die before his eyes. The dog, agitated at first by this predawn rising, wheezed and resettled on the floor. The moonlight weakened on the sills across the room, with their potted geraniums and violets and a night-blooming cereus that had been allowed to grow grotesquely long, so that its stem filled the window. His mother's shudders lessened, and eventually she told him to go upstairs, she would sit here a while longer. In her old age she had become almost grafted onto this chair of hers. On a previous visit, she had shocked him by refusing, when the evening run of television comedies that she faithfully watched was over, to come upstairs at all; morning found her still sitting there, in her clothes. This irritated him, along with her television watching. "Why do you watch all these idiots?" he once asked her. "They seem realer to you than I am."

She did not deny it. "Well," she had answered, "they're always here."

Now, her crisis past, he accepted her dismissal gratefully and yet reluctantly. He went upstairs feeling that this hour had been the most purely companionable he had ever spent with her in this house. To Joey in his father's fuzzy, overlarge coat, as he silently watched his mother struggle and the dog stir and doze and the night-blooming cereus cast its gawky shadow in the deep window recess beyond the tasseled bridge lamp and the upright piano, it had been like one of those scenes we witness in childhood, from under the table or over the edge of the crib, understanding nothing except that large forces are moving around us — that there is a heavy dynamism from which we are, as children, sheltered.

When she had her next attack of breathlessness, he was not there, and she called the neighbors, and they called the township ambulance, which came at five in the morning. For all her talk of "torture," she seemed to settle gratefully into the hospital's ministrations. "They said I was quite blue, the oxygen in my blood was down to nothing." Rather gaily, she described the emergency-room doctors thrusting some violent sucking instrument down her throat and into her lungs.

Her bathrobe was turquoise with a maroon hem; she ordered her clothes from catalogues now and was attracted to decisive colors. With her white hair all about her on the pillow, and the baby-blue tubes of oxygen making a mustache, and the identification bracelet looped on her wrist, she looked festive and hectic and feminized. All day, young men in antiseptic garb came and tended to her, cutting her toenails, interrogating her bowels. Her bowels, to Joey's embarrassment, had become a topic of supreme fascination to her. Her insides in general were brought uncomfortably close to the surface by the wearing away of her body. His father's method of coping with what seemed to Joey her unaccountable whims, including moving them all to the farm, had been to say, "She's a femme. Your mother's a real femme. What can you do?" He would shrug, and sometimes add, "I should have put her on the burleycue stage."

This had seemed one of the man's lofty, pained jokes; but now

her femininity, which Joey's father and succession of wives had
shielded him from, was upon him. In her slightly disheveled, re-
vealing gowns, in her gracefully accepted helplessness and fragility, in this atmosphere of frank bodily event, his mother had
her sex on her mind. She told him, remembering the first years
of her marriage in Pittsburgh, "There was this young doctor, Dr.
Langhorne over on Sixth Street, who when I went to him with
these pains on my chest I couldn't understand told me to take off
my clothes. Well, I trusted him, and did, and he looked me over
for the longest time, and then told me, 'You're not obese.' That
was all he said."

His own birth, her conviction that she couldn't do such a normal thing as conceive and bear a child, recurred in her self-ac-
counting; old Dr. Berthoff, who kept brusquely calming her fears,
who treated her as a normal woman and not as the monstrous
product of her own mother's agony, emerged as a kind of erotic
hero, and Joey suddenly saw that his own self, which he had
imagined she cherished for qualities all his own, was lovable to
her above all as a piece of her body, as a living proof of her womanhood.

And she recalled, of those straitened Depression days when he
was an infant, how she left him in the care of his grandparents
and went off on the trolley car to work in the drapes department
of the department store downtown. She had lost a tooth, a bicus-
pid, and the upper partial plate containing its replacement was
uncomfortable, and one day she didn't wear it to work and was
chastised by the department manager, Mr. Wirtheimer, for not
wearing it. The image of her missing tooth, this tidy black hole
leaping up within her young woman's smile, seemed erotic, too,
along with the thought of his then-slender mother's charm as a
saleswoman. "On my good days," she said, "I could sell anything.
But then the people would bring it all back for exchange on
Monday. As if I had bewitched them. Mr. Wirtheimer said there
was such a thing as being *too* good."

But not all her days were good days, she told Joey. She took
her periods too hard, they knocked her flat for thirty-six, forty-
eight hours; and this brought the conversation back to her body,
her body arching over his life like a firmament, and he would
leave the hospital building and find relief in the reality of the

city, Alton, with its close-packed suburbs, which he loved as his
mother loved her farm, because it had formed his first impressions, when the wax was soft. He ate at aluminum diners, shopped
at hardware stores for parts and tools the sandstone farmhouse
in its long decrepitude needed, and bought a new vacuum cleaner,
since his mother's old Hoover had hardly been used for years.
He even got himself a haircut in a front-parlor barbershop —
the kind of shop, with a radio playing and a baby crying in rooms
out of sight, and a spiral pole out front, that he thought had disappeared, because such shops had disappeared in New York. A
small child of his, years ago, had knocked the porcelain lid off
the toilet water tank and it had shattered. Now, between visits to
his mother, he went about the city with the cardboard box of
fragments, dusty and cobweb-ridden after years in the attic, to
plumbing-supply houses, where overweight, hard-smoking, not
quite sardonic men would return from digging in their cavern-
ous storerooms and give him, free, old spare lids that did not, it
would turn out, quite fit. He kept trying. Alton had lost factories
and population since he was a boy, and appeared in smaller letters on the maps of Pennsylvania, but it was still a place where
things were made and handled, where brute matter got its honest due, and he recognized as still alive in himself the city's blue-
collar faith in hardware and industry and repair, a humble faith
that had survived all his heady traffic in imagery.

Life was a series of plumbing problems. After a week, the hospital had cleared out his mother's lungs, and now the cardiolo-
gists wanted to operate on the malfunctioning heart that had let
the pulmonary edema occur. The angiography had revealed coronary arteries stenosed almost shut. "Oh, Joey — I could go any
day," she blurted to him after the test results had been described
to her. She showed him with a forefinger and thumb how small
the lumen had become. "Worse than they thought." She was sitting on the bed with her hair wild and one shoulder bared by a
loose tie in the hospital johnny, and her facial expression was
girlish, womanhood's acquired composure all dissolved. Their
intermittently shared life was being lifted into new octaves, and
they seemed in these moments of hospital conference simply a
man and a woman, both with more white hairs than dark, taking
counsel because no one else who mattered was left. They were it.

To his relief, she did not want the open-heart operation, sparing him the trouble, the expense, the tests, the trips to Philadelphia. He tried to suppress his relief and to argue for the coronary bypass that was recommended. She said, making a wryly twisted mouth just as her father used to when discussing the county's politicians, "Of course *they* recommend it. It's what they have to sell. They're in business, just like their fathers, only peddling different things. They pass me around, one to another; I've yet to see a Christian."

In the frankness that her closeness to death allowed, as her composed womanhood melted, an anti-Semitism was one of the things that emerged, shockingly. She could not see the doctors as saviors and allies but only as opportunists and exploiters. She even developed with one solemn young cardiologist a banter that cast her as a Palestinian: "You've taken me away from my village," she said. Joey was dismayed; his third wife, the briefest one, had been Jewish, and she and his mother had seemed especially friendly, and as he imagined now his mother's suppressed feelings in those years it was like seeing silverfish tumble out of old books. On her less lucid days, she seemed to think that the doctors and their allies ("One big fella, looked just like Danny Thomas, came and cut my toenails; now how much do you think *that's* going to add to the bill?") were scheming to do her out of her house and its priceless eighty acres — that she was territory they wanted to seize and develop. Each day she spent in the hospital, the little sandstone house pulled at her harder. "Get me home," she begged Joey.

"And then want?"

"Then we'll take what comes." Her eyes widened, watching his, and her mouth as it clamped shut over "what comes" was very like a child's, stubborn in its fright. For, however close their consultation and their agreements, both were aware that she was the star and he merely the prompter: though his turn would come, the spotlight burned upon her.

When, six months later, she died — instantly, it seemed to the coroner — in the kitchen, just under the room where she had been born, the neighbors, who were patient Mennonites and Lutherans, took a day to find her and another twelve hours to find

him in at his apartment telephone number. It was midnight when
he let himself into the house. The door keys had been lost long
ago, in that distant, fabulous era after they had moved. When his
mother would be away for more than a day, she would lock the
doors from the inside and go out through the cellar bulkhead.
Her neighbors knew this and had left the house that way after
her body was removed. Joey had brought no flashlight; after
parking the car by the barn, he walked to the slanted cellar doors
by moonlight, and within the dark cellar was guided by memory.
A Lally column here, a pyramid of paint cans there. His father
and he had laid this cement floor one frantic long day when three
cubic yards of ready-mix concrete were delivered in a giant gob
by a truck. He would have been fifteen or so, his father in his late
forties. The cellar floor of these old farmhouses was typically dirt,
the red clay of the region packed more or less hard, except when
the foundation walls wept in the spring and it turned to mud. His
father had talked with construction men, and set out boards to
frame the platform for the furnace, and dug a clay pipe into the
dirt for drainage, and stretched strings here and there to determine the level and pitch, but none of these preparations encom-
passed the alarming dimensions of the slowly hardening concrete when it arrived early that Saturday morning. With rakes
and shovels and boards and trowels they pushed and tugged the
sluggish stuff level, into the far corners, around the furnace and
the mouth of the drainage pipe. His father's face went white with
effort, as it had when struggling with the chimney stones several
years before, and the ordeal went on and on, by the light of a few
bare bulbs, this panicky race with time and matter, as the concrete grew stiffer and stiffer, and in drying pushed its water toward
the surface, and exuded its sonorous underground smell, its
inexorable stony scent. The floor had come out surprisingly well,
out of that day's sweaty panic — smooth and gray and delicately
sloped so that hardly a puddle lingered after a flooding. It sometimes seemed, in the mottled perspectives of hindsight, that there
had been a third man in the cellar with them, something of a
professional, for it seemed unlikely that he and his father, a history teacher and a would-be poet, could have made such a satis-
factory cellar floor. But if there had been such a man, Joey had
mentally erased him, jealous of this arduous day at his father's

side fending off disaster, doing a man's job. He was just becoming a man, and his father was wearying of being one; this was the
last project so ambitious that he tackled around the house.

In the blackness, Joey's city shoes slithered on the smooth cement, and then thumped on the echoing wooden cellar stairs; he
pushed the door open into the moon-striped kitchen, and a warm
whimpering hairy body hurtled up against him, and he thought
that his mother had not died after all. But it was the dog, who
took his hand in her mouth and unstoppably whimpered and
whined as if telling him a long story, the story of her hours alone
in the house with her mistress, with the body, with her hunger
and bafflement.

Things work out. One of his former wives, who had remarried
into the Connecticut suburbs, agreed to take the dog. The cats a
man from the county Humane Society came and trapped and
carried away to be gassed, a few each day. Joey stacked the magazines and catalogues and Christmas cards and tied them with
baling twine from the bucket and carried them to the barn to be
trucked to a landfill. The Boy Scouts no longer collected paper
and bottles; nothing was precious anymore. As his family assembled, Joey impressed them with his efficiency, portioning out the
furniture and heirlooms among his children, his ex-wives, the local auctioneer, the junkman.

For himself he kept little but odd small items that reached back
into his boyhood in the brick house they moved to the farm
from — a brass tiger that sat on the piano there, when he still
took piano lessons, and a curved leather-backed brush he remembered his grandfather using on his black hightop shoes before setting off to the Lutheran church. He kept some of his father's college notebooks, preserved in the attic, penned in a more
rounded version of his legible schoolteacherish hand. A set of
Shakespeare, with limp red covers, of which the silverfish had
nibbled some pages into lace. His mother's sun hats — these were
hard to throw away, though none of the assembled females wanted
them. His daughters sorted through the clothes for him. He
couldn't bear to touch and sort the dresses hanging in the closet,
dozens of garments pressed together in an anthology of past
fashions, all the way back to a fox-trimmed spring coat whose
collar he remembered close to his face, its tingling black-tipped

red-brown hairs. In the toolhouse, where his father had left a pathetic legacy of rusty screws and nails neatly arranged in jars, and oily tools, half of them broken, mounted on pegboard, there were also antique implements worn like prehistoric artifacts: an ancient oblong pink whetstone pointed at either end and soapily warped by all its use, and an old-fashioned square hoe worn into a lopsided metal oval, its edges had struck so many stones. Such wear couldn't have occurred in the merely forty years they were here, but must have been the work of generations; these tools had traveled back and forth across the county, surviving many moves, to end in his impatient hands. They seemed sacred — runes no one else could decipher. He was the last of his line to have ever hoed a row of carrots or sharpened a scythe.

Relatives and neighbors spoke to him with a curious soft gravity, as if he were fragile in grief. He knew he and his mother were regarded as having been unusually, perhaps unnaturally close; when in fact between themselves the fear was that they were not close enough. Why grieve? She was old, in pain, worn-out. She was too frail in her last half-year to walk to the mailbox or lift a case of cat food or pull a clump of burdock: it was time; dying is the last favor we do the world, the last tax we pay. He cried only once, during the funeral, quite unexpectedly, having taken his seat at the head of his raggedly extended family, suddenly free, for the moment, of arrangements and decisions, and seeing an arm's reach away the gleaming cherry-wood casket he had picked out in the undertaker's satiny showroom three days before. The lustrous well-joined wood, soon to be buried; the sumptuous waste of it; and the image of his mother as he first remembered her, a young slim woman dressed in a navy-blue suit, with white at her throat, to go off to her job at the downtown department store, hurrying to catch the trolley car. She had once reminisced, "Oh, how you'd run, and if you just missed it, there wouldn't be another for twenty minutes, and you wanted to cry." She had laughed, remembering.

His tears came and kept coming, in a kind of triumph, a breakthrough, a torrent of empathy and pity for that lost young woman running past the row houses, under the horse-chestnut trees, running to catch the trolley, the world of the thirties shabby and solid around her, the porches, the blue midsummer hydrangeas, this tiny well-dressed figure in her diminishing pocket of time, her future unknown, her death, her farm, far from her mind. This was the mother, apparently, he had loved, the young woman living with him and others in a brick semidetached house, a part of the world, youthfully finding her way. During the war she worked in a parachute factory, wearing a bandanna on her head like the other women, plump like them by this time, merging with them and their chatter one lunch break when he, somehow, had bicycled to the side entrance to see her. She was not like them, the tough other women, he knew, but for the moment had blended with them, did a job alongside them, and this too renewed his tears, his naive pride in her then, when he was ten or eleven. She had tried to be a person, she had lived. There was something amazing, something immortal to him in the image of her running. He remembered, from their first years on the farm, a crisis with the roof; it was being reshingled by a team of Amishmen and they had left it partially open to the weather on the night of a thunderstorm. Crashes, flashes. Joey's parents and grandparents were all awake, and he, boy though he still was, was expected now to wake and help too; they rushed up and down the attic stairs with buckets, to save the plaster of the walls and ceilings below. There was a tarpaulin in the barn that might help; he found himself outdoors, in the downpour, and he had retained an image of his mother running across the lawn in a flash of lightning that caught the white of her legs. She would not have been much over forty, and was still athletic; perhaps his father was included in this unsteady glimpse; there was a hilarity to it all, a violent health. Working his way, after her death, through all the accumulated souvenirs of her life, Joey was fascinated by the college yearbooks that preserved her girlish image above a line or two of verse:

> She's blest with temper, whose unclouded ray
> Can make tomorrow cheerful as today.

Group photographs showed his mother as part of the hockey team, the hiking club. With a magnifying glass he studied her unsmiling, competitive face, with her hair in two balls at her ears and a headband over her bangs. Her face seemed slightly larger than the other girls', a childlike oval broadest at the brow, its defenses relatively unevolved. As he sat there beside the cherry casket crying, his former wives and adult children stealing nervous peeks at him, the young woman ran for the trolley car, her breath catching, her panting mixed with a sighing laughter at herself, and the image was as potent, as fertile, as a classic advertisement, which endlessly taps something deep and needy within us. The image of her running down the street, away from him, trailed like a comet's tail the maternal enactments of those misty years when he was a child — crayoning with him on the living-room floor, sewing him Halloween costumes in the shape of Disney creatures, having him lift what she called the "skirts" of the bushes in the lawn while she pushed the old reel mower under them — but from her point of view; he seemed to feel from within his mother's head the situation, herself and this small son, this defenseless gurgling hatched creature, and the tentative motions of her mind and instincts as she, as new to mothering as he was to being a child, explored the terrain between them. In the attic he had found a padded baby-blue scrapbook, conscientiously maintained, containing his first words, the date of his first crawl, and his hospital birth certificate imprinted with his inky day-old feet. The baths. The cod-liver oil. Trying to do the right thing, the normal thing, running toward her farm, her death. In his vision of her running she was bright and quick and small, like an animal in a trap. This was the mother he had loved, the mother before they moved, before she betrayed him with the farm and its sandstone house.

Ruthlessly, vengefully, weekend by weekend, he cleaned the place out — disconnecting the phone, giving the auctioneer the run of the attic, seeing the refrigerator and stove hauled off for a few dollars each, by a truck that got stuck in the muddy winter lawn. With his new vacuum cleaner Joey attacked the emptying rooms, sucking up the allergen-laden dust from the cracks between the floorboards, sweeping the walls and ceilings clean of their veils of cobwebs upon cobwebs. How satisfying this was, one room after another that he would not have to do again. Joey discovered that his mother had been far from alone in the house; while the cats mewed and milled outside on the porch, a tribe of mice, year after year, ancestors and descendants, had been fed sunflower seeds, whose accumulated stored husks burst forth by the bucketful from behind where the stained-pine corner cupboard had stood, and the back of the dishtowel drawer of the kitchen sink. He set traps for the mice. He set out d-Con, and the next weekend tossed their small stiff bodies, held gingerly by the tail, down into the swamp, where the rocks were, and the ashes of his grandmother's mattress.

The old house had curious small cabinets built into the stone thickness, and they disgorged packets of his father's index cards, riddled with anxious, harried reminder notes to himself, and pads of old high-school permission slips, and small boxes of dull pencils and hardened erasers, and playing cards from the remote days when he and his parents played three-handed pinochle at the dining table. At first, he could scarcely hold the cards, sixteen fanned in one little hand, and would stifle tears when his meld was poor and he lost. Once at the farm, they never played cards again. There were animals of petrified Play-Doh made by Joey's children, and useless pretty vases and bowls sent distractedly as seasonal gifts, and plush-bound old-fashioned albums, with little mildewed mirrors on the covers, of stiffly posed ancestors he could not identify. His mother had offered, over the years, to teach him their names and relation to him, but he had not been interested, and now she was not there to ask, and his ancestors floated free and nameless like angels.

There were things she had offered to tell him he had not wanted to hear. "What didn't you like about him?" he had once asked her — a bit impatiently, wearying of her voice — about his father.

Sitting in her television-watching chair, her weight and strength so wasted that only her mouth and mind could move, she had been telling him about her youthful romantic life. She had gone to a one-room country school — when she was dead, he came upon a photograph of the student body and its corpulent mustachioed instructor, his mother's broad little face squinting toward the camera under a ponderous crown of wound braids. Among the other children there had been a dark-haired, dark-eyed boy she had fancied, and who had fancied her. But her parents had disapproved of the boy's "people," and of several other dark-eyed substitutes that over the years she had offered them. But no, not until Joey's blondish, pale-eyed father did she bring home a suitor they could endorse. "They liked him, and he liked them. I'll say this for your father, not every man could have lived with his in-laws that cheerfully all those years. He really admired my mother, that style of little woman. He loved energetic little women. He thought they could make money for him. It's true, Mother was a money-maker. She was the one who got up in the dark to drive the cart into Alton to market. The tobacco they retired on had been her project. But admiring Mother was no reason to marry me. I was *big*. It was a mistake, and we both knew it. We knew it the first day of our honeymoon." Joey had often heard his moth-er's views on little women, how they have the best of it, and take the men from the big women like herself, big women who have tortured their little mothers in the birthing. Behind these for-mulations there was something — about sex, he believed — that he didn't want, as a boy or a man, to hear. *A real femme.* Even as a very small child he had been aware of a weight of anger his mother carried; he had quickly evolved — first word, first crawl — an adroitness at staying out of her way when she was heavy with it, and a wish to amuse her, to keep her light. But now as they were nearing the end, and her flesh was dissolving, and her inner self rising to the surface, he had become more daring, less catering, even challenging. Her own blue eyes, that had never needed a cataract operation, widened at his question as if she were seeing ghosts over his shoulder. "Oh, Joey," she said, "don't ask. It was un*speak*able."

He had to smile at the old-fashioned concept. "Unspeakable? Daddy?"

A bit of flush had crept into her colorless creased cheeks. She was getting angry, once again. She kept staring, not so much at him as at the space in his vicinity. She knew from watching tele-vision what the talk shows permitted people to say these days. "Well, maybe you're old enough. Maybe I *should* speak it."

"Oh, no, no thanks, that's all right," he said, jumping up from his chair and heading into the kitchen, much as his father used to in the middle of a marital exchange. *Poor Daddy,* was his thought. Let the dead alone. Now she too was dead, and there were many things Joey would never know. Though he grew used to the sandstone house without her in it, he still found it strange, back in his Manhattan apartment, that she never called on Saturday mornings the way she used to, with her playful, self-mocking account of her week. The dead can't even telephone. The phone's silence more than any other conveyed the peace of the dead, their absolute and, as it were, hostile withdrawal.

The real-estate appraiser, an old high-school classmate, stood in his gray suit in the cobwebbed cellar, next to the rickety furnace, among the paint cans and rusty hot-air ducts, and said to Joey, "Seventeen years here alone. It took a lot of guts." Yes, she had been brave, he could now afford to see, all those years alone, alone but for the animals she fed, and the ghosts on television. Over the telephone, even when reporting an insomniac night of breathlessness and terror, she had tried to keep it light for his sake, and mocked herself, mocking her very will, at the age of eighty-five, to live. "It's strange, but I really don't intend to die. Though a lot of people would like me to."

"Really? Who?"

"The real-estate developers. The neighbors. They think it's time for this old lady to move over and make some room."

"Do they really?" He was grateful she had not included him among the many who wished her dead.

"Really," she mocked. "But I have a responsibility here. The place still needs me."

"We all need you," Joey said, sighing, giving up. The fate of the place was another unspeakable matter. She wanted the place to go on and on, as it was in her idea of it.

He had scanned her in vain for some sign of sunset resignation. She had choked down her pills and vitamins to the end, and her fear of life's sensations ceasing had seemed as pure as a child's. The last time he had visited, on a cool fall day, she came outdoors to supervise his planting, in two arcs by a curve of the cement walk, two dozen tulip bulbs she had ordered from a catalogue. At first he had arranged the bulbs point down, and then realized that the point was what would grow upward, toward the sun. His mother had stood there on her unsteady feet, in her gaudy bathrobe, looking down; the sight of the fat cream-white bulbs nested in the turned red earth startled a kind of grunt out of her. "Oh, how dear they look," she said. To Joey she added, "How nicely you do things."

In all of her leavings that came to light he was most touched by her accounts — her tax forms and used checkbooks, meticulously kept, even though her tiny backward-slanting hand had become spasmodic and shaky. (Could that big penciled handwriting on the back of the enlarged photograph have been hers after all, at the age of thirteen?) She had kept, on a large pad of green paper, spreadsheets of her monthly expenses, ruled off by hand at the beginning of each month. The last entries had been made the day before the morning of her death. This financial and mathematical niceness of hers was something quite unpredictable, like a musical passion in a banker. Among the stored sheets of figures were several drawn up before they moved, with lists of expenses side by side, taxes, heating, utilities, upkeep — absurdly small amounts they now seemed, from that frozen wartime world. By her calculations, their reduced costs in the little sandstone house, and the projected rentals of their eighty acres to the neighboring farmers, would save them five hundred dollars — a third of her husband's salary. It had never really occurred to Joey that their move here had had a practical side. When he came to sheets showing how the money for his college education could be squeezed out among their other expenses, he couldn't bear to keep reading.

Gradually, through the stark months of a winter that was, according to the forecasters, unseasonably cold, and then unseasonably warm, he reduced the house to its essence, removing every trace, even a rusty pencil sharpener screwed to a windowsill, of his life and the four lives that had ended. Here on this patch of now uncarpeted wood his grandfather had fallen, having convulsively leaped from the bed where, a year later, his widow would breathe her last. Here, in the bedroom adjacent, his father had sat up with such pains in his chest that he told his wife to call the ambulance. He had died in the ambulance. Here in this same space Joey had lain sleepless, wondering how to tell his mother of his next divorce. Here on the other side of the wall he would lie after a date, his head still whirling with cigarette smoke and the perfume-counter smell of the girl. Here on the worn linoleum his mother had died, at the base of a wall she had had the Amish carpenters make of old chestnut boards, boards left in the barn from the era before the blight, to cover the rough stones exposed when the big kitchen chimney had been removed. The rooms had a soft beauty, empty. The uncovered floorboards drank the sunlight. Joey looked through the curtainless windows, seeing what his mother had seen — the sloping old orchard to the north, the barn and road and fields to the east, the lilac bushes and bird feeder and meadow to the south, the woods and the tall blue spruce to the west.

On his final cleanup visit, Joey found something devil-like — a small dark stiff shape, in size between a mouse and a rat, its legs attached by webs — floating in the bathroom toilet. A flying squirrel. It had come down from the attic and drowned, sick and thirsty from the d-Con. Joey remembered watching at twilight, that summer he moved the stones, a pair of flying squirrels sail, as if sliding swiftly on a wire, from the attic window over to the blue spruce. The house had stood empty before his family had moved in the previous fall, and this pair had moved in ahead of them.

He had bought a padlock for the cellar bulkhead, and closed the house with a key, having installed new locks. The house was ready for sale in the spring. But in the meantime, as he lay awake in his apartment three hours away, its emptiness called to him. It needed him. Suppose a fire, or local vandals, jealous of the price the place would fetch . . . Housing developments were all around, and even Philadelphians were moving into the area. His mother had made a shrewd investment, buying back paradise.

Those weekends alone in the house, sorting, cleaning, staying away from the motel until moonlight had replaced sunlight on the floors, he had discovered himself talking aloud, as if in response to a friendly presence just behind the dry old wallpaper, in the thick sandstone walls. His own uncluttered rooms, suspended above Manhattan's steady roar, with an ornamental piece of porch banister hidden at the back of a closet, felt as if they were flying somewhere. He felt guilty, anxious, displaced. He had always wanted to be where the action was, and what action there was, it turned out, had been back there.

Contributors' Notes

100 Other Distinguished Stories of 1990

Editorial Addresses

Contributors' Notes

RICK BASS is the author of *The Watch*, a story collection, and four essay collections, of which *Winter* is the most recent. He lives in Montana.

▪ "The Legend of Pig-Eye" is, and always has been, about passions, and the purity of innocent obsession — obsession with an act rather than one's self. I think because there was some bare-chestedness in the story (albeit a man's bare chest) my agent sent it off to the editor of a famous men's publication: I mean to say, one of those magazines that runs fiction between the pictures of breasts and groins, pubic hair and hineys. Circulation three and a half million, I think.

"I loved your story," the editor wrote in the acceptance letter, "and we'll pay you $2500 for it." I was living in Mississippi, broke as a doorknob. I couldn't make up my mind if I was more pleased with the 2500 or the three and a half million.

It happened that I was going to be in NYC a couple of weeks later. When I got there, my agent gave me the message that Madame A. — the editor who had bought my story — wanted me to come by to talk some about the story: that she had a few suggestions. "Great," I said. It made me feel like a real writer.

Up in Madame A.'s office, she said that they couldn't buy the story yet — that it still needed a little "something." This was an alarming turn of events from the "$2500, loved your story" letter.

I tried to be reasonable. "It's a matter of pride," I said. "I'd feel bad about myself if I let you run over me this way. You go ahead and pay me what you said you would — and I'll work on this story some more — and if it still isn't for you, then I'll give you first rights on any story I ever write — *any* story — until you come across one that is. But you said you'd pay me, and I want to be paid."

Madame A. said that to be truthful, that might not ever happen. They'd already seen a lot of my stories, and none of them had worked yet; why should they expect that another one ever would? No, she said, looking out her window, they'd better pass on the lifetime first-rights exclusive.

"Also," Madame A. said, "I have a real problem with the death in this story."

"No one dies in the story," I said.

"Oh yes they do," Madame A. said. "I read it."

"I wrote it," I said. "Nobody dies."

"Oh, but they do," she said. "I'll show you."

I waited as she leafed through the story.

And then, when surprise crossed her face, she shrugged. That was when I got the idea that in my next draft someone *would* die. I was hot, and wanted *everyone* to die, or get injured; I wanted carnage, everywhere. I wanted a haven from bullshit, too.

"I don't understand why you won't do this," she said, when I was leaving her office.

It was hot and bright outside, and I walked for a long time, to the office of *The Paris Review*. I went up to see my friend Jamie, and Jamie introduced me to George Plimpton, the editor. Mr. Plimpton seemed surprised, even affronted, by Madame A's renege ("Why, she shouldn't have *done* that," he said, as if she'd hurt his feelings as well), and then we talked about the story some, and when he and Jamie discovered that it had some boxing in it — and that I wanted to put even more boxing in it — they grew even more interested, and Mr. Plimpton asked if I had any boxing experience.

When I told him I didn't, but was thinking about fighting a guy at Gleason's, Mr. Plimpton grew very serious. "Don't get in the ring," he said. "Whatever you do, don't get in the ring. Those guys are serious. They'll hurt you," he said. "They would love to hurt a writer. They *want* to hurt you," he said. "Don't get in the ring," he said, so insistent that I wondered if he was receiving some kind of vision in which I was killed or something. He pulled down a copy of his book *Shadow Box,* in which he had boxed Archie Moore, then the light heavyweight champion of the world, and toured with Muhammad Ali.

Mr. Plimpton's eyes took on an interested look, and he moved between me and the doorway.

"If I hit you in the nose, though," he said, "you'd become part of a hoaxy genealogy." He began limbering his right arm, rolling his shoulder a little, flexing and unflexing his fingers. "When I was fighting Archie Moore, Archie Moore broke my nose, and he had his nose busted by Ali, who had *his* nose punched by Joe Frazier, who had *his* nose punched by . . ." Plimpton recited, with pride, the chain of busted noses, of which I could become the most recent inductee — the geneaology of it going way back before even Jack Dempsey's time.

I made some lame excuse toward leaving. Plimpton lingered in the doorway, and the offer was made once more, with even more sincerity — but finally he took the half-step aside that would allow me to leave his office without becoming part of boxing history. I have always wondered what it would have been like, and if I should have allowed him to reach out and tag me with that long right.

My editor at Norton, Carol Houck Smith, helped me with the next draft — and more drafts, and more — we stripped and pulled, weeded out, and added, until finally, maybe a dozen drafts later, only one original paragraph (the last one) remained — a *catharsis*. There was *so* much more violence in it (noses smashing, hot-air balloons crashing, drownings, horse whippings, etc.), and I sent it to *The Paris Review*, and they published it. Carol understood the anger I was working out of, on the revising, and was lovely in helping me focus it — though she did fall prey to one eccentricity, always calling the boxer "Peg-Leg" instead of "Pig-Eye." (One of my dogs had had to go to the vet with an ailment that the vets called "pig eye" — a wonderful name, I thought.)

I was so angry! It wasn't enough to just *kill* Pig-Eye, in the revision. I had to kill him *twice* — once in the balloon crash, and then, as if with some kind of science fiction monster, I had to bring him back to life just to drown him.

I bear Madame A. no rancor.

CHARLES BAXTER is the author of three collections of short stories, most recently *A Relative Stranger*, published in 1990 (W. W. Norton). He is also the author of a novel, *First Light*. He lives in Ann Arbor and teaches at the University of Michigan and at the M.F.A. Program for Writers at Warren Wilson College.

▪ I worked in Detroit for fifteen years, and toward the end of that time, I wanted to make the city a character in a story — a story about people and things vanishing. Others have written about the city's social conditions; I didn't want to do that. The story seems to be concerned with fugitive spiritual feelings in a place where nothing is quite readable. As I wrote it, the presence of some god or other seemed to appear in it, and about six pages in, the story begins to suffer from a kind of fever. This story still unnerves me a bit. The Chevrolet billboard used to be down by East Jefferson; I owe the Acme Wrecking Company banner to Ira Livingston; and the church signboard belongs to Alvin Greenberg, to whom the story is dedicated.

AMY BLOOM was raised in the suburbs of New York City and now lives in a very small town in Connecticut. She has completed a novel and is finishing a collection of short stories.

▪ This is an adult fairy tale. At times, I think it would be wonderful if life could be a series of endlessly opening doors, with none of them ever shutting behind us. In this story, monogamy is trivialized by love of all kinds. The setting for "Love Is Not a Pie" came to me as I was sitting on a dock in Lake Caribou, watching my daughter swim.

KATE BRAVERMAN is the author of four books of poetry and the novels *Lithium for Medea* and *Palm Latitudes.* "Tall Tales from the Mekong Delta" is from her short story collection, *Squandering the Blue* (Ballantine, 1990). She is a professor of creative writing at California State University, Los Angeles.

▪ I never know what my stories are about until they are finished, until they choose to reveal themselves. I merely feel their power, how they breathe on me. I try not to write them. I prefer the rush of having them write me. "Tall Tales from the Mekong Delta" wrote itself.

It is only now that I recognize this story contains elements that have long fascinated me. I once said that "Tall Tales" is my version of "Little Red Riding Hood" at the millennium in Los Angeles. It's an ancient story, an archetypal tale, set beneath the tattered palms in the ruined California tropics under all that vivid and tawdry blue. It's about predators in a cutting-edge city at the end of a mean thousand years.

"Tall Tales" is about the legacy of Vietnam, which continues to infect the American conscience, often in unexpected configurations. It's about tarnished consciousness and some unspeakably sordid pulse at the core of the American Dream. On one level, it's about the irresistible lure of evil, its strange sheen. It's about relationships between men and women and some overwhelming darkness that may be intrinsic to this planet itself. It was here before us and it will remain when we are gone. It has something to do with sexual obsession and the glamour of danger and the fragility of ordinary life. It's about power and survival in a landscape where the boundaries between dream and reality have dissolved, probably to a rock-and-roll beat.

Writing is like hunting. There are brutally cold afternoons with nothing in sight, only the wind and your breaking heart. Then the moment when you bag something big. The entire process is beyond intoxicating. As soon as Lenny began speaking, I knew I had mainlined it. I felt like I was strapped in the cockpit with the stars in my face and the expanding universe on my back. In my opinion, that's the only way a writer should travel. When I finished "Tall Tales" I thought, this one is a keeper. This is a trophy brought back from the further realm, the kingdom of perpetual glistening night where we know ourselves absolutely. This one goes on the wall.

ROBERT OLEN BUTLER is the author of the novels *The Alleys of Eden, Sun Dogs, Countrymen of Bones, On Distant Ground, Wabash,* and *The Deuce.* A volume of his short fiction will be published in 1991. All the stories from the book have appeared in such magazines as *The Hudson Review, The Sewanee Review, The Southern Review, The Gettysburg Review, New England Review,* and *The Virginia Quarterly Review,* where he won the Emily Clark Balch Award. His work has also been anthologized in *New Fiction from the South, The Best of 1991.* He teaches creative writing at McNeese State University, in Lake Charles, Louisiana.

• "The Trip Back" is part of a book of fourteen stories and a novella, each piece written in the first-person voice of a different Vietnamese expatriate living in southern Louisiana. The book, entitled *A Good Scent from a Strange Mountain,* began with the gift of language. In 1969 I was ensnared in the pre–lottery-days draft and ended up in the U.S. Army and then in Vietnam. However, before shipping me abroad, the army sent me to language school in Arlington, Virginia, to learn Vietnamese. I studied seven hours a day five days a week for a year with a Vietnamese woman who wept with nostalgia for her homeland whenever she heard the cannon fire at dusk at Fort Myer. I was musical as a child and I picked up the tones of the language and was fluent by the time I arrived in Saigon.

I worked briefly as a military intelligence operative but mostly as an administrative assistant to the American foreign service officer who was the adviser to the mayor of Saigon. I had dozens of Vietnamese friends and close acquaintances, ranging from the mayor of Saigon to a leper beggar on Tu Do Street who was the most cheerful man I've ever known. My favorite thing was to go out late at night and wander the back alleys of Saigon and crouch in the doorways and talk with the people. I was extremely close to the Vietnamese, closer even than to the people I grew up with, and I've been close to the Vietnamese living in America, and so they have inevitably found their way into my work.

The more specific origins of "The Trip Back" include an old Vietnamese mechanic in the motor pool of Saigon City Hall who told me lovingly about all the automobiles he ever owned; an even older man, the Russian grandfather of my second wife, whose faltering memory on a winter afternoon in Manhattan in 1973 nulled his granddaughter's existence; and a stretch of Texas two-lane that runs from Beaumont to China to Nome to Liberty to the Houston airport.

CHARLES D'AMBROSIO was raised in Seattle. He earned his B.A. from Oberlin College and in 1991 he graduated from the Iowa Writers' Workshop, where he held an Iowa Teaching/Writing Fellowship. He was also the recipient of a Henfield/Transatlantic Review award.

▪ "The Point" began with an anecdote my friend Drew told me about a time when he was young and had to take an old drunk lady home from a party at his parents' house. Not too long after the story was written, I asked Drew to tell his anecdote again, and it didn't surprise me to find out just how completely my memory had screwed up the real-life events. I used to work as a reporter and get things goofed up in a similar way.

I wrote the story in fits and spurts over two months and I can't remember much about its composition. When I started writing the only thing I knew for sure was that the women all smelled like rotting fruit. At first the father was simply away on business, or something hokey like that, and then one night I found a drunk woman of my own, in a pile of leaves outside my apartment. I was terrified. Right away I thought — I just assumed — she was dead. I didn't really want to touch a dead woman, so I nudged her face with my shoe. When she showed no sign of life, I ran to my apartment and called the police. They came, felt for a pulse in her neck, slapped her, got her to stand up briefly, and, when she fell back down, dragged her to their car. After I found that woman, I knew the father in my story was dead, that the narrator would discover him in the car, and that he'd be a lot cooler than I was.

I'm of that age group too young for Vietnam but old enough to have worked jobs repairing washing machines and tending bar side by side with vets, and so the point of view of a kid whose father was in the war came quite naturally to me — a practical necessity, since I have no battle experience. The letter seemed like the most effective way of making the war real and dignifying a character who never shows his face in the actual story. But that sounds very calculated. In fact, I only realized there would be a letter after I wrote the scene where the kid says he doesn't know any bedtime stories, and then, immediately, I understood that he'd go home and pull a letter out from under his bed and read it to himself.

Mrs. Gurney is a compilation of drunk women from my days as a bartender. The Point itself is more or less a geographically real place in northwestern Washington.

MILLICENT DILLON was born in New York City and graduated from Hunter College with a degree in physics. She did not begin to write fiction until she was almost forty. She has published a book of short stories, *Baby Perpetua and Other Stories*, and two novels, *The One in the Back Is Medea* and *The Dance of the Mothers*. She is also the author of two biographies, *A Little Original Sin: The Life and Work of Jane Bowles* and *After Egypt: Isadora Duncan and Mary Cassatt*. Millicent Dillon has written two plays as well, *She Is in Tangier* and *Prisoners of Ordinary Need*. She lives in California.

▪ Once, many years ago, I actually did work as a petroleum engineering assistant in the Kettleman Hills Oil Field. At the time I was not a writer and did not even (consciously) think of myself as ever becoming a writer. As it turned out, however, so many years later, when the experience of working in that oil field had been almost totally forgotten, it emerged in the guise of a story, one that begins in vagueness but aims for precision.

HARRIET DOERR is the author of *Stones for Ibarra* (Viking Penguin, 1984) and is working on a second novel set in Mexico.

• My stories are set in Mexico more often than not and I cannot say why. Unless it is that fifty years ago, unknown to me at the time, I fell passionately in love with that fierce and gentle land.

Even now, unsummoned glimpses of people and places thousands of miles to the south intrude between my typewriter, flower bed, kitchen stove, and me. A hazardous curve on the international highway looms between me and a freeway exit. I open a book to a man and a woman alone in a desert at night. "A sky of stars," he says. She nods. But before I can find out what happens next, Fermín Díaz, my old watchman, materializes to block my view.

Fermín and I are naming constellations. "Orion," I say, and point.

Fermín contradicts me. "No. It is the three Marys and the four kings."

As a result of interposed images, I see much of my world today in layers. I have become addicted to echoes of voices, hints of faces, partial views of dry arroyos in Durango, ditches of hyacinths in Michoácan.

I regard these hallucinations as personal gifts from a nation. Mexico assembled them, handed them to me, said, "Here."

DEBORAH EISENBERG is the author of a play, *Pastorale*, and two collections of short stories, *Transactions in a Foreign Currency* and *Under the 82nd Airborne* (Farrar, Straus and Giroux, 1992). She lives in New York and teaches from time to time.

• How did this story come to be written? Well, how does any story come to be written? In my experience this is always something of a mystery, and even though it always takes me a very long time (usually between eight and twelve months) to write a story, when it's over I don't seem to remember much about the experience, except where I sat and what color notebook I used and that sort of thing. But to hypothesize a very approximate description, I'd say that the many elements that eventually fuse into a story just sit around cooking in a dark recess of one's brain, and as they develop they agglomerate. And by the time one of those elements becomes forceful enough to struggle its way into the light, it can manage to haul the others out behind it eventually. Usually when I write a story I like to find some new cliff to throw myself off, but when

I wrote this one, I remember, I was feeling timid and dull-witted. Also I was thinking I might sometime like to try to reclaim a certain simplicity of tone I felt I'd been sacrificing to achieve more complex or rarefied results. Also I'd been brooding a bit about class as an insufficiently acknowledged determinant of life in the U.S. And since I was having so much trouble locating in myself some initiating image or problem with enough charge to keep me going for a while, I settled for busying myself with some not very daunting tasks — exercises, almost — formal manipulations of time and tense, which I hoped might engineer various sensations of things as they are remembered. So I suppose that's how it all began to take shape (over the course of a number of drafts) as a story about a timid and dull-witted girl from a blue-collar background who's had a big but ordinary experience a long time before. And then the rest just filled itself in around that.

MARY GORDON was born on Long Island, grew up in Queens, and was educated at Barnard College, where she is now the McIntosh Professor of English. She has published four novels — *Final Payments, The Company of Women, Men and Angels,* and *The Other Side* — and a collection of stories, *Temporary Shelter,* as well as numerous essays and articles. She lives with her husband and two children in New Paltz, New York.

▪ The genesis for this story was watching mothers leave their children each morning in my son's nursery school class. One particularly extreme case suggested an even more extreme situation to me. But it was clear to me that the extremity was only another part of the story of all mothers and all sons.

ELIZABETH GRAVER grew up in Williamstown, Massachusetts, and was educated at Wesleyan University, Washington University in St. Louis, and Cornell University. Her stories have appeared in *Story, Southern Review, Southwest Review, Seventeen,* and elsewhere. Her story collection, *Have You Seen Me?,* published by the University of Pittsburgh Press, was awarded the 1991 Drue Heinz Prize. She lives in Ithaca, New York, where she is working on a novel.

▪ My story "The Body Shop" grew out of a picture. For years I've been saving newspaper and magazine clippings — science articles on the behavior of bats or how memory functions, news stories about missing children or a girl caught at the bottom of a well, odd photographs . . . anything that somehow strikes a chord. I paste the clippings in a big sketchbook where I also jot down writing ideas, and often the articles sit there for years without becoming stories. Sometimes, though, I flip through these sketchbooks when I'm stuck; other times an image or idea from one of the clippings comes to me as I'm writing — and only later do I become aware of its origin. "The Body Shop" grew out of a photograph and tiny article by Bruce Weber in the *New York Times* Sunday magazine. The photograph is of two bald, armless mannequins with extraordinarily realistic, staring, luminous green eyes. Those eyes stopped me and made me tear out the page; months later, they provided the opening image of my story.

The article next to the photograph told about a woman named Evangeline Calvin who ran a mannequin restoration business in Oregon. "We fix them up," she said. "I can paint them so they look like people. I can paint an eye on a flat surface and make it look like it's looking at you." This image, of a woman trying to make the inanimate look animate, and of mannequin restoration becoming a kind of passion and art, stuck with me. The article also mentioned that the woman had a son who ran a branch of her business in San Diego. All that — the mother and son, the business, the artificial eyes — gave me a setting, an ambiance, an image from which the rest could unfold. At some later point, in some unconscious way, the image merged with aspects of my grandmother, a dressmaker with a vivid imagination who moved to a Brooklyn nursing home after her leg was amputated.

When I begin a story, I never have any idea where I'm going, but the initial image, setting, or voice (any one of these can set things in motion) needs to be rich and full of possibility, and also somewhat mysterious to me, or else the story stalls. "The Body Shop" ended up being about a lot of things — disappointment and loss, one person's power over another, the attempt to construct a life — but it began quite simply with a sentence: "My mother had me sort the eyes." That sentence led to the next sentence, which led to the next, until the eye image became embedded in a larger fictional world.

SIRI HUSTVEDT is the author of *Reading to You,* a collection of poems published by Station Hill Press in 1983. Her work has appeared in *The Paris Review, Pequod, The Ontario Review,* and *Fiction.* Her story "Mr. Morning" was published in *The Best American Short Stories 1990.* She lives in Brooklyn with her husband and two children.

• "Houdini" is the second in a sequence of five "Iris" stories. All of them are rooted in some autobiographical event. Like Iris, I suffer from migraine and was once hospitalized because of it. The impulse behind the story was, I think, an attempt to investigate the experience of being a patient, which struck me as both a peculiar and a deeply comical state. But the work is a fiction, and despite the fact that it comes out of a particular moment in my life, what happens inside it is Iris's story, not mine.

MIKHAIL IOSSEL was born in Leningrad in 1955. He graduated from the Leningrad Shipbuilding Institute with a master's degree in physics, and subsequently worked as an engineer, free-lance translator, night guard, and coal stoker. His literary work was widely published in *samizdat*. In 1986 he emigrated to the U.S., where he received an M.A. in creative writing from the University of New Hampshire. A Wallace Stegner Fellow at Stanford University from 1989 to 1991, he currently lives in Minneapolis and teaches at the University of Minnesota. His first collection of stories written in English, *Every Hunter Wants to Know: A Leningrad Life*, was just published by W. W. Norton.

▪ I wrote this story at the University of New Hampshire in Durham, late in May of 1988. It was during the NBA playoffs and each night a friend of mine, also a graduate student, and I would go to Nick's, a local sports bar, to watch the Celtics on a big-screen TV. A pint of Bud Dry cost just ninety cents there, the place was filled with smoke and camaraderie. "What lousy beer!" my friend said. "The worst!" He usually spoke to me in simple sentences. I nodded and told him that I'd already used those words — what lousy beer! — in the story that I was beginning to write; it was called "Bologoye." Its original title was more literary and far-fetched: "Fountains on the Floor." In it, the main character and his friend spend a Saturday afternoon in front of a grimy-looking beer-stand in downtown Leningrad. Then they take a train to Moscow and back. It was going to be my fourth story in English. Of course, by then I'd begun to realize that all my stories written in New Hampshire, in English, were essentially about the same man. He could be me, but wasn't, because — who would want to write about himself? Still, that man was my age and seemed to follow in my unsure footsteps. So when the Celtics had lost the game — and the series — I went back to my first three stories and changed the names of their three protagonists to that of Yevgeny Litovtsev. The familiar excitement of a writer who can suddenly seem to see the end of his work made me want to finish "Bologoye" in a hurry. The rhythm I was striving for, that loping syncopated beat of mounting paranoia, corresponded, strangely, with the serenity of a New Hampshire night. The thought that I was thousands of miles away from Leningrad still drove me to despair. That was a long time ago.

DAVID JAUSS's stories have been published in various magazines, including *The Iowa Review, New England Review and Bread Loaf Quarterly,* and *Prairie Schooner,* and reprinted in the O. Henry Prize and Pushcart Prize anthologies. *Crimes of Passion,* a collection of his stories, appeared in 1984. He teaches at the University of Arkansas at Little Rock.

▪ Like many of my stories, "Glossolalia" began with an image generated by the intersection of two seemingly unrelated stories. Nearly a decade ago a student of mine, distraught at the death of his father, confessed to me that he hadn't spoken to his father for years. When he was in high school, he said, his father had embezzled several thousand dollars from the insurance company where he worked, and though he was fired, he continued to report to his office as if nothing had happened. When his supervisor finally changed the locks so he couldn't get into his office, he became enraged and threw a metal wastebasket through the glass door. He was arrested shortly afterwards and charged with destruction of property, but the charges were dropped after he suffered a nervous breakdown and had to be hospitalized. These events were the talk of the small Texas town where they occurred, and they embarrassed my student so much that he never forgave his father — until, of course, it was too late. The story affected me, and I tried several times without success to give its skeleton of facts a fictional body. Eventually, though, I abandoned the story and — or so I thought — forgot it. Then, about two years ago, my daughter went to a Pentecostal church service with a friend, and when she came home, she described how the parishioners had spoken in tongues. For some reason I still do not fully understand, a spark leapt between her story and my student's, and I saw the boy's father, collapsed on his hands and knees, his mind broken, babbling a glossolalia of anguish. From that image the story gradually grew over the course of an Arkansas summer so brutally hot that, for consolation, I set the story in my home state of Minnesota during winter.

LEONARD MICHAELS is the author of *Shuffle*, a book of autobiographical fiction; *The Men's Club*, a novel; and two collections of short stories, *I Would Have Saved Them If I Could* and *Going Places*. He lives in California and teaches at the University of California at Berkeley.

• In December 1987, I went to Havana to attend a film festival. People from all over South America, Europe, and the United States had arrived. There were parties every night. Toward the end of the festival, I went to a party given by a novelist who lived in the Miramar district, not far from the Tropicana nightclub, which had been built in the prerevolutionary days by gangsters who managed gambling clubs all over the city until Castro put an end to them. Very late at night, just when everyone was feeling most happily convivial, an argument started, an absurdly childish argument. Some boor from the United States said, "We are having a wonderful time, but we mustn't forget that Cuba isn't paradise." He'd met people, he claimed, who told him they were oppressed and fearful. He wanted the Cubans in the room to agree things were very bad. Our conversation and friendship would then be more open and natural, unqualified by lies. The Cubans disagreed with him, but they conceded some things — yes, there is street crime in Havana, and yes, a few political prisoners, among the unknown hundreds or thousands, had probably been tortured. The concessions always followed a remark like "Much as I love Fidel, it is true that . . ." or "I love Fidel more than my life, but who can deny that . . ." One Cuban, however, a woman of elegant facial bones and aristocratic bearing, would allow nothing said against Cuba or Fidel. People were surprised by her adamancy. Some insisted that she at least acknowledge what is real, even if only to admit that Cuba isn't perfect. I saw tears in her eyes, but, as if they too were a concession, she willed them to vanish. She was impossible, the sort who desires illusion more than truth, but, little by little, I found myself drawn to her. The rest of us had come to seem like common types, sentimental and self-righteous, without her beautiful and tragic machismo. Somebody whispered to me that she is the mother of one of Fidel's children. Later, I heard that Fidel kept many houses for personal use in Havana. By then my story was writing itself.

LORRIE MOORE is the author of a novel, a children's book, and two collections of stories, the most recent of which is *Like Life* (Knopf, 1990).
▪ I've forgotten how I came to write this rogue dream. I look at it now, see my name on it, and feel a little senile. Obviously, it's a narrative about dissolution and evanescence — in imitation of which the original source of inspiration seems to have done its work and flown off, withered away, like the Marxist state, or the training wheels of a bike. Might it suffice to say the piece is a mosaic, an agitated painting, and I have forgotten from what store I bought these particular paints? Though I could hazard a guess — to improvise a history, a birthday, a map — it seems a little unwise. Might I just say that this story lives on my steps like a stray?

ALICE MUNRO's most recent collection of stories is *Friend of My Youth* (Knopf, 1990). Born in Wingham, Ontario, Ms. Munro now lives in Clinton, Ontario. She has received Canada's Governor General's Award for two of her books.
▪ A friend was talking about the game of crokinole. This reminded him of some people he had known — the Cameronian family (who could play crokinole, but not cards) — and he told me about them. The drama in the family — the half-painted house, the desperate comedy — started me writing the story. I didn't know when I started that my mother and myself were in it, nor that the ways of looking at things and writing about them would become part of the story itself. I just found myself doing the story through my mother's story and then through mine. There must have been decisions made, but I don't recall them.

JOYCE CAROL OATES is the author of a number of novels, plays, and collections of short stories, poems, and essays. Her work has been included in previous volumes of *The Best American Short Stories* and the

O. Henry Awards, and she was the 1990 winner of the Rea Award for the Short Story. Her most recent story collections are *Heat* (1990) and *The Assignation* (1988). She is a member of the American Academy of Arts and Letters and holds the Roger S. Berlind Distinguished Professorship in the Humanities at Princeton University, where she has taught since 1978.

• "American, Abroad" is a fiction constructed out of a myriad of small authentic details, of the kind that impress us, as travelers, with an almost hallucinatory vividness. All its observable reality *is* real, and many of its conversations. There really was, in the late 1980s, in the European country where I had gone on a lecture/reading tour, an Iranian terrorist team that had "targeted" one of our ambassadors; there really was an ambassador's daughter, a yipping terrier, a false alarm at the palatial embassy residence where, one evening, I was being honored much as my character Caroline Carmichael is being honored. Of course, the fact that "American, Abroad" is cast in a certain mode of language makes it fiction, not memoir. Caroline Carmichael is not me, except as we overlap. Much of what she sees, I saw; much of what I saw, she sees. Sometimes we feel exactly the same way about what we see; in other, perhaps more crucial ways, we don't.

Without intending it, I have written, over the years, a small gathering of European-set stories, and these stories are all "real" — as a composite is real. The stories have a distinct family resemblance and are altogether different in tone, theme, and characterization from my more characteristic American-set stories, which are, despite authentic settings, much more fictional. When I travel, my imagination recedes; to use Emerson's surreal metaphor, I become an eyeball, a pure consciousness, avid to register all I can see, hear, smell, taste, absorb. The external world is a forest of signs and symbols, inviting, but always eluding, interpretation.

In "American, Abroad," even fellow Americans become mysterious, elusive. I must have imagined Caroline Carmichael into being in order to give a coherent dramatic shape to my sense of unease and vulnerability, yet my sense of wonderment too, a kind of generic American spirit that possesses us, sometimes, in foreign countries where we are both ourselves — private, solitary — and citizens of a rich, vast, legendary country into which, by sheer good fortune, we were born. This is precisely the kind of fiction an American writer can't write at home.

What I've liked about "American, Abroad" is the fact that it might have turned tragic, but did not. It might have ended in a wounding, devastating epiphany for its heroine, but did not. For sometimes, vulnerable and exposed as we are, we do triumph — to a degree.

FRANCINE PROSE is the author of seven novels and a story collection,

Women and Children First. Her most recent novel, *Primitive People* (1991), was published by Farrar, Straus and Giroux.

• "Dog Stories" comes partly out of my continuing interest in the way people tell their stories — in this case, stories about dogs. Like the couple in the story, I'd begun to find myself tuning out when people went on about the smart or cute or outrageous things their pets had done. But what I eventually realized was that I hadn't been listening hard enough. People never talk about *nothing,* not even when they seem to. There are always secret and interesting reasons for the stories they decide to tell and for the moments at which they choose to tell them.

The only part of the story that comes unedited from "real life" is the anecdote about the dog who runs away to be with his true love. The romantic dog was our Siberian husky, who died several years ago. It seemed like a personal compliment — a flattering reflection of ourselves — to have such a passionate dog. When I got wary of dog stories, I stopped talking about it. So it was nice to have a chance to tell it again, perhaps for one last time.

Finally, I think that "Dog Stories" may have been an unconscious homage to (or steal from) the great William Trevor story "Teresa's Wedding." I wanted to write a story about a wedding that was not exactly an expression of joy and hope for the future, but rather of some darker and less sanguine sense of acceptance.

JOHN UPDIKE was born in 1932, in Shillington, Pennsylvania, and graduated from Harvard College in 1954. After a year at an English art school and a stint as a Talk of the Town reporter for *The New Yorker,* he moved to Massachusetts in 1957, and has lived there since. His most recent book is his fourteenth novel, *Rabbit at Rest.*

• I wrote "A Sandstone Farmhouse" in a rush of liberation after fifteen months' captivity in the making of my last novel. The hero of this short story, Joey Robinson, figured, along with his mother and a Pennsylvania farm, in a novella of 1965, *Of the Farm.* So this is a kind of sequel, after many a year. I differ from Joey in that I lived only briefly in New York City, never was in the advertising game, and have not had three wives. But like him I did live, from the ages of thirteen to eighteen, in a sandstone farmhouse with four adults — my parents and my mother's parents. By keeping the focus on the house — its stones, its smells, its renovations — I hoped to convey the dizzying depth of life its walls have contained, and the poignant way that lives glimmer in and out of the more slowly transformed realities of environment. A Berks County friend of mine, in another connection, sent me his research on how the old houses were built, early in the nineteenth century, and I was happy to incorporate this information, with its extraordinary image of the carts shattering under their load. The story is about *things* — how they mutely witness our flitting lives, and remain when the lives are over, still mute, still witnessing.

Just last week, coincidentally, I visited the real farmhouse where I had lived for five years and where my mother had lived for sixty of her eighty-five years; the new owners have done wonderful modern things inside, and exterminated the mice and flying squirrels that kept my mother company, but they have retained the integrity of the thick sandstone shell, and the old knobbed clothes pegs on the wall, and they plan to put a fireproof metal lining in the crooked flue of the old stone chimney. It was a sunny day, and the place seemed dimly to recognize me, just as my mother's dog, happy with a new owner, wags her tail and whines when she sees me, trying to remember, but not having the words.

100 Other Distinguished Stories of 1990

SELECTED BY KATRINA KENISON

Smoke. *The New Yorker*, April 2.

CHECKOWAY, JULIE
Voice Lessons for the Writer. *The Iowa Review*, Vol. 20, No. 1.
Women in Antiquity. *The North American Review*, March.

CHEVIGNY, BELL GALE
Maggie's Dress. *The Michigan Quarterly Review*, Fall.

COE, CHRISTOPHER
I Couldn't Have Dreamed It. *Story*, Summer.

COOPER, RAND RICHARDS
Kerenyaga. *Harper's Magazine*, April.

DAVENPORT, DIANA
Rosie and Jake at Top Speed. *New Letters*, Vol. 56, No. 4.

DAY, ROBERT
My Father Swims His Horse at Last. *The TriQuarterly Review*, Fall.

DeMARINIS, RICK
Safe Forever. *Story*, Summer.

DeWITT, ABIGAIL
The Painter's Arrest. *The Carolina Quarterly*, Spring.

DORRIS, MICHAEL
The Benchmark. *Mother Jones*, January.

ERDRICH, LOUISE
The Bingo Van. *The New Yorker*, February 19.

FERRISS, LUCY
Outside Windhaven. *The Southern Review*, Winter.

FREDERICK, K. C.
Adding On. *Epoch*, Vol. 38, No. 3.

GEORGE, KATHLEEN
Rites of Burial. *Cimarron Review*, July.

GOLDMAN, E. S.
Earthly Justice. *The Atlantic Monthly*, October.

GORDON, MARY
At the Kirks'. *Grand Street*, Winter.

GRIMM, MARY
Before. *The New Yorker*, April 16.

GURGANUS, ALLAN
Nativity, Caucasian. *Harper's Magazine*, November.

HAAKE, KATHERINE
The Woman in the Water. *The Iowa Review*, Vol. 19, No. 3.

HAAS, BARBARA
The Most Private of Private Hells. *The North American Review*, June.

HALL, DONALD
Fifty People Talking. *The Gettysburg Review*, Spring.

HAMILTON, JANE
Rehearsing "The Firebird." *Harper's Magazine*, June.

HARRISON, JIM
The Woman Lit by Fireflies. *The New Yorker*, July 23.

HARTOG, DIANA
Theories of Grief. *Prism*, January.

HELLER, LINDA
Brown Town. *The Alaska Review*, Fall/Winter.

HEYMAN, ARLENE
Artifact. *Epoch*, Vol. 39, Nos. 1 & 2.

IOSSEL, MIKHAIL
Every Hunter Wants to Know. *Tikkun*, Vol. 5, No. 3.

JEN, GISH
What Means Switch. *The Atlantic Monthly*, May.

KIEDROWSKI, ANGELICA
Moonlight. *The Georgia Review*, Spring/Summer.

KIRN, WALTER
On Set-Aside. *Story*, Summer.

KLASS, PERRI
For Women Everywhere. *Glamour*, July.

KLASSEN, SARAH
Lake Sharon. *The New Quarterly*,
Spring/Summer.

LEVINE, PHILIP
The Key. *The Gettysburg Review*,
Winter.

MCCAFFERTY, JANE
Director of the World. *The Alaska
Quarterly Review*, Spring/Summer.
Thirst. *West Branch*, No. 26.
MCCORKLE, JILL
Waiting for Hard Times to End.
The Southern Review, Winter.
MCCRACKEN, ELIZABETH
Some Have Entertained Angels
Unawares. *Epoch*, Vol. 39, No. 3.
MCNALLY, JOHN
The Greatest Goddamned Thing.
Columbia, No. 15.
MASON, BOBBIE ANN
Tobrah. *Story*, Summer.
MATTHEWS, PATRICIA
A Perfectly Happy Woman. *The
Georgia Review*, Spring/Summer.
MAYTAG, TIA
The Way Things Are. *The Sonora
Review*, Fall/Winter.
MEYERS, KENT
Wind Rower. *The Sonora Review*,
Fall/Winter.
MILLER, ALYCE
Babysitting. *Great River Review*,
Spring.
MORRIS, MARY MCGARRY
Bingo. *Story*, Winter.
MUELLER, DANIEL
The Night My Brother Worked the
Header. *Playboy*, October.
MUNRO, ALICE
Pictures of the Ice. *The Atlantic
Monthly*, January.

NELSON, ANTONYA
Human Habits. *The Antioch Review*,
Spring.

NUGENT, BETH
Cocktail Hour. *The New Yorker*,
April 30.

OATES, JOYCE CAROL
Friday Night. *Antaeus*, Spring/
Autumn.
OBERMAN, SHELDON
This Business with Elijah. *Event*,
Vol. 19, No. 3.
O'BRIEN, TIM
Spin. *The Quarterly*, Spring.
OZICK, CYNTHIA
Puttermesser Paired. *The New
Yorker*, October 8.

PIERCE, ANNE WHITNEY
Abeyance. *The Massachusetts Review*,
Winter.
PRICE, REYNOLDS
His Final Mother. *The New Yorker*,
May 21.
Watching Her Die. *The Paris
Review*, No. 17.

RICHARDS, SUSAN STARR
The Screened Porch. *The Southern
Review*, Spring.
RILE, KAREN
Defection. *The Southern Review*,
Summer.
ROFIHE, RICK
Quiet. *Grand Street*, Winter.

SCHULMAN, HELEN
Boy, Girl, Boy, Girl. *Wigwag*,
November.
SCHWARTZ, ADAM
Where Is It Written? *Wigwag*,
February.
SEARLE, ELIZABETH
Round Objects. *Epoch*, Vol. 39, No.
3.
SECREAST, DONALD
When Loads Shift. *Carolina
Quarterly*, Winter.

SELLERS, HEATHER
  Hunting. *Chattahoochee Review*, Fall/
  Winter.
SELZER, RICHARD
  Whither Thou Goest. *Salmagundi*,
  Summer. Also published as '
  Follow Your Heart. *Redbook*,
  September.
SPENCER, DARRELL
  Song and Dance. *High Plains
  Literary Review*, Fall.
STAPLETON, LARA
  Maria Luna. *The Michigan Quarterly
  Review*, Winter.
SWICK, MARLY
  Moscow Nights. *The Atlantic
  Monthly*, August.
  The Rhythm of Disintegration. *The
  Gettysburg Review*, Summer.

TAYLOR, PETER
  Cousin Aubrey. *The Kenyon Review*,
  Winter.
THOMAS, ABIGAIL
  Modern Love. *The Missouri Review*,
  Vol. 13, No. 1.
TUDISH, CATHERINE
  The Dancing-Master. *The Agni
  Review*, Spring.

WILLIAMS, LYNNA
  Things Not Seen. *The Atlantic
  Monthly*, May.

ZABEL, RICHARD
  The Swan. *The Atlantic Monthly*,
  May.

Editorial Addresses of American and Canadian Magazines Publishing Short Stories

When available, the annual subscription rate, the average number of stories published per year, and the name of the editor follow the address.

Agni Review
Creative Writing Department
Boston University
236 Bay State Road
Boston, MA 02115
$12, 10, Askold Melnyczuk

Alabama Literary Review
Smith 264
Troy State University
Troy, AL 36082
$8, Theron E. Montgomery

Alaska Quarterly Review
Department of English
University of Alaska
3221 Providence Drive
Anchorage, AK 99508
$8, 20, Ronald Spatz

Alfred Hitchcock's Mystery Magazine
Davis Publications, Inc.
380 Lexington Avenue
New York, NY 10017
$25.97, 130, Cathleen Jordan

Ambergris
P.O. Box 29919
Cincinnati, OH 45229
$6, 8, Mark Kissling

Amelia
329 East Street
Bakersfield, CA 93304
$20, 9, Frederick A. Raborg, Jr.

American Literary Review
University of North Texas
P. O. Box 13615
Denton, TX 76203
$10, 7, James Ward Lee

American Voice
332 West Broadway
Louisville, KY 40202
$12, 7, Sallie Bingham, Frederick Smock

Analog Science Fiction/Science Fact
380 Lexington Avenue
New York, NY 10017
$25.97, 70, Stanley Schmidt

Antaeus
26 West 17th Street
New York, NY 10011
$30, 21, Daniel Halpern

Antietam Review
82 West Washington Street
Hagerstown, MD 21740
$5, 6, Suzanne Kass

Antioch Review
P.O. Box 148
Yellow Springs, OH 45387
$20, 20, Robert S. Fogarty

Apalachee Quarterly
P.O. Box 20106
Tallahassee, FL 32316
$12, 10, Barbara Hardy et al.

Appalachian Heritage
Berea College
Berea, KY 40404
$15, 5, Sidney Saylor Farr

Arete
715 J Street, Suite 301
San Diego, CA 92101
$18, 5, Alden Mills

Arizona Quarterly
University of Arizona
Tucson, AZ 85721
$5, 12, Albert F. Gegenheimer

Arts Journal
324 Charlotte Street
Asheville, NC 28801
$15, 5, Tom Patterson

Ascent
English Department
University of Illinois
608 South Wright Street
Urbana, IL 61801
$3, 8

Atlantic Monthly
745 Boylston Street
Boston, MA 02116
$14.95, 17, C. Michael Curtis

Aura Literary/Arts Review
P.O. Box University Center
University of Alabama
Birmingham, AL 35294
$6, 10, rotating editorship

Belles Lettres
11151 Captain's Walk Court
North Potomac, MD 20878
$20, 2, Janet Mullaney

Bellowing Ark
P.O. Box 45637
Seattle, WA 98145
$12, 7, Robert R. Ward

Beloit Fiction Journal
P.O. Box 11, Beloit College
Beloit, WI 53511
$9, 15, Clint McCown

Black Warrior Review
P.O. Box 2936
Tuscaloosa, AL 35487-2936
$7.50, 13, Alicia Griswold

Border Crossings
Y300-393 Portage Avenue
Winnipeg, Manitoba
R3B 3H6 Canada
$18, 12, Robert Enright

Boston Review
33 Harrison Avenue
Boston, MA 02111
$15, 6, Margaret Ann Roth

Boulevard
2400 Chestnut Road, Apt. 2208
Philadelphia, PA 19103
$12, 13, Richard Burgin

Brooklyn Free Press
268 14th Street
Brooklyn, NY 11215
$1, 10, Raphael Martinez Alequin

California Quarterly
100 Sproul Hall
University of California
Davis, CA 95616
$14, 4, Elliott L. Gilbert

Calyx
P.O. Box B
Corvallis, OR 97339
$18, 11, Margarita Donnelly

Canadian Fiction
Box 946, Station F
Toronto, Ontario
M4Y 2N9 Canada
$36, 23, Geoffrey Hancock

Capilano Review
Capilano College
2055 Purcell Way
North Vancouver,
British Columbia
V7J 3H5 Canada
$12, 5, Dorothy Jantzen

Carolina Quarterly
Greenlaw Hall 066A
University of North Carolina
Chapel Hill, NC 27514
$10, 20, Lisa Carl

Chariton Review
Division of Language & Literature
Northeast Missouri State University
Kirksville, MO 63501
$9, 6, Jim Barnes

Chattahoochee Review
DeKalb Community College
2101 Womack Road
Dunwoody, GA 30338-4497
$15, 21, Lamar York

Chelsea
P.O. Box 5880
Grand Central Station
New York, NY 10163
$11, 6, Sonia Raiziss

Chicago Review
5801 South Kenwood
University of Chicago
Chicago, IL 60637
$20, 20, Elizabeth Arnold

Cimarron Review
205 Morrill Hall

Oklahoma State University
Stillwater, OK 74078-0135
$12, 15, Gordon Weaver

Clockwatch Review
Department of English
Illinois Wesleyan University
Bloomington, IL 61702
$8, 6, James Plath

Colorado Review
Department of English
360 Eddy Building
Colorado State University
Fort Collins, CO 80523
$9, 10, David Milofsky

Columbia
404 Dodge
Columbia University
New York, NY 10027
$11, 9, Paul Gediman, Elizabeth Thomas

Commentary
165 East 56th Street
New York, NY 10022
$39, 5, Norman Podhoretz

Concho River Review
English Department
Angelo State University
San Angelo, TX 76909
$12, 7, Terence A. Dalrymple

Confrontation
English Department
C. W. Post College of Long Island
    University
Greenvale, NY 11548
$8, 25, Martin Tucker

Crab Creek Review
4462 Whitman Avenue North
Seattle, WA 98103
$8, 3, Linda Clifton

Crazyhorse
Department of English
University of Arkansas
Little Rock, AR 72204
$8, 13, David Jauss

Cream City Review
University of Wisconsin, Milwaukee
P.O. Box 413
Milwaukee, WI 53201
$10, 30, Ellen Barclay, Sanford Tweedy

Crescent Review
P.O. Box 15065
Winston-Salem, NC 27113
$10, 33, Guy Nancekeville

Critic
205 West Monroe Street, 6th floor
Chicago, IL 60606-5097
$17, 4, John Sprague

Crosscurrents
2200 Glastonbury Road
Westlake Village, CA 91361
$18, 38, Linda Brown Michelson

Denver Quarterly
University of Denver
Denver, CO 80208
$15, 27, Donald Revell

descant
Department of English
Texas Christian University
Fort Worth, TX 76129
*$8, 12, Betsy Colquitt, Stanley
   Trachtenberg*

Descant
P.O. Box 314, Station P
Toronto, Ontario
M5S 2S8 Canada
$26, 20, Karen Mulhallen

Elle
1633 Broadway
New York, NY 10019
$24, 2

Epoch
251 Goldwin Smith Hall
Cornell University
Ithaca, NY 14853-3201
$11, 23, C. S. Giscombe

Esquire
1790 Broadway
New York, NY 10019
$17.94, 19, Rust Hills

event
c/o Douglas College
P.O. Box 2503
New Westminster, British Columbia
V3L 5B2 Canada
$12, 18, Maurice Hodgson

Expression
P.O. Box 2429
Mesa, AZ 85214
$14, Caryn Martinez

Fantasy & Science Fiction
P.O. Box 56
Cornwall, CT 06753
$21, 75, Edward L. Ferman

Farmer's Market
P.O. Box 1272
Galesburg, IL 61402
$7, 10, Jean C. Lee

Fiction
Fiction, Inc.
Department of English
The City College of New York
New York, NY 10031
$7, 15, Mark Mirsky

Fiction Network
P.O. Box 5651
San Francisco, CA 94101
$8, 25, Jay Schaefer

Fiction Review
P.O. Box 12268
Seattle, WA 98102
$15, 25, Bob Spryszak

Fiddlehead
Room 317, Old Arts Building
University of New Brunswick
Fredericton, New Brunswick
E3B 5A3 Canada
$16, 20, Michael Taylor

Florida Review
Department of English
University of Central Florida
P.O. Box 25000
Orlando, FL 32816
$7, 14, Pat Rushin

Folio
Department of Literature
The American University
Washington, D.C. 20016
*$9, 12, William O'Sullivan, Anna
   Watson*

Formations
Northwestern University Press
625 Colfax Street
Evanston, IL 60201
*$16, 4, Jonathan Brent, Frances Padorr
   Brent*

Four Quarters
LaSalle University
20th and Olney Avenues
Philadelphia, PA 19141
$8, 10, John J. Keenan

The Gamut
1218 Fen Tower
Cleveland State University
Cleveland, OH 44115
$15, 4, Louis T. Milic

Georgia Review
University of Georgia
Athens, GA 30602
$12, 15, Stanley W. Lindberg

Gettysburg Review
Gettysburg College
Gettysburg, PA 17325
$12, 20, Peter Stitt

Good Housekeeping
959 Eighth Avenue
New York, NY 10019
$14.97, 7, Naomi Lewis

GQ
350 Madison Avenue
New York, NY 10017
$19.97, 12, Thomas Mallon

Grand Street
135 Central Park West
New York, NY 10023
$24, 20, Jean Stein

Granta
250 West 57th Street, Suite 1316
New York, NY 10107
$28, Anne Kinard

Gray's Sporting Journal
20 Oak Street
Beverly Farms, MA 01915
$34.95, 4, Edward E. Gray

Great River Review
211 West 7th
Winona, MN 55987
$9, 6, Ruth Forsythe et al.

Greensboro Review
Department of English
University of North Carolina
Greensboro, NC 27412
$5, 16, Jim Clark

Harper's Magazine
666 Broadway
New York, NY 10012
$18, 15, Lewis H. Lapham

Hawaii Review
University of Hawaii
Department of English
1733 Donaghho Road
Honolulu, HI 96822
$12, 18, Stewart Anderson

Hayden's Ferry Review
Matthews Center
Arizona State University
Tempe, AZ 85287-1502
$10, 8, Barbara Nelson, Dianne Nelson

High Plains Literary Review
180 Adams Street, Suite 250
Denver, CO 80206
$20, 7, Clarence Major

Hopeful Monster
Tiki Bob Publishing
842 Folsom Street, Box 102

San Francisco, CA 94107
$6, 7, Paul Benkman

Hudson Review
684 Park Avenue
New York, NY 10021
$20, 8, Paula Deitz, Frederick Morgan

Idler
255 Davenport Road
Toronto, Ontario
M5R 1J9 Canada
$24, 3, Paul Wilson

Indiana Review
316 North Jordan Avenue
Bloomington, IN 47405
$12, 9, Jon Tribble

Iowa Review
Department of English
University of Iowa
308 EPB
Iowa City, IA 52242
$15, 27, David Hamilton

Iowa Woman
P.O. Box 680
Iowa City, IA 52244
$15, 8, Carolyn Hardesty

Isaac Asimov's Science Fiction
Davis Publications, Inc.
380 Lexington Avenue
New York, NY 10017
$25.97, 27, Gardner Dozois

Jacaranda Review
Department of English
University of California
Los Angeles, CA 90024
$10, 9, Katherine Swiggart

Jewish Currents
22 East 17th Street, Suite 601
New York, NY 10003-3272
$15, 20, editorial board

Journal
Department of English
Ohio State University
164 West 17th Avenue

Columbus, OH 43210
$5, 5, David Citino

Kalliope
Florida Community College
3939 Roosevelt Blvd.
Jacksonville, FL 32205
$10.50, 12, Mary Sue Koeppel

Kansas Quarterly
Department of English
Denison Hall
Kansas State University
Manhattan, KS 66506
$20, 33, Harold Schneider

Karamu
English Department
Eastern Illinois University
Charleston, IL 61920
Peggy L. Brayfield

Kenyon Review
Kenyon College
Gambier, OH 43022
$20, 15, David H. Lynn

Key West Review
9 Avenue G
Key West, FL 33040
$17, 8, William J. Schlicht

Konch
Ishmael Reed Publishing Co.
P.O. Box 3288
Berkeley, CA 94703
$14.95, 1, Ishmael Reed

Lilith
The Jewish Women's Magazine
250 West 57th Street
New York, NY 10107
$14, 5, Julia Wolf Mazow

Literary Review
Fairleigh Dickinson University
285 Madison Avenue
Madison, NJ 07940
$18, 25, Walter Cummins

Little Magazine
English Department
SUNY
Albany, NY 12222
$6, 25, John Sandman

Lost Creek Letters
Box 373A
Rushville, MO 64484
$15, 10, Pamela Montgomery

McCall's
230 Park Avenue
New York, NY 10169
$13.97, 6, Helen DelMonte

Mademoiselle
350 Madison Avenue
New York, NY 10017
$28, 10, Eileen Schnurr

Madison Review
University of Wisconsin
Department of English
H. C. White Hall
600 North Park Street
Madison, WI 53706
$7, 8, Sara Goldberg

Malahat Review
University of Victoria
P.O. Box 1700
Victoria, British Columbia
V8W 2Y2 Canada
$15, 20, Constance Rooke

Manoa
English Department
University of Hawaii
Honolulu, HI 96822
$12, 12, Robert Shapard

Maryland Review
Department of English and
    Languages
University of Maryland, Eastern
    Shore
Princess Anne, MD 21853
$6, 7, Chester M. Hedgepeth, Jr.,
Cary C. Holladay

Massachusetts Review
Memorial Hall
University of Massachusetts
Amherst, MA 01003
$14, 3, Mary Heath

Matrix
c.p. 100 Ste.-Anne-de-Bellevue
Quebec
H9X 3L4 Canada
$15, 8, Linda Leith

Michigan Quarterly Review
3032 Rackham Building
University of Michigan
Ann Arbor, MI 48109
$13, 10, Laurence Goldstein

Mid-American Review
106 Hanna Hall
Department of English
Bowling Green State University
Bowling Green, OH 43403
$6, 10, Ken Letko

Mississippi Review
University of Southern Mississippi
Southern Station, P.O. Box 5144
Hattiesburg, MS 39406-5144
$10, 25, Frederick Barthelme

Missouri Review
Department of English
231 Arts and Sciences
University of Missouri
Columbia, MO 65211
$12, 15, Speer Morgan

Mother Jones
1663 Mission Street
2nd floor
San Francisco, CA 94103
$24, 5, Douglas Foster

Moxie
21100 Erwin Street
Woodland Hills, CA 91367
$24.95, Kathy S. Soverow

MSS
4820 Alpine Place

Building A, Suite 101-C
Las Vegas, NV 89107
$9.95, 30, Glenn Steckler

Nebraska Review
Writers' Workshop
ASH 212
University of Nebraska
Omaha, NE 68182-0324
$6, 10, Art Homer, Richard Duggin

Negative Capability
62 Ridgelawn Drive East
Mobile, AL 36605
$12, 15, Sue Walker

New Delta Review
Creative Writing Program
English Department
Louisiana State University
Baton Rouge, LA 70803
$7, David Tilley

New Directions
New Directions Publishing
80 Eighth Avenue
New York, NY 10011
$11.95, 4, James Laughlin

New England Review and Bread Loaf
    Quarterly
Middlebury College
Middlebury, VT 05753
$12, 15, T. R. Hummer

New Letters
University of Missouri
4216 Rockhill Road
Kansas City, MO 64110
$17, 10, James McKinley

New Mexico Humanities Review
P.O. Box A
New Mexico Tech
Socorro, NM 87801
$8, 15, John Rothfork

New Orleans Review
P.O. Box 195
Loyola University

New Orleans, LA 70118
$25, 4, John Biguenet, John Mosier

New Quarterly
English Language Proficiency
    Programme
University of Waterloo
Waterloo, Ontario
N2L 3G1 Canada
$14, 15, Peter Hinchcliffe

New Renaissance
9 Heath Road
Arlington, MA 02174
$11.50, 10, Louise T. Reynolds

New Yorker
25 West 43rd Street
New York, NY 10036
$32, 53, Robert Gottlieb

Nimrod
Arts and Humanities Council of
    Tulsa
2210 South Main Street
Tulsa, OK 74114
$10, 10, Francine Ringold

North American Review
University of Northern Iowa
Cedar Falls, IA 50614
$11, 18, Robley Wilson, Jr.

North Atlantic Review
15 Arbutus Lane
Stony Brook, NY 11790-1408
$13, 9, editorial board

North Dakota Quarterly
University of North Dakota
P.O. Box 8237
Grand Forks, ND 58202
$10, 10, Robert W. Lewis

Northwest Review
369 PLC
University of Oregon
Eugene, OR 97403
$11, 10, Cecelia Hagen

Oak Square
Box 1238
Allston, MA 02134
$10, 20, Anne E. Pluto

Ohio Review
Ellis Hall
Ohio University
Athens, OH 45701-2979
$12, 10, Wayne Dodd

Omni
1965 Broadway
New York, NY 10023-5965
$24, 20, Patrice Adcroft

Ontario Review
9 Honey Brook Drive
Princeton, NJ 08540
$10, 8, Raymond J. Smith

Other Voices
820 Ridge Road
Highland Park, IL 60035
$16, 30, Lois Hauselman

Paris Review
541 East 72nd Street
New York, NY 10021
$20, 15, George Plimpton

Parting Gifts
3006 Stonecutter Terrace
Greensboro, NC 27405
Robert Bixby

Partisan Review
236 Bay State Road
Boston, MA 02215
$4, 4, William Phillips

Playboy
Playboy Building
919 North Michigan Avenue
Chicago, IL 60611
$24, 20, Alice K. Turner

Playgirl
801 Second Avenue
New York, NY 10017
$35, 12, Mary Ellen Strote

Ploughshares
Emerson College
100 Beacon Street
Boston, MA 02116
$15, 25, DeWitt Henry

Potpourri
P.O. Box 8278
Prairie Village, KS 66208
48, Polly W. Swafford

Prairie Schooner
201 Andrews Hall
University of Nebraska
Lincoln, NE 68588-0334
$15, 20, Hilda Raz

Prism International
Department of Creative Writing
University of British Columbia
Vancouver, British Columbia
V6T 1W5 Canada
$12, 20, Debbie Howlett

Product
Center for Writers
University of Southern Mississippi
Hattiesburg, MS
$7.50, 9, Cynthia Hardy

Puerto del Sol
P.O. Box 3E
Department of English
New Mexico State University
Las Cruces, NM 88003
$7.75, 12, Kevin McIlvoy, Antonya Nelson

Quarry Magazine
P.O. Box 1061
Kingston, Ontario
K7L 4Y5 Canada
$18, 20, Steven Heighton

The Quarterly
Vintage Books
201 East 50th Street
New York, NY 10022
$36, 81, Gordon Lish

Quarterly West
317 Olpin Union
University of Utah
Salt Lake City, UT 84112
$8.50, 10, David Stevenson

RE:AL
School of Liberal Arts
Stephen F. Austin State University
P.O. Box 13007, SFA Station
Nacogdoches, TX 75962
$6, 5, Lee Schultz

Redbook
959 Eighth Avenue
New York, NY 10017
$11.97, 10, Dawn Raffel

Richmond Quarterly
2405 Vollmer Road
Richmond, VA 23229
$10, 5, Julia C. Killian

Rio Grande Review
Husdpeth Hall
University of Texas
El Paso, TX 79968
$6, 6, Jacob Moises Ramirez

Room of One's Own
P.O. Box 46160, Station G
Vancouver, British Columbia
V6R 4G5 Canada
$20, 12, rotating editorship

Round Table
Box 18673
Rochester, NY 14618
Barbara and Alan Lupack

Salmagundi
Skidmore College
Saratoga Springs, NY 12866
$12, 4, Robert Boyers

San Jose Studies
c/o English Department
San Jose State University
One Washington Square
San Jose, CA 95192
$12, 5, Fauneil J. Rinn

Santa Monica Review
Center for the Humanities
Santa Monica College
1900 Pico Boulevard
Santa Monica, CA 90405
$10, 16, Jim Krusoe

Saturday Night
511 King Street West, Suite 100
Toronto, Ontario
M5V 2Z4 Canada
$26.45, 7, Robert Fulford

Seventeen
850 Third Avenue
New York, NY 10022
$13.95, 12, Bonni Price

Sewanee Review
University of the South
Sewanee, TN 37375-4009
$15, 10, George Core

Shenandoah
Washington and Lee University
P.O. Box 722
Lexington, VA 24450
$11, 17, Dabney Stuart

Sinister Wisdom
P.O. Box 3252
Berkeley, CA 94703
$17, 25, Elana Dykewoman

Snake Nation Review
2920 North Oak
Valdosta, GA 31602
$12, 16, Roberta George

Sonora Review
Department of English
University of Arizona
Tucson, AZ 85721
$8, 10, Martha Ostheimer, Laurie Schorr

South Carolina Review
Department of English
Clemson University
Clemson, SC 29634-1503
$7, 2, Richard J. Calhoun

South Dakota Review
University of South Dakota
P.O. Box 111 University Exchange
Vermillion, SD 57069
$15, 15, John R. Milton

Southern Humanities Review
9088 Haley Center
Auburn University
Auburn, AL 36849
*$12, 5, Dan R. Latimer, Thomas L.
   Wright*

Southern Review
43 Allen Hall
Louisiana State University
Baton Rouge, LA 70803
$15, 20, James Olney, Dave Smith

Southwest Review
Southern Methodist University
P.O. Box 4374
Dallas, TX 75275
$16, 15, Willard Spiegelman

Sou'wester
School of Humanities
Department of English
Southern Illinois University
Edwardsville, IL 62026-1438
$10, 10, Donald Gilbert

Special Report–Fiction
Whittle Communications L.P.
505 Market Street
Knoxville, TN 37902
$14, 28, Elise Nakhnikian

Stories
14 Beacon Street
Boston, MA 02108
$18, 12, Amy R. Kaufman

Story
1507 Dana Avenue
Cincinnati, OH 45207
$17, 40, Lois Rosenthal

Story Quarterly
P.O. Box 1416
Northbrook, IL 60065
$12, 20, Anne Brashler, Diane Williams

Strange Plasma
Edgewood Press
P.O. Box 264
Cambridge, MA 02238
$10, 5, Steve Pasechnick

The Sun
107 North Roberson Street
Chapel Hill, NC 27516
$28, 30, Sy Safransky

Tampa Review
P.O. Box 19F
University of Tampa
401 West Kennedy Boulevard
Tampa, FL 33606-1490
$7.50, 2, Andrew Solomon

Taos Review
P.O. Drawer 1878
Taos, NM 87571
$12, 4, Annah K. Sobelman

Threepenny Review
P.O. Box 9131
Berkeley, CA 94709
$10, 10, Wendy Lesser

Tikkun
5100 Leona Street
Oakland, CA 94619
$30, 10, Michael Lerner

TriQuarterly
2020 Ridge Avenue
Northwestern University
Evanston, IL 60208
$18, 15, Reginald Gibbons

Turnstile
175 Fifth Avenue, Suite 2348
New York, NY 10010
$24, 12, group

University of Windsor Review
Department of English
University of Windsor
Windsor, Ontario
N9B 3P4 Canada
$10, 6, Joseph A. Quinn

Vincent Brothers Review
1459 Sanzon Drive

Fairborn, OH 45324
$4.50, 12, Kimberly A. Willardson

Virginia Quarterly Review
One West Range
Charlottesville, VA 22903
$15, 12, Staige D. Blackford

Vogue
Condé Nast Building
350 Madison Avenue
New York, NY 10017
$24, 8, Nancy Nicholas

Voice Literary Supplement
842 Broadway
New York, NY 10003
$9, 8, M. Mark

Wascana Review
English Department
University of Regina
Regina, Saskatchewan
S4S 0A2 Canada
$7, 8, J. Shami

Weber Studies
Weber State College
Ogden, UT 84408
$5, 2, Neila Seshachari

Webster Review
Webster University
470 East Lockwood
Webster Groves, MO 63119
$5, 2, Nancy Schapiro

Wellspring
770 Tonkawa Road
Long Lake, MN 55356
$7, 10, Vicki Palmquist

West Branch
Department of English
Bucknell University
Lewisburg, PA 17837
$5, 10, Robert Love Taylor

West Wind Review
Stevenson Union, Room 321
Southern Oregon State College
1250 Siskiyou Boulevard

Ashland, OR 97520
$6, 11, Dale Vidmar, Catherine Ordal

Western Humanities Review
University of Utah
Salt Lake City, UT 84112
$18, 10, Barry Weller

Whetstone
Barrington Area Arts Council
P.O. Box 1266
Barrington, IL 60011
Marsha Portnoy

Wigwag
73 Spring Street
New York, NY 10012
$19.95, 12, Alexander Kaplan

William and Mary Review
College of William and Mary
Williamsburg, VA 23185
$4.50, 4, William Clark

Willow Springs
MS-1
Eastern Washington University
Cheney, WA 99004
$7, 8, Lisa Graverholz Leitz

Wind
RFD Route 1
P.O. Box 809K
Pikeville, KY 41501
$7, 20, Quentin R. Howard

Witness
31000 Northwestern Highway, Suite 200
Farmington Hills, MI 48018
$16, 15, Peter Stine

Woodstock Originals
112 Brydcliff Road
Woodstock, NY 12498
11, Joseph Keefe

Writ
Innis College
University of Toronto
2 Sussex Avenue
Toronto, Ontario
M5S 1J5 Canada
$12, 7, Roger Greenwald

Writers Forum
University of Colorado
P.O. Box 7150
Colorado Springs, CO 80933-7150
$8.95, 15, Alexander Blackburn

Yale Review
1902A Yale Station
New Haven, CT 06520
$16, 12, Mr. Kai Erikson

Yankee
Yankee Publishing, Inc.

Dublin, NH 03444
$19.95, 4, Judson D. Hale, Sr.

Yellow Silk
P.O. Box 6374
Albany, CA 94706
$24, 10, Lily Pond

ZYZZYVA
41 Sutter Street, Suite 1400
San Francisco, CA 94104
$20, 12, Howard Junker